Works by Michael J. Sullivan

THE LEGENDS OF THE FIRST EMPIRE
Age of Myth • *Age of Swords* • *Age of War*
Age of Legend • *Age of Death* • *Age of Empyre*

THE RISE AND THE FALL
Nolyn (Summer 2021) • *Farilane* (Summer 2022)
Esrahaddon (Summer 2023)

THE RIYRIA REVELATIONS
Theft of Swords (contains *The Crown Conspiracy* & *Avempartha*)
Rise of Empire (contains *Nyphron Rising* & *The Emerald Storm*)
Heir of Novron (contains *Wintertide* & *Percepliquis*)

THE RIYRIA CHRONICLES
The Crown Tower • *The Rose and the Thorn*
The Death of Dulgath • *The Disappearance of Winter's Daughter*
Forthcoming: *Drumindor*

STANDALONE NOVELS
Hollow World (Sci-fi Thriller)

SHORT STORY ANTHOLOGIES
Heroes Wanted: "The Ashmoore Affair" (Fantasy: Riyria Chronicles)
Unfettered: "The Jester" (Fantasy: Riyria Chronicles)
Unbound: "The Game" (Fantasy: Contemporary)
Unfettered II: "Little Wren and the Big Forest" (Fantasy: Legends)
Blackguards: "Professional Integrity" (Fantasy: Riyria Chronicles)
The End: Visions of the Apocalypse: "Burning Alexandria" (Dystopian Sci-fi)
Triumph Over Tragedy: "Traditions" (Fantasy: Tales from Elan)
The Fantasy Faction Anthology: "Autumn Mist" (Fantasy: Contemporary)

Age of Empyre © 2020 by Michael J. Sullivan
Cover illustration © 2019 by Marc Simonetti
Cover design © 2020 Michael J. Sullivan
Map © 2016 by David Lindroth
Interior design © 2020 Robin Sullivan
978-1944145408
All rights reserved.

Published in the United States by Riyria Enterprises, LLC and distributed through Grim Oak Press.

Learn more about Michael's writings at www.riyria.com
To contact Michael, email him at michael@michaelsullivan-author.com

MICHAEL'S NOVELS INCLUDE:
The First Empire Series: Age of Myth • Age of Swords • Age of War • Age of Legend • Age of Death • Age of Empyre
Coming soon: Nolyn • Farilane • Esrahaddon
The Riyria Revelations: Theft of Swords • Rise of Empire • Heir of Novron
The Riyria Chronicles: The Crown Tower • The Rose and the Thorn • The Death of Dulgath • The Disappearance of Winter's Daughter
Standalone Titles: Hollow World

First Edition
Printed in the United States of America

2 4 6 8 9 7 5 3 1

Published by

RIYRIA
ENTERPRISES

Distributed by:

GRIM
OAK

Age OF Empyre

Age of Empyre

BOOK SIX OF

The Legends of the First Empire

MICHAEL J. SULLIVAN

Contents

Contents

Author's Note

Hello, and welcome to this final installment of the Legends of the First Empire. This book marks the sixteenth novel in my fictional world of Elan and the conclusion to the age of myths and legends that forms the foundation of my previous series.

This book is releasing at an unprecedented time in our history. As I write this, it is April 2020. The Coronavirus Pandemic is rampant throughout the world, and people are sequestered in "lockdowns"—families trapped in involuntary staycations. Early Kickstarter readers, who seem to be hoping to escape their four walls and perhaps the daily news, have been flooding my inbox with emails, clamoring for the book. Robin and I have struggled, but we managed to keep on schedule for the ebook and audiobook versions. We were thrilled the printer could produce the book at all, and it was just three weeks late.

While most people have struggled with stay-at-home orders, life here in the valley hasn't changed much. As most of you already know, we live in a cabin in the mountains of Virginia. Being a fulltime writer with a wife who is my editor, agent, business manager, and publicist means that we have long lived the lives of hermits—by choice. In the past, we have invited people from all over the world to the cabin. We have enjoyed the company of Pulitzer Prize-winning journalists, retired military generals, famous as well as aspiring authors, fans of my work, and even a few who had no idea who I am or what I do. All of that stopped in 2020, of course, and when we come out on the other side of this, I hope we can return to hosting people. So, if your travel plans ever take you to the Luray, Virginia area, drop us an email (michael@michaelsullivan-author.com), and we'll have you by for a drink.

For those who cannot come here, there is a possibility that we might come to you. Earlier this year, Robin and I bought a Jeep and a teardrop camper with plans of doing some traveling. Once the virus-imposed restrictions are off, we hope to start. Over the years, several people have said, if you are ever in <insert-various-place>, let us know, and because we have lived like hermits, we, unfortunately, didn't write those down. But we now have a system for recording such things, so if this is of interest, you can go to https://michaeljsullivan.survey.fm/if-you-are-ever-out-this-way, and let us know where you live. If it turns out that we'll be passing nearby, we'll see if we can meet up.

As it turned out, that teardrop camper came at just the right time. Robin became ill at the end of March, and she has been isolating in it. We are hoping she'll be able to emerge in a few days, but like everyone else, we are erring on the side of caution because we don't want those measures circumvented by moving too quickly.

Finishing this book has been interesting, to say the least. Robin and I work via Discord when she isn't resting to go over typos reported by the gamma and early Kickstarter readers. Usually, we would be in the studio while Tim records (something we always look forward to); however, that wasn't possible this time. We did receive the dailies and were able to communicate changes via emails. Thanks to Tim's in-home studio, he was able to stay mainly on schedule, and that saved the audiobook's release date. As always, our heartfelt thanks go out to Tim and our undying gratitude to the extra work he put in. He had to work alone without an engineer or director, but his efforts meant the audiobook's release wasn't affected by the crisis. Our heartfelt thanks go out to Tim for his added hard work.

So the long journey is finally at an end. I don't think I've fully processed that yet. Getting this book out in May fulfilled a promise Robin made; keeping that pledge was important to her. My hope is that this book has the power—in some small way—to help. I want to think we've created something good and lasting that can be shared—a doorway through which you can go to catch your breath, ease some stress, and perhaps even remember how to smile. Here's hoping that everyone who started reading this series will be able to finish it because that would mean the specter passed by your door. Stay safe. Keep your spirits up. And join with me now for the next, and last, journey into the Legends of the First Empire.

Michael J. Sullivan
April 18, 2020

HENTLYN

ERIVAN

Ervanon

Estramnadon

Harwood

Avempartha

Seon Hall

Swamp of Ith

Under the Dragon

Mount Mador

North Branch

Alon Rhist

The Forks

River

High Spear Valley

Bern

Nadak

Dureya

Gula

AVRLYN

Urum

Rhen

Melen

Merredydd

River

RHULYN

Menahan

Tirre

Warric

BROKEN LANDS

Green Sea

Neith

BELGREIG

Blue Sea

100 Miles

Fhrey towns
Rhune towns
Dherg towns

Age OF Empyre

CHAPTER ONE

Hitting Bottom

People often speak about "hitting bottom." They have no idea what they are talking about.

— THE BOOK OF BRIN

In the eternal silence and absolute darkness of the Abyss's unimaginable depths, Iver heard a scream. Faint at first, it grew to a piercing wail then stopped, cut short by a loud clap. Sounds were rare in his neighborhood, light even more so. And yet he did see a dim illumination seeping into the entrance of his cave. Prior to the howl, there had been a rapid series of booms. Iver hadn't bothered to investigate those, as he wouldn't have been able to see anything and the effort of crawling would have been wasted.

But the cry was different. Iver was certain the voice was familiar. Someone had fallen into the Abyss—someone he knew.

With great effort, he willed himself to stand. Few things drove Iver to such ridiculous extremes as walking, but this was a special occasion. He was certain who had fallen; he recognized that voice—that scream.

Iver held out his hands, searching for the wall, then followed it around to the narrow crack that formed the entrance to his *place*. He refused to call it *home*. Home meant something else: warmth and comfort. Even at the most miserable of times, a home served as a locale with merit, possessing an appeal beyond mere shelter. His cave served only as a place to be, a spot to sit, a hole to hide in.

He couldn't recall the last time he'd left his place. This didn't surprise Iver, as he was finding it increasingly difficult to remember just about anything. He still knew his name—the first part, at least. There had been more, a qualifier of some sort, but he couldn't figure out what that might have been. His life was fading, memories dissolving. The last significant event he could summon up was meeting Edvard, a Gula of Clan Erling. Iver had only been dead a short time when the man had beaten and dragged Iver to the cliff. It wasn't until he was falling that Iver realized why the man threw him over the edge. From high above, the Gula shouted, "This is for my wife, Reanna, you fat bastard! May you forever rot."

Iver had expected something horrifying waiting at the bottom. What he had found was nothing, which turned out to be even worse.

But now . . .

Creeping out of the cave, Iver saw a white glow coming off something on the ground not far away. At that distance, it appeared to be a bag of something, clothes perhaps. He remembered those. Drawing nearer, he saw it was a person. He shouldn't have been surprised. The biggest event in what felt like a century had turned out to be nothing more than a casualty of some brutal combat. Some poor wretch had fallen into the depths known to all as the Abyss—the absolute bottom from which no one returned.

He moved closer and found the small frame of a woman with dark, short-cropped hair—or rather what was left of her.

I'm certain I recognized that scream.

Iver felt excitement rise for the first time in . . . well, he hadn't a clue how long it had been. But his high hopes were dashed when Experience chastised him. *Not possible. There's no way it could be her.*

The fall had left the woman crushed on the hard frost: the price of admission to the worst level of existence. Iver surmised that every bone was broken, her skull shattered. Most of her body was lost in crumpled cloth, but Iver based the diagnosis on his own experience. It had taken an eternity to pull himself together. Even now, he had no idea how successful he'd been. In the Abyss, there were no reflections.

Reaching the woman's crumpled form, Iver realized she seemed to have fared better than he. Even so, her body was unnaturally twisted—her eyes open, alert, and still in her head. When they spotted him, both went wide. She attempted to scream again, but the only thing that came out was a wet gurgle.

"Roan," Iver said, shocked to discover his voice worked. "It *is* you!"

Broken as she was, the woman struggled to inch away. Mounted on a broken neck, her head swiveled to one side.

"Roan, you've come back to me."

"Nooo . . ." she managed to moan through broken teeth and pooling blood.

"Oh, yes," he said. "I'm here. We'll get you fixed up in no time. Won't that be nice?"

At the comment, her eyes grew wider still.

They might yet fall out.

Iver bent down and gathered Roan in his arms. Her snapped bones hung limp, feeling eerily like a bag of split firewood.

She moaned and a tear slipped down her cheek and fell to the frozen ground.

"Don't worry, my dear." He grinned at her. "Once you're put back together, it'll be like old times."

～

The moment Brin's fingers slipped off the edge of the bridge and she felt herself plunge into the Abyss, panic had taken hold. At first, her mind froze, locked by a singular idea: *This can't be happening.* Then, as she fell deeper into darkness, she wondered what hitting the bottom would feel like. She hoped she would bounce but figured the effect to be more like a dropped icicle.

Will I shatter into a million pieces?

After an inexplicably long time, Brin discovered she *wanted* it to be over. There was no avoiding the collision, no saving herself, and the waiting threatened to drive her insane. Anticipating the impact, knowing it could come at any time was the real terror. She closed her eyes, didn't want to see.

Get it over with already!

Then it happened. Brin touched down with all the force of having leapt from the front porch of the lodge, a whopping four steps. Landing feetfirst, the momentum pushed her torso forward. Her palms slapped the ground and prevented any real harm. Only the heel of her left hand suffered a wound—a slight abrasion from scraping the granular frost that covered the ground. It stung for a moment. She straightened and stood, staring at the frozen rock that formed the bottom of the world. Imagining herself breathing, Brin saw her exhalation created a fog, the way it always had in the depths of winter.

That wasn't so bad, she thought, relief pouring in.

The light, however, did catch her by surprise. Pure white and without an apparent source, it illuminated the new world around her. She could see from one side of the canyon to the other. Cliffs rose, their tops disappearing into darkness. She was at the bottom of the Abyss, and nothing was there except a vast, frost-covered plain of uneven ground and miserly ripples of snow that had been blown by a long-extinct wind.

"Roan?" she called out but got no answer. Brin had seen her friend fall, so she should be close by.

Perhaps she wandered off? It would be exactly like her to go exploring, curiosity eclipsing everything else.

Wondering if anyone else had slipped over the edge the way she had, Brin looked up but saw nothing.

I hope everyone else is all right. I'm alone down here—except for Roan. I really need to find her.

Walking in no particular direction, Brin found herself in a maze of fissures, which branched off into narrow canyons that zigzagged into the dark. These gashes were no doubt the reason for the many bridges they had traversed while traveling across the Plain of Kilcorth on their way to King Mideon's castle. The impossibly high walls were as porous as a sponge. Dark holes and caves peppered its surface: some were at ground level, others higher up and extending as far as she could see.

From time to time, Brin paused and called out for Roan. Her voice didn't travel far. The Abyss was a quiet place, its silence broken by the harsh crackle of her feet on the frosty ground. Roan didn't respond, so Brin picked an offshoot at random and ventured down one of the side branches. She guessed there were dozens of these tributaries, perhaps hundreds, and it could take a long while to search each one, but time was all she had now. Eventually, she would find Roan. This would be the Keeper's quest for as long as it took, and the reward would be maintaining her sanity. Searching gave her something to do beyond wallowing in self-pity for her failure.

The deeper into the ravine she went, the narrower it became. Given the open space where she had touched down, this confinement gave her an unexpected sense of security. Her dog, Darby, had often crawled under a table or bed when frightened, and Brin's father had explained that animals sometimes found small spaces comforting. Brin now felt that same sense of sheltered protection, and she was surprised that the Abyss wasn't frightening. The worst she could say about it was that it seemed more than a little cold.

And lonely. The idea popped into her head. *What if each person falls into their own separate Abyss? Is that why I can't find Roan?*

Now she was scared, and she recoiled from the notion the way she instinctively pulled back her hand after touching a hot pot. She tried to calm herself.

No reason to think like that . . . not yet.

She shook off the possibility and tried to focus. Roan might have crawled into one of the many caves the way Darby had wriggled under the bed. "Roannnnnn," she called out again.

This time she was rewarded by movement. From where she stood, she could see a shifting shadow some way up the cliff's craggy face where no vegetation grew. She watched, hoping to see the familiar figure of her friend. Crossing to the opposite side of the gorge, she got a better look and wondered why Roan would be up so high. Then Brin realized it wasn't Roan. This silhouette was too short and wide. Whatever it was, she didn't think it was human.

What would Moya do?

After taking a calming breath, Brin set her jaw, squared her shoulders, and inched closer. As she did, she spotted more holes in the honeycombed cliff. Most weren't big enough to be considered true caves, just little cracks and fractures. Drawing nearer, Brin saw more shadows. Figures crawled out of holes, each of them with two arms, two legs, and one head. They were generally in the shape of people, but it was obvious they weren't Rhunes, Fhrey, or dwarfs. These figures appeared to be made of partially melted wax. Shoulders were sloped and limbs elongated. Faces were merely vague contours with lumps where noses or cheeks ought to be. Some only had a slight indentation instead of a mouth.

Brin felt her stomach twist.

Dozens, scores, perhaps hundreds slipped out from cracks and ledges. Many appeared as shriveled as raisins. Others were not much more than lumps. And in some places, she saw only oozing pools of thick slime.

Brin stayed clear of the moving shadows, which was easy to do given how slowly they crawled. With them came a sliding, dragging slurp—the noise a snail might make if it were five feet long.

Splat!

The sound was so close, Brin jumped. Spinning, she discovered that one of the creatures had fallen from the heights, landing near her heels. Little more than a glob of ooze, it had one eye that peered up at her. Its mouth moved like a sock puppet, silently opening and closing.

Terrified, Brin stumbled backward, grimacing. *What in the name of the Grand Mother of All is that?*

Plop. Slip. Plop. Clap.

Dozens more fell from everywhere at once. They landed near and far, in front and behind. Hundreds oozed out of the ground-level caves, creeping, sliding, and dragging their misshapen bodies across the crackling frost—each one coming toward her.

❦

Gifford hit the ground, twisting an ankle and hammering a knee and a hip. The impact hurt, but it wasn't too bad. A lifetime of tumbling had made him an expert at falling and dealing with the aftermath. Despite the infamous reputation of the Abyss, Gifford didn't even think this was his worst fall. After only a moment to collect himself, he was able to stand. A fortifying breath allowed him to shake off the pain, and he straightened up to search for Roan.

When he'd last seen his wife, a flying creature had pulled her off the bridge. Moya had tried to save Roan by hitting her attacker with an arrow, but she'd been too late. When the bankor dropped Roan, she was a long way up and too far out to land on the span leading to the Alysin Door. Burned into his memory was Roan's terrified scream, which faded only with distance. He'd tried to follow, ran for the edge of the bridge, and planned to dive, but Rain had stopped him. Well-intentioned as the dwarf had been, he simply didn't understand. Rain wasn't saving Gifford's life; Gifford's life had already fallen into the Abyss.

Pivoting completely around, Gifford didn't find Roan. What he did see was . . . *snow.*

No flakes fell, but the ground was covered—a white sheet as far as he could see, which wasn't far. A light was nearby, but it had a limited distance. Where the brilliance came from, Gifford couldn't tell. Neither from above nor from behind, the radiance extended outward in every direction, casting back the eternal night like a lantern. Gifford was back in his traveling clothes. The armor made by Alberich Berling had disappeared, so that wasn't the source.

Getting to his feet, he took a step, and the light moved with him.

It's me!

He looked at his hands, but they weren't glowing.

I'm seeing what I expect, and I wouldn't be pleased with glowing hands. That would be more than strange; it would be frightening.

This new world was a barren landscape of frozen rock and washboard snowdrifts. Dark walls surrounded him—their height lost to the darkness beyond his radiance. Gifford took a few steps. Snow crackled under his feet. Nothing so pretty or welcome as deep fluff. This was a thin, bitter crust—more a frost than flakes.

Again, he made a quick circle, searching for Roan but finding nothing.

Then he heard screaming. From overhead and growing in volume came a pair of cries. They wailed toward him at an astonishing speed before being silenced by massive claps.

Gifford ran toward the nearest impact and found a woman lying unnaturally splayed out, one leg bent backward, her neck twisted too far, her head crushed the way one might expect a melon to appear after a drop from a second-story window. Her eyes were open but unseeing. A small stream of blood trailed from one nostril.

"Tressa?" he said.

No reaction.

The edge of Gifford's light revealed the other person.

Tesh lay facedown, arms and legs spread out. The left side of his face appeared to be driven halfway into the ground. Gifford guessed the stone was undamaged. It was Tesh's skull that had caved in. His jaw was unhinged, his teeth scattered in a spray of now-pinkish blood.

"You can't be dead," Gifford told them, or maybe he was trying to assure himself. At that moment, he couldn't be certain. There was something about seeing Tesh's scattered teeth that made Gifford want to vomit, yet he had no stomach or bile, just the horror revealed through his nonexistent eyes.

As he tried to cope with being trapped in a bad dream wrapped in a nightmare, Gifford was nearly crushed by a huge rock that smashed into the permafrost. Another boulder struck, then two more. Huge slabs fell, shaking the ground and exploding the ice into clouds of snow. He suspected Ferrol was lobbing stones to crush them. Gifford grabbed hold of Tesh and Tressa and dragged their bodies toward the nearest cliff wall, hoping for shelter. As it turned out, the rain of stone didn't last long.

"Gif . . . ford." The coarse croaking voice came from Tressa, a sound that scared him well past death. Her eyes were still open and remained unfocused. "Help me . . . Gifford . . . please. It hurts . . . please . . ."

The onetime-crippled potter looked from Tressa to Tesh. Both of them were stretched out from being dragged, and bits and pieces of each were left behind. *Helplessness* was too simple a concept for what he felt. "I don't know how."

"Fin . . . elp," Tesh managed to say, his jaw still attached, but just barely.

Find help? Here? Gifford looked around. All he saw was a vast, empty, and uninviting plain of cruel crystal-white frost.

There would be no aid. They'd reached the end, their eternal resting place. This was the Abyss.

CHAPTER TWO

Seasons Shift to Winter

Winter has a tendency to creep up like an old woman with a blanket who is intent on smothering the world.

— THE BOOK OF BRIN

Nolyn got up and rushed outside when they heard the shouting.

At five and a half years old, Persephone's sandy-haired son was as excited as a squirrel with two acorns and as agile as a mountain goat. The former she chalked up to being a child; the latter came from his father. Nolyn halted and waited for her. "Mama?"

Persephone drew back the flap. Snow was still falling, heavy flakes taking their time. This was the fourth snow of the season but the first stubborn enough to stick. The tent roofs were already white. The brown grass was covered, and the pathways that had been a muddy mess the day before were now pristine except for a pair of tracks left by an early riser. Persephone had always wondered at the irony of winter, a season that bestowed beauty and death in equal measure. The world had been transformed overnight in both appearance and sound. Even at such an early hour, the camp was usually ringing with activity, but the white blanket had smothered everything, leaving the world muffled until the shouts arrived with undeniable intent.

Cries of joy, they are not.

"What's happening?" Nolyn asked. Too short to see, he futilely jumped in place to get a look, tapping the endless reserve of energy that all children possessed. Persephone wished she could borrow some. The days were getting shorter, and she still didn't have the strength to push through them. She was forty-five going on eternity, but her age was only part of the problem. Guilt played its part, and fear took its toll.

Sikar appeared an instant later, hood up, his breath puffing clouds. As promised, Nyphron had appointed him as her new Shield. The onetime captain of Alon Rhist hadn't said so, but Persephone was certain he resented babysitting a Rhune.

"Back inside and get your cloak," she said to her son.

Nolyn looked at her, eyes wide, his little mouth forming a big O. For him, taking that additional minute to dress against the weather was absurd.

"Go on. You won't see what's happening until you have your wool."

Even with this threat, she still had to pull her son inside.

Justine was sleeping, curled up at the foot of the bed. Nolyn started to wake her, but Persephone stopped him. "Leave her be."

Persephone wrapped Nolyn in his mini leigh mor, pinning the shoulder while he huffed but didn't move. His effort to stand still was admirable but also calculated. He'd do anything to speed up the process. When she was done, he was a perfect image of a Clan Rhen child—except for the green eyes.

What does that mean?

In a world of brown-eyed Rhunes and blue-eyed Fhrey, Nolyn was unique. Snowflakes had stuck to her son's eyelashes, making him more striking than usual. Even taking into account her motherly bias, Persephone believed there had never been so beautiful a child. The brutish features of men were smoothed by the elegance of his Fhrey blood. Likewise, his Rhune heritage helped to dampen the inherent appearance of contemptuous superiority worn by his father's kin. Her job would be to ensure that Nolyn never rose to his full potential—an odd task for a mother, but no woman had ever birthed a son like Nolyn.

Persephone wasn't so naïve as to assume that her people would win the war, but if they did somehow, everything would change, and her child of two worlds could one day rule all of mankind. She had to make him worthy, and with Nyphron as a father, that would be a challenge. She needed to fight his influence, battle against Nyphron's unconscious prejudice and arrogance. And she'd have to get lucky. Persephone was concerned that being half human, Nolyn might have a shorter life span than his father. She wasn't certain of this, but the boy did look primarily human. He lacked the pointed ears and delicate frame of the Fhrey, and his hair was sandy-colored rather than a startlingly bright blond.

If the gods denied him a long life, what would happen when Nolyn, who would be raised as a prince-in-waiting, learned his father would outlive him by centuries? This made her worry that an egotistical son might resent an eternal father who blocked ascension to the First Chair. Either way, she wouldn't live to see the outcome and had only a handful of years to direct the course the future would take. She was swinging blindly into a fog at a foe that might not exist, and the fate of humanity lay in the balance. But that was a concern for tomorrow. On this snowy morning, she took the hand of an innocent boy who grinned up at her without a care. For him, the world seemed a wondrous place, and at that moment, it was for her as well.

In a heartbeat, all that changed.

ﾑ

Soldiers raced through the fresh snow, moving as if chased. Eight men in woodland armor ran across the field toward the camp. Bursts of white kicked up in front of their feet. Any deeper and they wouldn't have been able to run, but the snow was still falling, still building.

If it keeps up, no one will be able to walk, let alone run. Persephone reflected on the thought as if it were an unwanted prophecy. She hadn't been thinking in terms of flight, but seeing the dread in the faces of the men running at her, she wondered if she should have.

Persephone, Nolyn, and Sikar made it to the broad pathway that separated the Healing Quarter from the area where auxiliary troops were housed. The shouts had carried, and everywhere men opened tent flaps and exited with cautious eyes. Some threw on boots and cloaks, but still more remained wrapped in blankets, peering at the uninviting dawn and the unwanted gifts it delivered.

Reaching the camp's boundary, Nolyn pointed at the running men. "Who are they?"

"Techylors," she replied.

While she puzzled over what could drive a troop of Techylors to take flight, she saw they were not alone. More men emerged from the curtain of falling snow. In a broad dark line, they appeared as phantoms, a moving shadow wall along the plain.

"It's a full retreat," Nyphron said, coming up from behind. He said it softly, the words slipping out. He wasn't speaking to them. He wasn't speaking to anyone.

"Hi, Dada!" Nolyn grinned up at him, waving with his free hand.

"What do you think is going on?" Persephone asked.

"I suspect we'll know shortly," Nyphron replied. "But I wouldn't expect good news."

"Hi Dada!" the boy repeated, louder this time.

Nyphron looked at his son and frowned. "Why aren't you bigger?"

"I am big," the boy corrected.

"For a mouse perhaps, but if you're going to be my son, you need to grow, and faster."

"How?"

"Think bigger thoughts."

"Okay," Nolyn said as if the advice made perfect sense. Maybe to him it did, but somewhere in that idea Persephone felt a lurking dread.

A panting Edgar ran toward them. His face was red, nose a bluish beet. Snow gathered on his beard, and ice crystals had formed around his mouth.

"Report," Nyphron ordered while the Techylor commander was still several strides away.

Edgar stopped and puffed a fog for several seconds, giving Atkins the chance to catch up. The two men were still in their layered green-and-brown tatters that made them look like shambling mounds of leaves, the shoulders of which were frosted white.

"They've got one, sir," Edgar managed to say between gulps of breath.

Persephone took a faltering step. Concerned about discussing military matters in front of her son, she turned. "Sikar, escort Nolyn back to my tent. Wake Justine and tell her to take him to breakfast."

The Fhrey commander glared and made no sign of moving. Persephone wasn't in the habit of giving any of the Fhrey orders, much less the senior camp commander. He wasn't pleased, but Persephone had greater concerns than Sikar's pride.

"Have you forgotten the way to the *keenig's* tent, Sikar?" Nyphron asked.

"I'm not a nursemaid," the Instarya replied, keeping his tone even but cold. "This is—"

"You're Shield to the keenig and the keenig's son. Do your job."

Sikar frowned but took the boy's hand and led him back down the trail.

"Are you sure there's only one?" Nyphron asked Edgar.

"That's all we saw, sir. One was enough. We were on our way back to our station when it attacked the forward encampment. I don't expect there'll be any additional survivors."

Edgar looked back toward the wood. "The dragon set the camp and forest ablaze. You can't see the smoke because of the falling snow, but the trees are burning. I thought it was better to report than engage."

Persephone watched the snow, which at that moment made it seem as if the sky was falling, flake by tiny flake.

ꝰ

After dismissing the rest of the Techylors and the remaining men from the woods who had followed them, Persephone, Nyphron, and Edgar moved to the comfort and privacy of the keenig's tent. She ordered food to be brought, but her stomach was so braided in knots she couldn't consider eating. Nyphron also declined, but she suspected his reasons were different from hers. After years of deadlocked inaction, he had something to do. Something he was especially good at.

"The gilarabrywn has a limited range," Persephone said. "If it was created at Avempartha, it can't travel past the Harwood. Lothian's troops won't be able to use it this far out."

Nyphron rubbed his chin thoughtfully. "Do you know the exact range of the dragon?"

Persephone shook her head. "No, not precisely."

"Maybe Lothian doesn't know, either. He may not even be aware there is a limitation. If that's so, we remain at a stalemate—for now. They can't attack our position because of our dragon, and we can no longer approach Avempartha because of theirs."

"But won't they just make more and continue to advance?" Edgar asked after swallowing a mouthful of day-old bread and salted meat.

Persephone wished she could have offered better.

These men deserve so much more.

"That's what I would have done if I had a means to cross and Suri hadn't refused to make more," Nyphron answered. "But first I would have established a foothold on the other side of the river and used a dragon as protection while I massed my troops. Lothian has no military prowess, and if he is expecting his dragon to overrun and destroy us, he probably didn't plan for that essential middle step."

Persephone ignored the comment about Suri and appreciated that Nyphron didn't say more on the subject. He could have. He had every right. Maybe her husband saw no point in going down that rabbit hole. They both knew it was Persephone's fault. She had been the one who delivered the mystic to the fane.

Nyphron, who had been sitting in one of the soft chairs, stood up and looked to the north. "At this moment, there's nothing preventing the fane from advancing to the edge of this camp and making a dragon right on our doorstep. If he did that"—he let his arms fall in resignation—"it would be over."

"So what do we do?" Edgar asked.

He turned to face the soldier. "Is anyone left back there? Any defenders at all?"

"Don't know for sure. We left right away. Some at the river may have escaped, or were out of the camp at the time. If so, I suspect they'll be coming here."

"You will need to return to the forest."

Edgar looked shocked. "The Harwood is on fire, sir."

"That's not my concern."

Persephone interjected, "They can't fight a gilarabrywn."

Nyphron turned his attention to her. "Edgar and his Techylors are alive because Lothian's dragon has a limited range, just like ours. I need to know what that distance is, and I need to prevent the fane from gathering troops on our side of the Nidwalden. That army will *not* be limited. Most important, I need to ensure that no Miralyith escapes that wood. We cannot afford to let them anywhere near us."

"We'll need more men. I'll send for reinforcements. How many do you require?" she asked.

"All of them," Nyphron replied.

"Is it really so dire?"

"Our overwhelming numbers are the only advantage we still possess. And yes, it's precisely that ruinous. In fact, we should break camp as soon as possible." He hesitated, as if the words were poisonous. "We'll need to retreat. The reinforcements will have to be sent to our new rally point."

"Are you sure?" Persephone said.

"This position is no longer tenable. We should fall back to the farthest reaches of our dragon. The distance between Alon Rhist and Merredydd is about the same as between Alon Rhist and here, so the dragon ought to be able to come with us. Will it?"

"I'm not sure. Suri controlled it on the way here, but . . ." She hesitated.

"Even now." The words were seared into her heart.

"Yes. I think it will come," Persephone finished.

"Good," Nyphron nodded, his eyes shifting in thought.

"But what good will retreating do, sir?" Edgar asked. "Aren't we just putting off the inevitable?"

"No," Persephone answered. "Making a dragon comes at a terrible cost. Each one they are forced to make may weaken the resolve of the fane's forces." She looked at Nyphron. "With such bitter alternatives before them, it's possible they might seek peace."

"I think that option is forever off the table," Nyphron said. "Edgar, eat the rest of your meal walking. Get your men, gather those from the other encampments, and take half our reserves. Send a runner with daily reports about the number of Fhrey on our side of the river. Don't let them out of those trees unless they make another dragon."

"And if they do?"

"Fall back and join with the reinforcements."

"Yes, sir." Edgar saluted, grabbed another handful of food, and exited the tent.

With his departure, a long silence fell between them. Persephone was reticent about raising the subject again, but she needed to ask. "She's dead, isn't she?"

"Suri?" Nyphron asked. "Yes, I believe so. No reason to keep her breathing now that she's given up the only value she had."

It wasn't what he said but rather the matter-of-fact way in which he said it that Persephone found most upsetting.

"Would you have preferred that I lie?"

She shook her head. "No."

Nyphron wasn't the worst husband, but he wasn't the best, either. Reglan had had many faults, but he would have held Persephone's head to his chest and wrapped her in the security of his arms while she cried. He understood her need for such things. The Fhrey she married didn't have a clue. This failure wasn't Nyphron's fault; such behavior simply wasn't in his nature.

Without meaning to, she found herself staring at the black-bronze sword mounted on the center pole of her tent.

Birds fly, fish swim, she thought. Then, after considering further, she realized ducks did both.

"I see you're thinking the same thing I am," Nyphron said.

Persephone doubted that very much. "What are *you* thinking?" she asked, turning toward him.

He pointed at the blade she had been looking at. "We shouldn't have that sword here. It's a liability."

"How so?"

"The fane's forces are no longer contained, and it's the only thing that can kill Suri's dragon, isn't that right?"

Persephone was surprised he knew about that. They hadn't discussed it before. "Yes. The symbols on the blade are its name. It's the knot that binds the weave. If it penetrates the gilarabrywn's body, the enchantment breaks and the creature vanishes."

"Right, so what's to stop one of the fane's forces from stealing it and destroying our best defense?"

"Well, first he'd have to know that such a thing exists. Second, he'd have to learn that I have it. Third, he'd have to get close enough to use it, and I don't think the gilarabrywn will allow that. Malcolm gave it to me so that Suri wouldn't have to be the one to put it to rest, but now that I think about it . . ."

"What?"

"Maybe he knew Suri wouldn't be around, and that's why he gave it to me. He said to keep it safe. It never occurred to me to ask why. Lately, I've been suspecting Malcolm is a seer, able to foretell the future like Tura or Suri. He seems to know things he shouldn't."

Nyphron sighed. "Don't waste your time trying to figure Malcolm out. He's an enigma, but I'll grant you there is more to him than meets the eye. Still, at the very least, you should hide that blade. The tide has turned,

Persephone. We need to be cautious and use every advantage we have, or we'll lose this war."

She nodded and glanced at the sword once more. It glimmered in the early-morning light. "I'll ask Malcolm about it."

"Wonderful," he said sarcastically. "While you're at it, ask him what the weather will be like in Merredydd."

CHAPTER THREE

Saving Moya

If there is anything I learned from dying, it is the simple truth that no matter how bleak, terrible, or impossible things might seem, they can always get worse—and all too often they do.

— THE BOOK OF BRIN

Moya saw the bridge break and fall.

She'd been carried to the queen by a bankor and was now being restrained by a big man or perhaps a small giant. He gripped her from behind, so all she knew for certain was that he smelled of sweat and blood. His hands clutched her arms so hard it hurt. They prevented her from escaping, but as Moya watched the bridge shatter, they also kept her from collapsing. A moment before, the queen had asked her who had the key. Moya had tried to resist answering, but it was like holding her breath. No matter how much she wanted not to, eventually she had to inhale. The disappointment was how little time it took to break her—less than a minute. But it had been the fall of the bridge that took the strength from her legs.

She'd seen them go down. First Roan, then Brin, Gifford, and finally Tesh and Tressa. The route to the Alysin Door was destroyed and the key forever out of reach. Moya had failed Persephone and humanity as a whole, and she had lost her friends. Somehow, she still existed, but they did not. It made no sense. She had been in charge.

All of it is my fault. I'm responsible. How is it that I'm here, and they're gone? That's not how it should be.

For the first time, Moya felt truly dead.

The hands that held her let go, and she dropped, crumpling to the stone at the edge of the broken tongue of the bridge. She sat dazed, gaping at the missing piece near the center.

They're not dead. They can't be dead. You can't die when you're already in Phyre.

Waking from the depths of a nightmare, she looked around. The queen was gone, as were her hideous bankors and Orr. All around Moya, the armies were breaking up. Men, Fhrey, dwarfs, giants, and goblins were walking away, a quiet dispersal. The hosts neither cheered nor laughed. Melen and some others carried the brutalized bodies of Goth and Dian. Most remained where they had fallen. Hundreds of bodies littered the landscape. Fenelyus helped Mideon, who was slow to move, limping as he went.

"What's going on?" Moya called to them.

Fenelyus looked back at her. "We lost."

"And it's over? Everyone just goes home?"

"Yes. That's how it is here."

"But . . . no, it can't be over. We have to get them out. My friends who fell. We have to do something."

Fenelyus shook her head. "Not possible. And yes, it's over, and yes, it's pointless—it always is. That's why I stopped participating in these futile antics. I only returned because of you. This time was supposed to be different. Beatrice said you and your friends were special." Fenelyus sighed and shook her head again. "You weren't."

The Fhrey resumed helping Mideon walk away.

"It's not over!" Moya shouted after her. "There must be some way to help them."

"There isn't." Fenelyus's tone was as absolute as a slammed door.

"Come back with us, Moya," Mideon said, his voice weak and small. "We will drink and rest, and tomorrow will be better. It always is."

Moya looked back out at the void, at the yawning mouth of the Abyss.

No. I can't leave them like this.

She stood up.

I refuse to walk away and abandon them.

She took a step toward the brink.

"Moya?" Rain said. He was behind her somewhere.

"Leave me alone, Rain."

"But, Moya—over there. Look."

She was aware that the digger knew what she was planning. He'd tackled Gifford to prevent him from jumping off the bridge, and now he was trying to stop her, too. She wouldn't let that happen, yet something in his tone made her look.

The dwarf was pointing at a mass of bodies just before the bridge. These were the ones who had walked into Mideon's great ax and Melen's hammers. More than a dozen were left, abandoned by the queen. One face stood out.

"Tekchin!" Rushing over, Moya dropped to her knees. "Rain, help me!"

Together, they rolled bodies off the Instarya, revealing a grisly sight. Tekchin had fought valiantly. No mere stab wound had taken him down. Moya had seen butchered pigs that were more intact. An arm was missing, his head was nearly severed, and deep slices across his chest and thighs had gone through his armor as if it was cloth. Freeing him from the pile wasn't easy. They couldn't pull or drag for fear he would separate further.

"Tekchin! Tekchin!" Moya was nearly blinded as she sobbed. "Rain, help me!"

The dwarf was there. He'd found a cloth, a banner of some sort. Spreading it out, they gingerly laid Tekchin on it.

"We can drag him now," Rain said. "He'll be all right. It will take time, but he'll recover."

Moya continued to cry but managed to nod.

"He'll recover faster, and with less pain, if you're with him," Beatrice said.

The little white-haired seer was sitting on a shelf of stone a few yards away. She'd likely been there all along but became visible as the crowd thinned.

Moya spat on the ground. "You knew this was going to happen. This is what you refused to tell us."

"Yes," Beatrice said.

"You asked us to trust you."

"I didn't lie. I told you things would be bad—very bad—and then they would get worse. That's the truth, wouldn't you say?"

"But you withheld information. Why?"

The little dwarf stood up and looked out at the broken bridge. "Because you wouldn't have come if you'd known the cost, especially that it would be *them* paying the price rather than you. You would have taken the key and ordered the rest to remain safely in the castle.

"They would have protested with plenty of tears and shouts, but in the end, you would have gotten your way. As a result, the queen would have taken the key, the gates of Phyre would be thrown wide, and your little war centered on the Nidwalden River would be forgotten, replaced with a new conflict, one too massive and terrible to imagine. I know. I've seen it hundreds of times. The Golrok is the center of a maze that all paths go through. There is no way to avoid it. Not yet, at least."

"If there is no avoiding it, then why not choose an alternative where they didn't have to fall?"

"Because we need new paths, new options."

Moya spat again and wiped her nose. "You gambled with my friends, with the eternity of their souls."

Beatrice turned to face her. "This isn't a game, Moya, and you still have a part to play, so I can't tell you anything more except Tekchin needs you. Love—knowing someone cares about you—is a powerful medicine, both on Elan and, especially, in here. It gives a person hope, and that is unbelievably powerful."

CHAPTER FOUR

Losing the Light

*All too often, that which we are most certain of is that which we
are the most wrong about; and that which we are wrong about can
change everything.*

— THE BOOK OF BRIN

Gifford wandered the bleak landscape of craggy rocks, which were coated
with layers of crystallized frost. Each step made a declarative crunch.

Too loud, he thought, although he didn't know why.

The Abyss was desolate, deserted, and depressing. In comparison,
Dureya, with its brittle grasses, vast skies, and cloudscapes, was a paradise
of life and beauty. Gifford wandered the open plain between the two cliffs
with no specific direction. He searched for help in a place he suspected held
none. He felt heavy, burdened, and slow. Plus, his hip still hurt from the
fall. The injury got worse the more he moved, or maybe he'd misjudged the
initial extent of the damage. Walking was painful and noticeably tiring—at
least in comparison with how it had been since his death. Contrasted with
the thirty years he had lived, this was an almost insignificant hindrance,
certainly when viewed against the backdrop of his inability to help Tesh
and Tressa. And then there was Roan, or rather the lack of her, which made
his quest all the more desperate. The Abyss, he discovered, was a realm of
hopelessness.

As Gifford stepped down to a lower shelf of rock, his hip twinged in pain. He put a hand to his side and worked at rubbing away the hurtful spasm. The effort succeeded, and the sensation faded.

No body, he reminded himself. *The pain is self-inflicted.* This conjured a new and bewildering question: Why had Tressa and Tesh suffered so much more from their falls?

The two had resembled collapsed tents, spread out in gruesome displays. Despite knowing they lacked bodies, they puddled in pain and wallowed in anguish. Gifford stepped up onto another shelf, and felt the stab in his hip again.

And I can't erase the idea of a wound that is getting worse. This realization disturbed Gifford. *What does that mean? It seems we are our own worst enemies.*

A sound.

He heard it, or thought he had.

Gifford stopped and listened. Staring out into the dark, he tried to will it so.

Nothing. Just wishful thinking.

But in the absence of anything else, Gifford embraced hope and imagined the sound had come from a nearby rock wall, so he veered toward it. Vertical fissures appeared as violent scars in the dark-gray stone—the claw marks of some colossal beast. As he neared a cleft at its base, Gifford heard voices, or, more precisely, a voice.

Something is inside.

Gifford was aware he had thought *something* instead of *someone.* He remembered Brin telling him about a raow she had overheard in Alon Rhist, and that certainly couldn't be described as a person. But in this new world, anything might be possible. Only the mental picture of Tesh's and Tressa's mangled bodies and their pleas for help drove him inside. Entering slowly, Gifford took time to allow his light to peel back the mystery of the interior. The entrance was narrow, but the fissure widened as he went deeper. He paused to listen. No sound. *Maybe I'm mistaken.* Caves were usually empty things. The noise had been so slight.

I was wrong. This is the Abyss. It's nothing but a void.

"You've been a naughty girl, haven't you?" A voice issued from deeper in the cave. "A very, very bad girl."

I know that voice!

"You poisoned Daddy. Fed me something terrible and then watched me die, frothing like one of Gelston's sheep. I can see why you landed here. The gods can't forgive a killing like that."

Oh, dear Mother of All, not him! And who is he talking to? Gifford knew the answer, though he shoved it away, denied it the right to be. *No!* he thought. *Not her! Not him!* Moving deeper, rushing forward, Gifford's light revealed the answer.

Iver the Carver stood crouched in a small pocket-chamber. He looked soft, fat, and greasy. Gifford hadn't noticed before, but seeing that pasty face and bags for cheeks and that extra ring of neck, he realized Iver was the only one on the dahl to have cut such a round figure. He wasn't just fat and sagging due to his weight. He looked melted, like a candle left in the sun.

Iver stooped over something that lay on the ground.

"How's my daughter, eh?" Iver cooed.

Daughter?

Iver noticed the light and turned. The wax man was dressed in rags, remnants of a long-forgotten tunic. Torn and threadbare as spiderwebs, the unraveled ends waved with the same eerie undulating motion as long hair underwater. Spittle glistened on Iver's lower lip, and as small as his eyes were, they were wide with an eager joy. As Iver moved, Gifford gasped.

Roan lay at his feet. She didn't move except to quiver, didn't speak except to moan.

Instantly the cave grew bright as Gifford's rage flared. "Let go of my wife!" he shouted.

"Gifford? Gifford . . . the Cripple?" Iver stared in shock, backing up.

Gifford wasn't wearing armor, didn't have his sword, but none of that mattered. He charged in with fury and a raised fist. "I said let her go!" The quiet potter of Dahl Rhen shook, but not with cold. His eyes were wide and wild, his jaw clenched.

Iver cowered.

"'Touch her again and I'll find a rock and spend eternity bashing your head in! You got that?" He was screaming then. "Do you understand me, you sick son of a bitch? You stay away from her!"

Iver disappeared into the dark recesses of the cave as Gifford reached down and gently lifted Roan in his arms. She continued to cry as Gifford carried her out.

"Don't go out there," Iver said from the shadows. "It's not safe. The light . . . they will come for you."

At the sound of his voice, Roan shuddered.

"It's okay, Roan," Gifford whispered. "I've got you. He's gone. He won't touch you anymore. I promise. I'll tear him apart with my bare hands if he ever tries, so help me. With Eton as my witness and Elan as my judge, I swear it."

*

By the time Gifford had carried Roan back to the others, things had improved. While they still lay broken on the frost, both Tesh and Tressa had recovered somewhat. Instead of appearing crushed, Tesh's head merely looked as if he'd been horribly beaten with a stout stick. Teeth were still missing, and his nose was askew, but at least his jaw seemed to be working. Tressa had not recovered nearly so much, though she had rolled to her side, and her twisted limbs had resumed what resembled proper alignment.

Both could talk again.

"You found Roan," Tesh said. His head tilted slightly as he struggled to see. His jaw was working, but Tesh's voice was weak and shaky.

Gifford nodded as he laid Roan beside Tressa. He started to draw away, but Roan surprised him by latching onto his arm with surprising strength. "Don't leave me."

"I'm not going anywhere," he assured her. "And you should know by now, I'll never leave you."

Just the same, Roan pulled him into an embrace and held on. "So scared."

"If I could kill him for you, I would."

"Who?" Tesh asked.

"Iver the Carver."

"Iver is down here?" Tressa asked, then winced in pain from the effort.

Which wound troubled her was beyond Gifford's ability to reckon. The woman was battered such that he couldn't look at her. "He took Roan."

"And you found him?" Despite her obvious agony, Tressa managed a grin. "How'd that go?"

"I didn't need to do anything. I just yelled."

"Really? You let him go?"

Gifford rolled his shoulders. "Roan's all I care about." He brushed the hair from her face. When he'd first found her, she had looked terrible. Not as bad as Tressa, but not far behind. Her face had been black and blue, bleeding from a dozen cuts. Like Tesh, some of her front teeth had been missing, her nose crushed, and one eye was pooling with blood. Now her teeth were back. Her eye was still red but clearing, and her nose only had a bad bruise. Like the others, she, too, was recovering. Each reclaimed a sense of themselves but at different rates. Roan outpaced the others, and as he watched the bruises began receding.

"You look so much better," he told her, tears watering his eyes.

"You're bringing me back," she whispered, her lips trembling.

"Do you know where Brin is?" Tesh asked, his voice growing steadier as he spoke. "See any trace of her out there?"

Gifford shook his head. "There's nothing. Wouldn't have found Roan if I hadn't heard Iver's voice. He had dragged her into a cave." Gifford searched his wife's face. "Did he do anything to you?"

Roan shook her head, eyes fixed on him as if unable to let go even for a moment. "Didn't have time. He had more trouble carrying me than you did. He was exhausted from the effort. Thank you, Gifford. Thank you. I was so scared. To be alone—all alone . . . with him."

Roan shuddered.

"I love you," he said. "I always have and always will."

As if the words were magic, Roan calmed. She wiped tears from her eyes and under her own power rose to a sitting position. Then she smiled at him. "You're my hero."

At the sound of those words and the sight of her happy face, Gifford realized he no longer felt pain. The ache of his hip was gone, and he felt oddly lighter.

"You're brighter," Roan said. She took a moment to study him. "Your light—it's more brilliant than when you first found me."

He shrugged. "You bring me back, too, I guess."

"Good thing," Tressa said. "Dark down here—wherever *here* is."

Roan looked up toward the absent sky. "Did anyone else fall?"

"Brin did," Tesh said, then grunted as he struggled to lift his head. "So heavy. Can barely move."

"Like water," Roan said. "When you dive under, the weight increases the deeper you go."

They each looked up and nodded as if they could see the weight.

"I think this is what Tressa and Tesh were feeling up there." Roan pointed. "But down here, with depth, it's worse. It's terrible. You feel it, don't you, Gifford?"

He shrugged. "A little. It was worse before—not so bad now. Just feel a bit sluggish is all."

"I wonder what happened to Brin?" Tesh said. "This Iver guy, do you think he might have done something to her, too?"

"I didn't see her," Gifford said. "If I had—believe me—I would have brought her back, too."

"Of course, I didn't mean . . ." Tesh swallowed, and Gifford couldn't help but think it was blood filling his mouth. "I'm just scared."

"Trust me. I understand."

Roan shook her head. "Brin wasn't there. Just me and Iver. He talked as if I were a present sent to him by the gods. I couldn't move. Couldn't talk." She shivered.

"You're safe with me, now. I'm not a cripple anymore, and I might not be able to kill that old bastard, but if he ever threatens you again, I'll make him wish I could."

"I'm not scared," she told him, and once more she pulled him close and laid her head on his shoulder. "It's just that—it's cold down here."

She shivered again, and seeing her do so had the same effect as witnessing a yawn. Tressa began to shiver and then Tesh did as well.

"It is cold, isn't it?" Gifford looked around, searching for a solution, but he saw only the unending broken plain, the root cellar of the world. "Maybe we should make another fire."

Roan's eyes widened with fear.

"I don't think the queen can reach us down here, Roan." Gifford glanced up but saw nothing: no queen, bankors, or even the top of the crevasse. Everything beyond the reach of Gifford's light was the same—darkness. "Don't think anyone can."

Roan shook her head. "Nothing to burn."

"Don't need anything. It's not real fire."

Roan trapped her quivering lower lip between her teeth. She looked back at him with trepidation. "I don't know how to without wood." She seemed worried about letting him down.

"That's okay," he told her. "I don't even know if we can make fire here."

The Abyss felt like another place, a forgotten corner of the afterlife, and who knew what worked or didn't at the bottom of the world. In Rel and the upper levels of Nifrel, people were able to use their eshim to craft their surroundings into a place of their liking. But this place was a blank canvas—no, not a canvas, the frame. Gifford imagined all of Phyre might have been like the Abyss when the first dead arrived. The weight and pressure wasn't as crippling in the highlands, so those like Ferrol and Drome had been able to exert their wills and craft a place to their liking. But down in the depths of the Abyss, wills were crushed, and eshim in short supply. There wasn't enough to alter the landscape.

"It's not the fire that's important. We're looking at it all wrong. We're not really even cold. It's the *idea* of warmth that we need."

"I do feel warmer beside you," Roan admitted.

He nodded. "It's like the well in the Rhen village in Rel. More people, more eshim."

Roan looked at the open expanse. "The cold isn't real, but the idea is. We think it's freezing because it looks that way. Out here in the open, on this frozen ground, we can't help thinking icy thoughts."

"If we can find shelter, someplace small like Iver's cave, we might be able to imagine our body heat warming one another. I think that would help. Then we could work on finding a way out of here." Gifford considered driving Iver out and taking his cave, but he suspected that revisiting his place might be worse for Roan than sitting in the open.

"A way out?" Tressa said, stunned.

"We fell," he said. "Seems reasonable we can climb out, right?"

"No, it doesn't."

"Well, sure," Gifford admitted. "Right now, nothing feels possible, but once we find shelter, everything will seem better. Roan, can you walk?"

"I think so." She bent her legs, pushing to her knees. "I think maybe, yes."

Gifford looked at Tesh.

"I'm not going anywhere." The man was still laid out on the stone.

Gifford didn't bother asking Tressa. The woman resembled a sack of snapped sticks. He couldn't carry them all.

It's hopeless.

"Gifford?" Roan said. "What's wrong? Your light . . . it's dimming again."

"Sorry I—I don't know what causes that."

"Hope," she said. "Faith, maybe. That's what must give us the power to push back against the dark."

"Foolish optimism," Tressa said. "Which I just don't get, by the way." She lifted her eyes to stare at Gifford because lifting her head appeared impossible. "You lived a life of misery, spat on by everyone including the gods—no, *especially* the gods. I was better off than you—for a time, at least. Then you're granted a handful of not entirely appalling years, and now you're Mister Sunshine, all bright and cheerful. How's that possible?"

"I have Roan," he replied. "And very low expectations. It doesn't take much to make me happy."

"But you're not happy," Roan said. "Your light, it's still getting weaker. What's wrong?"

Gifford tried to will himself brighter, but that didn't work. "I don't know what to do. All of you are hurt. I want to help, but I don't know how. I'm feeling—I'm feeling a bit overwhelmed and a lot scared."

"We're dragging you down with us," Roan said.

Gifford's light grew fainter. "You're no weight to me, Roan."

"I'm certainly no support," Tressa said.

Tesh, who had been trying to roll to his side, gave up. Roan, too, settled back to resting on her elbows.

I'm losing them, Gifford thought, and once more his light weakened.

"Giff . . . ard," Roan said, squeezing him. "Dun't let it git to ouu." Her words were slurred. Her mouth—something was wrong with it. Her front teeth—*she's missing them again!*

Gifford felt the cold rush in. He shivered, and his light, once as strong as a lantern in the night, became little more than a flickering candle. He felt the weight pushing down, pinning him to the frost.

He clutched Roan, wrapped his arms around her, squeezing tight. There was still warmth there as long as he had her. "I love you," he said, hoping the magic would work again.

Roan looked up and smiled, showing perfect teeth.

Tressa, who by then was lying with her cheek on the frost, staring out across the plain, whispered, "What in Phyre is that?"

In the distance, a light appeared—a dazzling sight just above the horizon.

"It's like the morning star," Roan said.

"Don't go out there," Iver had warned. *"It's not safe. The light . . . they will come for you."*

"It's getting bigger." Gifford hugged Roan tighter, until he was afraid he might hurt her. "It's coming at us."

Fearfully gazing at the brilliance that grew larger by the second, the four held their collective breath. They lay directly in its path.

Who are they? Gifford wondered.

A moment later, he realized it wasn't a *they,* but a *who,* and she was beyond brilliant.

℘

Running up to them, Brin shouted, "Tesh!"

To find anyone in the Abyss was wonderful; to find *him* was a joy. Yet this was the last place she would have wished Tesh to be.

He looked terrible, all mangled, mutilated, and sprawled out on the hard ground. Tressa looked worse. Roan was better, Gifford the best, but none of them looked good.

"You're alive—" Brin caught herself. "You're *okay.*"

Tesh put up a hand to shield his eyes and peered at her. "Brin?"

She came close and watched as his face, bruised as it was, shifted from confused to elated.

"It's me," she told him.

"You're all right."

"I'm fine. Well . . ." She looked behind her. "There were these scary things after me, but I think I lost them. They don't move very fast, and I'm pretty quick. I'm hoping that once I got out of their sight, they stopped. Even if they didn't, it ought to take them about a year to get this far."

Tesh's hands inched off the ground. They shook with the effort, but he managed to cup Brin's face. Cradling it ever so gently, he pulled her to him and they kissed. He was shuddering, his whole body quaking. "I'm so sorry, Brin. I failed you. Raithe begged me to take you away, to find a peaceful little place where we could make a new life together. He was showing me how to live, to *really* live. I should have listened. I was the last Dureyan, and because of me—because I didn't listen to the man who was like a father to me—my entire clan is gone."

Tears welled in Brin's eyes. The man who had been so strong, so confident and capable, now lay before her, broken and frail. She didn't trust her voice to speak.

"It doesn't even matter if you can't love me," he went on, filling the silence. "I love you, and I should have married you. I should have listened to Raithe and taken you away and had children . . ." His voice broke. He gave up the effort and hugged her.

"I love you, too," Brin managed. "And we can still have all those things Raithe wanted as soon as we get out of here."

"How can you love me? You know what I did."

"Yes, I do. You followed me into the pool."

"That's not what I meant."

She smiled at him. "I love you, Tesh. Don't ask me to explain it. I just do."

"I don't understand."

"Tesh, loving you isn't something I *decide*. It isn't a choice. Maybe I shouldn't love you, but I do. It's not something I control."

"That doesn't make sense."

"Doesn't have to. Not everything is logical. Scales don't need to be balanced. Wrongs don't need to be righted. I'm not like you, Tesh."

"He's not like you, either," Tressa said. "He's an idiot."

"Maybe," Gifford said. "But he's standing."

CHAPTER FIVE

Inconvenient Daughters

You never know who you will meet—even after you have met them.
— THE BOOK OF BRIN

I don't know what's wrong with me.

Imaly felt sick. She'd been feeling horrible and getting worse.

Maybe I'm too old for this.

The thought had rattled inside her head for days, growing louder as it fought to be heard over the noises in the house.

Revolution is for the young, she considered before remembering the tragic fates of Makareta and Aiden. *No, that's not true. The young are too foolish.*

Although the youthful benefited from drive, ambition, and an unwavering faith in their ideals, having those tools wasn't enough. *Experience* was an essential missing ingredient. The young hadn't seen enough to understand how the world worked. They took everything at face value because that was the entirety of their reality, and that limitation locked the door to alternative possibilities.

To those who had glimpsed just a fraction of the landscape, assumptions were rampant and dangerous. Only by riding the slow river of time could a person distinguish the *what-is* from the *what-was* and determine the likelihood of *what-could-be*. That comparison granted wisdom and understanding. Some things were eternal, others could be temporarily altered, but a few things—a very few—could be changed such that the world shifted forever. Sacrifices made for the unchangeable or even the short term were foolish. But like those who are colorblind and faced with a red, green, and yellow door, the young couldn't tell the difference.

So it's up to me.

Imaly sighed.

From the other side of the wall, the banging started again. Muffled shouts were followed by laughter coming from the bedroom. When Suri had first arrived, Imaly had been concerned that the mystic and Makareta would clash, and such a conflict would drive Makareta into a deeper depression. If that had happened, it could have made both of the Artists useless to the Curator. To her surprise and good fortune, bonds of friendship had risen from their recent tragic pasts.

Imaly's second concern was Suri's presence attracting attention from the neighbors. Adding such a high-profile individual to her home was bound to draw interest. Imaly had nightmares of Fhrey from the outer villages knocking on her door and asking to see Suri. As it turned out, that didn't happen. No one wanted anything to do with *the Rhune,* and everyone avoided Estramnadon now that the fane was making dragons. Even those already in the city sequestered themselves in their homes, fearing a knock on their door.

Vidar had made the first dragon and had done so not far from Avempartha. Imaly often wondered what that trip had been like. Had he talked to his sister? Explained that he didn't have a choice? Or had he spent the time weeping and begging for forgiveness? Suri had explained to Imaly what was necessary to "play the deep chords," which explained why the Rhunes only had a single dragon.

Lothian wanted more.

Imaly knew that. Everyone did. And that's why the residents of Estramnadon stayed in their homes, hiding behind doors and hoping the knock wouldn't come.

The only two people who didn't worry about being sacrificed were the ones roughhousing in the next room. For all Imaly's fear that Suri and Makareta would coexist as well as fire and water, it turned out the two were remedies for each other. Their unlikely friendship had done wonders for Makareta's depression, and hopefully dulled the sharp edge of mistrust Jerydd had fostered in Suri by his mistreatment of her.

Thump! The portrait of Gylindora Fane that hung on the wall rattled and tilted askew.

"Stop it!" Imaly erupted. "Whatever it is you two are doing, stop!"

The Curator collapsed into a sunlit chair in the little nook that looked out on her vegetable garden, now lost in snow.

"Did you call us?" Makareta came around the partition wearing her filthy smock and a guilty expression.

Suri lagged behind. She wore Imaly's best asica, which was now tailored to fit.

"Must you tear my house apart!" Imaly got up and straightened the picture.

"We were just—"

"I don't care what you were doing. I can't take much more."

"What's wrong?" Makareta took a tentative step, and Imaly noticed the young Fhrey had a hammer in her hand.

What in the name of Ferrol are they doing?

"Nothing," Imaly lied, this time out of convenience rather than anything else. She didn't want to explain how she felt like a grape being pressed into wine. The members of the Aquila were losing their resolve, and Vasek seemed to be wavering as well. He was a fragile piece of expensive crystal she'd left at the edge of a table, and the wind was rising.

On top of everything else, innocent people were dying—or would be soon. So much had been laid on her shoulders: the legacy of her ancestors, the outcome of the war, and the future of the Fhrey people. She held the lever and the burden of pulling it. And each night she came home to the antics of Suri and Makareta.

Imaly sighed. "But it is time to go over a few things, so please sit down. Both of you."

The two pulled over chairs, moving them to the shadows to avoid the blinding sun that pierced the windows. Realizing the drapes were open, Imaly closed them before returning to her chair.

It'd be cosmic justice if someone spotted Makareta and reported me. Especially now that this is almost over.

"By *a few things,* do you mean . . ." Makareta began, her voice dropping in volume and rising in seriousness.

Imaly nodded as she took her seat once more, then focused on Suri, who, despite Imaly's efforts to keep an open mind, appeared ridiculous when dressed in an asica. Even with the alterations, it was both too big and the wrong style. This was the dress Imaly usually reserved for formal settings, and to see a Rhune wrapped in it was to witness the clashing of extremes. In many ways, this collision was appropriate, as Suri was a monument to contradictions.

"I don't know if you've heard," Imaly began, "but a dragon has been successfully created."

"Where?" Suri asked, her grim tone making Makareta's sound casual.

"Avempartha." Imaly tensed. This was the first of three dangerous hurdles she would have to clear, and none of them would be easy.

"I told you I wouldn't allow my people to be hurt." Suri's words were delivered as a threat.

Imaly wasn't surprised. She'd expected it, but there was a difference between suspecting a pet bear could turn on you and actually hearing it growl. Imaly had already learned that Suri wasn't a subtle person, so the Curator knew the tone wasn't being used to intimidate.

Imaly faced the point of a sharpened spear as she spoke her next words carefully. "I have not forgotten our agreement, and please note that I could have kept this information from you but didn't. That event has accelerated our need to act quickly. Tomorrow night I'll hold an official meeting of the Aquila where we will pass a resolution to remove Lothian from the throne. The following day, we will kill him, fulfilling my part of our bargain."

Imaly waited and watched Suri, who knitted her tattooed brows in thought.

As much as Imaly wanted to get through this quickly, she understood the value of patience. She couldn't rush. Accidents happened when people pushed ahead too fast.

"Has there been an attack on my people?" the mystic asked.

"As far as I understand the situation, the dragon cleared the river camp and drove off the soldiers stationed there. This first beast's purpose is for defense. More will be made for attacking, which is why—in order to stay true to our agreement—I have moved up my schedule. Is that satisfactory? Or will you kill me now?"

Makareta's eyes widened, and she straightened up, turning to get a better view of Suri and looking at the mystic like she had just morphed into something else. "What kind of deal did you two have?"

Neither answered as Suri stared at Imaly. From the cold glare, the Curator wondered if she had overplayed her hand, misjudged the girl.

"You're not telling the whole truth," Suri said.

Imaly swallowed, holding still, fearful of betraying anything.

She's using magic, but she can't read minds. No Miralyith can.

Silence had never been so deafening as when those three sat facing one another. To the ignorant observer, they were three females chatting in a kitchen when a disagreement arose. For Imaly, the world, and everyone in it, swung on what would happen next. She forced herself to take even breaths as she wondered if Makareta would defend her if Suri decided to melt off the Curator's skin.

"You're lying to me," Suri said. "But . . ."

With the thought of her skin hissing and crackling as it dripped down her body, Imaly was never so happy to hear the word *but* in her life.

"Yes?"

"But that doesn't matter. Arion's path goes through you. It has to. I'm sure of it."

"So you'll let me live?"

Suri nodded.

"Well, that's good to hear," Makareta said with exaggerated nonchalance. "What just happened?"

"Fortunately, nothing." Imaly took a deep breath as she prepared for the next hurdle.

Might as well get all of them over with at once.

Addressing the young Miralyith, she said, "But that doesn't mean we're done. Now it's your turn."

"Mine?" Makareta asked. She looked at Suri and then back at Imaly as if they were co-conspirators in some fiendish plot.

"I have a favor to ask, a rather terrible one."

Once more, Makareta straightened in the chair, bracing for bad news. After that last bout, the Miralyith appeared unquestionably frightened.

"The fane is protected by two bodyguards: Synne and Sile. I suspect Sile will be of little consequence, but Synne is a Miralyith, and she has a reputation for being incredibly fast. In order to kill the fane, Synne must be eliminated first."

"You want me to kill her?" Makareta asked.

Imaly fixed her jaw and returned a grave nod.

"Is that all? That's the terrible thing?"

"Yes," Imaly replied. "I'm asking you to murder her."

Makareta smiled, then began to chuckle. "Not a problem."

Imaly found her cavalier response unexpected and a bit disturbing. "Are you certain?"

"She killed Aiden," Makareta said. "I'd be more than happy to *eliminate* her. One more death won't make a difference."

"Well then . . . good." Imaly paused and smoothed the wrinkles on the lap of her asica where she had unconsciously been squeezing a fistful of material.

Time for the last hurdle.

"All of this will happen very quickly. Everyone needs to know what to expect. So let's go over this, shall we?"

Suri and Makareta glanced at each other. Both shrugged, childish gestures for those who would soon hold the fate of tens of thousands in their hands.

For this next part, Imaly stood up. She wasn't prone to pacing back and forth, but she found walking to be calming. The room was small, so she was forced to orbit the little nook's wooden table. Legend held that it was the one her great-grandfather, Eyan, had crafted for Gylindora, and it had been the reason her great-grandmother had fallen in love with him. Why something as mundane as a table had formed the foundation of their love was a mystery to Imaly, and everyone else. It didn't matter. Some things just were.

"At my urging," Imaly started, "the fane will give a State of the War address in the Airenthenon the day after tomorrow. When he does, I want both of you there. Suri won't be allowed inside, so she will need to wait on the steps."

"Why should I be there at all?" the mystic asked.

"Absolutely no reason—*if* everything goes as planned, and let's hope that will be the case. My greatest wish is that you spend an hour being bored while watching the proceedings through the archway. But should things not follow my plan, you're my insurance, and I expect you to step in and protect me, the members of the Aquila, and the peace we intend to offer your people. Is that too much to ask?"

"I'll be there," Suri said, but it didn't escape Imaly's notice that she hadn't answered the question.

"And what about me? Exactly how and when should I act?" Makareta asked.

"You will come to the Airenthenon the same way you visited Vasek, with your hood raised and using that blocking shield that hides your Miralyith powers. Since it's winter, no one will find it odd that your hood is up. Inside, people will be standing around talking in small groups. I'll be in the center. Find me. Volhoric and I will position you behind the dais. There are two massive staggered sets of pillars there, eight or nine feet in diameter, at least. That'll be more than enough to disappear behind. Everyone in attendance has been handpicked and briefed, so no one will take notice. I'm only concerned about someone unexpected wandering in, and of course, Sile and Synne. So keep yourself out of sight. When the fane sits down, Synne will position herself on Lothian's right and Sile will be on his left."

"Won't they search the Airenthenon before the fane enters?"

"They never do."

"Why not?"

"Why would they?"

Makareta glanced at Suri, who gave no indication of caring one way or the other. "Oh, I don't know. Maybe to make sure no one is lying in wait to kill the guy they're protecting, perhaps? We did try to assassinate him once before, after all."

"No—not we," Imaly said. "That was you and your friends. But that was years ago, and we both know what happened to those who participated in the Gray Cloak Rebellion. Lothian feels quite safe these days. He sees himself as our beloved god-leader who is shielded by the fact that Fhrey don't kill Fhrey. He only fears the Rhunes, and they are across the river, much too far away to be of any concern."

"I'm not across the river," Suri pointed out.

"True." Imaly nodded. "But he still believes you are inhibited by the Orinfar collar. Any threat from you would be physical and Synne and Sile would be more than enough to stop you before you got too close. The only true threat would be a Miralyith, and as far as Lothian knows, all of them are several days away except for his bodyguard, himself, and his son."

"Vasek knows I'm still alive. What if he or someone from the Aquila has had a change of heart and warned Lothian?" Makareta asked.

"Then I suspect where you stand won't make the slightest bit of difference. Besides, if that were so, we would have been arrested. Are you still concerned? Or can we move on?"

Imaly waited, but Makareta remained silent.

"Now then, as the fane delivers his speech, you will kill Synne. Yours will be the action that triggers all else, so time it for a minute or so into his address. Afterward, it would be in your best interest to eliminate Sile, as he will likely be coming for you."

"Shouldn't I kill Lothian first?"

"No. You're only there for Synne and Sile."

"Then who will? And how?" Makareta asked.

Imaly stopped walking. "We're hoping to convince Mawyndulë."

At the mention of the name, both of them reacted. Suri's brows rose, and Makareta began shaking her head as she leaned forward in the wooden chair.

"No. No. Mawyndulë can't kill his father. If he does, he'll lose his soul."

"He won't."

"Imaly, we've talked about this. I can't allow it. I won't let him . . ."

Imaly held up her hands. "He won't lose his soul—not for this. I have it on the highest authority."

"What are you talking about?"

"Volhoric, Ferrol's high priest, has pointed out that Lothian has shattered his covenant with Ferrol. When he murdered Amidea, an innocent, he forever revoked his standing as a Fhrey who is protected by Ferrol's Law. This one act—just like yours—has ejected him from our society, so he can be killed without any repercussions whatsoever."

"Are you certain?"

"Volhoric has assured me of this, and he will testify as such before the Aquila when we reveal our intentions and ask Mawyndulë to save us."

"But . . ." Makareta hesitated. "Having him kill his own father? That's a lot to ask."

"It is, but we have no choice. Mawyndulë knows better than anyone about the perils of having Lothian's rule continue. He'll do what's needed."

"But what if you're wrong about his soul being safe," Makareta said. "Mine is already gone, so I should be the one."

"You can't kill Synne *and* Lothian *and* Sile—not without taking down the whole Airenthenon and everyone else with it, can you?" Afraid that her own lack of understanding about the Art might grant Makareta a means to dispute the statement, Imaly quickly added, "Even if you could, it's too risky. Synne is formidable, and this is too important for half measures. We'll need two Artists."

"Then why don't you have Suri do it?" Makareta asked.

Imaly was genuinely shocked at the suggestion. "You might not have noticed, Mak, but Suri is a Rhune. A race we are presently at war with. What do you think will be the reaction when the people discover the Aquila invited our enemy to kill our leader? Mawyndulë has the best chance of success. Synne, Sile, and you will be behind Lothian, and the fane will have to turn to see what is happening. This will provide Mawyndulë, who will be seated with the other Aquila members in the gallery in front of Lothian, with the perfect opportunity to attack without his father having any chance to defend himself. Moreover, Lothian won't expect his son to be an assassin. It *must* be him."

Makareta considered this. She didn't look like she agreed, but the fight was draining from her. "And then he will be fane, correct?"

"Yes, Mak," Imaly said. "With Synne dead and Vidar on the frontier, I can't imagine anyone else—any non-Miralyith—would take the risk to challenge him. Even you can't do it. The horn won't sound for you because you're no longer a Fhrey. Besides, after the fane is dead, I'll be presenting the horn to Suri."

"Why?" Makareta asked, glancing between them.

"For two reasons. One, it was part of the deal I made with Suri, an even trade. She gave Lothian the ability to create dragons, which threatened her people, and I promised her the horn to restrain ours. We both have the means to rule over each other, but this whole affair has been a gamble that we both are sincere about seeking peace. Giving her the horn will provide the appropriate leverage to ensure Mawyndulë negotiates with the Rhunes."

"How does her having the horn do that?"

"Normally the Aquila holds it. When a fane dies, his eldest child is instantly recognized as a candidate for the throne. By virtue of keeping the horn, the Aquila decides who can blow it—who can challenge the heir to be fane. But that isn't actually a requirement. We could refuse to let anyone use it and the child will become fane . . . sort of."

"What do you mean by *sort of?*"

Imaly took a big breath and blew it out so her cheek quivered.

What I wouldn't do for a chalkboard right now.

The Horn of Gylindora wasn't a simple artifact. Its rules were detailed, arcane, complex, and often confusing to outsiders—meaning those who were not the Curator or Conservator of the horn. Explanations were never easy, but in this case, providing one would be necessary.

"If the horn isn't blown, no challenge has been declared, and there is no time limit to make one. So while Mawyndulë will have the powers of fane, any Fhrey can still blow the horn at any time to challenge him. Which means, if Mawyndulë doesn't work toward peace, then Suri can seek a challenger of her choosing. Then Mawyndulë would need to fight her choice or concede his position. Of course, Suri won't need to do that because Fane Mawyndulë's first act will be to declare peace between the Fhrey and the Rhunes, or at least that will be my counsel. And Mawyndulë has grown to trust my opinion over the years."

Makareta asked, "So there's normally a time limit?"

"Yes. For instance, when the fane dies and he has no heir. In that case, there would generally be two challengers. The first person to blow it starts a cycle that ends after the passing of a full day and night. If no one else blows the horn during that time, the first person becomes fane."

"So if the horn is used to challenge for the throne, why wouldn't an heir just blow it himself? Wouldn't that prevent him from being challenged?"

Imaly shook her head. "No. It wouldn't work. The horn already accepts the heir as a blood candidate, and it only sounds to announce a challenger. But if there isn't an heir, the first horn blast starts a day-night cycle. Since all Fhrey hear its call, it gives everyone time to put forth their names so that the Aquila can choose both candidates."

The Rhune girl sat with arms folded across her chest in an obstinate manner. "I didn't know Mawyndulë would be the new fane. He killed Arion."

"Suri, do you want revenge or peace? Take your pick. You can't have both."

Imaly waited. When neither had anything more to say, she nodded decisively. "Good. Now we all know where things stand, and may Ferrol help us. Mak, at the Aquila meeting, we'll need your help convincing Mawyndulë he has to be the one to kill his father. I think once we give him assurances that he'll be in no danger of losing his soul he'll go along. But you should also stay with him afterward and gauge his resolve. If you think there's a chance he won't go through with it, you'll need to let me know right away. Can you manage that?"

Makareta grinned, and Imaly felt a stab of pain. Makareta was the obvious choice to help persuade the prince. She'd already seduced him once, so she could again. By all accounts, the girl seemed to genuinely like Mawyndulë and had always wanted the prince to be fane. She might even be in love with him. It was possible she expected Mawyndulë to forgive her crimes, accept her back into Fhrey society, and marry her. Then the two would live thousands of years together. Such were the dreams of youth—that bliss could be achieved so easily and sustained indefinitely. It weighed on Imaly's conscience that she didn't set Makareta straight about the realities of life.

Guilt. That's what's making me feel so terrible.

Imaly had always wondered if she had missed something by not having a child, a daughter, someone who would bang on the wall of her bedroom when she was trying to think. Now she had two. And instead of bestowing her love, she was using them. Every day together made matters worse.

I like them too much. This betrayal is going to kill me. But they're not my daughters, Imaly reminded herself.

Even if they were, she would still have to go through with it. The stakes were higher than any single life, or two, or three. Imaly wondered where the pros and cons finally evened out. At what point did the deaths and betrayals become too great?

They aren't my daughters.

Imaly let the thought repeat in her head as it fought to be heard over the cries of her own heart.

CHAPTER SIX

The Cave

Hope is a fragile thing, despair a hammer.
— THE BOOK OF BRIN

Brin couldn't understand what had happened to them and why her drop had been so easy. Gifford told her about how ghastly everyone had appeared right after impact, explaining how some hit harder than others. She was sorry she hadn't been there to help but pleased she hadn't seen it. The thought of Tesh's crushed head and scattered teeth was difficult to hear, let alone witness. According to Gifford, the trio were much better than when he had found them.

They had been the only ones to fall. According to Tesh, Moya and Rain had been taken by Ferrol. Miraculously, Tekchin had turned up and freed Tesh from the queen's tower, but the two had been separated during the battle at the bridge. Tesh and Tressa had fallen when he broke the stone span to prevent the White Queen from getting Eton's Key.

The news that Moya wasn't with them was both a blessing and a curse. More than ever, Brin felt the need for their confident, headstrong leader. While she was concerned about what Ferrol might do to Moya and Rain, she suspected they were better off than the ones who had fallen.

"Those lost to the Abyss are never seen again." That was what Ferrol had said just before Brin fell into the Abyss.

Was she just being overly dramatic? I mean, yeah, it's far, but given enough time we should be able to climb out. And I don't think time is the same in Phyre as it is on Elan.

Looking at the sorry state of the others, she knew scaling the cliff walls wasn't possible . . . not yet.

They just need more time to heal.

After finding them, the group had sat in the open for a long time. Brin waited for Tesh, Gifford, or even Tressa to step forward with a plan. Being the youngest—and an extraneous member of the group—she didn't think it was her place to step forward.

When none of them had shown any sign of doing more than sitting, Brin had asked for suggestions, but none were given. The only conversation revolved around being cold and wanting shelter. Which way to go, or when to set out, seemed too difficult a problem to overcome. Brin had tried for consensus, calling for votes on various options. Even that proved to be too much, so she accepted the unwanted role of leader. Summoning her inner Moya, she barked them to their feet, demanded they walk, and kept everyone moving with the promise they could rest soon.

She helped Gifford with Tressa, who could barely move. Between them, the older woman slumped and dragged her feet, leaving furrows in the frosty crust, torment displayed in the taut lines of her face. Tesh and Roan followed, helping each other. Neither looked good, as if every step was an agony.

Brin searched for a place that was sheltered, a niche or crevice, but she remained hesitant to get too close to the ravines for fear of discovering more of the slug-like creatures. She had easily outrun the globs that had been drawn to her light like moths to flame but didn't think Tressa and Tesh could do the same. Perhaps those creatures were harmless, but Brin didn't want to risk finding out otherwise. Frustrated with her inability to find anything but open expanse and plagued with complaints from the others about being exhausted, Brin took note of some bits of shattered rock. In desperation, she steered them that way and found more. Pieces lay strewn across the ground. They ranged from boulders to chips. She followed the fragments and wondered where they had come from.

A landslide? In the Abyss?

She tracked the growing mounds of stone to the foot of a cliff. Quickly glancing around, she found the place devoid of globs. What's more, there was a cave, but it was a strange thing. Nothing about it appeared natural. The opening was huge, and—

"Looks like something ripped the stone open," Gifford said, standing beside her, Tressa's opposite arm over his neck. He pointed at the distinct grooves in the rock, the same sort of marks a person left when digging in mud. "Something big."

Big didn't begin to describe the opening before them. By picking such a mundane word, Gifford was likely trying to minimize the possible implication, perhaps for her benefit. What Brin saw was a hole ripped in the side of the cliff that would have required something with appendages larger than Goll the one-eyed giant or Balgargarath from Neith. Even if she and the rest of their group stood on one another's shoulders, they couldn't touch the top of the entrance's archway.

"What could have made this?" she asked.

"Dunno," Gifford replied. "This is real stone, not created by eshim. What could dig through that? Should we go in?"

"I'm not sure."

"I hear something," Roan said from behind them. Both she and Tesh were looking back over their shoulders. "Something is coming."

They listened. It didn't take long before Brin picked out the throbbing resonance. She'd never heard anything like it. Delivered in a constant rhythm, the sound was deep, below what normal, living ears could hear. It reverberated off the cliffs and shook the frost-covered ground.

"I think we should give it a try," Gifford said, pointing at the huge gaping hole.

Brin nodded. "I agree. Everyone inside."

"Are you sure?" Tesh asked. "We don't know what's in there, and I can't fight. I can barely walk."

"We don't know that *anything* is in there, Tesh," Brin replied, "but something is absolutely out here. It's getting closer, and I don't like the sound of it." Focusing her attention on Gifford, she added, "Just to err on the side of safety, let's lift Tressa for this last part so we don't leave a trail."

"Good idea."

Stepping through the opening, they saw less a cave and more a deep tunnel. Its interior was littered with more wreckage, piles of shattered rock shoved to the sides. Much of it was the porous sort that Brin had observed before, but as they went deeper, the rock changed. She saw streaks of lighter gray, and white-lined layers like stripes of marble, even some yellow and speckled sections of a rusty orange. At a place where the primary stone was a kind of slate, some of which was broken into thin sheets and piled along the sides, the tunnel ended near a trio of boulders. Here, deep in that passageway to nowhere and hidden behind stacks of rubble, Brin called a halt to their march.

Instantly the others collapsed like rag dolls. Tressa curled up into a ball. Tesh dropped beside her, and Roan and Gifford settled together against the tunnel's wall. They were a sorry sight.

Not great, Brin thought, *but better. At least the stone isn't frosted.*

Looking back, she listened but didn't hear the sound anymore.

I just hope that whatever we heard outside doesn't live in here.

They waited, and for a moment, Brin thought she heard the rhythmic rumbling sound again, but it soon faded. They were alone in the tunnel, a feeble pack of moles clustered in the dark. No one spoke. They were all too sick, each one suffering. Brin wanted to help but didn't know how. This was the Abyss, the bottom, the lowest of the low, the dry well of the afterlife.

"Those lost to the Abyss are never seen again."

But why?

Brin held onto the hope that they would eventually climb up, pass through the door to Alysin, finish their mission, and save Moya, Tekchin, and Rain on their return trip. While the plan was optimistic, it was no more impossible than anything else they'd gone through. And yet while looking at the others huddled on the floor, she had to ask herself, *If climbing out is so easy, why hasn't anyone ever done it?*

When Moya had been in anguish from the loss of her leg, Brin had gone in search of help and found it. Buoyed by the memory of that success, she felt that searching was worth trying again, given that she didn't know what else to do. "I'm going to go explore. The rest of you wait here."

"Brin, be careful," Tesh said. He looked so pale, so weak.

"I'll be fine. I'm just going to look around. Maybe I can find help, or an easy way out, or something useful. While I'm gone, everyone needs to rest. Get your strength back. We won't be staying for long. We have a mission to complete, remember?"

Everyone nodded except for Tressa, who didn't move at all.

Brin slipped outside. Free of the others, she moved quickly, surveying their surroundings at a brisk trot. The Abyss was a quiet place, and when she stopped to listen, she heard nothing—not a drip, squeak, rattle, or breath of wind stirred the place. Absolute silence was absolutely frightening. This time Brin stayed clear of the ravines and the pitted cliffs. She was out in the open again, and at her speed, it wasn't long before she returned to the fallen slabs of the bridge. The remnants had landed in a rough line. Assuming they'd fallen straight down, Brin figured she could use them as a perfect reference point to align herself to the upper tier of Nifrel. Straight up was where the bridge had been. One end of the line of debris pointed at the Plain of Kilcorth, while the other was an arrow aiming at the door to Alysin.

For a moment, Brin felt wildly brilliant.

I'm a veritable Roan, I am.

The moment faded as she saw no practical use for the knowledge—at least not yet. What she needed was a way to help the others regain their strength. She was also unable to determine which end of the series of stones was which. That would be important later. When they did climb out, it would be best to scale the pillar that led to the Alysin Door.

Hoping to find a clue, she followed the row of bridge sections until she reached the end. Peering out into the darkness, she spotted a series of large, rocky mounds. One moved, and Brin gasped and nearly bolted. A moment later, she recognized what she was seeing—the Breakwaters. The giants appeared to sit or lie where they had fallen. Three still had their arms linked together. None spoke; nor did they move much. Each appeared befuddled. Watching them, Brin was reminded of how Tesh, Tressa, and Roan had just sat where they fell.

Slowly the giants' heads turned. They could see her, of course. Without anything to block her light, it must be visible for miles, and in that eternal dark, light would be . . .

Hope.

The idea came to her then. In Phyre, nothing physical existed. Everything was manifested from the spirit. Brin had no legs or feet, yet she understood that's how she moved. Light was the same. There was no true illumination. Or perhaps she was simplifying too much. Light might also encompass confidence, belief, faith. Each generated a kind of power on the spiritual plane, and that power showed itself in the form of light. That was why the blobs had chased her. She was a beacon of hope.

Not wanting to get any closer to the Breakwaters, Brin returned up the line of debris in the opposite direction. Eventually, she reached a rough column of stone—the Alysin Pillar.

"Some call it the Needle." Fenelyus had said.

Brin paused at the base and looked up.

The door to Alysin is at the top.

Her light revealed jagged rocks with ledges and plenty of cracks and crevices. Brin reached up, gripped one of the many handholds, and pulled. Hoisting her body to the nearest ledge was like lifting a pillow filled with no more than ten feathers. She climbed to the next ledge, and the next, feeling exhilarated. As inspiration took over, Brin's excitement grew and she found herself jumping through the air and catching one outcropping after another.

This is so easy! Climbing out is *possible.*

She let go and floated down.

Elated at her discovery, Brin grinned. Not only had she found the pillar and proved that the climb was possible, she had also managed to develop a mental map of the Abyss. The broken bridge was at the center of the canyon, and the Breakwaters were at one end, nearest the queen's tower. On the opposite side was the Alysin Pillar. To the right lay the giant tunnel where she had left everyone. To the left lay . . . she wasn't sure what.

Just one way to find out, she told herself.

Returning to the center of the bridge's debris, she turned left and began walking—in the direction she arbitrarily proclaimed to be north. She hadn't traveled far on the open expanse of frost-covered ground when she reached a wide track of bare rock. One portion led due *north;* the other curved toward one of the many fissures heading roughly in what would be *east.*

It's like a road, but to where?

She'd begun to follow it north when far ahead she saw something—a light. It was the only thing she was able to see at such a distance. Outside of Gifford's pale glow, Brin had found no source of illumination beyond her own.

People! she thought. *Maybe it's a whole city of them, helping one another cope and drawing strength from the entire community. Except . . .*

This light was different, not the pale-white or bluish color that she and Gifford gave off. This one had a decidedly red glow, and it wasn't firelight because it didn't flicker. There was nothing warm about it. Appearing like a rose-colored rising sun, it had to be enormous given the great distance between her and it. Then, as she watched, she realized it was moving—coming at her. That's when she heard the sound again. That horrible rumbling beat.

Not a city. The source of that light is something that moves along this road, whose passage has worn it away.

This time Brin did not ask herself what Moya might do. She didn't care. She wasn't Moya, and the red light scared her. Every instinct she possessed told her to leave, and quickly. Turning away, she ran.

❧

"We can get out," Brin told them. "I've found the pillar that leads to the Alysin Door, and it's easy to climb. We shouldn't have much trouble."

The news, Brin was confident, was the remedy. Once they heard their troubles were over, hope would return. They would glow with the joy of relief. Strength would surge back into them in the same way that Roan and Tesh had managed to restore themselves after receiving the power of love and reassurance that Gifford and Brin had administered. They would rise up and as soon as she was certain that nasty red glow had gone its normal route up the road, she would lead them out and they would begin scaling the pillar. Together they could do it. Brin was certain of that.

But they did not glow or rise.

They looked back with those same tired eyes.

"How?" Gifford asked, sitting up with his arms around Roan, whose head was nestled on his chest.

Brin knelt down before them. "I just told you. I found the pillar, the one with the door to Alysin on top. It's so easy to climb."

Gifford blinked. Tesh rocked back. Roan opened her mouth, but no words came out.

Tressa simply laughed, a cold miserable sound. "Did you say *climb?* As in—all the way back up to where we fell from?"

Brin frowned. "Yes, of course."

"Brin," Tesh said, "I don't think I could walk up a flight of stairs."

"I *might* be able to climb," Gifford said. "But, Brin, you're talking about—I don't know—miles maybe—miles straight up."

"But we don't get tired—not in here, not really. And it doesn't look that difficult. Besides, *difficult* hasn't stopped us before. Defying Konniger was hard; getting past Gronbach was hopeless; defeating Udgar and subduing the Gula was futile; fighting Balgargarath was absurd; winning against the full force of the fane was impossible—but each time we succeeded. I think we can again. The handholds are plentiful, and there are lots of ledges to rest on. It will be easy."

"For you, maybe," Tressa said. The woman was sprawled against the wall, her head slumped off to one side as if she were a rag puppet that a dog had just finished playing with. "I swear I weigh a thousand pounds down here. It's so much worse than when we were on the Plain of Kilcorth. And my bones are still broken."

"But you don't actually *weigh* anything, and you don't have bones. If you really weighed so much, you'd have cracked the stone when you hit. Did you?"

"Honestly, I didn't check. Maybe."

"Come on. You have to try. Stand up. All of you. Let's go. Right now. You'll see. Once you get started, when you understand how easy it is, you'll gain confidence and strength, and with each step, it will get easier."

"It's not that we want to stay here, Brin," Tesh said. "But it's like you're asking us to sprout wings and fly. I can't do that. It took every ounce of effort I had just to walk over here."

"He's right," Roan said. "I'm exhausted, too."

"Okay. Fine. We can wait *a while*. You rest, but as soon as you're able, we climb."

ॐ

The crack in the back of the cave bothered Brin, like when a tongue probed the empty spot after a tooth came loose. She'd been staring at it for . . . she actually didn't know how long. That was one of the problems with the afterlife. There was no way to tell time. Maybe it didn't exist. There were events certainly, one followed the next, but *time* as she had always understood it didn't seem to apply anymore. If nothing happened—if she sat in one place like the Breakwaters, as she was doing right now—she was certain time stopped. Maybe not for everyone, but it would for her.

The others remained clustered near the wall where they had first collapsed. She could see Gifford's light, and Roan glowed, but with far less radiance. Her light was overwhelmed by his. Tesh had no light at all, and Tressa . . . Brin had refused to believe it before, but there was no denying it now. Tressa emitted a darkness. All of them together didn't come close to Brin's brilliance, which illuminated one whole side of the cavern.

For a long time, she had waited near the tunnel's entrance, keeping watch for the source of that red glow and horrible noise. On a regular basis, she heard it approach before fading away once more.

Whatever it is, it's following a route, patrolling. Is it habit or is the red light looking for something?

Brin didn't know how, but she sensed the red light was bad, something to be feared and avoided.

She returned often to check on the progress of the others. They never appeared any better. If anything, they seemed worse. Knowing their weakness wasn't physical, she tried to cheer them up. She told them stories, the ones Maeve had forced her to practice so long ago, tales of heroes overcoming massive adversity. Chronicles of men and women who—even when they were certain they couldn't win—tried and somehow persevered.

That's what stories are for, Brin realized. *They are magic that aid people in times like this. They provide hope, a light to see by when all others are snuffed out.*

Her companions appreciated the tales, and they looked a bit better as she recited them, but the healing properties weren't good enough. Tressa was hardly able to lift her head.

Brin was getting frustrated by their lack of progress and went off to sit on her own. That was when she noticed the opening in the back of the tunnel. She moved toward it and sat down, chin on hands, elbows on knees, staring for what could have been hours.

"You're looking at the crack, aren't you?" Roan said, shattering Brin's timeless bubble. She'd crept over so soundlessly that Brin jumped.

"Sorry. I didn't mean to startle you."

"No—no, it's wonderful," Brin said and shifted over, giving Roan a space to sit. "I'm glad to see you up and moving around. Are you feeling better?"

"A little. Your stories help."

"That's great. I'll tell more then. We need to get out of here, Roan. Think of Moya, Tekchin, and Rain up there with the queen. She might be torturing them. If we can just—"

"It's too high for us, Brin." Roan said, shutting her down. "Your stories help, but they're not enough. They treat the symptom, not the malady."

"It's only another problem, Roan. A puzzle to be worked out. You're so good at that—the Land of Nog, remember?"

"I didn't name it that."

"No, you *made* it that. All I'm asking is that you figure a way to get everyone up that pillar."

Roan looked away with defeat in her eyes. Brin realized that Roan couldn't do it—wouldn't do it—because she didn't think it was possible. This was a side of her friend that Brin had never seen before. Usually, Roan thought anything was possible. She often speculated that with the right resources she could fly, make it rain, and eliminate sickness from the world.

What's happening to her? How can she believe that escaping the Abyss is beyond her reach? And if it's too far for the Wizard of Nog, what chance do the others have?

"Those lost to the Abyss are never seen again."

"Wait!" Brin raised a finger, holding up the point she was about to make. "What about Rain? Beatrice saw that in the future he would be a king, and he can't leave without Tressa's key. So getting out must be possible. She saw it happen!"

Roan looked uncomfortable and drew her feet in as if to stand. She was going to leave.

"Or maybe Beatrice is crazy," Brin quickly said. She smiled. "Don't go."

Roan hesitated, as if deciding.

"And yes, to answer your question," Brin added. "I was looking at the crack. It's stupid, but I feel like I've . . . I don't know, that I've seen it before."

"You have," Roan said, letting her legs stretch out across the stone again. "We've both seen the three boulders over there, too."

Brin turned around and gasped. "You're right." She still couldn't remember where, but she *had* seen them—them *and* the crack. "How—" Then the two clicked together in her mind and everything made sense. Not according to reason but rather a sort of dream logic. She remembered. The whole thing was impossible, and yet . . .

Brin stood up. Her light extended farther, but not far enough. "If this is the crack—if this is *that* crack—then . . ." Brin began to walk toward it. "But it can't be."

"We were down pretty deep." Roan slowly got to her feet and followed.

"Not *this* deep." Brin purposely moved very slowly. She wanted Roan to stay with her as the two crept toward the back of the cave.

"Then how do you explain the crack?" Roan asked. She was directly behind, her words giving voice to Brin's own thoughts.

"It *is* the same, isn't it?" Brin said. "And it's hard to forget *that* opening. We stared at it for so long."

Brin felt Roan take her hand. Roan had never touched her before—by accident sometimes, but not intentionally and certainly not for more than a second. Roan was better about contact these days. She didn't panic the way she used to, but as far as Brin knew, Gifford was still the only one whose touch she was comfortable with. Brin was so shocked that she looked down to make sure it was Roan's fingers she felt. Together they moved forward, watching as the far edge of Brin's light revealed more and more of the rock and floor. Then Roan stopped and gasped. Brin saw it, too. On the ground was what looked like a stick, but it wasn't. Too straight, and there was a sharpened stone tip: a tiny spear—an arrow.

"Mother of All," Brin said, wide-eyed.

Brin bent down and tried to pick it up, but she was unable to affect it, just as she couldn't alter the stone they stood on.

"It's the practice arrow," Roan said. "The one Persephone made Moya warm up with before going after Balgargarath, the one she flung into the dark."

"How can it be here?"

Roan didn't answer. The two moved ahead once more, slower this time.

"There." Roan pointed.

Brin caught the glint of silver metal on the floor near the wall. "I can't believe it."

Reaching down, Brin tried to pick up Persephone's lost torc, but just as with the arrow, she could feel but not move it. Then Brin stood and looked at Roan. "We're in the Agave again."

Brin noticed that Roan's light was brighter.

Was it hope? Maybe with Roan, a puzzle of this magnitude is fuel.

They advanced to the crack at the rear wall, but now Brin realized it wasn't the *rear* but the *front*. Beyond it, there would be the pool with the blue glowing lichen and the stair that led up. They could get out as they had before: by climbing the steps through Neith to emerge at Caric, on the banks of the Blue Sea.

Brin was only inches away from the crack. When she stepped forward, intending to pass through the rip that Balgargarath had torn open, she hit something solid, bounced back, and fell.

Roan reached out, and her hand was likewise blocked. "It's the division between the worlds." She looked back. "When the little men and Moya were exploring, they found something like this, but it was back there." She pointed past the boulders. "This place, the Agave, is like a bubble that extends into both worlds. The area between is common to each but there is also a separation that keeps the two worlds apart. Coming from Neith, the barrier is back there, but coming from the Abyss, the barrier is at this crack. But beyond it . . ." Roan rotated slowly, her eyes taking everything in, nodding as she put the pieces together.

Brin had her own revelation. "This is where the Ancient One was. He wasn't imprisoned—he was dead! But he got out, so we can, too."

Roan shook her head.

"Don't do that," Brin snapped. This was the answer, their salvation. Maybe they couldn't climb the pillar, but they could get to the back of the stupid cave. She and Gifford could drag them if necessary. The weight of Nifrel, which had intensified in the Abyss, would be gone once they were back on the face of Elan. "We can get past this barrier. We have the key. This makes everything work out. Beatrice wasn't crazy. Malcolm is right, and the key really can open any door!"

Roan nodded. "Yes, the key will likely work, but it won't help us."

"What do you mean?" Brin thrust a pointed finger at the crack. "That's our way out."

"I don't think so."

Brin wanted to slap her. "Why not?"

"Three reasons. One, our bodies aren't nearby. They're back in a mud puddle in the Swamp of Ith, and—"

"So we'll travel as—I don't know—as ghosts, I guess. We'll be like Meeks. We can sneak aboard a trade ship going from Caric to Tirre. Then we can walk back to Ith and get our bodies."

"It will take too long. Our bodies will rot. We'll remain ghosts."

Brin frowned. "Well, it's better than being in here."

"We'll also fail our quest. Give up on Suri. We'll have died for nothing."

This reason had more impact, and Brin paused to consider it. As she did, Roan added one more rock to the pile.

"Third, we can't pass through stone."

Brin struggled to understand. "Why would we need to—"

"Suri collapsed the mountain, remember? Neith is buried under a mountain of rubble. We won't be able to get through it."

"You don't know that for sure. You're only guessing."

"That's true," Roan conceded. "But it's likely."

"We need to at least try. I'm getting really tired of everyone just giving up. C'mon, let's get the key and—" Brin saw the apprehension in Roan's eyes. "Okay, fine. You wait here. I'll go fetch it."

Roan smiled, nodded, then sat down right where she was. Their little stroll must have been difficult for her.

Brin returned to the others. They hadn't moved. If anything, they appeared more settled, less upright. Everyone appeared to be sleeping.

"Tressa," she said gently, "can you hear me?"

The older woman opened her eyes but said nothing.

"May I borrow the key?"

"So you're leaving us at last?"

"No, but I think I might have found a way for everyone to get out."

Tressa looked at Tesh, then at Gifford and gave a sigh. "Fine. But you'll have to take it off me. I can't . . . I don't have the strength."

Brin crouched down beside her. As she reached around Tressa's neck and the two were cheek to cheek, Tressa reached up and grabbed Brin's arm. The older woman whispered in her ear, "There's a secret you need to know. Something Malcolm told me, the last thing. He said I had to wait until the very end because as he explained, 'Brin is the only one who's going to make it, so she's the only one who needs to know.'"

Brin gasped. "What?" she said, trying to pull back, but Tressa's grip was too tight.

Tressa went on, her voice barely loud enough to hear. "We didn't come for Suri. This quest was never about her. Malcolm needed us to do something far more important but knew we wouldn't go unless I said it was to save the mystic. The real reason for this trip is to return with something called the Horn of Gylindora. It's like the key, made of both Eton and Elan, so you'll be able to carry it back through Phyre."

Brin shook her head. "I don't understand."

"Did you really think the doors to the afterlife were opened for us to save the life of one wild mystic girl? Suri would have to die if she were to return with us, and I'm shocked none of you geniuses realized that. This has always been about more. Much more. If you can get that horn to Nyphron, not only will it end the war, but we'll also help fix the world that Malcolm broke. And that will be beneficial for everyone . . . everywhere."

Brin stared at Tressa, then once more started to draw back, but Tressa held on.

"I also want to apologize about lying, but it was necessary. That's why Malcolm picked me. He knew I was good at it. You see, when you want to build a wall, you ask a mason, and . . . and . . . nothing. I'm sorry I . . ."

She let go of Brin, who staggered backward. With tears in her eyes, Tressa continued, "I'm sorry I threw your book in the river. You didn't deserve that. You were trying to help me and I—I just couldn't believe you were being sincere. Seeing your face . . . I had no idea how much your book meant to you. It's stupid, but of all the terrible things I've done, I think I hate myself the most for that. I had nightmares afterward. Terrible dreams where I kept looking for the pages and couldn't find them. I've got plenty of reasons to hate myself. Believe me. I've done much worse, but not to a person who was so . . ." Her lips squeezed tight in a Padera-like frown. "I'm just sorry, okay?"

Brin nodded. "It's all right. I forgive you, Tressa."

The older woman's head came up, and her lips quivered. "Don't say that. Just take the damn key. I think—" Tressa swallowed. "I think he always meant for you to have it. Malcolm was just letting me feel important by being the one to carry it. He was being nice. So few ever have been."

Brin slipped the key's chain over Tressa's head. "We'll get out, Tressa. We all will. You'll see. I'm going to make sure about that." She stood up. "You rest now. I'll make it right. I promise."

Brin walked back to where Roan waited, looking like a lost puppy, her dim glow washed away by Brin's brilliance.

"What's wrong?" Roan asked.

"Nothing—well, I'm concerned about Tressa. I think maybe this place is messing with her mind. She's talking nonsense." Brin looked back. "At least I think she is. Doesn't matter, I have the key. Let's go."

Brin held the end of the key out and moved to the barrier, then stopped. "What if I get out, but then can't get back in again?"

Roan shook her head. "It opens all doors. Besides, getting in doesn't seem to be the hard part."

Brin nodded. "Right. Of course. Here goes."

Ducking her head, Brin took a step into the crack. Her light went out and almost immediately she hit something hard. As she jumped back, her light returned.

Turning, she saw Roan staring at her with that typically curious stare of hers. "What happened?"

"Nothing. It doesn't work," Brin said. "I'm still hitting the barrier. But my light went out."

"No." Roan shook her head. "I saw you disappear."

"You did?"

"You passed back into Elan and vanished."

"Would my light work on Elan?"

Roan shrugged. "Probably not. The light is spiritual strength. You can't see that on Elan."

"Right." Brin turned back and took a breath as if going underwater, and once more she stepped forward.

Again, her light went out, and again she immediately encountered an impediment. This time she let her fingers explore. What she felt was different from the barrier. She felt the edges of the crack and beyond it, stone—rough and cold. She felt sharp edges, flat blocks, and gaps. She was feeling the cave-in that was just beyond the bubble of the Agave. What lay beyond the crack was an impassable mound of debris.

Stepping back, Brin's light returned, and once more she saw Roan. "Don't you hate always being right?"

CHAPTER SEVEN

Faith on Trial

Faith is trust pushed to the limit of what is considered sane, but the question most people ignore is: How do you know where the boundary of sanity lies?

— THE BOOK OF BRIN

Malcolm dusted snow off his arms and shoulders as he entered Persephone's tent. "Sorry I'm late. I only just heard you wanted to see me."

Justine and Nolyn were still at the Padera Memorial Meal Tent for breakfast, a luxury Persephone no longer had time for. They were leaving. Nyphron was designating priorities for the preparation to break camp, and Sikar was mercifully absent from his post, leaving Malcolm and her alone. Such a private moment wouldn't last. This was the calm before the storm.

"What is it you need?" he asked.

"Oh, let's not go there, for I have a long list. From you, however, I'd be satisfied with a few answers. For instance"—she pointed at the black-bronze sword—"you mentioned I needed to keep that. Nyphron feels it's a danger to our security. Is there any reason I can't get rid of it? Can I melt it down, bury it, or toss it in a lake? If not, can we at least send it miles away?"

"Yes."

"Yes, what? Destroy, bury, toss, or send away?"

"None of the above. I was answering your first question: Yes, there is a reason you *can't* get rid of it. It will be needed."

Persephone waited. She stared at the tall, thin man, but he made no move to elaborate. Instead, he began searching his sleeves for snowflakes he might have missed. Finally, she sighed. "Can I hide it?"

"No."

"Why?"

"Because that'll make it difficult to find." Malcolm smiled sweetly.

In frustration, Persephone slammed her hands on the arms of her chair: Habet's makeshift First Chair that he had brought from the ruins of Alon Rhist.

She stood up because she couldn't sit any longer. "What's going on, Malcolm? When last we spoke, you told me a fairy tale about Moya leading her party into the afterlife on a mission to save Suri and win this war. Now the Fhrey have dragons, which means Suri is dead, and we must now pull back. We'll be going to—"

"You can't retreat."

"Why?"

"Because you *have* to stay here." Malcolm spoke as if his words were common knowledge and she was spouting nonsense. "Nyphron especially. If you want to win this war—if you want everyone to survive—that's what is necessary."

"At the risk of sounding like my son, I must repeat . . . *why?*"

He shook his head, appearing frustrated. "Explanations require too many details. Everything would be so much easier if people simply accepted what I say."

Persephone pursed her lips, laboring to suppress a scream. She fought the impulse to throttle Malcolm to make him understand she wanted—no, *needed*—answers, not games. Instead, she tried logic. "Your hesitation to be forthright creates doubt and suspicion. It's natural to be wary. If I have nothing to fear regarding your motives and methods, why keep secrets?"

"If Moya were forced to shoot an apple off the top of Nolyn's head, would you badger her with questions while she did it? Would you demand that she explain the minutiae of archery while taking aim, even though you couldn't possibly understand anything she said?"

Persephone's mouth hung open for just a moment at both the words and the gall. "Did you just say I'm an idiot? And are you actually equating my desire to learn more before risking the lives of thousands of people to a distraction? I don't think you should brush my concerns aside so casually. This is important."

"Even more than you could guess," Malcolm said, "and it's far more dangerous than whether a few thousand people will live or die." He looked up at the canvas ceiling for a long moment, then sighed. "Every word I tell you has repercussions. Pebbles tossed into a pond send out ripples. You don't see them, but I do. Many of them are needed, others are counterproductive, and some are downright disastrous. You're asking me to walk across a frozen lake of thin ice for no reason."

"And you want me to risk the fate of the human race on faith."

"Exactly. And my question to you is this: Why isn't that enough?"

The sounds of people working came through the canvas walls: belongings being packed, wagons being loaded, tent stakes being pried up. The camp was awake, and the news was spreading. Persephone felt derelict by not helping, and Malcolm was delaying her further.

She threw up her hands and shook her head. "Are you joking?"

"No . . . no, I'm not. When Moya told you she could defeat Udgar, you had faith. When Arion said she could handle a giant, you believed. When Nyphron declared you could take Alon Rhist with a handful of Galantians, you took him at his word . . . on trust."

"Because I had proof of their abilities. I saw Moya kill Balgargarath, Arion fight Gryndal, and the Galantians dispatch an attack of giants."

"And what of me?" he said as if he alone had failed to receive an invitation to her exclusive party.

"That's just it, Malcolm. I don't know anything about you—not really. You seem as if you can tell the future, but I don't know how accurate you are. I have no proof of your abilities, no reason to trust you."

Malcolm frowned. He looked hurt even as he nodded. "That's what this comes down to: trust and belief, two commodities which are obviously in short supply. You see, when I mentioned Balgargarath, Udgar, and Alon Rhist, I wasn't giving examples of others you trusted. I was presenting evidence to support why you ought to believe me. All those events, and so many more, came to fruition through *my* efforts."

She raised a skeptical eyebrow.

Malcolm counted on his fingers as he talked. "Udgar was defeated because you challenged to be the keenig, and you were able to do that because you were chieftain, and you were chieftain because you were Reglan's wife. Reglan married you because years before you were born, I told Tura to make sure Reglan's father would pair you two."

Persephone opened her mouth to protest, but Malcolm went on. "Balgargarath's defeat was in large part due to Suri, but she wouldn't have been there if I hadn't told Tura to look for an infant near the cascades on the first full moon after Summersrule of that year. Nyphron revolted against Petragar at Alon Rhist because I convinced his father to challenge Lothian. This set his feet on a path toward rebellion, which led him to Dahl Rhen. In truth, you have far more reason to trust me than anyone you know."

Persephone had no idea what to think. He was lying to her, had to be. There was no way Malcolm could have arranged for her marriage or known about Suri, and yet . . .

Why would he lie about such things?

She'd known him for years; he'd always been a good friend. And Malcolm always seemed wise, in an awkward kind of way.

"You knew Tura?"

"Since she was born. I was the one who brought her to the Crescent Forest, so she could be the Mystic of Rhen and the fulcrum of so many events."

"Tura was ancient, but you're—"

"A bit older than I look." He smiled.

"It sounds so unlikely."

Malcolm nodded. "And yet when most put a paddle in the water to steer their boat, the water never demands explanations or reassurance about the choices made." He shrugged. "However, we're getting close to the end. Little can affect the outcome at this point. So as long as you promise not to ask questions, I can tell you some things."

Persephone waited as Malcolm took a deep breath. Despite remaining undecided on whether he was being truthful, a liar, or utterly mad, she braced herself for his next words as if he were about to proclaim an irrevocable sentence on the guilty.

"What Tressa told you was close to the truth. I sent them into Phyre as a means of reaching Suri in Estramnadon."

"So are you saying Suri is still alive?"

Malcolm rolled his eyes.

"Sorry . . . I'm sorry." She held up her hands in penance. "No questions. I forgot. Please go on."

"I can only see—foretell, if you will—what happens outside Phyre, so I have no idea what is going on inside or how those events will play out. I only know that there will be a race against time, and if this camp moves from this spot"—he pointed at his feet—"that race will be lost and along with it the war and quite possibly a great deal more."

"And *you* did all this?"

"No," Malcolm said. "You, Suri, Raithe, Nyphron, and untold others accomplished it. I merely put the right people in the correct place at the needed time."

Persephone took a seat on her bed and ran a hand through her hair.

"Your decision is simple." He spoke to her with warmth and compassion, yet she felt he was belittling her struggle, her pain, and the terror that caused all her muscles to tense. She was a table bearing too much weight, and Malcolm was dismissing the pressure as if it were nothing and her decision easy.

"Oh, is it?" She looked up, irritated.

"There is but one thing you must do—answer a single question: Do you trust me? Everything else is irrelevant."

"That's a pretty big question, Malcolm."

"Yes, but it's an easy one to resolve." He turned and pulled the collar of his cloak up. "Because you knew the answer to that question before I came in." Then, as he walked out, he added. "And so did I."

ॐ

Persephone found Nyphron in the Healing Quarter, where a small crowd had gathered outside one of the tents.

Stepping inside, Persephone saw a man lying on a cot.

"What's happening?" she asked.

"They found him lying facedown in the snow just sixty yards outside the camp," Nyphron replied.

He looked familiar. She thought his name might be Norch or perhaps Nachman. Born of Clan Tirre, he was one of the commanders of the troops Nyphron had sent to establish a safe route across the Nidwalden south of the falls. He was covered in blood, his fingers black, as was the tip of his nose.

Frostbite.

She'd seen it before; his feet would likely be worse.

Anyval, the attending Fhrey physician who had helped heal her after the raow attack, was heaping fur blankets on the injured man. Two men and three women rushed around his cot, carrying heated water and carting away the clothing that had been cut off.

"Will he live?" Persephone asked.

Anyval nodded. "After a fashion, I suppose."

"Prymus Noch, report!" Nyphron barked.

Persephone was taken aback by his forceful address to a man barely clinging to life, yet her husband knew the soldier's name better than she.

Noch's eyes fluttered and slowly lifted. "Sir . . ."

"I said report! Why are you here? What happened to your men? Where is First Prymus Adham?"

"Eaten, sir."

No matter what they were doing, everyone in the tent paused.

"Did you say . . . *eaten?*"

"Yes, sir," Noch managed through cracked and bleeding lips. "Goblins, sir. Thousands of them. We saw their ships. Black sails on the water. Huge things, like floating cities. None of us ever saw the like. Then the boats disappeared."

Corry, a Melen woman, placed a warm cloth on his head, and Noch jerked.

"Leave him alone, woman!" Nyphron snapped. "Nurse him later." He turned his attention back to the soldier. "Go on with your report. What happened then? Did you reach the river?"

"Yes, and it was beautiful. Seen from the bottom, the falls are—"

"I don't care about the view, man. What happened?"

"We found a good spot and set up camp. Cut trees to make a clearing. The First Prymus planned to use the logs to make a platform bridge to get across. We were all in high spirits. The river was so calm, we thought we were looking at the end of the war. Then the sun went down. Darkness came, and so did the goblins. They were all around us. Couldn't see them, but we heard their chattering in the dark. They stayed away from our fires, but all night long we heard cries as they took our scouts. Next day, we found . . ." His eyes closed as he trailed off.

"What?" Nyphron shook him awake.

"Bones. Piles of bones, as if they'd had a pig roast. But these weren't from no boar. All day long the First Prymus worked us hard to make rafts. He figured if we could get across the river, we'd be safe. But the river widens out as it becomes the Green Sea." He shook his head. "No, not the Green Sea, the Goblin Sea. They own it, every square inch. More ships came. We planned to cross the river at first light, but that night they burned our rafts and took more men. By morning, we saw a new forest. This one was on the water, masts from all their ships. That's when the First Prymus ordered me and ten others to leave, to try and slip through their lines to come back here and report. As I crept out, I saw shadows in the trees. The whole place was moving. I still don't know how I managed. Got lost. Slept in a cave. Didn't dare make a fire. How many others made it, sir? How many besides me got back?"

Nyphron looked at Persephone briefly, then turned so abruptly that his blue cape whirled. Without answering Noch, he walked out. The soldier shifted his worried eyes to Persephone.

"You need to rest now," she told him. "Take care of him, will you?" she asked Anyval before she, too, left, following her husband.

⨘

"They're all dead," Nyphron told her as soon as they were clear of the Healing Quarter.

He led her away from the hub of the camp. She didn't think he had a destination in mind; he just wanted to be anywhere else. All around them, the camp was a hive of activity as people hauled boxes and sacks out of tents. Their slumping shoulders screamed of defeat.

"So no others returned?"

Nyphron shook his head. "Half of the Second Legion—a thousand men. Gone. And they weren't even fighting our enemy. What a waste."

They passed a group of men using a pry stick to unfasten a primary tent peg. Two were already free, and the canvas had fallen. Inside the deflated canvas, the main pole listed and threatened to fall.

"*You can't retreat.*" Malcolm's words rang loud in her head. "*Because you have to stay here . . . Nyphron especially.*"

"Nyphron? I—"

"The worst part is that Malcolm predicted it," he said. "Well, no. The worst part is losing so many troops for nothing. But still, having him be right adds that special twist of the knife."

"Malcolm did what? When?"

"Just after I sent them off. He even said it would be the goblins, and that the men would be eaten."

Together they reached the end of the road where the snow went deep.

"You're not going to like what I'm about to say," she said.

"Then maybe you shouldn't." He offered a half-hearted smile. "What is it?"

"We can't leave. We have to stay here."

"What? Why?"

Persephone bit her lower lip. "Malcolm just told me that if we move— even a short distance—we'll lose the war."

Nyphron let go a sad imitation of a laugh. He gestured with his arms toward the camp. "Look around, Persephone. We already have."

"Then what good will it do to retreat?"

"Stalemate," he said. "You're right about the cost of making more dragons. Death among the Fhrey is rare and as such harder to accept. It could become too high a price for Lothian to bear. Besides, retreating *is* doing something. It's better than just sitting here and waiting for death to descend upon us."

"But Malcolm . . . he says we can still win. And all that we have to do is just stay here."

"I don't see how that's possible, do you?"

"No, but he knew about the goblins, and he knew about Suri's capture before she was even sent, and he knew about Nolyn's birth. He said I would have a son."

"That's hardly remarkable. He had a fifty-fifty chance of being right."

"He told me that my child would be born on the banks of the Bern River in the High Spear Valley."

"I still don't see—"

"He predicted it while we were still in Alon Rhist, and you were chasing Lothian. At the time, I wasn't sure if you would return. He *knew* you'd make it back and that you'd be moving our position—and where it would be. He knew we would wed even before I had made my final decision."

Nyphron had no response to that. Instead, he looked out across the white expanse into the infinite, his breath making tiny clouds that vanished as quickly as they formed.

"I think we should stay," she said, making the decision as she spoke the words.

"That's incredibly risky. It will mean our deaths if Malcolm is wrong."

"Since when are you afraid of death?"

"You weren't there," he said in a deadly serious tone that was aided by the frigid air and bleak landscape. "You didn't see what Lothian did to my father in the Carfreign Arena. He wanted to make an example of what happens to those who defy him. Zephyron was a good and a proud Fhrey, and he followed the law. He exercised the right that our society—that our god—granted him. Lothian could have given him an honorable death. Instead, he turned my father into a puppet, made him defile and mutilate himself before all of Erivan. He died slowly, painfully, forced to eat his own fingers before a vomiting crowd. That's what Lothian did to a law-abiding citizen who dared to challenge his authority. What do you think he'll do to us?"

The wintry wind blew a cold chill between them.

He sighed. "We'll stay for now if you want, but the day we see the fane's army assembling on the eaves of the forest—accompanied by dragons—that's when we must leave. And I don't care what Malcolm says."

CHAPTER EIGHT

The Past and the Future

Continuing to fight against insurmountable odds is difficult, even insane, but giving up was the hardest thing I have ever done.

— THE BOOK OF BRIN

Roan had been studying one of the stone tablets when she stopped, looked up, and stared off into the dark, as if listening for something.

"What's wrong?" Brin asked.

"Hmmm?" Roan blinked her way back to reality—at least their present version of it. She looked down at the tablet before her as if she'd forgotten what she was doing. "Oh, nothing. I was just thinking that this symbol here has to make the same sound as this one." She pointed at the markings. "And this one, and this, too. They all make the same sound, but they're all different symbols."

Brin smiled and nodded. "I call it the *schwa*. It's the most common sound people make when talking, a short quiet one, almost never stressed. But, yeah, in order to capture it in writing and have the rest make sense, it requires some flexibility and varies depending on the adjacent symbols."

"A lot of the sounds come from the same markings, at least in combination. These sets here . . ." Roan pointed again. "They're identical, yet for the phrase to make sense they would have to be pronounced a little differently."

Brin nodded, bit her lip, and made an embarrassed face. Her system wasn't without flaws; she knew that, and this was the first time anyone had ever studied it—the first time it had been taken apart and critiqued. Teaching Roan to read had become an act of humility.

Maybe teaching someone to read wasn't such a good idea. I sort of imagined it would be fun. While Tressa never learned much, at least she never made me feel like an idiot.

"And these symbols that appear at the end. They set the timing, right? When the thing happened—in the past, the present, or the future?"

Brin nodded.

"So why are there eight? And why are there so many of these items added in front of words that designate the opposite of the thing that follows? There should only be two states, but, again, you have eight: *un* important, *il* logical, *dis* agree, and so on. You seem to have a thing for *eight*."

"It's just how people talk," she defended herself. "I didn't invent the language."

Brin had invited Roan to search through the scattered set of tablets, looking for any information on how to escape. Neither of them could move the stones, so several couldn't be read, and none could be reordered. As a result, Brin went around the chamber on her hands and knees reading all the ones she hadn't had a chance to go over on her first visit. Teaching Roan to read gave the Wizard of Nog something to work on. Brin hoped it would help her recover. The speed at which the woman grasped ideas was astounding. In a world of mental sloths, Roan was a diving peregrine. Problems, however, developed given the way Roan's mind worked. She wasn't the type to accept *what was*—she always focused on *whys* and *hows*.

"But if you are going to make a system, why not make it the best? Why not clean it up and standardize?"

Brin shrugged. "Because everyone already knows how to talk. It's been difficult to get Tressa to learn while using words she already knows. If I'd tried to make her use new words like *undecisive* or *unpossible*, it would have been a lot harder."

"Hmmm." Roan's single tone sounded judgmental, disapproving.

Brin felt altogether miserable. The written language was her one thing, her life's achievement. She'd spent years creating, refining, and polishing the system. It was the accomplishment she was proudest of, at least until a moment ago.

Maybe it's best that I never taught anyone else. Apparently, it's a mess.

Roan sat back and sighed heavily, a scowl on her face.

She hates it. Roan hates what I created.

"I'm tired," Roan said. "I need to rest. Being *up* like this is exhausting. I feel like we've gone back in time, like Arion is draining us again."

Brin nodded.

Roan slowly stood and began to walk back toward the others—to Gifford—leaving Brin alone. After a few steps, she stopped. "It's beautiful, though."

"What is?" Brin asked.

"Your writing. It's an amazing thing you've created. I wish I could study more of it. I wish I had more strength. It's wonderful."

Brin felt her heart swell so much it pushed tears to her eyes. "Thank you." Then, feeling uncomfortable under the weight of such massive praise, Brin sought an escape. "I don't think I did much. The person who wrote these tablets did most of the work. Malcolm thinks he saw me in the future and used my own system. Truth is, the Ancient One filled in some gaps, improved what I was trying to do, and made me see what was possible."

"Maybe," Roan said. "But even without the tablets, you would have figured it out eventually, or those who you taught would have. How else could he have learned this? He must have seen the language you eventually made. You taught him first."

Roan left her alone with that idea to ponder and another score of tablets yet to read.

❧

Tesh knew what he had to do; he just wasn't sure he could manage it.

They had all agreed it was the only way, and that he was the man for the job. He'd faced deadly Fhrey in the Harwood, fought Sebek and whatever a raow was, but none of those things had scared Tesh as much as the battle he was about to wage—one he couldn't afford to lose. But deep down in his selfish depths, he hoped he might. He knew victory would be bitter; it would hurt more than anything he'd previously experienced and last an eternity. Still, he had to do it.

Tesh walked across the cave, feeling like he was going to his execution while carrying the weight of the world. His feet dragged across the stone, and his arms hung as if boulders swung from his wrists. He didn't have the will to lift them. He didn't have arms or feet, either, but he was past trying to understand such things, beyond caring. This place was killing what was left of him. Soon, very soon, standing and walking would become things he *used* to be able to do.

Finding Brin was easy. She shone out as a beacon in the dark, and he noticed that the closer he got, the lighter he felt. Something about Brin had a way of lifting his load, now and always. She was sitting on the floor near a wall with dozens of flat tablets gouged with markings strewn about. She was doing her "reading thing." Tesh had never understood, but he knew it was important to her. She hadn't seen him yet, and he paused while still several yards away. Crossing the cave was exhausting, and he needed a rest before taking those last difficult steps, but he also wanted to look, take her in. She was beautiful, never more so than at that moment. She leaned over a tablet, studying it with her fingers as well as with her eyes.

I never deserved her.

He'd been telling himself that for some time. He thought it might make his quest easier. It didn't. A mouse trapped in a corner by a bear will still fight for survival. Love, he came to realize, was like that. No matter the odds, love refused to give up. That's what made those last few feet so hard, what made any and all excuses useless.

"Brin?" he said softly.

Her head came up. She drew back the curtain of hair, saw him, and smiled.

Don't do that. Please don't smile at me.

Tesh could feel the pain again, deep in the place where his chest used to be.

"I never thought I'd find these tablets again. Roan and I have been reading them, trying to find something that can help us get out."

She pointed at the one she had been working on. "The Ancient One . . . the being whom the dwarfs let out of the Agave—wasn't a prisoner at all—I mean, well, he was, but he was dead, just like us. His name wasn't The Three; it was Trilos. You can see how I made that mistake, right? I'm still trying to figure out how these tablets were made. Nothing of Eton can affect anything on Elan. Unless . . ." Brin lifted the key, which now hung around her neck. "I bet I could scratch on stone with this. I wonder if he had something like it? Anyway, Trilos was in the Abyss, and he managed to get out. Out of this cave, out of the Abyss, out of the afterlife—or the *Afterworld,* as he called it. He's probably the only one to have ever done that. And he did it *without* a key."

"How?"

"I don't know, exactly. I can't read all of the tablets. Trilos wrote on both sides, and I can't turn them over or move them. That means there is still a lot of missing information, but I've learned a lot. You see Trilos—an Aesira—was murdered by his brother. He was the first ever to die."

"Aesira?" Tesh said. "Isn't that what Fenelyus called Ferrol?"

Brin nodded. "According to Beatrice—she's a dwarven seer we met—there were five Aesira: Turin, Trilos, Ferrol, Drome, and Mari. Trilos was the first to die, and he became the first inhabitant of Phyre—aside from the Typhons."

"Who?"

"According to these tablets, they were spoiled brats with the power of the elemental forces of nature. When they lived on the face of Elan, the Typhons ripped the place apart, destroying everything they came in contact with. It's one of the reasons Eton hated them. Eventually they were cast into Phyre. The Typhons' continued efforts to escape are still felt on Elan in the form of earthquakes. They're the ones that made this tunnel, probably trying to dig their way out. But there's a barrier between Elan and Phyre that even they couldn't get through."

"Brin, I'm glad you found the tablets. I can see how much you enjoy this stuff, but I—"

"Oh, you have no idea!" She pointed toward a tablet a few feet away. "From that one, I learned that the Abyss was created to hold the Typhons, but the shackles strong enough to restrain them were harmful to an Aesira, and devastating to the likes of us. So Elan created an upper tier to Phyre. The low plains of Nifrel, the midlands of Rel, and the highlands of Alysin. This gave her children a place where they could live comfortably. Anyway, Trilos wasn't alone long. With the First War, others died, and as Trilos's siblings joined him, he learned the tragic truth that Turin had given the gift of eternal life to his daughter Muriel."

"Why is that so bad?"

"Because she and Trilos were in love. The tablets are filled with his thoughts and memories of Muriel. Oh! I even found the message Padera gave me."

"Padera?"

"She died. We found her in Rel, and she said Malcolm told her to tell me, 'When trees walk and stones talk.' At the time, I didn't know what that meant. But I found it in the tablets. It's a phrase Muriel uses when she's frustrated that something will never happen." She paused and shook her head. "When I think of the cruelty, it . . . it's no wonder Muriel hates her father so much."

"I'm not following you."

"Oh, well, Muriel is immortal so she can never come to Phyre, but Turin killed Trilos to keep the two of them apart. When Trilos found out Muriel would never be joining him, he threw himself into the Abyss. The tablets don't actually say why. Maybe he thought there would be a way out down here, or it could be he was hoping the Typhons would obliterate him from existence. But then he found this tunnel and the thin barrier between the two worlds. This gave him hope. The Typhons' brute force wasn't able to breach the boundary, but Trilos found a way. Rather than bashing a monster-sized opening, he chose to focus on creating a teeny-tiny pinprick, just big enough for a bodiless spirit to pass through, but he faced two problems. The first was that he lacked the power to break through the barrier even with a small hole. The second was that he would still be buried under layers and layers of rock. Eventually, the dwarfs provided a solution. He heard them burrowing and called to them, promising secrets in return for his release. That's how he got out of Phyre."

"And you got all that from these tablets?" Tesh stared at the scattered stones.

"Yeah."

"But you didn't actually find anything that can get us out?"

"Well, no."

"And you read all the tablets, right?"

"All the ones I could. Like I said I can't—"

"Brin, I have to tell you something, and you're not going to like it." He paused and licked his lips. His head drooped from the weight. He had to get this done while he still had the strength.

She turned to face him fully, and her light was blinding. He wanted to lift a hand to shield his eyes, but that wasn't going to happen, so he turned away. "Brin, the others and I have been talking, and we've made a unanimous decision. You have to go on without us."

"Go on? What do you mean, *go on?*" There was a harsh, suspicious bite to her tone. She knew exactly what he meant.

"You can climb up. You can reach the door to Alysin. You can finish what we can't."

With a nervous laugh, she shook her head. "I can't do that—not alone. We all have to get out of here. I can't just leave you all—not here. Oh, dear Elan, no. I can't leave *you* here."

"Tressa told us what Malcolm said. That you, and *only you*, would make it all the way through."

"I think Tressa might be suffering from—"

"Look at us, Brin. I know you thought we'd get better, but you know we won't. The longer we're here, the more we are drained. You have to leave us behind and—"

"No! Roan will figure out some brilliant solution, or we'll find another tunnel made by the Typhons that isn't blocked. Or—"

"Brin, all those things take time."

"So? We have plenty of that. We have eternity."

Tesh took her anger as a good sign. If she thought he was spouting nonsense, she would have laughed. Instead, she barked at him, her face twisted up, showing teeth. It hurt to see that expression, to know he was causing her pain. Tesh had become acutely aware of such things. He was a raw wound, sensitive to what he did and what he caused. It was a shame he'd only recently acquired this talent. Gritting his teeth, he pressed on. "We don't have a lot of time, and you know it. If you don't go now, you'll never be able to."

"What do you mean?"

"We've all noticed. You're growing dimmer. Don't try to deny you aren't starting to feel the effects of the Abyss. How much longer before you're like Roan, then me, and eventually like Tressa?"

Brin looked at her hands self-consciously, then set her jaw. "I'm *not* leaving." She was shaking her head, and Tesh reached out. "Brin, you—"

"No!" she shouted and jerked away. She stepped back, nearly falling.

"You have to," Tesh said as gently as he could.

"No, I don't! I *don't* have to. I'm—"

"You're the only one who can. At the very least, the key has to be taken up. If this was only about Suri, I might concede, but we're talking about the fate of the world. Tressa explained it all."

"Malcolm might be wrong." Her mouth folded up in a hateful, hurtful, determined pucker.

"Brin   " Tesh fought to find words, struggled to talk. His tongue was working against him. He didn't want to speak. He didn't want her to leave. He shredded his insides with every uttered word.

"If I leave you"—Brin's eyes grew moist, the beginning of tears brimming—"the weight of this place will . . . Tesh, it will crush you, melt you, make you into . . . you don't know. I've seen some of the *people* who've been here too long. They're—they're . . ." Tears slipped free and ran down her cheeks. With her glow shining through, they sparkled like diamonds.

Dear Mari, she's beautiful.

More than anything he longed to grab her, hug her, hold her, and agree to stay together forever. He wanted to dissolve, melt away with Brin. He could accept his fate if she were with him.

Summoning all the strength he had left, he said, "You don't belong here, Brin. Not with us—not with me."

"Don't say that!"

"It's true. Look at you. See the light you give off? You deserve better."

"I don't *deserve* anything! And you're just trying to make me go because . . ." She put a shaking hand to her mouth to rest on quivering lips. Her whole body jerked and shook. "Tesh, I love you. Leaving you—oh, Grand Mother—leaving you here in this place. You'll lose yourself—that's what's happened to those horrible blobs that chased me. The Abyss—this place—it isn't for people like us. We can't endure it. The pressure, the weight that it exerts crushes, erodes, and wears away the very understanding of ourselves until . . ." She shuddered. "I can't abandon you to waste away, to dissolve—I can't do that. I can't. I won't!"

Tesh had battered her weak, forced her shield aside, clubbed her sword away. Brin was exposed for the thrust that he had been leading up to. He didn't want to do it, and the pain flashed hot and sharp in his chest even as he opened his mouth. Tears slipped down his own cheeks, and he hated himself for knowing they would only serve to drive his blow deeper. He would win this battle, slay his opponent, and then hate himself for all eternity. But he had to do it for everyone, but mostly for her.

"Brin," he said, his words so soft that they barely overcame her weeping. "You once told me that the only way I'd ever lose you was by refusing to let you go. You were right. I had a hard time seeing it then because I cared so much. I love you, Brin. We all do. The question is, do you love us? Do you love us enough to let us die?"

Her weeping turned to a sob.

"Brin, you have to let us die the same way I had to let you. Don't you see? You have to let us go."

He saw it then. Her light flickered. It blinked hard. In her eyes, through those windows to her soul, he saw her break. He'd seen the same look on men in the instant of their deaths: shock, pain, resignation. Tesh had won, as he'd known he would. Brin would leave, taking her light away and leaving them in darkness, but none more so than Tesh. And he was certain she was right—seeing her go would crush him.

"Oh, Tesh." Brin fell to her knees. "Tesh, it hurts so much."

"I know . . . believe me . . . I know."

CHAPTER NINE

The Climb

Extended trips are the most frightening to begin, sheer cliffs the most difficult to climb, long falls the most painful to endure, but it is invisible chains that are the hardest to break.

— THE BOOK OF BRIN

"Well?" Tressa asked when Tesh and Brin returned to the others.

Tressa and Roan looked like dead bodies left to be picked over by crows after a massive battle. Each was propped up against the cave wall on either side of Gifford, as if he were a campfire—one that had burned down to coals. Like everyone else, he, too, was dimming.

"She'll do it," Tesh told them.

"But you can't give up," Brin added. Her cheeks were dry, but her eyes were puffy and red. "You have to promise me that you'll keep looking for a way out. You especially, Roan." Brin pointed at her. "Maybe I missed a tablet, or I read something that meant nothing to me but could provide you with an answer." Roan didn't look capable of much more than clinging to Gifford's arm. "You have to think. Put that imaginary hair into your nonexistent mouth and chew harder than you've ever done before. There has to be a way. There's always a *better* way."

"In the world of the living maybe," Tressa said. "But no one can cheat death."

Brin glared at her. "You and your husband once told everyone in Dahl Rhen that you can't fight the gods. Remember? Maybe you don't, but I do." She poked her own chest with a finger. "Keeper of Ways. I don't forget anything. You once asked Persephone, 'Will you have us take up spears against the Grand Mother Elan for not sending sufficient rain this year? The finest warriors of this village couldn't defeat a bear, and you expect us to make war with the Fhrey?' And then Konniger added, 'Men can't kill gods.' Well, guess what, Tressa? We didn't just kill those *gods*. We've nearly wiped them out. So don't lie there and tell me what can and can't be done. For starters, *I'm* about to cheat death. I'm going to climb that pillar, something no one has ever done. I'm coming back from the Abyss. But I won't do so unless I get pledges from each and every one of you that you won't give up. That you'll keep trying. Understand?"

"I'll accept your condition with one of my own," Tesh told her. "I promise to keep trying, but only if you promise not to hold out hope. If we make it, so be it, but I want your word that you won't expect it. You have to let us go. And, Brin, if you manage it—if you cheat death and somehow find your way back to a life under the sun—I want you to forget me and find a new life, a new love."

She was shaking her head again, her jaw locking down. "I can't possibly—"

"You have to. Brin, you need to accept that I'm dead. That we all are. If you get out, you really need *to get out*. Don't leave any part of you behind to suffer. If I can believe you're free—truly free—living happily somewhere, then that will be my reward, my little comfort to hold onto here in this place. My sacrifice will have been worth it. Do you understand?"

Brin nodded.

"Then I swear by my deceased parents and my lost tribe that I'll try, and keep trying."

Brin looked to all of them and received similar assurances.

"And by the way, Tressa, I forgive you."

"No, you don't. You can't. You don't know all the things I've done." Tressa was holding her lips in a tight frown.

Brin nodded. "Maybe not, but I *can* forgive you for destroying my pages. And whether you believe me or not, I already did, and a long time ago." She rolled her shoulders. "As for the lies that brought us here? I don't know how it all works, but you came knowing you'd be sacrificing your own life. That has to count for something, you know? People change, Tressa. I think you have. Or maybe you've always been a good person, but the world never gave you the chance to show your true colors. Either way, I see them now. And I think you're something. Something special."

"And *that's* why you're as bright as a morning star," Tressa said.

Brin gave Tressa a tight hug and kissed the sobbing woman goodbye.

ॐ

Gifford was the only one to walk out with her, the only one who could. The rest stayed anchored to the floor of the cave. She said her goodbyes to everyone but Tesh. In the end, she couldn't face him. She knew if she tried, she wouldn't have the strength to leave. He seemed to know it as well and kept his distance. That was for the best. Even so, if it hadn't been for Gifford pulling her free of the cave, she might not have left.

The potter walked with Brin to the base of the column. Black cracked rock with angled strata of varying shades of gray rose up, a great pointing finger, or massive stone tree.

Yes, a tree.

Brin wanted to think of it that way. She would simply be climbing, like when she was a girl. Walking to the base, she placed a hand on the stone. "This is it." She wiped tears from her cheeks.

Gifford looked up and nodded. "You can do this, Brin."

"You could, too."

Gifford didn't answer.

"You know you can. The weight afflicting the others has less of a hold on you."

He reached out and laid his own hand on the rock and nodded. "You and I, I guess we didn't have enough opportunity to get into too much trouble." He smiled at her, and she missed the old lopsided grin. "Turns out, not having much of a life has its advantages."

"We could do it together, Gifford."

He shook his head. "You know I can't."

"You could."

"I won't." His voice was firm and stern.

Brin sighed. "If Roan had died, you'd have to go on without her. This is like that."

Gifford shook his head. "You remember your aunt Needa's dog, Apple?"

Brin nodded. "My uncle Gelston said my aunt ruined him. That all he was good for was following Needa around. He couldn't herd at all."

"What did Apple do when your aunt died?"

"You're not a dog, Gifford."

"That dog stayed at her grave, day and night. I tried to lure him to my house with meat. But he wouldn't budge. After days without food or water, he up and died. I couldn't figure it out. Just didn't make any sense. It does now. I won't leave Roan. Certainly not in a place where Iver still walks around." Gifford patted the rock. "I had a better life than I should have, and I had more than five years of true happiness. That's enough. No, it's more than enough. I'm sorry, but you'll have to climb by yourself."

"You're a good man, Gifford." She hugged him tightly. "A very good man. No—you're a *hero*."

Brin let him go and looked at the column's face, tilting her head back. It seemed to go on forever. "Gifford, don't tell the rest of them, but I'm scared. I don't know if I *can* do this."

"You said you already tried a bit, and it was easy."

"Not the climb—but yeah, maybe that, too . . ." She frowned. "If I do make it, if I reach Alysin, how will I cross it alone? And if I manage that, what challenges wait in the Sacred Grove? And I know nothing of Estramnadon. I honestly don't know what it is I'm supposed to do now. Tressa said I need to get a horn, but how do I do that? And even if I succeed, how can I ever get all the way back through Phyre? Nifrel's bridge is gone. The queen will still want the key, and she'll know I have it. And what about Drome? There are so many obstacles still ahead of me. I'm not Moya. I'm not Persephone. I'm not like you or even Roan." Brin slapped her thigh in desperation. "Tressa would have been a far better choice than I—at least she has grit. All of you are so much more capable. I'm not smart. I can't fight. I'm not brave. I'm nothing. I shouldn't even have been included on this trip."

Gifford smirked. "Before I got on Naraspur, I was a cripple who couldn't talk whose biggest accomplishment was making pretty cups. So don't tell me you don't have what it takes to be a hero. No one had less clay to work with than the god who made me. You're *the* Keeper—the best that's ever been, which means you know everything. You willingly drowned yourself to come here, so I think we can safely say you're very, very brave. And do you think I wasn't scared when I rode out of Alon Rhist that night? I thought—no, I didn't think at all, I knew—I'd die. What are *you* afraid of? Falling? You've already done that. Dying? Done that, too."

"Not falling—*failing*," Brin said. "If I do that, then all of your sacrifices will have been for nothing."

Gifford nodded. "Excellent point, except you're going to succeed."

"How do you know?"

"Malcolm said so."

Brin pretended to smile, but she knew the truth. Malcolm, Turin, Uberlin, no matter what name he went by, he was evil and manipulative. If by some miracle she *did* succeed, she would be playing into the hands of someone too nefarious to fully understand.

Why should I do what he *wants?*

"So he can be twusted?" Gifford had asked Muriel.

Her answer had been, *"As far as you're concerned, yes. It seems he wants you to succeed, and as I said, if Turin wants something, he usually gets it."*

Brin didn't know what to believe, and her thoughts were interrupted by a hug from Gifford. "You're gonna be fine. Keep your focus on Suri.

Remember she's alone, too. Once you two are together, you'll muddle through. I'm certain."

"Sure," Brin said. "For Suri."

Gifford gave her another hug and kissed her cheek. "I'm sorry I can't help, and that everything has to fall on your shoulders. I'm sorry to let you down."

"You didn't let me down, Gifford. None of you have. You all did your part." She looked up. "Now I have to do mine."

Brin grabbed hold of the rock and pulled herself up. She jumped to a ledge and looked back at Gifford. "And know this, Mister Crippled Potter. I'm going to make you a legend in *The Book of Brin*. You, Moya, Roan, Tekchin, Rain, Tressa—and Tesh. When I'm done, each of you will be more famous than Gath, Mideon, and all the rest combined. People everywhere will remember *all of you* as the heroes who saved the world."

"I'd like that."

"So would I," Brin said. "So would I."

The climb didn't go as easily as she had expected. She wasn't weightless, and the ascent seemed to go on forever. The higher she went, the more fatigued she became, and she found fewer ledges for resting. Time and distance couldn't be gauged with any degree of certainty.

And there was the cold.

While the Abyss had been constantly freezing, the rock was more than icy. The stone seemed to steal heat from her—not that she had much to give. The rests weren't just to stave off weariness but to provide her fingers a chance to warm and recover. She knew they weren't real, but *something* hurt and then went numb. When trying to latch onto little jagged outcrops, she preferred her hands to have feeling.

Fear of falling should have been an issue, but it wasn't. She wasn't scared of hurting herself or dying. She just didn't want to start over. During her time in Nifrel, Brin had found nothing to appreciate, and everything in the Abyss had been a misery. But climbing that pillar brought a whole new level of agony. In retrospect, she didn't think Gifford could have made it after all.

Brin guessed she was still quite far from the top. Instead of the light of the queen's false sky, that winter haze, she saw only darkness beyond the reach of her light. And with some concern, she noticed that it wasn't as bright as it had been.

When she'd first fallen into the Abyss, Brin guessed she illuminated an area roughly the size of Dahl Rhen, and the light was bright enough to make people shade their eyes. Now, as she pressed her back against the icy column's face and her toes hung over a narrow lip the size of half a milking stool, she estimated that with this paltry light, she would have trouble doing needlework in a roundhouse. She was just so tired and heavy.

Yes, I'm definitely heavier. Why is that? What makes me that way? Why now? As I get farther away from the base, shouldn't the weight decrease?

She'd wondered about that several times during the ascent. Toward the bottom, when she used to leap for handholds, she'd been fearless, and a fall wasn't anything to be concerned about. Now she no longer attempted jumps.

During the climb, her thoughts kept returning to Tesh and whether he and the others would find a way out. Deep down she knew it wouldn't happen.

How can it? Tressa can't even walk to the pillar, much less climb. And Tesh's and Roan's treks to the tablets all but did them in.

Every time she thought about Tesh trapped at the bottom, her heart reminded her it had been shattered.

Sitting here won't help. That's what It *wants.*

Brin had come to think of the Abyss as a living thing, where the term *living* was used in the broadest possible sense. She pictured it as the stomach of a beast that was digesting Tesh and everyone else. She was trying to claw her way out through its throat, and the creature kept swallowing.

Each minute she remained, she got weaker. Lingering, even to gather her strength, only resulted in shrinking her reserves.

Brin reached up, groping for the next handhold, and wondered if it was possible for the rock to get even colder.

It doesn't want me to get out.

"Those lost to the Abyss are never seen again."

And yet Trilos escaped.

The thought came from nowhere, and it gave her the reserves to pull herself up another foot. Instead of focusing on the cold and difficulty of climbing, she concentrated on the tablets. Running them through her head, she worked to remember what she had learned, so she'd be able to include it all in *The Book of Brin*.

Some of the tablets spoke of brothers and sisters and their days of happiness and joy while wandering a garden of perfection. Other portions talked about the deceit of the dwarfs, and the broken promises they made before eventually letting Trilos out. But most of what was written was a love story.

Tablet after tablet was etched with thoughts of *her*. The author called the subject of his admiration Reely. A nickname, a pet name, a secret name for Muriel. But Reely was treated with great care both in the etching of the word on the tablets and in the respect paid her in the text. Brin got the sense that the name had a double meaning, maybe more than one. This person was both *real* to him and the most *real* thing he knew.

Included in the tablets was the tale of how they'd first met in a golden field on a spring morning. This scene had been explained in great detail, right down to a description of what Muriel had worn. Then there were whole tablets devoted to nothing but random thoughts about her or snippets of conversations the two had shared.

SHE HAS A GAP BETWEEN HER TWO UPPER FRONT TEETH
THAT SHE CAN MAKE AN EAR-PIERCING WHISTLE THROUGH,
BUT SHE THINKS IT'S IMPROPER TO DO SO. THERE'S A

SIZABLE FRECKLE ON THE TOP OF HER LEFT EAR, AND SHE
ALMOST ALWAYS DROOLS WHEN SHE SLEEPS. SHE'S ALWAYS
USING THE PHRASE, "WHEN TREES WALK AND STONES
TALK," WHEN SHE'S FRUSTRATED ABOUT SOMETHING THAT
WILL NEVER HAPPEN.

Pondering why Malcolm thought that one line was so important kept her mind occupied for what seemed like hours while she climbed.

Why is it so important for me to know that Trilos and Muriel were in love? There has to be something I'm missing. Didn't he know that Beatrice would tell me about the two of them? He knew I had read the tablets when I was here with Persephone. Was he counting on me remembering that line? Funny thing is, I didn't see that phrase back then. I only found it when I was searching the tablets for a way out. And now that I have, what does it matter?

She still didn't know what to think about Malcolm. His divinity—if that was the right word—was no longer in question, but what he was up to was still a mystery.

Malcolm isn't an idiot. He must have known that by coming down here, I would learn the truth about him.

He'd always appeared so genuine, unassuming, and supportive, especially regarding her *Book of Brin.*

"It sounds wonderful, this idea of making a permanent record of everything that's happened. But you need to be careful. Don't allow personal opinion to distort facts."

He'd said that the last time they met, back in Alon Rhist after the Battle of Grandford. She thought he was talking about her own opinions, but maybe he was trying to warn her about the negative comments Malcolm's siblings and daughter would make.

She pulled herself up another two feet and found what was becoming an increasingly rare sight, a ledge. She didn't pause there. Keeping her mind busy was helping her forget the trials of the climb. Unable to unravel the mystery that was Malcolm, she focused once more on Trilos and his writings about Reely.

Why did Trilos devote such an enormous amount of time and effort to jotting down trivialities about the love of his life? Was it boredom, longing, or something else?

There were dozens of tablets filled with insignificant details about this woman, and more devoted to his love for her. He described how a mere smile from Muriel had the power to erase a whole day of misfortunes. How tears in her eyes made him physically ill. No detail was too small. He poured his feelings for her onto the tablet . . . but why? Brin felt she was missing something—something important.

And how did he escape? If Phyre is able to hold the Typhons, where did Trilos find the power to punch through worlds?

Pins and needles in her fingertips were becoming an agony once more, and Brin took a brief rest even without a ledge. Fatigue of spirit translated into sore arms that quivered as she pulled on them and watery legs that protested when pushing up. Weight continued to increase, and her light had dimmed by more than half. She realized Gifford was probably brighter now.

Air moved.

Startled, Brin looked around.

Wind?

At no point in all of Phyre had she felt a breeze.

The Abyss doesn't want me to escape.

Brin clutched the stone. Flattening her body as best she could, she clung to the column as the wind brushed by. Her hair whipped, but the air had a hard time getting a grip on her. Eventually its icy fingers found a hold, pulling her back from the pillar, jerking first left, then right.

The wind is actually trying to tear me off!

Brin shifted around, working to get to the lee side, but this was no ordinary gale. The wind followed her, clawing harder. She hugged the rock, her fingers frosting with the relentless blow of freezing gusts. She pressed a cheek against the pillar's face. Her entire body trembled from stress and exertion.

Brin searched for another handhold. She had to keep moving upward because her light was fading faster, reduced to little more than a candle's flame, a lonely flicker.

She could feel the hopelessness seeping in, stealing her strength.

I'm not strong enough. Tressa was right. No one can cheat death.

She squeezed her eyes shut and fought against the growing weakness. Then she remembered, *Trilos cheated death, but how? Where did that power come from?*

The wind gusted and howled, and nearly tore her off the pillar. She shifted her weight, finding a better spot, a larger foothold. It wouldn't matter. Brin could feel her muscles failing. Soon she wouldn't have the strength to hold on. Before long she'd let go.

"I'm sorry," she cried, but the wind stole her words, too. While her failure was a blow, the knowledge that she'd convinced Tesh to die for nothing was so much worse.

Brin felt the weight even more than before. Her light flickered dangerously low. The disappointment of her failure was bitter, her remorse palpable.

Regret. Regret is the weight.

Her foot slipped, and Brin cried out from the pain in her hands as they fought to hold on. She was panting in fear, huffing against the rock. The dangling foot was as heavy as if a weight were tied to it. She couldn't pull it up.

How did Trilos escape?

Brin concentrated on that, feeling there had to be a clue, something she could use.

SHE HAS A GAP BETWEEN HER TWO UPPER FRONT TEETH
THAT SHE CAN MAKE AN EAR-PIERCING WHISTLE THROUGH,
BUT SHE THINKS IT'S IMPROPER TO DO SO. THERE'S A
SIZABLE FRECKLE ON THE TOP OF HER LEFT EAR.

He wrote as if he didn't want to forget even the most trivial detail. Trilos was recording his memories—he was making his own *Book of Brin*. He was being a Keeper—but not of a people and their deeds. He was recording the specifics of the one he loved. Why?

Why do I write? Brin thought for a moment. *Because I don't want to forget anything. I'm trying to preserve what I've learned for the future. But I'm also writing about the people I love, so they won't be lost when I die.*

But he was already dead, so why would he . . .

Sacrifice.

Gods demanded it. So did the Art when making dragons. The greater the sacrifice, the stronger the power.

Then Brin understood the horrible truth of it all. She realized where the power had come from to punch through worlds and create Balgargarath.

That's how he got out. He sacrificed her. That's what I have to do, too.

Brin shook as she clung to the pillar. She finally understood.

Tesh is my weight.

The mere thought allowed her to replace her foot and relieve the pressure on her hands.

I have to let him go, but how can I do that?

She couldn't forget Tesh any more than she could forget—

What he did.

The wind shrieked in her ears and clawed at her face.

No, the weight isn't what I've done to Tesh. That's not how it works. The weight comes from me.

Brin's breath deteriorated to short gasps.

What do I have to let go of?

She lost footing again, and this time the sudden movement pulled both feet free. She hung only from her fingertips as the wind whipped, pulling then slapping her dangling body against the rock. Yet she hardly felt it. Her mind was hard at work, searching for the answer.

Love can't be a weight, but . . . do I love him? Can I love a murderer? Should I? I was able to forgive Tressa, but . . . can I forgive Tesh? Can I truly and completely forgive him for luring Anwir out into the forest and killing him slowly? Can I just look past all the Galantians he murdered? How can I forget that he pretended to be their comrade while plotting their deaths?

The wind went to work on her fingertips, biting with icy teeth.

None of the Galantians were innocent, she reminded herself. *They had murdered his family, his whole clan. And for what reason? To start a war where thousands of other innocent people would die. But does that excuse Tesh?*

No, that's his weight, not mine. He has to deal with that. All I need to address is how I feel after knowing what he did. My weight is my judgment.

The wind whipped into a fury, and the cold raised a frost on the stone, turning it white. But still, Brin hung on.

My regret, my failure, is that I never truly forgave him. Not really. That weight is mine to carry, or mine to let go.

Who am I to judge him? Was I there? Am I him? Who granted me the right to arbitrate the transgressions of others?

The moment the thought entered, the second she gave it room, she realized she wasn't an authority on the matter. She hadn't killed anyone, never even helped her father slaughter a sheep. But she had made mistakes and was far from perfect. She could have seen the good in Tressa years before. If she had, Tressa might not have turned out to be the bitter woman she grew into.

I could have been a better friend to Moya and Padera, and most of all, to Roan. And I certainly could have been a better daughter.

And then there was her uncle Gelston. The lightning strike had left him enfeebled. If ever he had needed his family, it was then. But she had avoided him out of fear. She was his niece, the only living family he had, and she did nothing for him. Only Tressa, the dahl's anointed "evil one," took care of him. She was kinder to Brin's uncle than Brin was herself.

Yes, she'd made mistakes . . . like anyone. Everyone fell, some harder and farther than others, but . . .

Who am I to judge?

"I forgive you, Tesh," she said aloud. "And I'm sorry for taking so damn long to do it."

Just then, Brin had no choice but to close her eyes. If she hadn't, she would have been blinded by her own light.

CHAPTER TEN

Yellow and Rose

Some homes are haunted by spirits. Some spirits are haunted by homes.

— THE BOOK OF BRIN

Suri put a heel of the loaf of dark bread into her bag and added a wedge of orange cheese. She'd always had a fondness for little pouches. Big bags encouraged carrying too much. Little ones invited the gathering of such wonders as polished pebbles, colorful leaves, string, animal teeth, or shiny pieces of metal. Suri didn't have such treasures anymore, but the cheese and bread would do.

"What are you doing?" Makareta asked. She was working on her sculpture again, her hands caked with clay.

"Going for a walk."

Makareta's brows rose. "Oh, the old lady's not gonna like that."

"I can't continue staying inside. Makes me crazy. I think it drives everyone a little nuts." Suri gave Makareta an insinuating smile, and then glanced at the Fhrey's mouse slippers.

Makareta replied with a smirk.

"*You* went out," Suri said.

"I had to," Makareta replied, dipping her fingers into a bowl of water and letting the runoff drip on the heads of the statuette. "I had to invite Mawyndulë to the meeting."

"I have to go out, too."

"Where are you going? I only ask because Imaly will want to know where to look for the body." Makareta smiled back.

"Mine or my victim's?"

"Ha-ha," Makareta said, impersonating a laugh. "Seriously—be careful." She looked over her shoulder at a blank wall, as if she could see through it. "There's a lot of scared people out there."

She meant that there were a lot of Fhrey who might think hurting a Rhune would make them feel less frightened.

"I can take care of myself," Suri replied as she slung the bag's drawstring over her head so that the pouch hung under her arm.

Makareta tapped her own neck. "Collar, remember? No one is supposed to know."

Suri reached up and touched the metal band around her neck. She'd worn it for so long, she'd forgotten it was there. "I grew up among wolves, bears, raow, leshies, green apples, and really nasty pricker-bushes. I was able to handle all those things long before I knew the Art. As long as I don't bump into Mawyndulë, everything will be fine."

"He's not the only Miralyith in the city."

Suri shook her head. "That's not the problem."

Makareta frowned. "Be nice. He'll be the next fane and my husband, and I'd like you two to be friends."

Suri chuckled. "Oh, that's not going to happen."

"Fine. Be that way. And here I was planning to invite you to the wedding. Guess it wouldn't be appropriate now that I know you want to kill my fiancé."

"Could be awkward." Suri started toward the door.

"Arion's house is north. It's been empty since she left. Easiest way to go is through the Garden, which is pretty empty this time of year. Head up the widest street out of the plaza, then straight through the Garden. Follow the street and you'll see it, a little house with a bright blue door."

"What makes you think I'm going there?"

"I didn't, but where else would you go? It's not like you have a lot of friends in Estramnadon."

"Good point," Suri said.

"Don't be too long," Makareta called after her. "When you get back, we'll play a string game."

⁂

Suri would have liked a real walk, one that would take her into the forest, but she guessed that wasn't such a good idea. She had to get out, needed to know she *could*, but she wasn't trying to escape. As much as she longed to disappear into the arms of the trees, she knew better than to risk everything. Imaly had called for the meeting, setting everything in motion. Suri could afford to wait one more day. Regardless of how things turned out, the world was going to be very different.

It looked and felt like snow was on the way, and there weren't many Fhrey wandering around. Those who were out and about took little notice of her passing. From a distance and while wearing the asica and a borrowed cloak, she looked much as they did. A light snow did begin to fall as she moved through the plaza, leaving a thin film of white dust on the street. Suri followed a fresh set of single prints, which were joined by another. Suri knew how to read tracks, and these were especially easy. One small, the other large—male and female.

Suri enjoyed the walk between the house and the Garden, even though it was short. It felt good to stretch her legs and to see the world. Even the cold spray of snow against her cheeks was nice. She remembered such wintry kisses from her childhood when she played wild and free in a forest full of grand adventures. Her world had grown, and her adventures were bigger by far, but somehow less grand. Everything was that way: duller, grayer, smaller. She had gained the power of magic, but this had only served to render the world less enchanting.

Suri knew Arion's home the moment she saw it, a bit off the road and mostly shaded by a tree; it would be beautiful in spring. The place was small, delicate, and unassuming. The front door was unlatched. She stood there, listening to the flakes fall—working up the courage to push the door open. She had no idea what she would find. Nothing, most likely. Yet Suri was afraid without knowing why.

The interior was musty. She found a pegboard where a hooded cape hung. Suri touched it, rubbed the thick material between her fingers.

Probably put it there on her way out.

In the center of the first room, a small, round table stood covered in dust. After running her finger over its surface and removing the grime, she found it had been polished to a fine gloss. A vase sat in the middle; long-dead flowers had rotted away. She could see the remains of them like shadows on the side of the vase, marring the existing design. Chairs were pushed under the table and carefully spaced. Light came through open shutters framed by yellow drapes, making the room bright and cheerful. The walls were painted a festive rose color, and a plush carpet matched the drape's sunny disposition. Suri's toe caught an edge of the rug. She took a moment to smooth the corner back down and straighten the tassels.

How long has it been since Arion was here? Did she suspect she would never return?

A half-moon arch led to a room with a high bed topped by a pretty canopy. The thick mattress was covered by a wonderful quilt with embroidered flowers in the colors of—what else—yellow and rose. Suri ran her hand over the cloth that was still beautiful despite being shrouded in dust. Inside closets, several colorful asicas hung, one with pretty blue piping.

She would have looked beautiful in that.

Suri made sure to close the closet door before sitting on the bed.

Arion's world was so perfect and bright. When Suri had first met Arion, the Fhrey had been lying on Persephone's bed in a dark, smoky lodge, bleeding and hurting. How horrible that must have been after this—after a world of yellow and rose, a place of sunlight and softness.

Suri reached into her bag and felt around until she touched the knit hat. When Suri was captured, she'd thought it had been lost forever. Imaly had no way of knowing how much giving it back had meant. The gift, that tiny gesture, had made all the difference. Suri held it to her face and breathed in. The scent of Arion was gone from the wool, and Suri laid it on the bed beside her. She pressed it out, making it lie flat.

"You're home," she said, and for the first time since being lied to, captured, dragged across the Fhrey lands, imprisoned, buried alive, and forced to give up a terrible secret, Suri cried.

꘏

Even fewer Fhrey were out by the time Suri left Arion's home. All around, windows were shuttered against the cold. After reaching the Garden's gate, only Suri and her shadow remained. She followed the curving path around the snow-covered bushes until she came to a set of benches across from a whitewashed door. Surprisingly, someone was there. Suri hadn't noticed anyone her first time through, yet here was a person in a dingy robe with the hood pulled up, sitting across from the Door.

"Do you know how long before it opens?"

Suri stopped, and the hood tilted upward to look at her. She shook her head.

Shoulders slumped. "Neither do I. But I think we're getting close— very close now."

Beneath the hood was an odd face: youthful yet old, friendly and frightening, innocent and guilty. All of the contradictions were built upon one another, and he stared back at her with a pleasant smile. Suri didn't know why, but she was certain his question wasn't as simple as it seemed to be.

"You're Suri. Is that right?"

She nodded, even though she assumed he wasn't actually questioning her identity. She was, after all, the only Rhune in the city—the only one on that side of the Nidwalden, for that matter.

"How did you learn to make the sentinel?"

"The what?" she asked.

"What everyone calls a dragon."

"Oh," Suri said, and relaxed a bit, realizing this person was just the curious type.

Anyone would be, I suppose. Even I would ask a deer about how it managed to climb a tree.

Given that Neith was buried, she didn't see any point in hiding the facts. "I found instructions on a stone tablet under a Dherg city."

"You were in the Agave?"

Suri was surprised he knew the name, but didn't find it alarming. She assumed a lot of people in the wider world knew about many places she didn't. Perhaps the Agave was as famous as Phyre. "Yes."

"Was there a . . . did you encounter . . . an, ah . . ." He made gestures for something large with his hands.

"Balgargarath? Yes."

"I'm guessing that's what the Dherg named it?"

She nodded.

He became intensely interested and leaned toward her. "What happened?"

"We destroyed it."

Suri expected the next question to be how, but she wouldn't answer. Not only was it painfully personal, but given that she'd already provided Lothian with the secrets to making and destroying dragons, she felt she had said all she needed to on that subject.

"So you found Hilderagozneroraha's name?"

Suri stopped breathing.

Seeing her face, he nodded. "Yes, I made him." He paused. "Not actually a *him* so much as an *it*—just a thing, really."

"How—how did you do it?" The irony of her own question, pushed her to add, "I mean, I know how, but what did you use to reach the deep chords? You must have sacrificed someone important, but weren't you alone?"

"I doubt you understand half of what you're asking." A shadow crossed his face as he looked back at the door. He didn't speak for quite some time. Then he said, "I wasn't alone. I still had my memories."

"You sacrificed your memories? How?"

"You simply erase them the way you do anything else. The chords of creation can destroy as well as create. You pull the threads and alter the pattern of the weave that makes you who you are."

"And that's enough?"

He looked at her surprised, even a bit appalled. "Sacrificing the life of a loved one is horrible, but through your memories a part of them lives on. You can still talk to them, share stories with others, and sometimes they visit you in dreams. During those comforting moments, it's as if they are with you again. But removing their memories erases everything. Afterward, it is painless, but the act is beyond horrific. You aren't killing the person you love—you're killing your love for the person. Because love is one of the most powerful things in the universe, breaking it like that is . . . yes, it's more than enough."

"What memory did you erase?"

He laughed a sad chuckle. "How would I know?" He stopped staring at the Door and shook off his melancholy. "I must say I'm impressed you were able to defeat my sentinel. He looked nasty."

"It wasn't . . ." She was going to say *easy*, but couldn't. She searched for another word, but found none. Anything she came up with trivialized the horror she had gone through, the twin nightmares she still suffered. She considered whether she should hate this person. He had created the creature, and because he did, she had been forced to—

No, I can't pass on that blame. I killed Minna, no one else. I have to be the one to live with that. The memory is painful, and yet . . . he's right, at least I still remember her.

"Never mind," the fellow in the hood said and waved her off. "I understand. We all do what we have to when the time comes. And we hope that in the end everything will work out such that our sacrifices will be worth the cost. But the future is a fickle thing, and you never really know what it will bring."

She nodded.

"You haven't asked who I am."

"Should I?"

He shrugged. "Most people do."

"What do you tell them?"

"I give them a name that means nothing."

"You're the Ancient One."

He thought about this and nodded, his lower lip judging the pronouncement. "I guess that works. I am old, and I am one."

When he said nothing more, Suri started to walk past. Then she stopped and glanced at the little door. "You've been waiting for that door to open for a long time, haven't you?"

"Yes."

"What will you do when it does?"

A smile formed, and the fellow on the bench laughed softly to himself. "I'll go in."

CHAPTER ELEVEN

Alysin

Alysin is the sort of place only a child can believe in. The longer you live, the more you know it cannot exist.

— THE BOOK OF BRIN

Reaching the top of the pillar and once more beneath a hazy gray sky, Brin saw that the bridge across the Abyss really had been torn apart. It shouldn't have been a surprise. It wasn't that she doubted what Tesh had told her, but it was shocking to see.

Not surprisingly, the armies, the queen, the bankors, and the dragon were also gone. Brin couldn't say she was disappointed about their absence.

Others might have previously walked to where she now stood—when there was a bridge—but being the first to *scale* her way to it from the Abyss gave her a feeling of authority over the place. Like some grand explorer, she officially renamed it the Pillar of Lost Regret. She felt she deserved the privilege.

Anyone else in Nifrel would have named it after themselves. Fenelyus was right. I don't belong here.

Looking out at the desolate chipped-slate landscape of Nifrel, Brin couldn't see anyone. Not a soul waited; no one looked for their return.

Why bother? No one ever returns from the Abyss.

If the queen had stationed someone to keep a lookout on that far side where the broken tongue of the bridge stuck out at the Alysin Pillar in a most insolent manner, they would certainly see her. Brin was as bright as the sun at midday, and there was no way to hide. As it turned out, no one was watching. Wouldn't have mattered if they were. Brin had no fear of being spotted. She was just a few steps away from the door. Having ejected the last of her weight, Brin knew she could cover that distance in less than an instant. Looking back at the missing section of bridge, she also realized she'd have no trouble leaping over it.

I bet I could run the whole length of Nifrel in the blink of an eye.

But that was for later. Turning, she faced her future.

The gate to Alysin was visible, a shimmering light inside a cave. The twinkling beckoned her with its beauty, and she walked inside. The door was smaller and narrower than those leading to Rel and Nifrel. She wondered if it was because getting in here was harder.

She couldn't see anything through the opening except light. As Brin approached, she squinted from its brilliance. Coming closer, she spotted movement. Someone was coming toward her, approaching the door on the far side. She was a wondrous being of radiance and power, dressed in fantastic armor. The person wore no helm, revealing long hair that cascaded over her shoulders—an amazing woman with a fierce determined look and sad but serious eyes. This was no one to trifle with. In all her underworld travels, Brin had never seen the like of her before. *Impressive* was too small a word.

Am I looking through the doorway and seeing one of the heroes who dwell in paradise, or is this another of the gods?

The woman who had been walking toward her stopped when Brin did.

Brin raised a hand to wave.

So did the woman.

Dear Mother of All . . . that's me!

The light didn't come from the other side. The brilliance was her own. The door was a mirror.

Brin's eshim armor, which couldn't exist in the Abyss, had returned, more beautiful than before. And that wasn't all. Staring at herself, she noticed something strange. She could clearly see the key dangling from her neck, but . . .

Brin reached up and the key wasn't there—not exposed, at least. It remained tucked under her shirt—which was now beneath the grand breastplate, but in the mirror, she could still see it hanging on the outside. The door to Alysin *knew.*

Brin reached out and touched the mirrored surface but felt nothing. Her hand passed through.

I guess I just need to have the key.

She drew back and stood for a time, staring at herself, at that impossible image. She appeared like a crimbal queen, a goddess.

Is that really me? Or an illusion I've invented?

Brin looked into her own eyes. Mirrors within mirrors going on into infinity, into an Abyss deeper than the one she'd climbed out of.

Or is this the real me and the other an illusion?

She found no answers, just more questions that, like the reflections in her eyes, multiplied upon themselves.

Maybe the answers are on the other side of the looking glass.

With that thought, Brin closed her eyes and stepped through.

❧

Before she looked, before she opened her eyes, she heard music. The delicate plinks, plunks, and quivering strings of instruments filled her ears. Warmth was on her face. A breeze, cool, sweet, and filled with the smell of spring flowers, greeted her. She didn't want to look. Nothing could match the beauty she imagined in her mind, grown from the sounds and smells—a paradise, a perfect place. Because Rel and Nifrel had been so terrible, she had expected this, too, would disappoint. Alysin would end up being a place of lost hope, of false dreams, and—

"Brin?"

She opened her eyes.

The first two things she noticed overwhelmed and surprised her, but in retrospect, neither should have. Color was the first. She'd grown so used to the fiery red of Nifrel's battles and the black-and-white dullness of Rel that the sudden abundance of greens, blues, browns, reds, and purples staggered her.

Brin's second thought was far simpler: *Raithe?*

"Welcome," Raithe said.

He didn't look the same. Sort of, but not quite. Years had passed since she'd seen him last. Some differences would make sense—a few more wrinkles, perhaps. But Raithe didn't look older. If anything, he looked younger. There was more color in his face—or maybe she was just obsessed with color now that it was back. The weariness she'd always associated with his eyes was missing. That was it. He stood straighter, and there was a smile on his lips.

Have I ever seen Raithe smile before?

The big Dureyan was dressed in a long beige shirt, the sort of garment one might sleep in, except that it had a belt made of white rope. Although the shirt was of excellent quality and made from an amazing material, the style and simplicity resembled the clothing of someone who was poor, certainly when compared with how elaborately people dressed in Nifrel or even Elan.

"Welcome to Alysin," he repeated, extending his arms.

She felt like she'd just crossed a desert, and he was holding out a bucket of water. To someone fresh from the Abyss and starved for kindness, comfort, help, and hope, he represented a refuge from an unforgiving world. She threw her arms around him, and Raithe caught her. She reveled in his embrace, strong, friendly, and familiar. Since leaving the Dragon Camp, she'd done her best to be steadfast. She couldn't cry in the swamp, express terror as they marched to battle, or scream at the others' resignation in the Abyss. And she certainly couldn't allow herself a moment's worth of self-pity while climbing the pillar. But all that was behind her. This was Raithe, and she could surrender to him.

"I'm the only one—the only one left," she cried. It didn't matter if he understood or not. A dam had burst within her. "I had to leave them behind, every last one: Moya, Tekchin, and Rain; Gifford and Roan; Tressa and—and Tesh. Oh, Grand Mother, I abandoned *him!* I left them all in Nifrel, most of them in the Abyss. I'm sorry. I'm sorry. I'm so sorry. I failed them, and I don't know if I can do the rest by myself!"

"It's okay, Brin." Raithe held her tight. "Shhh, hush now. It's all right."

"But you don't understand. We were supposed to come through together, but I'm all that's left. I don't think I can do it. I don't know how. It's all so hopeless, and everyone will die for nothing. It'll all be my fault."

"You're here, Brin. You made it out."

"But I wasn't even supposed to go. It should be Gifford standing here, or Moya, or even Tressa. Anyone but me."

Raithe smiled at her, and in that look was both pride and a dash of amusement. "Oh, Brin, this has *always* been about you. This is your destiny, and it has been from the start. Don't you see that? Before the war, before I came to Dahl Rhen, everything has been about you. And it will continue to be long into the future."

"What? No. You don't understand."

"Yes. I do. We all understand. Trust me, we do."

His big hand was on the back of her head, gently holding her as she cried. Then she lifted her face out of his chest. *"We?"*

Raithe nodded.

"Who are you talking about?" She wiped her eyes clear and looked around. They were on a broad dirt trail that led through a lush land of forest and field. Gentle green hills dappled by golden light made waves across a lovely valley of lush grass and wildflowers. In the distance were blue mountains, with a matching sky overhead.

"It's beautiful."

"You should see it on a nice day."

Brin took a step forward and peered up at the clear sky. No sun—no ball of light, at least. But a beautiful radiance did shine down. *"This* isn't a nice day? What's wrong with it?"

"We'll get to that later." Raithe placed his hands on her shoulders. "You're taller than I remember."

"I grew up."

He made a disapproving sound in his throat. "You should try to avoid that in the future."

"Well, I'm dead, so that shouldn't be too difficult."

"Perhaps." He offered a wink and a smile. "But for now I want you to look down that path and take a deep breath."

"Why? We don't need to breathe, right?"

She heard him sigh. "I don't remember you being so quarrelsome."

"I told you, I grew up."

"Just do as I ask."

Brin drew in a deep breath, and her eyes went wide. After her climb, she'd thought all her burdens had been discarded. They hadn't. For as she breathed, she felt all the hidden apprehension and fear she still carried in the tiny pockets of her soul fall away. The weight she'd unknowingly carried from one side of Nifrel to the other, and the burden of leaving everyone in the Abyss slipped from her. *Light* didn't describe the sensation of buoyancy she felt. The closest thing she could compare it to was being tossed high into the air on a big cloth stretched taut by members of Dahl Rhen during summer celebrations. Up she'd flown, her stomach rising, and she had felt a giddy, tingling sensation that left her laughing. That rush, the same wonderful feeling surged through her now. She was high in the air, caught at the apex of the toss, that perfect moment of exhilaration that she only had glimpses of when on Elan. Here, she rode that single note as it stretched and lingered.

A note. Yes, that's what this is. Everything is music. Not just the sounds, but the light, smells, and sights.

Everything was woven together into a perfect tapestry of music: the droplets of dew, the breeze in the branches, the quiver of petals on flowers.

She looked at Raithe and saw him smiling back again. "My first day, I did a jig."

She offered him a skeptical smile.

"Expressions of joy aren't something to be ashamed of, especially not here. On Elan, if you enjoy a good meal, you belch. It's how we express appreciation to the cook. In Alysin, dancing, singing, and laughter are like that."

He took her hand and pulled. "Come. There are a few people who want to meet you. More would have come, but time is short, and you'll need to hurry."

"People want to meet me?" Brin asked, confused. "Who?"

"You'll see."

Raithe led her up the path into the light which, unlike the light in Rel, gave warmth. They jumped a fallen log and walked past a little hill where an orchard grew. Red, yellow, orange, and green fruits dangled from branches. A few had fallen to the hillside and rolled down near the path.

"Can you eat those?"

Raithe glanced over. "Of course."

"What do they taste like?"

"Whatever you want them to."

Brin laughed, but Raithe didn't.

"You're serious?"

"Try one."

Brin snatched up a perfectly round orange thing with a smooth skin and no stem. "Do I just bite into it?"

"Do whatever you like. It's your fruit."

Brin licked it.

Sweet. Like honey.

She took a bite and was shocked when a flood of juice ran down through her fingers. It made no sense, but the orange ball the size of an apple tasted like a blueberry. And it was the sweetest, most luscious berry she'd ever eaten. "This is fantastic!"

"Usually are. People generally don't choose things that taste terrible."

Around the bend was a quiet pond in a lovely field. To one side was a great tree that looked like a massive oak; friendly branches spread over three figures, each a woman.

"Allow me to introduce you." Raithe spread out his hand. "Brin, Keeper of Ways of Clan Rhen, meet Gylindora Fane." He gestured to the first Fhrey Brin had ever met who wasn't dressed in either shimmering cloth or bronze armor. She wore a simple, ankle-length pullover dress of light blue. In her hands were the makings of a basket. She smiled and nodded gently in greeting. "So pleased to finally meet you."

How could a Fhrey in Alysin know I exist? And why would she be waiting to meet me?

"Gylindora is—" Raithe began.

"An excellent basket weaver," the Fhrey interrupted him and smiled.

"So I see," Brin replied. "Nice to meet you. My mother was a weaver, too—of wool, mostly."

Gylindora nodded. "And a fine raiser of daughters, apparently." She grinned at the others, who laughed.

"Is there . . ." Brin paused. "I feel like I'm missing something."

"Not at all, child," Gylindora said.

"We're just so excited to see you," mentioned one of the two remaining women, who stood up and grinned in amazement. The woman was small, delicate, and so young. Not much more than a girl. "Isn't she something?"

"Do I know you?" Brin asked. She was a stranger, but her smile, eyes, and the sound of her voice were familiar.

"My name is Aria," she said. "I believe you know my son, Gifford."

"You're Aria?" Brin clapped her hands to her cheeks, then foolishly looked behind her down the path, as if Aria's admission would somehow summon forth her son. But of course, he wasn't there. Cruel sadness followed. "Oh, Grand Mother of All." Tears filled her eyes. Light as Brin was, her legs gave out, and she fell to her knees. "I'm sorry. Oh, I'm so sorry. Gifford—your son—he was with me. He could have—"

"I know." Aria knelt down and took Brin's hands. Her touch was ... the only way Brin could describe it was magical. Instantly she felt better.

While alive, Brin had never met Aria, but everyone in Dahl Rhen who had, spoke highly of Gifford's mother. Although she died when not much older than a child, she was a hero to the clan. Her whole life had been lived fearlessly. She had been the last to take and the first to give, beautiful, gentle, understanding, forgiving, and wise beyond her years. Not a soul had ever had a bad thing to say about her. Despite the full-throated claims of people like Padera, Brin had suspected the stories were too good to be true. She assumed Aria's faults had been sanitized and forgotten. No one could be so perfect. It wasn't possible.

Or was it?

"He—he looked for you in Rel," Brin told her. "Then we fell into the Abyss."

Aria nodded, and the woman's expression was like seeing love looking back at her.

"Gifford won the race. He went faster than any man ever, and he saved everyone."

Tears welled in Aria's eyes. "I know, my dear. I've heard the tales and expected nothing less."

"Gifford stayed in the Abyss because he wouldn't leave Roan. She's his wife."

"Sounds like someone we know," Gylindora said, smiling at Aria.

Gifford's mother sniffled as she wiped tears from her cheeks.

"He wanted to meet you so very much," Brin said. "He loved you even though he never met you."

"If he's his mother's son," Raithe said, "he may yet do so."

Brin wiped her face again. "I feel so stupid. Here I am in this wonderful place, and I keep bawling my eyes out." She sniffled and looked at the third woman. She appeared about the same age Brin was when her parents died.

"Brin," Raithe said. "This is my sister, Dedria. She's been wanting to meet you for a long time now. She's a storyteller."

"Nice to meet you." Brin nodded to the girl.

"I've never met a real Keeper," Dedria said. "We didn't have one in our village, and certainly not one as important as you." The girl looked embarrassed, and gestured at everyone else. "I'm not like the rest of you. I didn't do anything great to get in here, I didn't earn my place. Raithe invited me."

"You can do that?" Brin asked.

The girl nodded. "Of course. How can a person be truly happy if someone they love isn't allowed to be by their side? Alysin wouldn't be a paradise if that meant separation from loved ones."

Raithe nodded. "The hard part is getting people to accept that truth. Some people, like my father and brothers, don't understand how it works, so they deny themselves entry. Others, like my mother, aren't ready. Those who walk in here on their own are the ones who were always here—in a way. It's hard to explain. And I was never as good with words as you."

After Brin's visit to the Abyss, she felt she understood better than he thought. She never would have believed it, but people were their own worst enemies. Tesh could climb out if he could get past what was weighing him down. They all could. The problem was they felt they deserved to suffer. Guilt anchored them to the bottom.

"We should get going," Gylindora interrupted, putting a hand on Dedria's shoulder. "She has a long way to go yet, remember?"

"A shame you couldn't be here on a better day," Aria said as they began to stroll up the path leading toward the blue mountains.

"Raithe said it was a bad day, too, but I don't understand why," Brin said.

Aria looked at Raithe, who looked at the Fhrey.

"Because it's storming out," Gylindora explained.

Brin looked up at the clear sky.

"Not in here, dear," the Fhrey told her. "Not in here."

≈

The trip across Alysin was lovely, and Brin lost her concern about storms and why everyone was acting so oddly around her. They weren't telling her everything . . . or anything, for that matter, but watching the four of them laugh, sing, and at times dance had a way of making her feel like there was nothing to worry about. Aria danced the best, performing with fearless abandon. Raithe's sister did cartwheels. Gylindora had a beautiful voice for song. Brin didn't understand the words, but she didn't need to. She couldn't understand the messages in birdsongs, either. Brin hadn't imagined Raithe to be a dancer, but he was wonderful. At one point, he took her hands and spun her around until her feet came free of the ground. Joy was air in Alysin, ecstasy the grass beneath their feet, and delight the brilliance that shone upon everything. But even surrounded by all of it, Brin couldn't be carefree. The banquet they feasted on wasn't for her. She was just passing through.

And it isn't a good day.

By the time they had crossed the valley and entered the foothills, the reality of leaving started to weigh on her. Alysin was a warm home filled with the light of a crackling hearth, the smell of baking bread, and good friends laughing heartily, but outside that house, a thunderstorm raged. Brin knew she would soon be forced back into that dreadful tumult. And when she left, she would go alone.

During their travels, Brin discovered that Alysin was more sparsely populated than either Rel or Nifrel. For a time, she wondered if it was just the five of them, but every now and then she spotted a distant figure walking on a far-off hill. Gylindora or Aria would wave, and the others would return the gesture. Brin should have asked who the strangers were. She was neglecting her Keeper duties, but her mind was on the storm. She grew quiet, and the others left her to her thoughts.

Brin realized that each realm of the afterlife was imperfect. Rel was calm but stale and dull. Nifrel was exciting but also scary, violent, and cruel. While joyful and bright, Alysin suffered from the knowledge that the rest of the world remained in pain, a particular remorse tailored for the inhabitants it drew.

The world is broken. Both Phyre and the face of Elan are shattered and in splinters.

Brin thought she could glimpse how the parts might fit, and could guess at the final shape once it was made whole again. The equally obvious problem was the massive scale of the required restoration.

Is it even possible to fix it all?

A pretty house appeared along the path, perched on a rise that overlooked fields and, farther down, the sea. The home was small, made mostly of stone, and was topped with a thatched roof. Window boxes held red flowers, and a walkway of cleverly fitted stones serpentined from the road to the door, which was painted bright green and had a half-moon top. They stopped, and Aria knocked.

"Who lives here?" Brin asked.

Before Raithe could answer, the door opened, and a beautiful woman looked out at them. She had a luxuriant mane of golden hair that reached down to her waist, but her eyes were dark as rich soil.

"So she's arrived at last," the lady said without a hint of surprise. "Please, come in."

Brin couldn't make even a guess at her age. She had a youthful beauty, but the grace of her movements and the confidence in her voice suggested profound wisdom. And for no reason at all, or perhaps all of them at once, Brin loved her. The lady held the door open and smiled. The others went inside, but as Brin drew closer, tears filled her eyes once more. By the time she stood before the lady, Brin was sobbing without knowing why. There was no pain or sadness. The tears were the same as those she'd cried when she found her parents in Rel, but Brin didn't know this woman. A moment later, she had fallen into the lady's arms.

"It's all right," she whispered, brushing the wet hair from Brin's face. "You'll be fine."

Brin continued to cry. The lady held her patiently as they stood in her doorway. Finally, Brin found enough voice to ask, "Who are you?"

"I'm your mother."

Brin looked up, confused.

"All right." The lady smiled in a whimsical way. "I'm your very, very great-grandmother. My name is Mari. I'm the third daughter of Eton and Elan."

Brin gasped, shuddered, and felt completely lost. "Should I—I don't know—should I kneel?"

"I have chairs." She smiled, and to see it was to look full-faced at love.

She gestured at the interior of her house, which was what Brin imagined the perfect home to be. A wood floor, cushioned window seat, bright green shutters that were thrown wide open, soft chairs, and a stone hearth with a steaming pot. Brin stared in amazement. The painted walls were covered in circles and curving lines of yellow and orange, celestial swirls with stars above them.

The others took seats around the hearth. Mari waited for Brin to do the same. There were plenty of chairs, but she sat on the floor the way she used to at home. Brin half expected to see her mother at the loom and Moya working the spinning wheel. Sitting cross-legged, she couldn't shake the feeling that this place felt more like her home than the one she'd grown up in. It seemed like the place that her parents—that everyone—had been trying to make.

Mari sat beside her; the white gown she wore settled like mist.

"I asked the others to bring you by so we could talk," she said.

Brin nodded, trying her best to look serious, but it was hard to concentrate.

This place is just so perfect. This is where everyone should live.

"Brin, you need to focus. I know it's hard to do here, but up that path lies the exit from Phyre and the entrance to the Sacred Grove. When you go through, you'll be returning to Elan."

"To the storm," Brin whispered.

"Yes."

"But . . ." Brin looked out the open window and saw a bird land on a berry bush. "Couldn't I just—" She stopped before saying more. She wasn't a child, yet she felt like one. "I want to stay here. I wish . . . but it's more than that. I don't think I can do it. I'm supposed to go to Estramnadon, but that's the home of the Fhrey." She glanced at Gylindora. "Tekchin was supposed to be our guide. He knows the city and the language. There were others with me, all of them heroes—real heroes. They would be able to see this thing through, but I can't. I'm not even sure anymore why I came at all." She brushed the hair from her face, feeling the residue of tears on her cheek. "At the time, I said it was because I wanted to help my friend, but I think that wasn't true. I guess I just didn't want to be left out. I didn't want to be the only one who did nothing. But there's a reason why I never did anything—because I *can't* do anything. I'm not a hero. I only write about them."

"Brin." Raithe caught her attention. "You climbed out of the Abyss."

Aria nodded. "*No one* has *ever* done that."

"So okay, that was hard, but only because I was dragging stuff with me. Once I let go of it, the climb wasn't so difficult."

"But you were smart enough to figure that out," Gylindora said. "And strong enough to do it."

Brin nodded. "Yeah, okay. Sure, I get that, but the rules are different in here, aren't they? Out there, I'm nothing special. And this time I'll be alone. I'm not like the others. All I've done is create a book that only two people can read, and both of them are lost to the Abyss. I don't even know what I'm supposed to do. We thought we came to save Suri, but Tressa told me that was a lie. Instead, I'm supposed to get some kind of horn and give it to Nyphron. But I don't know where to find such a thing, or even what it looks like."

"It's about this big," the Fhrey said, holding her hands about a foot apart.

Just then, the Keeper's mind clicked a piece into place. *"The real reason for this trip is to return with something called the Horn of Gylindora."*

She stared at the Fhrey, stunned. "Your name is Gylindora! It's your horn!"

She nodded. "I'm the first fane of my people, and it was given to me, to all Fhrey, to keep us from destroying one another through infighting. It's our most sacred relic. But it doesn't look like anything special. To most, it looks like a battered ram's horn. But it has markings on it."

"Writing?"

The Fhrey nodded. "No one knows that—not yet. Right now, everyone thinks they're just decorative markings. Some might even speculate they're magic runes like the Orinfar. But in fact, they are words—words you can read."

"How is that possible?"

"Because you invented the language they're written in."

Brin should have refuted the idea as being impossible. The horn was obviously ancient, and even if that weren't the case, Brin had never been on the Fhrey side of the Nidwalden River. But there was no denying her ability to read the tablets in the Agave that were written by the Ancient One. Trilos had used her language as well, or maybe she had used his. The whole thing was confusing, and it was impossible to know how much came from her and what had come from him. She had no idea how any of this was possible, yet there was no denying it was.

"What do the words say?" Brin asked the question with riveted anticipation. She guessed the writing must contain something wise, or magical, or profound. She was certain the fane would shake her head, dismiss the question and say, "It is beyond your understanding, child." Instead, Gylindora began to chuckle.

"They are instructions on how to use it." She put a hand to her mouth and laughed in embarrassment. "Ironically, at some point in the future, reading will be common, but the nature of the horn will be forgotten. Strange how these things sometimes work out."

"Can all of you see the future?"

"No," Mari said. "But the person who wrote on the horn could. He can see everything quite clearly."

"Turin," Brin said.

They all nodded. Until that point, Brin hadn't realized that a simple rocking of one's head could communicate so much emotion. Each nod was incredibly sad.

Brin looked down at the patch of light that entered the window and created an elongated, skewed rectangle on the floor. The color was golden, far richer and more vibrant than anything on Elan.

Here, even light on the floor is a wonder. I could spend an eternity staring at it. What a wonderful place this is. I want to stay.

"I'm not certain I should do anything that he wants." Brin blurted out the words that she'd kept inside so long. Like the tears she'd shed on Raithe's shoulder, the confession burst out. "Malcolm"—she looked at Raithe—"told you his name was Turin, but he's also known as Uberlin. Did you know that?"

"I didn't then," the Dureyan said, "but yes, I've heard the tales."

"Given that, I have to wonder whether completing any quest that *he* initiated makes me complicit with evil." She looked at Mari. "Can you tell me?"

Mari stood and walked to the window, where she drew the curtains. As she did, the room darkened.

"That's why you're here—why I asked you to be brought to my home." She crossed to the other window. "It's important that you are well informed, but I should warn you, it's not a pleasant tale, and I can't tell you all of it because I wasn't there for the end." Mari closed the other set of drapes and darkness reigned.

She resumed her seat near the hearth, where a small fire began to glow.

The goddess of mankind sat up straighter than before, and as she did, the others shifted. Apparently, Brin wasn't the only one interested in the story. Mari placed her hands on her thighs and leaned forward, assuming the posture that all storytellers reserved for their best tales.

Perhaps the technique is inherited, passed down from parent to child for eons. Or have I somehow channeled Mari when reciting the old stories?

Brin had always felt there was something mystical in the power that Keepers had to transport others to different times and places.

Maybe it's a kind of a spell.

Brin was discovering that magic was far more common than she would have ever believed.

It's not that magic is so rare in everyday life, but perhaps it's just ignored or overlooked.

"Turin waged the First War upon us, his brothers and sisters," Mari began in a soft but ominous voice that captured the attention of everyone in the room. Brin imagined that even the birds outside—those who could hear—had stopped to listen. "Our father, Eton, did not approve of what he saw. It confirmed that he had been right. He punished Alurya instead of my mother, or us, or Turin. In his finite wisdom, he determined that it was she who was at fault for giving Turin eternal life. She was the lawbreaker, so she was the one to face his wrath."

"What did he do?"

"Eton disowned her. He turned his face away." Mari clasped her hands together, placing the tips to her mouth. As she did, the last of the remaining light that bled through the material of the drapes and from the other rooms, was snuffed, casting them all in darkness. "Alurya cried and begged for forgiveness, but Eton refused to listen. He sealed her in stone, cutting her off from his gifts: rain, warmth, and light."

As they sat in the dark, only a faint glow from the embers of the hearth illuminated their faces. Each stared wide-eyed at Mari. Outside, the birds *had* stopped singing. The breeze stopped playing with the leaves. The whole of Alysin paused as Mari told the tale. And as she did, her voice grew in depth and volume.

"Turin was unstoppable and proclaimed himself to be King Great One. His forces—the many who remained loyal to Rex Uberlin—poured out of Erebus, laying siege to each of our cities. His war escalated. He killed Ferrol first, and made a sport of it. You see, she was the first to defy him after Trilos's death. Turin humiliated Ferrol before the walls of her own city. Then he made her watch as it burned and her people were slaughtered." She closed her eyes, and in the embers' light, Brin saw Mari's pain.

"Drome was next. Uberlin destroyed him, and while he wasn't as cruel, he killed Drome just the same. By the time Rex Uberlin showed up at my walls, he was tired, so he made my death mercifully quick. I think he regretted it. I believe—yes, even then I was sure—he didn't want to kill me. I was his little sister. But by then he was traveling down a path that had no turns, no way to reverse course. At the time, he didn't know about Alurya's fate. He'd been too busy slaughtering us. Once all his brothers and sisters were dead and safely imprisoned in Phyre, he turned his attention to what remained of their children, who were fleeing across the sea to the west. While chasing down Ferrol's people, he came upon the Sacred Grove and discovered what Eton had done. That's when Turin challenged his own father. He brought war to the sky itself."

Mari stopped. Her hands came down to her lap once more as she stared silently at the floor.

After a long pause, Brin asked, "What happened?"

Mari offered a sad smile. "Forever the Keeper. I wish I could tell you, my child, but I don't know. I wasn't there. I was dead." Mari gave her a little smirk, like a friendly aunt who was once a very mischievous child. As she did, the room brightened. "For the rest of the tale you have to go to the source. You must enter the Sacred Grove."

"But you know—you *know* what happened."

"I've heard about it. *Everyone* has. The afterlife is rife with gossip. That's what the dead do: We spread rumors. There is plenty of talk about what we would have done, what should have happened, and what some believe did occur. But we're in here, and it's not possible to separate truth from speculation. It's best that you hear the story from one who was actually there."

"Who?"

Again, that impish smile formed on Mari's face as she stood and took the effort to open the drapes once more.

"Mari knows how to motivate a Keeper, doesn't she?" Raithe said as light once more filled the homey space.

"Can you at least tell me why you have a wonderful place while Ferrol is in, well, where she is?"

"Nifrel isn't a punishment." Mari returned to her seat. "That's like asking why you don't tie your hair back like someone else does, even if you think their choice looks ghastly. To Drome, the world was always this or that, black or white. When we were children, he would stay in the clearing while the rest of us explored the woods. After we came back, he would have a sculpture made out of branches or a little house built from sticks. He was content and didn't need more. Ferrol was always smart, arrogant, and insecure. She admired her older brothers, but resented them, too. She believed they got all the glory. If Turin hadn't invented war, she most certainly would have. To her, Nifrel is as near to perfection as she could ask for."

"And you?" Brin asked. "Don't you hate your brother for what he did?"

Mari stared out the window at a distant point on the horizon. "I can't say I'm happy with him—but *hate?*" She scrunched up her nose and pressed her lips together, shifting them back and forth as she searched for an answer. Since Mari had had so long to contemplate it, Brin was surprised she didn't just know. Maybe she had at one time, but Mari had the look of someone reevaluating. "For a time I did hate him, but for me, hate is difficult. Hate is like holding your hands over your head on a dare. You can do it for a long time, sure, but it does get tiring and bothersome after a while. It's not possible to do much with your hands over your head, and given enough time, you wonder why you are inconveniencing yourself. You question what is to be gained, and then you feel just plain silly. When Uberlin reached my walls, I went out to meet him. He didn't look happy. He was supposed to be evil incarnate, a conquering madman. But I only saw my brother. You see, Drome and Ferrol—being twins—bickered all the time. Because I was the youngest, I was left behind. But sometimes Turin and Trilos would take me adventuring. They were my big brothers, and I loved them." Mari pressed a hand to her lips and sighed. "I guess I still do. Doing so makes me mad sometimes, but I can't help it."

She wiped her eyes. "Turin—or Uberlin by then—had come to kill me, dressed in his shimmering robe that shifted color and a mantle that had a mind of its own. He held his spear, Narsirabad, and wore a silly-looking crown. He seemed so sad, and for a moment, he was my big brother again.

I asked him to spare my people, to let them go. He agreed, and to his credit, he honored that promise." She paused, looking past Brin again, focusing once more on something too far in the distance to be seen. "I would have died anyway, eventually. I only lost a few years."

Brin shook her head. "I don't know if I could be so understanding."

"You?" Mari said with a laugh. "You have no idea what you are capable of—not yet. All of that lies beyond the door to the Sacred Grove. It's time you were on your way. Come."

With that one word, she ushered them all out of her house and up the stone-fitted path to the road. There Mari threw out her arms, closed her eyes, and tossed her head back as if basking in the rays of an invisible sun. She took deep breaths as if needing to rejuvenate herself. Once more the birds sang and the breeze blew.

Brin looked up the road at the stretch she had yet to walk. "I'm still not certain I should do this."

"Rex Uberlin, the Great King of the World, the lunatic who fought the sky, has gone through an incredible amount of effort to get you where you are now," Mari told her. "He doesn't do anything without a reason, and more than anything he hates to lose. I understand it's upsetting to feel manipulated, and no one likes to learn they've been lied to, but having the first king on your side does come with benefits. And you should consider this . . . he knew you'd find out, but he had faith you'd do the right thing. My oldest brother is many things, but stupid isn't one of them. He can't make you continue. You have Eton's Key around your neck, and Turin is immortal. If you decided to stay, there's nothing he could do to you. He can't come in here. But know this, Turin entrusted the key to you, and he isn't a trusting person."

"Malcolm didn't trust me. He gave the key to Tressa."

Mari smiled and let her hand drift across the tops of ivy that grew on a trestle alongside the road. Where her palm passed, purple flowers bloomed. "The fact that you are here, and you have it, says differently."

"I know it's difficult to trust him given what you know," Gylindora said. "I had it easier than you. I didn't know anything about the First War when I met him, and he went by the name of Caratacus. But if it helps your decision, know this. He did bring order to my people at a time when it seemed like there was no stopping us from orchestrating our own destruction. He stopped Fhrey-on-Fhrey violence and instilled a system whereby leadership could pass without the death of thousands. I can find no nefarious reasons for him to do that, so if you ask my opinion, my counsel is to put your trust in him. And know that he has without question put his trust in you. He knew you would succeed, even before you were born."

"But you're not listening—he didn't send me. I—"

"Brin," Aria said, stopping her. "You are the *only* one that matters. Don't you understand that? This hasn't been about Tressa, or Moya, or any of the others. They were sent to ensure you made it through, and you have."

Brin shook her head but couldn't find the words to explain how wrong they all were. They had to be. And despite Mari leading them at a casual pace down the road, Brin felt rushed, pushed toward a fate that terrified her. Already Mari's house was far behind them, and the road had narrowed to a path and then vanished entirely. Now, they walked through a field of swaying grass with flowers that bowed as they passed. At first, Brin thought it was just the wind, but that wasn't it. Daisies and goldenrod dipped their heads whenever the group came near. Birds swooped as if to get a better look, and the light that had no source followed them like a friend.

If only Tesh were with me. If he could just see this place. If only they knew what waited.

She sighed, remembering her promise to forget them. Some promises were harder than others to keep, and she doubted she would ever manage to forget any of them. She was, after all, a Keeper.

"You won't be alone," Gylindora said.

"That's right," Raithe added. "The greatest of the great awaits you in the Sacred Grove."

Mari nodded. "Eton gave an exemption from his laws for those who proved themselves deserving of his trust. For them, death has no hold.

They alone have the freedom to go where they will, and do as they please. Sadly, only one has been found worthy."

"I heard about that." Brin nodded. "Fenelyus said there are only two in the Sacred Grove, Alurya and her Guardian."

"That's our understanding as well," Mari said. "And with the exception of brief absences that hero has chosen to spend eternity in the Sacred Grove next to Alurya."

By all accounts, the Grove was the pinnacle of all. Average people went to Rel. The ambitious were rewarded with Nifrel. And the true heroes came to Alysin. Given that, Brin wondered what it would be like in the place where the greatest of all heroes dwelled. Brin figured it had to be a place of even greater reward, and yet . . .

Can there be a better place than this? What can surpass Alysin?

She also began to speculate about the great hero whom Eton had found worthy. She'd come across every person of great renown: the First Fane of the Fhrey, Gath of Odeon, Atella, Raithe, Mideon, Fenelyus, Aria, and four of the five Aesira, including the goddess of mankind. None of them had earned the right.

"Who is it?"

"I believe you're about to find out." Raithe stopped and pointed at a small pool.

Of course it's a pool. A dark sinister pool. And I bet it's the only one of its ilk in all of Alysin.

"You can do this." Mari grinned at her. "You've entered my realm dressed as a Belgriclungreian warrior and shining like a star. You, Brin of Dahl Rhen, Brin of the Book, Conqueror of the Abyss, Holder of the Key of Eton, and—whether you like it or not—Champion of the First King, Rex Uberlin. You are greater than you think."

"Have faith, Brin," Gylindora said. "Remember, I, too, have been where you are now. Putting your trust into his hands. When he found me, I was sitting on the bank of the River Gan, crying so hard I couldn't finish weaving the basket I was working on. He told me that if I trusted him, together we could save my people and eventually the world. He made good on his first promise, and I believe he is working through you to fulfill the second. I witnessed miracles. My people were saved. I don't believe he's going to destroy them now."

Brin nodded.

There's no getting out of this. If nothing else, I must see what lies beyond.

She faced the pool and gritted her teeth.

"Thank you," Brin said.

One by one, they hugged her. Raithe was the last.

"You'll do fine," he whispered in her ear. "You're the only one who doesn't know that."

She squeezed him back. "Persephone loves you. You know that, right?"

"Yes. She talks to me all the time."

Brin stared at him for a moment, unsure what he meant.

"Go on. Become the hero we all know you to be."

Brin nodded and walked forward, wading into the pool. As the water rose to her chest, she thought of all those she had left behind, and once more her last thought was of Tesh.

CHAPTER TWELVE

Venlyn

I have long wondered about Mawyndulë and why he did it. When presented with such a terrible choice, why did he take that path. Was it fame? Was it fear? Or was it something else entirely?

— THE BOOK OF BRIN

Mawyndulë had first entered the Airenthenon as a junior councilor, then as a senior member of the Aquila, and later as an ex-councilor. Now he arrived in the ancient chamber as a potential traitor. Makareta was at his side, and the sense of déjà vu was thick in the air.

Together they stood in the doorway, bathed in the warm glow of the late-night braziers. Mawyndulë had never been there at night. He turned back and saw how the moon cast a cold light on the snow-covered marble outside the entrance. Across the valley and standing on its own hill was the palace, bathed in shadow. The Airenthenon had supposedly been built at the same elevation as the Talwara, a fact that Mawyndulë disputed. Now the equality seemed deserved.

"It will be fine," Makareta whispered in his ear. "You'll see."

He wanted to believe her, but she'd lied before.

No, that wasn't right. She simply hadn't told him everything. And in a way, each of them had been led astray, both of them victims. Yet in the aftermath, they lived very different lives. While he slept in the Talwara and ate at banquets, she lived on scraps and slept in the forest, under bridges, and in cellars.

Makareta had filled him in on the tragedy that had been her life since the failed rebellion. She hadn't asked for pity, hadn't been melodramatic about any of it. She spoke openly of her hunger-filled days pretending to be a Gwydry when she ate fly-covered trash and dressed in rags because she was too scared to use the Art for fear it might be detected. She had almost died more than once. She didn't talk much about those times, just said she took desperate chances.

The most dangerous moment was when she revealed herself to someone she hoped might be sympathetic. That had been terrifying because she knew her life was on the line. Makareta believed the odds were against her but felt she had no choice. The next step would be suicide, so she had one chance in three to survive. She would either be rescued, turned in, or die by her own hand. Thankfully, she won that bet. Makareta never said who the mysterious benefactor was, but he guessed he was about to meet her patron.

Mawyndulë imagined her alone on the streets, hiding, cowering, and eating whatever she'd hastily stolen from a filthy compost pile. He wished she had come to him sooner. He wanted to be the one she came to when making that desperate gamble. He would have liked to wash the dirt from her face and make it perfect again. At least she had eventually come to him.

This night, Mawyndulë wore his heavy black cloak. Normally it hung in the back of his closet because he never went out when it was this cold. It became his final defense against the bitterest of days. The wool was four layers thick and cinched tightly with a leather belt. He'd pulled its large hood up, making a tiny cave for his head. Even as cold as it was, snow was still possible, and it swirled around them. His body shook; his eyes watered, and his cheeks burned from the wind, but his hand was sweaty where it touched hers.

Mawyndulë was surprised to see so many people inside. He'd anticipated only four or five unknown faces, perhaps another renegade Miralyith who had also escaped the fane's retribution. He certainly didn't expect what he found.

Nearly the entire Aquila had gathered.

Four councilors, Nanagal of the Eilywin, Volhoric of the Umalyn, Hemon of the Gwydry, and Osla—newly appointed as senior council of the Asendwayr—were in their usual seats. Family and some friends of the Aquila sat behind them in the lower tier, but the junior councilors were absent. In the center of the chamber—in what was supposed to be the fane's seat but was clearly her chair—sat Curator Imaly, representative of the Nilyndd. Vidar of the Miralyith was the only seat left vacant. He was still at Avempartha, teaching the Artists on the frontier how to conjure dragons.

The assembly's whispered conversation halted the moment Makareta led Mawyndulë in. Everyone in the chamber rose and applauded. Mawyndulë stopped short at the sight. The Aquila only did that when the fane entered.

Makareta led him to Vidar's seat, and he realized *he* was meant to take his place as a representative of the Miralyith, making this as complete an Aquila meeting as possible without the always absent Instarya. Everyone sat when he did. Makareta took the junior councilor's position that she'd occupied years ago for those few minutes before she attacked Imaly. He watched the Curator, expecting an explosion of outrage. What she did was even more shocking. Imaly smiled approvingly and bowed respectfully toward Makareta.

"We are complete," Imaly announced. Her voice was as it had always been, making the proceedings on that dark winter's night sound official and untainted. Still, Mawyndulë wondered if she wasn't speaking just a tad quieter than she usually did in the light of day.

"Thank you, Mawyndulë, for coming. I realize—we all do—that this couldn't have been an easy decision or a casual walk. The weather does fit the proceedings, does it not?" She stood up and faced them, clasping her hands before her in a solemn pose. "All of us braved the bitter storm and gathered here this night because we have come to realize that something is fatally wrong with our world." She tilted her head back and gestured at the ceiling and the paintings of Gylindora Fane and Caratacus. "Out of a great disaster, my great-great-grandmother led our people to this place to create a better life. In Gylindora's youth, Fhrey fought Fhrey, and did so with great zeal. Death and destruction was our existence until Caratacus found her weaving baskets on the bank of a small creek. 'The last virtuous Fhrey,' he called her. She, who had no desire to rule, was the one he anointed to be the first fane of our people—the one he knew could lead us out of the darkness and into a new future of peace. It is in this spirit that we are gathered here tonight."

Imaly walked around her chair and gripped the back of it with both hands, speaking to them over its top. "To fill this seat, a Nilyndd was chosen. Not a powerful Instarya warrior, nor even a pious Umalyn, but a lowly basket weaver from the crafters' tribe. The lowest of us was understood to be the best choice because she had no vanity, no sense of superiority." Imaly revealed an inner humor that spilled onto her lips in a modest smile. "Except in her basket weaving, about which I was told she was unbearably conceited." In a normal meeting of the Aquila, this bit of humor might have elicited laughter. That night the best it raised was appreciative smiles.

Imaly let her arms fall away from the chair. "The true talent and success of Gylindora was wholly due to her ability to see all Fhrey as her family. Her fairness and understanding are what allowed her to establish Estramnadon and this council. She understood that she needed help to govern. More recent fanes have forgotten that—the ones who never had the benefit of having woven baskets."

The Curator moved around to the front of her chair. "The spirit of Gylindora Fane no longer sits on the Forest Throne. As a result, our people face annihilation. We who once ruled the known world have been brought low out of arrogance, pride, and our own crippling traditions." She said this while looking at Volhoric.

The high priest frowned and shifted uneasily in his seat.

"The laws Caratacus brought to us along with the divine horn were given and accepted as a means to save us from ourselves. Now those very laws may be our undoing. Blind adherence is foolhardy at best and at this point suicidal." She clapped her hands against her thighs. "Fane Lothian is killing us. First, he refused to allow the Instarya to have a voice in this august body. He maintained the entire tribe's banishment and killed their leader in a despicable manner. This was a message not just to the Instarya, but to all of us. The fane wanted to demonstrate that the spirit of Gylindora Fane was dead, her horn no longer needed to be blown, for only the Miralyith would sit on that woody throne from now on. Out of his arrogance, he elevated his tribe above all others, sowing mistrust and dissent. When the Rhunes discovered that the Miralyith were not gods, he sought to destroy them." She sighed, bowed her head, and then lifted it to address those assembled. "Well, that didn't work out so well, did it? Everyone here knows the pain of losing someone who died during Lothian's needless war with the Rhunes. There was a time, not so long ago, when Death was a stranger, a rare and bewildering visitor. Now it lingers in every shadow, every song unsung, each silenced set of footsteps. We all sat here and listened as Fane Lothian told us how the death of Amidea would save us. Instead, she died in vain. She died for nothing, and the blood was on his own hands. Now our fane has ordered Miralyith families to be ripped apart. To create his dragons, he is forcing mothers to kill their children, husbands to execute their wives, and friends to kill friends. What kind of insanity condones the murder of the ones we love?

"The enemy that threatens to destroy us is not being held at bay on the banks of the Nidwalden. He sits on the Forest Throne."

She sighed again and once more clasped her hands before her. "We can be foolhardy, or we can be as brave as a basket weaver."

Imaly sat down, and a silence allowed the sound of the winter wind to enter the chamber.

Then Makareta stood up. "You'll need a Miralyith to fight other Miralyith," she said, "and everyone knows how I feel about the fane. I'll do whatever is needed, but I don't think I can handle Synne, Sile, and Lothian by myself."

Imaly appeared to consider this, and Mawyndulë was lost in the surreality of the discussion.

They really mean to do it. This isn't just speculation.

A figure Mawyndulë hadn't noticed—apparently no one had—rose from where he sat in the balcony and stepped into the light near the rail. Like all of them, he wore a dark winter cloak, this one with silver trim. Reaching the rail, he drew back his hood.

At the sight of Vasek's face, Mawyndulë's breath caught in his throat.

We're all dead! The Master of Secrets has finally found Makareta and with her a whole new nest of traitors.

Vasek made a subtle coughing sound to gain everyone's attention. Heads turned. Mawyndulë expected there would be cries, maybe a few would try to flee, but he knew it would do them no good. Vasek was too smart for that. The Airenthenon would already be surrounded. Synne and who knew how many others would be waiting.

Mawyndulë remembered Vasek questioning him. *"I was wondering if you've had contact with, or have heard about any resurgence of, the Gray Cloaks?"*

Perhaps Vasek had suspected him this whole time and had been following his movements and Makareta's.

To Mawyndulë's surprise, no one attempted to flee. They didn't even appear worried.

Shock, that's what's going on. It has to be.

"She's right," Vasek said. "Makareta will need help. Someone who can get close, someone the fane won't expect—would *never* expect." Vasek looked at him then. "The one to kill Lothian must be the prince."

Heads turned to Mawyndulë, who sat lost in an unimaginable world. The whole of the Aquila were in on the conspiracy. Vasek, too.

Mawyndulë felt Makareta's hand on his. It gave him strength. It gave him courage. He stood up, slowly feeling the weight of his heavy cloak. He didn't know what he would say until the words came out. "He's my father."

"He's a tyrant," Vasek replied, his voice falling down from above with an unaccustomed emotion and surprising authority. "And he'll bring forth the end of us all."

Master of Secrets was a title Mawyndulë had always assumed meant that Vasek knew the private dealings of everyone else. While that might be true, the greater truth was that Vasek was the master of his own secrets.

"He's also a Fhrey," Mawyndulë said. "If I were to—" He couldn't bring himself to say it. "If I did *this*, I would break Ferrol's Law."

He saw Imaly look to Volhoric, who stood with as much reluctance as Mawyndulë had.

"As high priest of the Umalyn tribe and spiritual leader of the peoples of Erivan, I can assure you that ending Lothian's reign as fane will be sanctioned by Lord Ferrol. Through his actions, your father has abdicated his role as fane, broken his covenant with his people and our god. By murdering Amidea without just cause and forcing others to kill their loved ones, he has cast himself out of the protection afforded by Ferrol's Law. You will not anger Ferrol by taking this action because in the eyes of our lord Ferrol, you will be executing an outlaw."

"There you have it," Hemon of the Gwydry proclaimed. "Ferrol's blessing—not his wrath—will be upon you."

Imaly spoke then, "This is a heroic act, *and* with Lothian removed, *you* would receive the throne. I propose that if you do this great service to our people, the least we can offer in return is to guarantee no challenger will be put forth. You will receive the throne unopposed. Do we all agree?"

Each of the senior councilors responded with a communal "Aye."

Mawyndulë was still standing, still holding Makareta's hand, still thinking.

"There is one more thing I should mention," Imaly said casually from her seat, where she leaned on one of the arms, her legs crossed beneath her winter cloak. "A secret that I suspect even Vasek isn't aware of because everyone else here has faithfully kept it for years, as is our charge under the law. I'll break that covenant now because as Curator, I feel this situation warrants it, and because there's no sense in protecting one who is already dead."

She focused on Mawyndulë. "When your grandmother Fenelyus died, I as Curator and Volhoric as Conservator agreed that the Instarya leader Zephyron should be given the opportunity to challenge your father. We did this because we were uncomfortable that an entire tribe of the Fhrey was being denied a voice in this chamber, and thus a voice in the ear of their fane. We felt this was Ferrol's will. The result wasn't what we expected."

"With all due respect," Mawyndulë said, "I already know all this. I was there. I saw the fight."

"True, but you don't know what no one but the voting members knew."

"Which was?"

"There was another applicant who was denied."

Mawyndulë shook his head. "Who?"

"Gryndal of the Miralyith."

Mawyndulë stared in disbelief. He wanted to say it was a lie, but he knew better because he remembered Gryndal's words to him during their trip to Dahl Rhen: *"I know it's wrong for me to say this, but sometimes I honestly wish some tragedy might befall your father. Not anything fatal, of course, just something rendering him unable to rule so that you could take over. I know that sounds terrible, but I fear your father isn't suited to guide us into the future. His rule will lead to disaster. Trust me, Mawyndulë, your father's reign will threaten our whole way of life."*

Mawyndulë now saw that those words had not been idle musings. At the time Gryndal said them, he had already tried to challenge the fane.

"Ever wise, Gryndal spoke of the danger your father posed to our people," Imaly said. "Sadly, this body did not fully appreciate his fears. If only we had listened. Instead, we chose to go with an Instarya challenger because there were concerns that continued rule by the Miralyith tribe would forever be the norm. So, we avoided pitting two members of the same tribe against each other. We didn't want to give the impression to the other tribes that the challenge was obsolete. We were wrong. Our judgment was clouded, and we denied the candidate. As a result, our people have suffered. If you are willing to step forward, you can correct our error. I'm sure I speak for everyone here when I say it is *you* who should rule. You proved your bravery when saving the Airenthenon; you were tested at the Battle of Grandford; and it is you who is the worthy successor of Fenelyus's legacy. While Gryndal would have been a better choice than Lothian, it is you who has always been the *best* choice. We look to you, Mawyndulë, to save our people."

The room erupted in applause and shouts of "hear, hear." All the senior members were on their feet, expressing full-throated agreement.

"You won't be alone," Makareta said, squeezing his hand. "I'll protect you from any threats from Lothian's bodyguards. I'm already soulless, and I swear I'll kill anyone who tries to hurt you."

"So then . . ." Mawyndulë began while looking around, "it's the—the unanimous will of the Aquila that I do this?"

Heads continued to nod, but Imaly shook her head. "No, it is not our will, Mawyndulë. We do not come to you with a decree, nor a petition, nor recommendation. This is no council of advice." Imaly stood up, and with the effort that age required, she took hold of the arm of the chair and knelt in the center of the Airenthenon. As she did, the others followed her lead, each taking a knee.

"We—the Aquila," Imaly said, "we *plead* to you for the good of our people, for our very survival. We *beg* you to save us."

❦

Everyone else had left the Airenthenon. The last brazier, the one behind Volhoric's seat, was almost out, leaving Mawyndulë and Makareta in the single flicker of a lonesome flame. Mawyndulë didn't want to leave. He would have to return to the palace, back to his father's house, to the home of the fane he now planned to kill.

And I will have to leave Makareta.

Having reunited with her, he could no longer bear it when they were apart. He didn't know how he could have been so oblivious to someone who was now as necessary as water and air.

How have I lived all these years without her?

The answer was obvious.

I didn't.

He imagined this was how birds felt the first time they flew.

"Do *you* think I'll make a good fane?" Mawyndulë asked.

They were still holding hands, huddled close against the cold, his arm around her waist, her head on his shoulder. Outside, the snowstorm still raged, wind gusting with a hurried violence. Yet in the Airenthenon, they were safely hidden and protected from the blowing snow, a pair of mice below the frost line.

"Think? No, I *know.* You'll be a legend." She pointed at the ceiling. "Your face will be up there."

"Think so?"

"Absolutely. And it will be nice to see someone handsome on that ceiling for a change." She giggled, a child's laugh.

He rubbed the back of her fingers with his thumb, feeling how thin and delicate they were. "So, you think I'm handsome?"

"Of course. I thought you knew that."

He shrugged. "I hoped. I wished."

"Wish granted." She threw up a hand as if tossing something invisible in the air.

"Can you do that? Grant wishes?"

She raised her head and looked at him with a serious, suggestive flash of her eyes. "Try me."

Just then, the braziers blew out, leaving them in darkness. Mawyndulë leaned in and kissed her. He didn't know what to expect. He didn't think she would pull away, but she might. Still, a person who is about to commit regicide and patricide at the same time shouldn't be afraid of stealing a kiss in the dark.

She didn't pull away. Instead, she pressed against him and tilted her head slightly so their noses didn't collide. He felt her hands, hot and moist, pressing on either side of his head. Her palms warmed his cheeks, holding him there as her lips parted. It felt as if she stole his breath, that she was sucking the air from his lungs. He couldn't breathe. Didn't want to. His eyes were closed, his heart pounding when he wrapped his arms around her waist and drew her close.

So much clothing lay between them, so many folds. She was in there somewhere. He felt with pressing fingers, which he used to explore in a manner as violent as the storm and soft as a sigh.

"You're shaking," she said after drawing her lips away, concern in her tone. "Are you cold?"

"Not even slightly." He didn't like that she knew he was trembling. That didn't strike him as brave, so he said, "When I'm fane, I'll pardon you. Reinstate you as a Fhrey."

"I'm not sure a fane has that power but thank you. It means a great deal that you want to."

"What's it like? To be—to not be Fhrey?"

She looked sad for a moment. "We thought . . ." She paused and looked away. "The Gray Cloaks thought the loss of one's soul was just superstition. But then, we also believed ourselves to be gods. We were young and foolish on both counts."

"It's real?"

Makareta nodded while pressing her lips tight, as if holding back a tempest of emotion. "I can feel it—this coldness, this horrible emptiness. It hit me a second after I killed Jinreal, a Gwydry who got in the way. I was fighting a member of the Lion Corps, a soldier who ducked at the last instant. I really didn't expect to lose my soul, especially not from killing a Gwydry."

Makareta started to cry.

He drew her tighter and kissed the wet of her cheeks and then her eyes. "I'll make it better. I promise."

"You realize we could die tomorrow. It's actually a very real possibility. This could be the last night we have."

She pushed farther away and rubbed her hands together, humming a simple Torsonic Chant. All twelve of the braziers came to life. The bronze urns burst into blue flames that licked upward like living things. Below the dome, the room was cast in a wondrous indigo glow.

Mawyndulë smiled and added white lights, firefly sparks that billowed and swirled. The light from them filled the chamber.

Wiping away her remaining tears, Makareta raised her brows mischievously and flicked one finger. A bird made of light appeared and flew in a circle around the chamber.

Mawyndulë found her weave and drew out a long, colorful tail that left shimmering sparks as the bird flew. For a moment, they were both that bird, intertwined and linked through the Art—both flying as one. The Airenthenon was no longer a dark and solemn place. It became a light show of warmth and humor.

"We shouldn't," he said, and loathed himself for saying it. "We'll attract attention."

"So?" she asked, that playful look turning blatantly wicked. "What are you afraid of?"

"What about the fane's guards? What if they see the lights through the windows and come to investigate?"

Makareta laughed. "It'd be their worst night ever; don't you think? Them with their spears, swords, and shields and us with everything else? Together we are *venlyn*."

"Ven-lyn? Land of Hope? Is that a word?"

"It is now." She nodded with that wonderful smile. "Venlyn is what we make together. A place where anything is possible, a sort of paradise. I may not be able to enter Phyre when I die, so we'll make Alysin right here, right now. We are venlyn, what should have been and what will now always be."

"What about Sile and Synne? What if they come to investigate?"

"I'll kill them," she said in a dull, flat tone, the words as cold and uncaring as the winter wind that could no longer reach them. "And if it was your father?"

"I'd do the same. I don't want anything, anyone, to come between us. Tomorrow we both might die. But tonight—"

"Yes, for this one wonderful evening—we are venlyn." She clapped her hands, and the entire Airenthenon transformed. Plants lush and flowered burst forth as spring surrounded Makareta and Mawyndulë. Vines snaked up the pillars. Birds sang and butterflies flew.

"It seems so real!" he said, amazement in his voice.

That wicked smile continued as she slipped off her cloak and began to untie her asica. "I'll show you what's true."

CHAPTER THIRTEEN

The Door Opens

Life can surprise you. Death will astound you even more. Trust me;
I know.

— THE BOOK OF BRIN

Darkness.

Stepping into the pond was like wading into the dark hollow of a forest where the air felt colder for no apparent reason. Instead of feeling buoyancy or the sensation of any fluid's resistance, Brin simply continued to walk until she seemed to reach the bottom of the pond and just stood there, stupidly. With few options, Brin started walking again. Before too long, the ground tilted, and she was ascending an incline, perhaps the other side of the pool. She continued to walk until, at some point, the light disappeared. That should have been her first clue that something had changed. The only time Brin had been without light since entering Phyre was during the few moments when she passed through the barrier in the Agave. Still, Brin didn't consider herself an authority on the afterlife, so she didn't know for certain what was happening. Neither the trip down nor the one up was very long, and in just a short while, she found level ground again. Brin tucked the key back under her shirt.

She wasn't sure if she was clear of the pool. Brin didn't feel any wetness, but then she never had felt anything, so it was hard to tell. Then a sound emanated from somewhere in the dark. Not a comforting noise. A growl, deep and threatening, came from not too far away, making Brin do her best imitation of a statue.

If only I could see!

Brin waited, expecting sounds of movement.

Will there be any? Or will the ripping of my throat be the first thing I notice? No, of course not. I don't have one.

For the first time, the lack of a body was a comfort, but a small one as she stood in the dark, listening to more growls.

After several minutes of standing still, which, not surprisingly, got her nowhere, Brin took a step, then another. Everything was still dark, and she had no idea which way she ought to go.

This is insane. Even in Nifrel, it wasn't this dark. There was always a sky of sorts. And in the Abyss, I was able to use my own light. This is . . . this is just frustrating.

She bent down, feeling with her hands, and found dirt. She tried to scrape up a handful to see if it was wet, sandy, or worm-filled. She was looking for any clue, and she got one—her hands failed to move so much as a single grain. She could feel the soil, but not affect it.

The dirt is real. I'm back on Elan . . . and my light is gone because I'm a ghost. But why is it so dark? Where am I that there is no light at all? And if I'm a ghost, shouldn't I glow? Meeks did. If I can't see, what should I do next?

"Grand Mother of All, help me," she whispered.

Instantly lights appeared.

Faintly glowing mushrooms appeared here and there. The little fungi began to light up in luminous greens, blues, and reds. Clusters materialized on the ground and grew brighter until the Sacred Grove emerged from the gloom and became as enchanted as the Land of Nog—the real one from the stories of old. Brin was on a patch of barren soil, and at its center stood a tree. Brin had no idea what sort it might be. She wasn't an expert on flora, although living most of her life on the eaves of a forest gave her better knowledge than most. She cycled through every variety she knew and couldn't find anything to match the one before her.

It had the friendly spread of an old oak, but the majesty of an elm or hickory. The tree was perfect in its symmetry, huge and wonderful. But it was dead. No leaves dressed it. The bark had fallen away, and several of the withered branches had cracked and fallen.

Brin looked around, bewildered.

The Sacred Grove was supposed to be a wondrous garden, the heart of Elan, the most marvelous place in existence. This was where the greatest of all heroes came to dwell in beauty beyond even that of Alysin. Having seen the former, Brin's expectations had been high. As it turned out, the Grove wasn't just disappointing, it was puzzling and not a garden at all.

She stood in an enclosed room with a dirt floor and no visible ceiling. The sides were smooth white stone that formed a continuous circular wall, completely uniform except for a single small door that appeared to be made of wood. The only thing in the room other than herself and the pool was the very large and extremely dead tree.

Brin heard the growling again.

It came from the tree.

~

"Hello, Brin."

The words didn't come from the tree, and they didn't sound like a voice at all. They were like rushing water, wind in leaves, and the call of a loon on a summer's night.

"Hello?" Brin sounded small.

"Do you know where you are?" The not-voice was the drone of bees, the chatter of crickets, and the flutter of birds taking flight.

"The Sacred Grove," she whispered, but she didn't know why.

"Do you know who I am?" said ice receding on a lake, the unfurling of a flower, and the cracking egg of a soon-to-be-born chick.

The question was simultaneously absurd yet perfectly reasonable. Brin did know. That voice was as familiar to her as her own breath and heartbeat, both of which continued to be missing and sorely missed. The words spoken to Brin were the songs by which she had lived her days, a rhythm and melody she hadn't heard in, oh, so long. They summoned memories of morning dew, dandelion tufts drifting on a breeze, sunshine glimmering on the surface of a lake. In that instant, Brin knew who was speaking, and her strength gave out. Down she fell, plopping onto the dirt.

Brin quivered in shock and amazement and answered, "You are Elan, the Grand Mother of All."

"It's good to have you back. I've missed you. I doubt you remember when we first met. You were so small, such a tiny thing. Now look at you."

"I'm still small." At that moment, Brin had never felt so insignificant.

"Bah!" Responded the sound of a sheep, and Brin knew she would never hear a bleat the same way again. *"There are many means of measure, and at this moment, you may well be the biggest person in existence. You've come a long way, my child, so very, very far. You are only the fourth to stand in this place."*

The growl rumbled in the dark, a terrible, frightening sound.

"What is that?"

"The Guardian. Except for just a few absences—extended holidays so to speak—she has protected this place for eons, since the early days. Fear not, she is merely making her presence known. She doesn't like anyone to get too close to Alurya—my firstborn."

"The tree?"

"Yes, that is the shape Alurya took. She is the mother of trees, plants, and all things green. She also gave birth to animals, all things feathered or furry. And she was my beloved daughter and dearest friend to all who met her."

"She's the one who gave Mal—ah, Turin—the fruit, isn't she? The food that granted immortality."

"Yes, and when she did, this became her tomb, the prison Eton sealed so she was denied my husband's light and rain. In here, she withered and died while Turin was killing his brothers and sisters. When he finally came to her, it was too late."

"So that's why he challenged his father to combat?" Brin asked.

"Yes. And now you must learn the rest of the story. Make yourself comfortable."

Brin hesitated. "What about the Guardian? Is it safe for me to sit?"

"Absolutely."

Brin wasn't about to second-guess Elan herself, so she pulled her legs up as she would have in the lodge when Maeve began to tell a tale. As she did, the glow of the mushrooms dimmed and the shadow of the great tree was cast upon the wall opposite Brin. It stretched upward, looking utterly grand and alive in its silhouette.

"First, you have to understand that Turin loved Alurya. We all did. Even Eton. How could anyone not love her? This is what makes the events all the more tragic. Turin arrived covered in the blood of his family. He'd killed all of them and was a terrible sight. What a monster he had become. Eton added the door and left it open so Turin could see what his rebellion had wrought. I suppose he expected Turin to understand the error of his ways, bow down, and ask for forgiveness. That's the way of fathers. But of course Turin no longer saw himself as Eton's son. By then he was Rex Uberlin, King Great One, and Uberlin didn't bow to anyone.

"Turin loved Alurya more than anything in the world. I honestly don't think Eton could have done anything to hurt him more. I didn't know what would happen. As it turned out, he went sort of mad, lost all self-control, and it wasn't as if he had a lot to start with. In his insanity, he challenged Eton to battle. Having murdered his brothers and sisters, Turin intended to do the same to his own father."

"Is that possible?" Brin asked.

"To destroy the sky? No. Eton is eternal."

The light of some of the mushrooms went out while others lighted and turned red, and on the wall, Brin saw flashes of yellow as other forms of fungi flared near the base of the majestic tree. Then, as the room filled with a ruddy light, the shadow of the tree on the wall appeared to stand amid tears of blood. As she watched, it seemed to Brin that a haze of smoke drifted across the wall. Violence and sorrow were painted on this mammoth canvas. They appeared as abstract colors and shifting shapes, but Brin had never experienced anything so disturbing. What she saw was the emotions of hate and sadness depicted with the artistry and beauty of a sunset.

"I've never seen such a terrible fight, and I shuddered beneath their blows. Turin had no hope of defeating his father, but the battle raged on and on. Eventually, Turin's madness fled and his reason returned."

Brin saw a great shadow on the wall in the shape of a man. He was tall, thin, draped in a shimmering robe, and wearing a whipping mantle and a crown of light. In one hand, he held a spear.

Then the light softened to a gentle pink.

"It's difficult to explain, and maybe only something a mother could see. But I knew Turin wanted Eton to prevail."

The shadow on the wall shrank, becoming smaller and smaller.

"I'm not speaking of his desire to die and join his brothers and sisters in Phyre. I think he wanted Eton to unmake him, to dissolve him back into the universe. Perhaps my son understood his transgressions and wanted to be punished. Or maybe he just couldn't go on with her death on his hands. The spoiled child who had always gotten his way lost the one thing he cherished most, and nothing he could do would ever change that. In a rage, Turin threw himself against the sky. Eton was unmoved and refused to grant his son anything—not even death. Oblivion would not make up for what Turin had done. Letting Turin die would only allow the child to once more escape his mistakes."

The shadow of the king lost its crown as it continued to diminish. The mantle disappeared; the robe vanished. Soon the shadow was of a simple man holding a common spear.

"Knowing there was no other outcome except for Eton to imprison Turin in Phyre, for that was where my husband put all his unsolvable problems, I stepped in. Too many of my children had been thrown away. And having both murderer and victims in the same place would only serve to harden the divisions, forcing every one of them to suffer eternally. I had to do something, and having seen what I thought was a glimmer of change in Turin, I opposed my husband and defended Turin. Eton saw it as a betrayal. In disgust, he gave up.

"Then I demanded the key."

The light in the room changed to illuminate the little door with a white glow.

"I knew Turin would want to visit Alurya, but I also knew it was the same key that Eton had used to lock the doors of Phyre—the prison he kept my children in. Even now, I am not sure if Eton understood why I wanted it. He and I, we don't speak much anymore. Father and son have so much in common: They are not fools, but frustration can get the better of them, which makes them unbearably stubborn. Maybe Eton wanted to be done with it all, but perhaps he understood that for a child to grow up, he needs to first be granted the ability to fail, and having failed, the opportunity to learn from it."

The shadow of the man threw away his spear and sat down.

"Afterward, Turin remained here, not far from where you are now. He sat and he cried. Ages went by out there while he wept in here. Without his leadership, his people emulated the memory of their murderous missing king. Likewise, the children of Ferrol, Mari, and Drome found themselves similarly without guidance, lost and afraid. The abandoned remains of Erebus fell into decay and ruin."

Brin watched as the shadow play on the wall continued. The silhouette of the man sat to one side as in the background Brin witnessed the destruction of a great and noble city. Towering buildings tilted and fell. The ground shook and broke. Water from the sea rushed in, flooding everything. People fled. Some climbed over mountains, others fought their way through dense forests, and the last group fashioned crude, feeble-looking ships and paddled out into the unknown darkness.

"The children of Ferrol, Drome, and Mari fled west across the sea and were scattered in forest, field, and mountain. Turin's followers remained in the east, but left with his legacy—his example—they became cruel, hateful, twisted things."

Brin saw a group of people left behind, and as she watched, they changed shape, becoming bent and hunched. Their arms lengthened, fingers sprouting claws.

"*Being the ones to stay, they called themselves the ghazel, which in their language means both 'the loyal' as well as 'the forgotten.' Deprived of his presence, they no longer served Uberlin as king. They began to worship him as a god.*"

The monsters faded, as did all else save the small man sitting on the ground.

"*By then, Uberlin was dead. All that remained was Turin. I thought he might never leave. It was clear he wanted to die but couldn't. The gift that Alurya had once given him, which had caused her death, denied him even that solace. Her love kept him alive long after she had passed, long after he wanted it to.*"

"*They all hate me,*" he said.

"*Yes,*" I replied. "*You destroyed their homes, killed their children, taught them war, murder, hate, and revenge. Through your selfishness, you destroyed the world.*"

"*Do you think I don't know that?*" he asked.

The reddish light cast by the mushrooms faded and shifted from crimson to purple.

"*That's when I knew there was a chance. I had been optimistic from the start, but when I heard those words, I knew there was reason for hope.*"

I told him, "*Turin, I don't hate you.*"

"*You should,*" he replied.

On the wall, the man was standing, his head bowed, his body weak.

"*You're my son.*"

"*I am evil.*"

"*You were not born that way.*"

"*But I became so.*"

"*Yes, which means you have the power to unbecome it.*"

On the wall, the man's head tilted up.

"*He looked puzzled at that. You have to understand that Turin was never puzzled. He was always so sure of everything. I took this as another good sign.*"

"*How?*" he asked me.

"You ruined the world, Turin—fix it. Make things right."

"I don't know how."

Another good sign, I thought.

The light shifted farther from the red spectrum, becoming more and more blue.

"Then you'll have to learn."

"How? From whom? You?"

"No." I told him. *"I love you and always will, but I cannot teach this lesson. To learn how to change the hearts of those you wronged, find a teacher, someone who hates you."*

"That should be easy enough," he said.

"Then make them love you," I told him.

"I'm not sure that's possible."

"With time, everything is possible, and forever is what you have. It is Alurya's gift and your curse."

The color was a deep blue now, once more revealing the tree. Not the majestic thing it had been, but the broken, withered body it now was.

"He stopped speaking then. I could see he'd thought of something, and that brought me joy. Turin had wrought unspeakable evil, but there is no denying that he's a formidable force when he has a goal. He had been on the wrong path, but I feel his feet are now leading him in the right direction. If anyone can fix what he broke, it is he."

Brin saw the man turn his back to the tree and walk out. He closed the door and locked it with a key that he had on a chain looped over his neck. Then he walked away.

"Has he ever come back?"

"Once. His first task was to help those he wronged the most—Ferrol's children."

Again, the room darkened with the red light. On the wall, shadows fought one another. The room in which Brin sat was utterly silent, but the imagery was so powerful that she felt she could hear screams of pain and fear and sobs of sorrow. People in a forest beside a river were slaughtering one another.

"They were in a terrible state. Though Ferrol would never admit it, she is very much like her brother, and her children followed her example. They fought one another and were nearly erased. That's when Turin appeared. Like a good uncle, he gathered the best and led them west—here, to this place. So they could be as close to Alurya as they could get. As penance, Turin's first act was to give the most sacred site he knew to Ferrol's children. And then he stayed and taught them to live in peace."

Once more the red shifted to blue and then to a warm and friendly green.

The happy light didn't last long. An instant later the walls were growing red again.

"But then a war came. The children of Drome fought against the children of his twin sister—a war of foolish greed."

Short shadows battled against tall. For a time, it appeared as if the tight, disciplined ranks of the diminutive silhouettes would devour the others. Then the situation shifted. The smaller shadows retreated, dogged by the enemies who hunted them through forests, fields, and finally their mountain fortresses.

"Ferrol's offspring gained the advantage, and it was in their power to erase the children of Drome forever. But once more Turin intervened. He went to the leader of the Fhrey and invited her inside the Sacred Grove. He showed Fenelyus the First Tree, and he allowed her to see the body of his beloved Alurya—to witness the cost of war and the penalty of hate."

"Did she know who he was?" Brin asked as she stared at the wall, captivated by the image of the tall noble lady standing beside the thin man, both looking up at the withered remains of the tree. The shadow of the first Miralyith fell to her knees, crying.

"She called him Caratacus—the name he'd used centuries before when he fashioned the horn—so she guessed that much, but there's no telling if Fenelyus realized she was speaking to Turin—to Rex Uberlin himself. Or if she even knew what those words meant. Still, the visit worked its magic, and Fenelyus spared the Belgriclungreians."

The light faded. The images on the wall disappeared.

"And that was the last time he came here?"

"That was the last time anyone did."

"But . . . you said I was the fourth."

"You pay such close attention."

"I'm a Keeper of—"

"I know all about you, love. I remember the sound of your first cry."

While Brin couldn't see it, she both heard and felt Elan smile like the first warm day of spring.

"Yes, you are indeed the fourth. Turin, of course, is the first. Then he returned with Fenelyus."

"And the third?"

"The greatest of the great, of course. Eton exempted from mortality those he decreed were the most worthy, but by setting the requirements so high only one has ever met his standards. She is the third to enter this place. You see, the Guardian has been granted the privilege to freely travel both the realms of the living and the dead. As such, she needs no key to enter this place. With just a few brief exceptions, she has guarded Alurya's body, slept on her roots, and kept watch for the end of days, for the Golrok. For you see, it is believed that Turin will unlock Phyre. But as with all rumors, they are easily distorted. Most think that Turin can't stand the fact that there is a realm beyond his control. Those in Phyre are convinced that the creator of war will wage a final campaign against them, and this is what they plan for. It is commonly thought that the start of the final war will begin here. The Guardian will not allow any desecration of Alurya, and for that reason, the Greatest Hero stands her vigil, guarding the body of my firstborn against any who might do her harm. But given the task that lies before you, she may once again take a leave of absence to offer assistance."

"Who is she? Who is this hero?"

Brin heard footsteps. She turned, and a shadow stepped out from behind the trunk of the great tree.

"Oh, Grand Mother of All! It can't be!" Brin exclaimed, as she immediately recognized the face. The light in the room grew in that joyful reunion as Brin saw bright-blue eyes and snow-white fur.

め

"The world's wisest wolf!" Brin said and smiled. "Suri wasn't kidding, was she? Did she also know you are the greatest of heroes?"

The wolf licked Brin's face.

"Oh, Minna, I've been sent by Malcolm to find Suri. I couldn't hope for a better guide. Will you help me?"

The wolf responded by bounding to the little wooden door and scratching at it.

"Good luck to you, my dear one," Elan said. *"And remember I'll always be with you, no matter where you go."*

Brin walked to the door as the light from the mushrooms faded. She fished out the key, then paused. Brin wasn't nearly as frightened, now that she realized she was a ghost.

What worries can I have? she thought. *What harm can befall me on the face of Elan? If an army with spears and swords attacks, what could they do?*

Minna scratched on the wood again.

Brin reached out and was surprised to discover she could touch the door—really touch it. The wood was as real to her as it was to Minna. Reaching over, she found the walls to be the same.

Another scratch.

"Okay, okay," Brin said and looked for a place to insert the key. Rain had explained locks when they were at the gate to Rel, but . . .

There's no hole, no place to insert it.

Minna scratched again.

I didn't see what Tressa did when we entered Nifrel, but I didn't have to do anything to get into Alysin. I only had to have the key with me, and that was enough.

Another scratch, and Brin noticed the door move. Putting her hand to it, she gave the door a shove and felt it give. A sliver of light entered around the edges.

Brin became giddy at the sight. Not only was the door open, but it was daytime. She hadn't seen the sun in so long. There was reassuring comfort in that yellow light, such that she wanted to bathe in it. She pushed on the door again and noticed something was impeding its swing. With effort, she moved it a bit more.

Minna leapt up and clapped her forepaws against the wood. The opening grew wider—enough for Brin to slide out through the gap.

Snow. Everything was covered in winter white, and large lazy flakes fell through the last rays of a setting sun. A drift had been pressed against the door.

I've made it. I'm back.

CHAPTER FOURTEEN

The Last Meal

*I did everything I could. I jumped. I waved. I shouted and screamed.
At one point, I tried to hit her—anything to get Suri to notice. None
of it worked.*

— THE BOOK OF BRIN

Suri stood at the counter, watching Makareta push the chestnut porridge around on her plate. Imaly often made it for the midday meal, frying the leftovers for the evening's supper. That day, with Imaly gone, Suri had volunteered to cook, since Makareta had proven to be inept in all endeavors related to food preparation except for making tea, which to Suri meant she was incapable of doing anything sensible.

Imaly had explained that Makareta's upbringing was to blame. She had been raised a Miralyith, and they were taught at a young age to rely on the Art, to use it for just about everything. Total immersion was said to be the best way to learn a language, and the Art was a tongue of sorts. But it had left Makareta, and many other Miralyith, stunted when it came to basic tasks. "The least of which is her inability to cook," Imaly had once told Suri. "Being so removed from the common shared experiences of a normal, natural life, the Miralyith have lost their connection to others. Untethered as they are and free of traditional drudgeries, it is easy to see why they made the mistake of believing themselves to be superior."

"Something wrong with the porridge?" Suri asked as Makareta continued nudging her meal around the plate.

Makareta was confused for a moment; then she noticed her plate and understood. "Oh, no. The food is fine. At least it's as good as fried chestnut porridge is capable of being. I'm just not hungry. To be honest, my stomach is already filled with butterflies."

Suri stared at her, appalled.

Makareta rolled her eyes. "I didn't eat any *butterflies*. It's an expression that indicates being nervous or excited, that sort of thing. Honestly, did you really think I ate insects? Aside from the obvious *eew* factor, how do you think I managed such a feat? It's winter. There's, like, a foot or more of snow out there. Not a lot of butterflies this time of year. You ought to know better. Didn't you grow up living inside a tree or something? You must know a thing or two about butterflies."

Butterflies. Butterflies. Butterflies.

The way the word was being thrown about and repeated disturbed Suri. That word—that idea—carried with it a personal and ominous portent. Whether Makareta knew it or not, Elan was speaking through her.

Filled with butterflies . . . I didn't eat any butterflies . . . not a lot of butterflies this time of year . . . You must know a thing or two about butterflies. There are too many mentions to be a coincidence. Is it a warning? An alarm? What is Elan trying to tell me?

That had always been the problem with Elan's discourse: It was never straightforward. Rarely did she say, *"Don't step there because the wood is rotted."* Or, *"Those berries will make you sick."* Or, *"Don't knock down that big fruit you think must be sweet because all the bees are around it."* The *fruit* hadn't been food after all. It had turned out to be the bees' home, and they didn't appreciate Suri whacking it. Now Elan was shouting about butterflies—practically screaming the word at her as if Suri were blind, deaf, and dumb.

Suri guessed Elan had decided to break with her tradition of vague innuendo and subtle hints. For years, Suri had been waiting for the time that Arion had foretold. The end of her own Gifford's Race. The time she would do the thing she had been meant to do for her entire life. As far as Suri could tell, Elan was jumping up and down and waving her arms, letting her know the time had come.

Get ready to show off your wings, butterfly!

"Suri?" Makareta was saying.

"What?"

"You all right?"

"Uh—yeah. I'm fine. I was just thinking about something."

"Yeah, me, too." Makareta looked down at her food for a moment, then asked, "Have you ever killed anyone?"

Suri frowned as she abandoned the skillet and took a seat opposite the Miralyith at the table where she had laid out a meal neither of them would eat.

Stupid butterflies.

"I know it's not polite conversation, but"—she glanced at the drawn drapery—"in another few minutes it will be dark, and I'll be doing that . . . again. You might have to as well, so I was wondering if you ever had."

"Yes," Suri quietly admitted. "More than once."

"So you know what it feels like?"

"All too well."

"Did you feel . . ." Makareta placed palms on her chest. "Was it like a part of you died?"

Suri nodded.

"And did you feel hollow afterward?"

Again, Suri nodded.

"Are you afraid you lost your soul?"

Suri had been with her up to that point, but this was a sharp turn in a new direction. She didn't even know what a soul was, which would make it pretty hard to know if she had lost it.

"What do you mean?"

Makareta pushed aside the plate of fried porridge and spread out her hands on the wood as she leaned forward and whispered, "When I killed the Gwydry Jinreal, I felt like a part of me was ripped out. You see, Fhrey believe that if we kill another of our own kind, Ferrol will banish our soul, prevent us from entering Phyre. For years, I thought that was a myth or lie used to keep our people in line. But after I killed Jinreal, I *knew* it was true. Priests have blathered on and on about how the afterlife is a place of peace and beauty. But nothing is ever mentioned about what awaits the likes of people like me. Do I just spend eternity standing alone, listening to the music and laughter I can never reach? Or when my body dies, do I just stop existing?" She touched her face and arms. "Is this all that remains of me, and when it's gone, I will be, too?"

"I don't know," Suri said. She thought about it for a moment, and added, "But I don't know of a single thing that *stops being*. Trees seem to die, but they come back. Even after they fall down, new shoots spring up. Creeks dry up but return with the rain. When Tura passed away, I burned her body, but there were still ashes that drifted on the winds. And the stars are always there, following the same course they have always travelled. It's like they take a trip each year and then return. The moon is the same way, it just takes shorter, more frequent, trips. Maybe everything does that. Goes away, but eventually comes back."

"But now that you've killed, are you afraid of death?"

"Huh?" Suri stared at her, shocked.

For a moment she thought Makareta might be joking. Sometimes she did that—made jokes that didn't make sense. The Fhrey would say something pointless and then break into guffaws for no reason. Suri wondered if this was one of those times, but Makareta wasn't laughing. She had her serious face on. This was important to her.

"No, I'm not scared." Suri realized the idea was funny after all—the absurd sort of humor like asking if a person was all right after they had clearly suffered a painful injury. But she knew Makareta wasn't joking.

"Dying is easy. Anyone can do that," Suri said. "Living—going on after you've lost those you love, having to face each new day under the weight of their absence—is what's hard. You have to witness a sun that is never again as bright and hear music that is no longer cheerful. Eating food will never fully satisfy, and you wake each morning to a shattered world that can never again be whole. Despite all this, you have to find a reason to breathe, to move." Suri stared at Makareta. "You've killed, and so have I, but that doesn't compare to losing someone you loved. That's when you really lose a part of yourself. Have you gone through that?"

Suri hesitated long enough to give Makareta time to answer. She didn't.

"Try going through that a few times, and I doubt you'll give a damn about what happens to *you* after you die because it couldn't possibly be worse."

The two sat in silence. Then Makareta said, "The sun is going down. I need to get to the Airenthenon. You're going to wait outside on the steps, right?"

Suri nodded. "And you're going to go in and kill."

"I don't want to," she said defensively. "I don't have a choice. It's just destiny, I guess."

"You're lucky." Suri stood and collected the plates. "I'm still unsure what my fate will eventually be, but I don't think I'll have to wait long." She glanced toward the draped window. She didn't need to see outside to know the sun was nearing the horizon. They had less than an hour. "I think a lot will be revealed very soon. Good luck."

"You, too," Makareta said. She stood, pivoted on her left heel, and walked to the door where she took her cloak off a peg. "I'm sure it will be fine. Imaly is smart. I'm certain she's planned this out perfectly." With that, she left.

Suri cleaned up the dishes and put away the food. No matter how this evening turned out, she had no intention of coming back to this place, and she didn't want anyone to think Rhunes were either messy or lazy. Then Suri grabbed a cloak off the peg, and as she, too, left Imaly's little house, she reflected on how she didn't share Makareta's confidence in the Curator.

Butterflies!

Suri didn't think Elan did, either.

૮ৡ

Suri took her time reaching the Airenthenon because she expected a crowd. Imaly had called the meeting, which would draw the full membership of the Aquila, the fane and his entourage, and who knew how many others. While Suri wasn't forbidden from climbing the marble steps, she didn't think it would be smart to be there as all those people walked by. She waited until the fane and his bodyguards went in, figuring they would be the last to arrive.

As Suri climbed the broad steps past fountains and sculptures, the sun's face was fully set, the last hints of light quickly fading. Looking out across the city from that high perch, Suri witnessed a tranquil scene. The cold, dark winter's night didn't invite people to wander, so the streets were empty, and no one gathered in the plaza. Aside from the sounds of shuffling feet and the murmur of low conversation emanating from the interior of the Airenthenon, the evening was as quiet as any other night during that time of year.

Suri took a seat on the top step, sitting sideways so her legs dangled while still granting a decent view into the Airenthenon. She couldn't see much, just a thin slice of firelight through the door that was left open a crack. Maybe they did that for her, or perhaps it was just warm inside with so many people gathered. She could see a bit of them—tiers of seats where folks in heavy winter robes sat. Suri had no idea where Makareta was, but she guessed Imaly would be toward the middle.

My last night here, Suri realized, swinging her legs as a smile came to her face. *I can go home after this. The goulgans are going to rue the day when I return to the garden. It will be good to get back.*

She should be happy, but the idea frightened her a bit, and she bowed her head.

This will be the first time I'll be by myself in the Hawthorn Glen. After Tura died, I still had Minna. I had no idea I'd be away for so long. What will it be like to be back there by myself?

She wouldn't be completely alone. Suri remembered that no one is ever truly alone in a forest. Still, it wouldn't be the same without Tura and Minna.

If I still had Minna—if it was the two of us again—I'd be fine. It's easy being brave with a sister, especially when she is a courageous and wise wolf. Oh, how I miss you, Minna.

Suri's eyes refilled with familiar tears when—

Yip!

Suri's feet stopped swinging, and her head came up. "Minna?"

She looked out across the city, searching the streets, then shook her head.

I've done this before.

Suri remembered climbing stairs out of Neith, believing Minna was somehow following her.

Must have something to do with stone stairs—that and wishful thinking. Talking to Makareta got my mind going, so of course, I—

Yip!

Suri stood. Below her, a quickly moving figure ran up the street, a fleeting shadow racing toward her.

"Minna?" She stared down as the shape revealed itself to be a wolf.

As it crossed the plaza, the animal was illuminated by one of the lamps, and in its light, Suri could clearly see white fur.

A great grin filled Suri's face. "Minna!"

At the sound of Suri's voice calling out, the white wolf sprinted to the base of the stairs and charged up the steps, taking them three and four at a time.

"Minna! Oh, Minna! You're back! You came back!"

The wolf leapt to Suri, who threw her arms around her sister's neck.

Suri fell onto the marble, hugging the wolf to her. Tears ran down the mystic's cheeks, and she wiped them by burying her face in the wolf's thick fur.

"Oh, Minna," Suri cried. "I can hardly believe it! It's been so long. And . . . and here of all places! Oh, Minna, I've missed you so. Are you all right?"

The wolf licked her face.

Suri laughed.

"Such a wise wolf you are to find me again, coming back to life, just like a river with the rain." The thought came to her, a strange wonderful notion. All messages from Elan seemed to come from within but were too profound to be homegrown. "Minna? Did you . . . did you know? Is that why you came to me in the Agave?"

She continued to hug Minna, who licked the mystic's face, cleaning the tears that kept rolling.

Inside the Airenthenon, Suri heard a hammering, and the murmuring stopped. The fane was about to give his speech.

At that moment, Suri remembered how once when she was young, she had broken a toe while leaping up a particularly difficult dry riverbed in the Crescent Forest. The pain was incredible and her eyes watered. What made matters worse was she was miles from the Hawthorn Glen, which meant she'd have a long and painful trip back. As bad as that was, there were storm clouds rolling overhead. Getting wet usually wasn't much more than a nuisance, but at that time, she was in a dry riverbed. When the rain came, it was fierce, forcing Suri into thick brambles that added to her misery. Worse still, night arrived because—as usual—she had lost track of the time. So there she was, struggling in the dark through heavy underbrush with a broken toe in a rainstorm that turned out to be a gully washer.

Why? The question had come to her as she had hobbled along, wincing in pain.

The broken toe had been her fault—bad jump and all—but why did it have to occur right then? This wasn't the first time Suri had noticed this phenomenon, the piling on of bad luck, one hardship coming on the heels of another. Problems were like crowds of people. If a few gathered, several more would surely come. And this pattern wasn't limited to problems. Big events of any sort held an attractive, cumulative aspect. If you plan for something important, then you're guaranteed that a host of unexpected things will pop up, as if major events could only happen at precise moments, so as many incidents as possible squeezed their way in simultaneously.

Imaly's plan to overthrow the fane was underway in the Airenthenon. The moment they had planned for had finally arrived, so of course, it was at that precise moment that Minna came back from the dead.

As inexplicable as Minna's appearance had seemed at first, Suri realized it was her best friend's death that had been the odder occurrence. *That* had never felt right. The idea that Suri wouldn't see her sister again had been impossible to believe. Holding tight to Minna's warm bundle of fur was the most normal Suri had felt in years. The *how* of Minna's return was quickly swept under the *who-cares* rug in favor of the sheer joy that enveloped Suri. It took chaotic, harsh sounds reaching her ears to remind Suri that she and Minna were not the only two that existed.

There had been a crash—a great boom—followed by a chorus of screams. Suri glanced through the open door and saw a rush of movement and a flash of fire. She felt she ought to enter and see what was happening, but Minna was there, and besides, Imaly had instructed her to stay outside unless called for. Suri would be given the horn, and she'd drop it off with Persephone before heading home. But she wouldn't be alone now. Minna was coming.

"Those goulgans are in for real trouble, now."

CHAPTER FIFTEEN

Breaking the Law

Some decisions we make ourselves. Some are made for us by others.
And some are simply the way they have to be.

— THE BOOK OF BRIN

Mawyndulë sat at the front of the Airenthenon in Vidar's seat. He had no legal right to the chair, but then neither did Vidar. The pair of seats had always belonged to the Instarya representatives and were redesignated when the newly formed Miralyith tribe decided the warriors no longer needed seats on the council. Vidar had left that crucial fact out of the history lesson he had given so many years ago. Mawyndulë had been a junior councilor then; now there wasn't one.

Makareta was hiding somewhere. He couldn't see her but guessed she'd be toward the rear of the Airenthenon, in that forest of massive columns that acted as an impressive backdrop, a sort of dramatic curtain. Mawyndulë reached out tentatively with the Art, but he only sensed his father and Synne. Makareta was blocking. After her exile, she had a lot of practice walling off her powers. Mawyndulë kept his eyes on his father, who took his designated seat in the center of the room. Synne stood just off the dais to the left; her eyes looked like those of a cat searching for prey: pupils swollen as they shifted and darted, studying every face. But her gaze was fixed forward on the most obvious threats: the crowded tiers of attendees dressed in winter hoods. Sile was to the right. The huge bodyguard loomed over Lothian. Someone had finally made armor big enough to fit him, and Sile looked like a wall of bronze. Mawyndulë had decided long ago he couldn't be a pureblood, must have been some sort of sick crossbreed. How that had happened, he didn't want to guess. Such an abomination was wrong. The idea that the fane used Sile as his personal guard was disgusting.

The fane—my father. This is it.

In a few moments, he would kill his father. Mawyndulë would execute the fane before a packed session of the Aquila and claim his place as their new ruler. His heart was pounding, and he could feel his asica sticking to the sweat on his skin, tugging with each panted breath as the defining moment of his life approached.

Imaly was relegated to her senior council seat between Volhoric and Nanagal. She leaned over and whispered to her junior, a fellow who already looked old but appeared like a child beside Imaly. Many of the councilors were ancient. Mawyndulë made a quick check and corrected himself. *All* of them were old. That had to be part of a larger problem, and something he would correct. Picking the Fhrey who represented each tribe wasn't normally in the fane's purview. Historically, councilors were appointed by their tribes, and those selected were almost always the leaders. This current crop had made a fatal mistake that had kept Lothian in power. Had they picked Gryndal to be Lothian's challenger, Mawyndulë wouldn't have been required to clean up their mess. As far as Mawyndulë was concerned, the fane was endowed by Ferrol with absolute power to act in his stead on the face of Elan, and once he replaced his father, changes would be necessary.

Imaly's plan was simple, as all good plans should be. When the fane rose to speak, all eyes would be on him, and Makareta would strike Synne—the only real threat.

Sitting where he was, Mawyndulë had a close and unobstructed view of the fane. The moment after Makareta made her surprise attack on Synne, Mawyndulë would kill his father. He hadn't decided exactly which weave to use. Fire was his most reliable attack. He felt the most confident with it, but such a weave was so rudimentary that he was concerned his father could easily counter. Mawyndulë's advantage was surprise. If done quickly, the fane wouldn't have time to understand what was happening, much less fight back.

It would have to be fire. Mawyndulë didn't think he could cast anything else with enough speed. He was nervous and his hands were shaking, so he tucked them under his thighs. Unsteady hands weren't good for the Art. Anything more complicated than a fire weave, and he was certain he'd screw up. He couldn't afford to make a mistake. He had one chance. If he failed, he would be dead. They all would be. Mawyndulë remembered what his father had done to Zephyron in the arena, which did nothing to quiet his trembling.

Maybe I'm in over my head.

People were still climbing tiers and shuffling across rows to their seats. The occasional cough sent an echo over the soft murmur of the congregation. There were more attendees than usual. All the seats—except the one next to Mawyndulë—were filled. The balcony was packed, and people were forced to stand two and three deep at the back, peering over one another's shoulders. For a typical winter address, this was unexpected.

How many know what is about to happen? How many came just to see it?

He leaned forward and looked down the line of seats at Imaly. She didn't look back. None of them did. Not a single soul in the entire Airenthenon looked at him. Again, he had to correct himself. One did. His father.

The fane smiled at his son, an oblivious expression. Mawyndulë was struck by his father's blindness, how unaware Lothian was in regard to what was about to happen. This, above all, demonstrated that the fane wasn't fit to rule. Mawyndulë tried to focus on that thought because another idea was knocking to be let in.

He's my father. Does he deserve this? And from his own son?

At that moment, Fane Lothian didn't look monstrous, didn't seem dangerous. Sitting wrapped in his gold asica and heavy winter robe, he was just an old Fhrey who looked cold. His hair was whiter. Mawyndulë noticed new lines adorning his face, new cracks and shattered crevices around his eyes and across his brow. His lips sagged, pinned up by the two points of the smile that his son had unwittingly and unintentionally put there.

Is he really so terrible that he has to be executed? And must it be at the hands of his son?

The fane stared across the short distance that lay between them. His father trusted Mawyndulë. He could see that in his eyes, a look that said, "You and me, boy. It's us against the world, you know? You're the only one I can rely on because we're one and the same."

Yes, Mawyndulë thought. *There is pride on his face. Maybe everyone is wrong about him. Isn't he just doing what he thinks is best for all of us?*

The moment arrived.

The administrative officer hammered his staff on the marble, and the murmuring quieted. "This two hundred and fifty-seventh meeting of the Aquila in the Age of Lothian is hereby called to order." The speaker was a tall, thin fellow with a loud, but nasal, drone. "May our lord Ferrol grant us wisdom."

Mawyndulë watched his father rise, while in his mind he shouted at him not to. But it was too late. The fane got to his feet and faced the Aquila.

"This winter has been a long one, and it isn't half over," Lothian said. He sounded exhausted, as if he'd just run from the palace to the chamber.

Mawyndulë was stunned. Nothing happened.

Has Imaly called the whole thing off but didn't have time to tell me?

Relief washed over Mawyndulë.

His father leaned to one side, looking wounded and showing the price each dragon's creation had exacted. While Lothian hadn't personally made any, he had ordered the creation of each one. Mawyndulë knew this because the fane communicated with the frontier via Mawyndulë and Jerydd. Through them, the fane learned who was to be killed: wives, husbands, children, lifelong friends, mentors, apprentices, and lovers. Mawyndulë had witnessed firsthand how his father had spoken to each and thanked them for their sacrifice. In each conversation, the fane explained how they needed to do their part for the good of the Fhrey, for Ferrol, and the survival of their entire race. When none of that was convincing enough, he threatened. The fane said the chosen victim would die one way or the other, and the loved one's approach was certain to be more merciful. That always did the trick. Mawyndulë often wondered what his father would actually do if they continued to refuse. Probably nothing, Mawyndulë concluded, and even though Lothian didn't have to torture the victims, the meetings had taken a toll on him. Now there was a bulwark of dragons along the Nidwalden, and his father bore the weight of each one on his face.

"Many of you want to know how the war goes. I am pleased to report that we are launching a major offensive. We finally have enough dragons, and they and an army are gathering in the Harwood. They will lay waste to the Rhune encampment at the base of Mount Mador. After that, we'll sweep south across the Bern. Unfortunately, we will need to create more dragons as we go because they have a limited range, so this will require more sacrifices. Regrettable as that is, I am here to announce that our victory is coming soon. We are already safe from invasion, and the long darkness is near its end."

"You have no idea how right you are." The words were spoken by Makareta. Mawyndulë still didn't see her—no one did—but he knew her voice.

In his desire to believe the plan had been called off, Mawyndulë had forgotten she was there. He was listening to his father speak, lost in his words and the familiar normality of the moment.

The voice had come from everywhere at once, giving no indication where Makareta was hiding, but talking hadn't been part of the plan. Knowing Synne's prowess for speed, Makareta wasn't supposed to give any hint of her presence. Maybe some part of her rebellious nature couldn't be suppressed, or perhaps memories of her friends' deaths at Lothian's command had demanded acknowledgment.

Makareta was no slouch with the Art, and she launched the spell even before her words ceased. For anyone else, Makareta's attack would have landed in plenty of time, but Synne—being who she was—had managed to raise a shield. If Makareta had cast fire as Mawyndulë was planning to use, Synne would have lived, but Makareta gave no quarter, no chance. She wasn't relying on half measures. She didn't cast directly on Synne, which rendered her block pointless.

Instead, she hit several of the pillars between them. Blocks of marble that had taken a thousand Fhrey with ropes and ramps to set into place rushed toward Lothian's bodyguard with the force of a burst dam. The first slab would have smashed into her face if the shield hadn't deflected it. But personal shields worked best against the purity of a conjured assault: fire, cold, and lightning, not tons of marble, and the force threw Synne onto her back. The unprotected crown of her head hit the stone with a *clack,* which was audible to Mawyndulë from the first row. The impact likely cracked Synne's skull. It certainly broke her concentration and with it, her shield weave. Lying stunned on the dais, she screamed as the next stone pillar crushed her legs to meal. To her credit, and Mawyndulë's amazement, she managed to cast one last weave before dying, before the last of the pillars crushed her. Working in pain and faster than ever before, Synne managed a wind weave that was enough to throw Makareta off her feet.

Nothing more happened for a heartbeat.

With the air knocked from her lungs, Makareta fell to the floor in full view of everyone. She was just as stunned from the impact as Synne had been. The room gasped.

This was Mawyndulë's moment. The time for him to act. The fane was facing away, his back turned as he stared in shock at the crushed body of Synne. Mawyndulë got to his feet along with everyone else. If he took two steps forward and reached out, he could touch his father. At this range, he couldn't possibly miss, and the fane would have no time to react. But his way wasn't clear.

Is he really so terrible that he has to be executed? And must it be at the hands of his son?

The questions stood between them, blocking Mawyndulë's attack.

He's my father!

"Makareta?" the fane exclaimed. "You! How could—"

Sile jingled a symphony of bronze as he strode across the chamber, aiming his spear.

At a withered whisper and a hand gesture from Makareta, the bronze began to melt. Sile, that great monster of a Fhrey, screamed as he struggled to rip the armor off his body even as it charred his skin before burning through muscle and bone. He shrieked, high-pitched and shrill, like a rat being boiled alive.

Makareta looked to Mawyndulë then. He saw confusion in her eyes. *What are you waiting for?* they said.

Then, as Sile collapsed, the fane raised his hands.

Before Mawyndulë could speak, step forward, or do anything, his father shouted, and he made a gesture as if ripping something invisible apart. In that instant, blood exploded in a singular burst, spraying the white marble. Half of Makareta was thrown across the chamber to slap against one of the braziers, making it wobble. Her torso clapped against a pillar, leaving an ugly red stain. Around Mawyndulë came screams, whimpers, and tears. People shuffled, moving to get away, to get clear of the violence, to escape.

The prince didn't move. He stood frozen, staring at the blood staining the white pillar, as it formed tears that cried.

"This could be the last night we have," he had told her.

"And if it was your father?" Makareta had said.

Mawyndulë focused on Lothian. The fane was hunched over, breathing hard, and still facing away.

"You deserve to die," he whispered under his breath and cast fire.

⟿

Most of the Airenthenon had emptied out. Mawyndulë knew this, but the thought was only a faint understanding. His eyes and his mind were still fixated on the charred remains of his father. The fire summoned by the Art went out several minutes before, but natural flames still flickered in places. His father's hair—that being a Miralyith he should never have grown so long—had burned away in an instant, but his shoes still smoldered. The thick portion of his heels continued to glow, and whenever an errant gust of wind blew, a flame jumped up and danced.

Like the remaining embers, his father had refused to die quickly; he had screamed and thrashed. His arms and legs flailed. Blackened, cracked hands slapped the dais until charcoal bits of his fingers broke off, leaving a greasy stain on the marble. As the flames dissipated, his father grew quieter. Soon, the sound of his hissing body was louder than the moans. Then even those ceased—about the same time the flames on his heels finally died.

That's when Mawyndulë felt the cold. Not a mere chill, nor even an icy wind. Those things came from the outside; this was *inside*. There was an ache like that of an empty stomach, only it came from deeper than that. This gaping, frigid winter bloomed in that hallowed space within Mawyndulë that was greater than the sum of all his parts. And now that place was as empty as if some internal flame had been snuffed out.

Ferrol's Law!

Mawyndulë placed a groping hand to his chest and looked at his father, at the still-smoking body. Then he turned and searched the room for Volhoric. He spotted the high priest fleeing for the door, his heavy cloak whipping side-to-side as he ran.

"Stop!" Mawyndulë shouted. With a grasping motion, he locked the high priest's legs together. The old Fhrey fell and skidded to a stop, causing those running behind him to jump over or dodge. One not-so-agile follower stepped on the priest's hand, making Volhoric cry out. He clutched his injured fingers and rolled over. Seeing Mawyndulë staring at him, the priest's face filled with terror.

Everyone knew I was going to kill Lothian, so why is he so scared of me?

That was the moment realization landed, the truth of the comedy he starred in revealed.

"You lied to me. You knew I'd lose my soul, and you lied!" Mawyndulë shouted at Volhoric.

He heard a pop and sizzle and looked back at the heap on the dais, cooked flesh in the shape of a person that the breeze stirred up. As Mawyndulë stared, the full weight of what he'd done landed.

I broke Ferrol's Law. I'm no longer a Fhrey. But I'm the fane! How can the leader of Ferrol's children not be a Fhrey?

Mawyndulë struggled to hold his breath against the nauseating smell that was sweet, putrid, and meat-like. The odor was so thick and rich that he could taste it on his tongue as he breathed through his mouth. He crossed the dais to the charred body and ripped the circlet from his father's head, causing the blackened face to rock in protest. Mawyndulë put it on and shouted, "I'm fane now!"

The few people still in the Airenthenon froze, halting their efforts to escape. They looked his way, every face filled with fear—almost every face.

Imaly, who hadn't left her seat until that moment, rose. "No, you're not," she told him and took a moment to brush the creases out of her purple-and-white asica.

"Of course I am!" he shouted. "My father is dead. That makes me the fane!"

Imaly shook her head, showing him the familiar mentor-like expression that he finally recognized as condescension. "Fhrey cannot kill Fhrey. You did. You broke Ferrol's Law, so you are no longer Fhrey. You cannot be fane."

Mawyndulë whirled and pointed at Volhoric, who was still lying on the floor with his legs trapped by the Art. "He said there was an exception. He told me Lothian had already revoked his standing as a Fhrey and could be killed without repercussion."

"That's true," Imaly said. "And as you already pointed out, he lied."

Mawyndulë glanced at the priest who struggled to drag himself to the door using only his arms. Then he looked at Imaly. "So you knew, too. You knew and you convinced me to do it anyway? Why would you do that?"

"Because we cannot be ruled by Miralyith forever, and that was the course that lay before us." Imaly spoke in that same powerful, commanding voice she'd always used when orating to the Aquila. "That was not what Gylindora—what *my great-grandmother*—intended. The Miralyith have tried to vanquish Ferrol and replace him with themselves. Today we restore our god to his throne, and his will to our laws. The horn will be blown by a worthy Fhrey, one who—"

"The horn!" Mawyndulë burst out. "That's it! Gryndal told me that the fane of the Fhrey must be Fhrey, that there's a crack in Ferrol's Law. If I blow it and survive The Challenge, I must be reinstated. If I do that, I will be fane. Where is it?"

Imaly hesitated. Mawyndulë could tell she hadn't expected this. For the first time ever, she looked genuinely concerned. She glanced at Volhoric, still pulling himself across the floor.

Mawyndulë punched his fist into the air, and the two rows of marble seats just to Imaly's left smashed against the walls, cracking the rock. "I have a very long reach, Imaly." Mawyndulë glared at her. "You were behind this whole thing, weren't you? All those times we talked." He sneered at her as the full extent of her betrayal registered. She had deceived Mawyndulë for . . . years.

"You were only feigning respect. You pretended to help, when all along you were manipulating me to this." Mawyndulë's mouth hung open in disbelief. "I saved you!" He pointed at the far wall. "When the Gray Cloaks attacked and this whole building was about to come down, it was *I* who saved *you!*"

Imaly could have been a marble statue. Not a hint of remorse nor a trace of sympathy appeared on her face. "You saved yourself, or have you forgotten telling me that? I only fanned the flames of your own ambition. You're not the type of person we need as our next fane."

"And who *do* we need? You?" Mawyndulë glanced between Imaly and Volhoric. "Where is the horn? It's here, isn't it? You planned to blow it. Being the *great-granddaughter* of Gylindora Fane, you believe yourself to be the rightful choice. Isn't that so? That's what this has been about from the beginning. You're stealing the Forest Throne for yourself. I was warned about you. Vidar said you were dangerous. He was right about that. But he also said you were smart, and on that score he was mistaken. You forgot one important thing. I may not be a Fhrey, but I'm still a Miralyith. With Synne dead, I'm the *only* remaining Miralyith in this city, the only one who isn't three days away at the Nidwalden River."

Mawyndulë sucked in a deep breath, and with it, he drew power from the people around him, from the dormant trees outside, and from the fires burning in the braziers. Extending his arms, he began smashing holes in the walls. He tore down the balcony, which shattered on the floor. The whole of the Airenthenon shrieked and rocked. "I'm done holding up tradition." With a grunt, he destroyed another of the great pillars holding up the dome, and the whole ceiling slipped dangerously. "The old ways are gone," he shouted. "I am fane, if not by law then by might. Everyone here will serve me or die. Now where is the horn!"

Imaly didn't answer, but her eyes were on Volhoric.

With a sweep of Mawyndulë's arm, the priest slid across the floor toward the prince. The old Fhrey cowered in a ball, his cloak and robes a chaos around him. Mawyndulë had assumed he was huddling out of fear, but he now suspected that wasn't the case. The primary job of the Conservator was to keep the horn safe and present it to the Curator when called for. Imaly would want things done properly for her coronation. Mawyndulë pulled strings in a weave and manipulated Volhoric like a puppet, spreading his arms and lifting him up to reveal a strap over one shoulder and a bulge at his side deep in the folds of his robe.

Mawyndulë gestured for the priest to come closer, and Volhoric acted as if each wave of Mawyndulë's fingers were a forward shove. Using the priest's own hands, Mawyndulë forced him to strip off his clothes and reveal the horn at his side. Mawyndulë had never seen it before. Always kept in secret by the Aquila, it was a relic that most Fhrey had never laid eyes on. But they'd heard it. The moment the horn was blown, all Fhrey everywhere perceived its cry. Mawyndulë had always imagined it to be a jewel-encrusted treasure. The *thing* at Volhoric's side looked like just an old ram's horn with decorative markings.

"Bring it to me," Mawyndulë ordered.

The priest no longer needed to be manipulated by the Art. He walked forward and handed the horn to the prince. Then he and Imaly stared at each other, their faces reflecting fear.

"It won't work," Volhoric said. "You're no longer Fhrey. The horn will only sound for a child of Ferrol, and you've cast yourself out." His words were brave, but his tone was just hopeful—less declaration and more wish.

"My soul is gone. You are right about that." He smiled a wicked grin. "But Gryndal theorized that the only thing required to blow the horn is to possess a single drop of Fhrey blood, and I still have plenty of that running through my veins. Let's see who is right—you or Gryndal."

He lifted the horn to his lips and blew.

CHAPTER SIXTEEN

Uli Vermar

She did not go with us, but she suffered nonetheless. I do not think anyone will ever know just how much.

— The Book of Brin

Persephone's feet crushed the snow as she walked. The paths between the four quadrants of the Dragon Camp had been packed down with traffic, melted by the daytime sun, and refrozen at night such that sections were turned to ice. The heels of her boots managed to leave divots, creating little footholds that kept her from falling.

I need to ask Habet to toss wood ash along the glossy parts. And get the other fire tenders to do the same. It'll look terrible but could prevent a few broken bones—not the least of which might be my own.

Persephone made daily visits to each of the quads to hear grievances and learn what was needed. Not that she could do much about the growing concern over Lothian's dragons or the worsening weather, but sometimes it made folks feel better just to be heard. People could withstand hardships if they knew they weren't alone and felt their sacrifices were appreciated. Persephone had learned this as a chieftain's wife and honed her empathetic skills as a keenig. Simply listening made a difference.

Returning to the center of the camp after completing her rounds, she found Nyphron waiting in her tent. In his hand was the bottle.

"Who?" she said, no longer needing to ask what the container held.

"Elysan," Nyphron replied. He said nothing more for so long that Persephone grew aware of the snap and crackle of the fire that, under Habet's single-minded care, eternally sent sparks into the dark sky. Eventually, Nyphron tightened his lips and added, "He had his arms torn off by giants and was mounted on a pole while still alive, turned into a Grenmorian battle flag."

The image was explicit, the delivery blunt, but Persephone held steady, watching him with a firm jaw and steady hands at her sides.

"I sent—ordered—him north to the giants to persuade Furgenrok to assist us."

"I know," she said.

He didn't seem to hear. "I felt he was the best for the job. He gets—got—along with everyone and was blessed with insight and artful with words. I've never known a wiser Fhrey. He made the perfect ambassador. I was certain he could persuade them." He looked up at her then. His eyes were dull, only casting back the flicker of the fire. "Didn't work."

He pulled the top off the bottle, making a deep, hollow sound.

Persephone remembered the night they toasted the deaths of Tekchin and the others who'd gone to the swamp. Nyphron had been cheerful—after a fashion—wearing a classic, brave warrior's face. He joked, smiled, and made light, silly conversation. That—along with sharing a drink of erivitie—was how Nyphron mourned.

This time he was different.

Nyphron seemed angry but also sad, and there was an uncharacteristic dash of confusion. She thought a bit and realized Nyphron had often deferred to the recommendations of Elysan, and he sometimes sought out the older Fhrey's opinion.

"He was like a father to you. Is that right?" she asked.

Nyphron appeared to think the question over. "No," he finally said. "Zephyron was like a father to me. Elysan was something better. He was ..." Nyphron paused with a finger up, his eyes chasing a thought. Then he shook his head. "There's no word for it. Not in Fhrey, nor Rhunic, or even in Dherg. There just aren't words for some things. I think perhaps it's—"

Nyphron's head jerked sharply to one side. His mouth dropped open in surprise.

Persephone turned to look but saw nothing unusual. He was staring northeast toward the forest and the river, which was a bad sign. The Fhrey had better hearing and more acute eyesight. She looked above the tops of the tents.

Dragons? Is he hearing them? Will I see them in a minute? Are we all about to die?

Persephone braced herself for the sound of leathery wings and the blast of fire.

Nothing happened.

She peered up at the Dragon Hill. The gilarabrywn was still there.

If dragons are coming, surely it would know and get up. Even if the danger was just the approach of the fane's army, it should lift its head.

"Nyphron, what's wrong?" she asked.

"The horn," he said. "Someone has blown it."

"What do you mean—"

Persephone heard running feet on snow. Turning, she saw Sikar, Erye, and Anyval coming toward them. The one bringing up the rear was still in the process of pulling on his cloak.

"It's the horn," Erye said.

As a Fhrey resident of the Dragon Camp, Erye stood out as doubly odd because she was neither male nor an Instarya. Erye was an Asendwayr. Since she hadn't moved to Merredydd like all the other noncombatant Fhrey of Alon Rhist, Persephone suspected that she shared a bed with someone. Anyval was the obvious choice, but Persephone couldn't rule out anyone, including Nyphron.

"The Uli Vermar has ended," Anyval announced.

Just then, Poric and Plymerath joined them, coming from a different direction. Together they appeared as two ends of the Fhrey spectrum: Poric was small, fastidious, and pretentious, while Plymerath was big, smiling, and relaxed.

"Lothian is dead," Sikar stated.

All of them looked east, stunned.

Poric asked, "How do you think he died?"

"Someone killed him," Nyphron said hotly.

His anger baffled Persephone. Not only was it unlike him to exhibit such emotion, but there appeared no reason for it. The mystery was solved with Nyphron's next words. "Someone who isn't me."

Anyval continued to stare out at the dark winter's night with a dismal expression. "I don't understand. Who would break Ferrol's Law? And why replace Lothian now that he has the advantage?"

"Is it possible he was eaten by one of his own dragons?" Plymerath asked.

Persephone thought this might have been a joke, but no one laughed or smiled. She didn't, either. "I don't understand what's going on. You all heard a horn? I didn't hear anything."

"You're not Fhrey," Anyval told her. The physician who had helped her after the raow attack recognized what all the others appeared to miss— that she wasn't knowledgeable about the Fhrey laws of succession. What's more, he realized how rude it was to ignore her ignorance. Snapping closed the clasp on his cloak, he took a step closer. "It's Ferrol's pact. We're all bound to the horn by birth. If you have Fhrey blood, you hear it sound when someone announces their challenge to be fane."

"Why do you assume Lothian is dead? Couldn't someone be challenging him?"

"No. Lothian has already been opposed, so the horn remains silent until his reign ends. His son has first rights to the throne, so it's Mawyndulë who is being confronted."

"Not necessarily," Poric said. "It's possible he's dead, too."

"Maybe." Anyval nodded. "But the horn would need to be blown again by this time tomorrow for that to be true."

"It's possible whoever blew it might go unchallenged." Poric spoke as if he was an expert.

Persephone had her doubts. Poric was the sort to always assume he was right.

"Doesn't matter," Nyphron replied and finally drank from his bottle. "It will be another Miralyith."

Persephone didn't want to drink. She had questions and needed answers that no one gathered there could give her. With Lothian dead, perhaps the next ruler of the Fhrey would be willing to seek peace. Maybe a Miralyith had been forced to murder a loved one to make the dragon at Avempartha, and they killed Lothian in retribution. If that were so, there was a chance they could be reasoned with. Nyphron and the others didn't know who was challenging to replace Lothian, but she knew someone who probably did.

Persephone climbed Dragon Hill in the dark. She stood twenty feet from the sleeping beast and waited. After several minutes—when her feet had sunk into deep snow and grown cold—she suspected she might be an idiot.

I don't know what I was thinking. He's just a man. He doesn't actually know the future. If he really knew everything, he would have known I would come here even before I started this way. He should have been waiting. He should have been—

She heard the crunch of snow as a tall figure came toward her out of the night.

"Good evening, Persephone," Malcolm said in greeting, vanquishing her doubts.

He looked the same as always: tall, thin, and not at all special. That night he wore a heavy winter cloak.

Does he even need it? Is he affected by the cold?

They stared at each other for a moment.

Why doesn't he just tell me what I want to know?

Everything suddenly felt absolutely absurd.

They were standing in the cold snow at the foot of a dragon-like beast where she planned to ask Malcolm questions—the answers to which he couldn't possibly know. Except she knew he did.

"What just happened? And don't feign ignorance. Lying won't help either of us."

He shrugged casually. "You already know. Lothian is dead."

"How did he die?"

"Murdered by his son Mawyndulë."

"Oh." Persephone was surprised Malcolm was forthcoming with information. "Will I be able to broker peace with the new leader of the Fhrey?"

"No. But that won't be necessary as long as you keep Nyphron here."

Persephone's fingers were cold. She didn't have mittens, so she tucked her hands into her armpits. "You keep saying that as if this is going to be a problem. Will there be a time when Nyphron wants to leave?"

"Yes."

"My husband is many things, but flighty isn't one of them. He doesn't do anything without reasons—usually good ones. If he thinks we need to pull back, I suspect the retreat will be warranted."

"I wouldn't make such a point of it, if staying will be an obvious choice."

"But you promise everything will work out?"

He didn't answer immediately. The pause bothered her. "Nothing is absolutely certain."

"What's that supposed to mean? If what you say is true, I'll likely be risking the lives of everyone I know on just your word. I might be risking the future of unborn generations as well."

"I don't control the universe, Persephone. I can't *guarantee* success."

"What are you talking about? Of course you can! You can see the future."

"Not all of it." He said it casually, almost like a joke.

Maybe to him it is.

Persephone had already begun to question whether Malcolm was human. If he was something more, it could be that everything happening to her people was nothing more than entertainment. She struggled to reconcile the Malcolm she'd first met with this one. They seemed so different, or perhaps she just hadn't been paying attention.

He was the one who struck Arion on the head with the rock. Everyone else had been terrified. Even the Fhrey were helpless against her, but Malcolm got away with an assault that debilitated someone as powerful as Arion? Why hadn't anyone thought that was peculiar?

"What do you mean *not all of it*?" Her voice rose to an octave beyond what she felt a keenig's tone should.

Malcolm sighed. "You can see this field, can't you? Can you tell me where every snowflake has fallen? Or exactly how many there are? Do you know their relation to one another?"

She stared at him incredulously. This wasn't what she wanted to hear. She wanted him to say it was all going to work out in the end. She didn't need to be told about snowflakes. "Recent reports say the Fhrey have"— she took a breath—"*dozens* of dragons. Edgar's men have spotted them. They are also massing troops on our side of the Nidwalden. They won't wait for spring, Malcolm." She pointed at the Harwood. "Every scout tells me they are preparing for a winter assault. Tomorrow, a Fhrey army could appear on the forest's eaves." She pointed down the slope toward the trees. "Malcolm, we can't fight *dozens* of dragons." She looked at the sleeping behemoth beside them. "Maybe one, possibly two if we're lucky, but not dozens. If we retreat, we can get out of their range. By going beyond Alon Rhist, our dragon can still protect us, and Lothian's dozens will be powerless. The new fane will have to make more."

"If you leave, you will lose the war."

"How? Explain that to me. How?"

He thought a moment, then looked up at the stars. "It is extraordinary how so much is determined by timing. Being at one place rather than another at a singular moment alters the world. It happens all the time. Raithe and his father being at the Forks at the precise moment that Shegon, Meryl, and I passed is a perfect example. Didn't have to happen that way."

The mention of Raithe's name so close to the gilarabrywn unsettled her, but the beast showed no sign of recognition, and it continued with what she suspected was a false nap.

"So many events are connected to thousands of others—another reason why it isn't possible to be absolutely certain of the future. There are focal points, however, instances when so many paths converge that it would be foolhardy to ignore the pattern. Even the slightest alteration to these major crossroads can cause the world to veer wildly. Oftentimes, it is necessary to stand quite still while a blow that looks like it will destroy you lands just a hairbreadth away. We are coming to one of those moments. The magnitude of this intersection is so great that I'm sure even you can feel it. That's why you tested me by coming up this hill tonight. You're nervous and worried."

"Damn right I am! And I do feel it. Something terrible is about to happen." Persephone frowned and clutched herself tighter. "I'm just—I'm scared."

He nodded. "Just know this: We need to be *here* when she comes back, and so does Nyphron—right here." He pointed at his feet. "We can't afford to flinch. Timing is everything."

"Timing for what? And who do you mean by—*she?*"

He looked down. "Snowflakes, remember?"

"I think you're being vague because you don't want to answer me."

"Well, you mentioned lying won't help, so here we are."

Persephone wanted to scream. He was just so . . . so infuriating. Knowing something—anything—would help. She put her hands on her head, came very near screaming, then spotted the dragon and thought better of an outburst. Instead, she made fists and shook them in tandem. "I just need a little reassurance, that's all."

"That's good because at this point a little is all I can offer."

"Then do so."

He nodded. "I saw a white wolf in Estramnadon."

"You saw what?" She stared dumbfounded. "I don't understand."

"As far as I can tell, Brin is coming close to completing her mission. She doesn't know it yet, but she has very little time left. If everything transpires as I have seen it—and keep in mind it's very hard to guess at this point—the difference between success and failure will be determined by a matter of minutes, possibly seconds. If we are not here when Brin returns, *everything* will fail. And more than you can possibly imagine will fall apart. Such a setback could unravel centuries of hard work."

Persephone stared at him. She wanted to believe, but all she had were the words of one man to cling to weighed against the fate of the entire world. "What about the others?"

Malcolm said nothing.

"It's just Brin, then? She's going into Estramnadon alone? She's going to save Suri all by herself?"

"She's not there to save Suri. I didn't send her to save one person. I sent her to save everyone."

"You keep saying *her,* but what about Moya, Tekchin, Roan, Gifford, Rain, Tesh, and Tressa? And don't you dare mention s*nowflakes!*"

Persephone looked into his eyes and immediately stepped back. For a moment, for a brief instant, she saw more than she wanted. The man before her, the simple, pleasant, awkward, ever-pleasing ex-slave, was missing. In his place was a stranger. Within those eyes she saw rage and hate on a scale so vast, it caught her breath. And she saw sadness so profound that for that moment, she forgot her own. In his eyes, she'd glimpsed eternity stretching out like a road so lonely, it hurt her heart to think of the steps needed to walk it.

"This place," he told her, "this hill and this time is a focal point, the center of a web. You've heard Suri and Arion speak of the Art? How it's like a string game and all life is connected by threads. Well, they are right. The Miralyith feel those connections. They sense them, but I can see them. They are endless, countless, and more abundant than flakes of snow or grains of sand on all the beaches."

Persephone continued to stare at the man before her. She must have started breathing again, but she didn't know when. She'd also started shaking. Maybe it was the cold.

Malcolm didn't notice. He had turned away and was facing the camp. "Most of the time I can follow the paths, see the cross-points, but this hill, this singular moment . . . is like tying a million threads to a single knot, all of them smaller than a human hair. Imagine them being all tangled and twisted—more than a million—more than a million-million-million—more than you can conceive of. That's what I see when I look at this hill tomorrow. It all leads to this one point. Everything runs through a tiny hole to this epic knot. I've been trying to untie it, but I can't. It's too hard. It has to be cut."

He looked back at her, and as he did, she saw the old Malcolm, the apologetic man with the spear named Pointy. "Be thankful that Brin made it through. Make sure we are still here tomorrow and that Nyphron is as well. That's all you need to think of just now."

"For the love of Elan, Malcolm, we're talking about *Brin*. She's just a young, inexperienced woman. How is she going to—Oh, dear Mother of All." Persephone clasped her face in her cold hands. "What have I done?"

"This isn't over yet."

"Did you know what would happen?" She could see in his eyes that he hadn't. She could see he, too, was worried. And if Malcolm was worried, what did that mean?

"Oh . . . and one more thing," he said. "Either assign someone else to feed your fire, do it yourself, or let the eternal flame go out."

"What are you talking about? That's Habet's job."

"Not right now. I gave him a new one."

"My Habet?" she said, bewildered. "You gave *him* a job to do?"

"A rather important one, too, but I trust he is up to the challenge. It will all make sense tomorrow. You'll see. The thing is, I hate to lose. I *really* hate to lose."

He left her then, and walked back down the hill.

Persephone looked out across the white-covered land at the forested horizon.

Oh, Brin, please be strong.

CHAPTER SEVENTEEN

We Call Him Malcolm

That day, I discovered that animals can see and hear ghosts, but apparently mystics need proof.

— The Book of Brin

The sound was clear and loud. It lacked any musical quality, sounding instead like a cry—a scream of hate and loathing. Imaly and Volhoric stared openmouthed.

Mawyndulë lowered the horn, refilled the air in his lungs, and said, "It would seem you are wrong." Then he held it out to Imaly. "Go on. Take it."

Imaly looked at the horn in his hands as if it were a poisonous snake.

"Blow it," Mawyndulë taunted. "It's what you wanted to do, isn't it? Blow it, and tomorrow we can face off in the Carfreign. And if you thought what my father did to Zephyron was a spectacle, just imagine what I'll do to you after so many years of lies and deceit."

"That was promised to me," a small voice said, and Mawyndulë turned to see the Rhune step into the ruins of the Airenthenon. With her came a white wolf that Mawyndulë remembered from a battle between Gryndal and Arion in a Rhune village so many years ago.

How did it get here?

The wolf hung back near the door, where the guards had abandoned their post.

"We had a deal." The Rhune entered the circle of marble that was the central floor of the Airenthenon. "I gave up the secret to making dragons, and in return, you are supposed to give me that horn." She wasn't looking at him. Her eyes were on Imaly.

Mawyndulë laughed. He was in a decidedly better mood than a moment ago. He sensed pain circling him and could still smell the scent of burnt hair, but he refused to look to his left to where Makareta had been. All such things would be examined in time, but right now he was riding the high of unexpected victory over unforeseen treachery. "Get in line," he said. "Imaly lies to everyone."

"Is that true?" the Rhune asked.

"Of course not," Imaly said. "But . . ."

"But what?"

"Mawyndulë wasn't supposed to be *able* to blow it."

"Why does that matter? You told me and Makareta that he was to be fane," Suri said.

"No. He was *never* supposed to be fane."

"And yet here we are." Mawyndulë grinned.

"But Makareta—" The Rhune looked at the place Mawyndulë couldn't. Shock and horror filled her face.

"He wasn't supposed to be capable of sounding the horn," Imaly went on. "He should have been cast out and ineligible. I should have been the one, and Volhoric was going to blow it after me and immediately concede. I would have been fane, and . . ." She faced the Rhune. "I would have honored our agreement. I would have made peace with your people. I swear it!"

The Rhune swallowed hard and pulled her sight away from the forbidden place. She focused on Imaly. "After you became fane."

"Yes," Imaly said. "It made the most sense. I could fix everything. I could stop the war, restore the balance between the tribes, and return Erivan to how it used to be."

The Rhune continued to stare at Imaly, and the Curator looked back as if pleading to be believed. Why Imaly cared what the Rhune thought was beyond Mawyndulë's ability to understand.

"We trusted you," the Rhune said, and once more she looked at the forbidden place. "She trusted you."

The Rhune took a step toward Mawyndulë and held out her hand. "Give me the horn."

Of all the nerve!

Mawyndulë was so stunned that he didn't do anything for a moment. He couldn't understand—and then he remembered the collar around her neck and smiled. "I see. You think because you have that collar on, I can't hurt you with the Art. Or maybe you believe that your agreement with my father protects you?" Mawyndulë pointed at the body on the floor. "Your safeguard went up in smoke. And as I learned when fighting at Alon Rhist, there are ways around the Orinfar."

With a small weave, Mawyndulë lifted a huge stone bench and threw it at her. The size of it was so great that it wasn't merely going to kill her, but would likely crush Imaly and Volhoric as well. This suited Mawyndulë just fine. The Curator and Conservator both screamed and cringed as tons of marble came at them. The Rhune appeared unconcerned and clapped her hands as if applauding.

The instant her palms met, the marble burst into dust, finishing its flight as a cloud.

Mawyndulë stared in shock. "How did—?" He pointed at the collar. "You're wearing the Orinfar."

"No. I'm not. It's just a collar." The Rhune reached up and touched the metal around her neck. She muttered a word of breaking. The circlet cracked open, and she threw it on the ground.

Mawyndulë turned on Imaly. "You did this!"

The Rhune appeared to sigh, and Mawyndulë sensed a bloom of power. Then she coughed, and he felt the horn ripped from him. It flew the distance between them, landing in the Rhune's hands.

"Thanks," she said and turned to leave.

"You're not going anywhere with that," Mawyndulë told her.

"Watch me."

Mawyndulë waved his hand, and the door Suri had entered slammed shut.

The Rhune sighed and looked at the wolf. "Minna, you should stay out of this. You know that, right?"

The wolf moved in a circle twice then lay down on the steps. The Rhune looped the horn's strap over her head and faced Mawyndulë, but did nothing more.

She's waiting for me to make the first move. A tactical mistake. Gryndal was a big proponent of First Strike–Last Strike tactics.

Mawyndulë went once more with fire

క్

Suri watched Mawyndulë with a puzzled curiosity as he attacked her with a blast of flame. The torrent grew around Suri's body like a cyclone of hot wind. Fire had been a poor choice, but she already knew Mawyndulë was an idiot.

Winter was a terrible time for everyone. Birds were forced to leave. Hardwoods, after being stripped naked, suffered ice and snow. Flowers were killed outright, something Suri had always thought of as unfair. A few months of sun and then wham! Frozen to death and promptly buried. Deer mice, hedgehogs, skunks, and bats all just gave up and went to sleep for the whole season. No, winter was a rough time. Elan was asleep, and she didn't want to add to her burden. Suri felt the sleepy trees, their groggy thoughts far down the slope. She didn't want to take strength from them. Doing so would be rude. Wind was a better choice. It didn't mind being tapped, and in winter, wind was plentiful.

With a flick, the fire he'd sent her way winked out—just a momentary flash and a puff of smoke.

Mawyndulë hadn't expected that. His eyes went wide, then narrowed in anger.

Suri had seen that look before. She'd seen it *all* previously. But the last time was in spring, and the irritated Fhrey Miralyith was Gryndal, with his long, ugly fingernails, metal-ring piercings, and cape of gold. Mawyndulë had been there, too. But he and Suri had stood and watched as Arion and Gryndal fought. Now it was their turn.

"Imagine that as you alter the patterns in that string, you are also altering the world around you, and because you are part of this world, you are also transforming yourself," Arion had instructed. *"If you can see this, then you'll know the truth: The string you weave is really yourself, and the pattern you make is your own life."*

The string was life. The lines connected directly or through points to others. This one just happened to be a straight line from that first fight between Artists in Dahl Rhen and where she stood now. Her life had threaded between the two moments, one long loop tied and knotted, and *this* was that knot, and she had come around to it once more.

She selected her retaliatory strike: wind and ice. The weave was easy. Suri was surrounded by everything she needed. The breeze rose and swirled. With it came ice, forming sharp shards and foot-long icicles. She saw him struggling to counter as her attack grew larger and larger.

He will use fire to block because he's too flustered to think of anything else. It won't work.

A cyclone of deadly ice roared as it attacked.

Mawyndulë flinched as the icy tornado struck, then vanished the moment it hit him. The wind died; the ice fell; the roar ceased. Mawyndulë looked as puzzled as everyone else that he had survived.

"Protection of Ferrol," Volhoric said. "He's blown the horn and cannot be hurt by anyone except a challenger."

Suri thought that was solved easily enough. She took hold of the old ram's horn and blew on the little end, but no sound came out, not even an ugly note like the one Mawyndulë had made. Suri looked at the horn, puzzled, then tried again.

"Only one of Fhrey blood can sound that horn," the priest said.

Mawyndulë's confusion was replaced by a great grin, and he attacked once more.

Suri was baffled. His stance, fingers, and the words he muttered were all wrong. He was trying to be quiet, attempting to hide his attack, but he was clumsy and inept.

He's actually casting fire again! Doesn't he know anything else?

This time she snuffed out the weave before it even got going, leaving only a telltale puff of black smoke between them. His face was a mask of frustration. Arion had done something similar to him in Dahl Rhen, cutting him off before he even finished, and he hadn't liked it then, either.

It had to be embarrassing—to know your opponent was so much faster and better than you that it was impossible to get a swing started.

How humiliating it must be to find a Rhune better in the ways of the Art.

The two stared at each other, neither certain what to do next.

"Give Imaly the horn," Volhoric said to Suri.

"Why?" Imaly glared at him.

"You can blow it and challenge Mawyndulë."

"And you can go to Nifrel and rot," Imaly told him.

"You are forgetting that a champion can be named to fight in place of the challenger. There's no restriction; it doesn't have to be a Fhrey. This Rhune knows the Art and can fight for you. If she wins, you'll be fane."

Imaly's eyes shifted left then right before looking at Suri. "Would you do that?"

Tempting, Suri thought.

She'd long wished for Mawyndulë's death for killing Arion, and she was frustrated by the protection that blowing the horn was providing him. But then she once more spied Makareta's body—one part here, another over there—and realized she couldn't believe anything either Fhrey told her. For all she knew, giving Imaly the horn might grant the Curator the same safeguard that Mawyndulë possessed. It could even be a trick that would cut her off from the Art the way the Orinfar had.

"No," she replied. "Fhrey lie as frequently as Belgriclungreians."

"If you don't act as her champion," Volhoric said, "Mawyndulë will rule. He'll have a fleet of dragons at his command and will kill all your people."

"If you support me now," Imaly told her, "I'll fulfill my promise and work to make peace between our peoples. That was always my plan."

"She's lying," Mawyndulë said. "Imaly won't stop the war any more than I will. She's only telling you what you want to hear. You can't trust her."

Mawyndulë gathered power. He was doing it subtly, muttering softly, trying to catch her off guard. Suri had no idea what he planned this time, but it didn't matter. With a word, she canceled his weave before he even raised his hands. He let out a grunt of anger and stamped his foot.

"Look," Volhoric said. "I know you're suspicious of Imaly, and with good reason. But it's Mawyndulë or her. One person has blown the horn. If another Fhrey doesn't do so before this time tomorrow, then Mawyndulë is fane by default, and he'll rule for the next three thousand years. The Miralyith will continue to dominate the Fhrey people, and every last Rhune will be hunted to extinction. You know that as well as I do. With him, you know what you're getting. With Imaly, you at least have a chance for peace."

Imaly softened her gaze and added a little smile, a motherly expression. "Suri, you were a prisoner, and I freed you. You lived with me. I took care of you. Don't you owe me this?"

"No—I don't." Suri shook her head.

"But I got you out! I took the collar off!"

"To be kind? Why did you wait so long to do this? How many gilarabrywns did Lothian make? And what would have happened to Makareta if your plan had worked?"

Suri looked again at the torn body of her friend, then narrowed her stare at the old Curator, who didn't dare reply.

The four of them stood facing one another across the stained marble.

"Suri," Imaly said after no one spoke up. This time she did so without the pleading or the false motherly tone. "You're right. I didn't tell you the whole truth, and you can't trust me, but that doesn't change the fact that it is still him or me. No one else will challenge because only a Miralyith can hope to win, and there are none within three days of here. You have to choose. Who do you want to be fane?"

Suri remembered Arion saying, *"Suri, you can be the difference. You can change the future. It's up to you."* And in that moment, everything made sense.

The future was hers to decide. The problem was she didn't like her options.

꙰

No one moved or spoke for a long time.

Suri shifted her gaze from Mawyndulë to Imaly with occasional short trips to the still-smoldering body of the fane and the remains of Makareta. She also took notice of Lothian's larger bodyguard, whose name she didn't know, and Synne, who had gone unnoticed as she was almost totally buried beneath a fallen column.

Imaly's plan had led to this. She didn't care what happened to the people she manipulated. Would her rule bring further disasters?

On the other hand, Mawyndulë had killed Arion, and Suri had learned firsthand what sort of person he was during her time in a cage on her travels to Estramnadon.

As she stood and thought, Suri began to wonder if there might be a third option. She could wait until a day had passed—hold out until Mawyndulë became fane—and *then* kill him. The problem with that idea was that she wasn't certain if the whole Protection of Ferrol thing would still remain in effect. She considered asking, but doubted she could trust their answers. That was the problem: She couldn't rely on any of them.

As Suri struggled to find a solution, an annoying sound pestered her—a nearby scratching noise.

Suri looked at each of them. Imaly wasn't moving, neither was Volhoric or Mawyndulë.

The sound came from right in front of Suri. Looking down, she noticed small scratches appearing on the marble floor. Suri took a step closer.

Imaly looked at her. "What are you doing?"

Suri shook her head. "Nothing."

Imaly faced Mawyndulë, who was also watching the scratches as they appeared in front of Suri. "Is it you?"

Mawyndulë shook his head.

"It's not the Art," Suri declared.

"Well, someone has to be doing it!" Imaly exclaimed, growing more agitated as she stared at the ground.

Suri looked at Minna.

First, I broke my toe, then it rained, then . . .

Big events have an attractive, cumulative quality. Suri reflected on this and quickly modified her statement. *Maybe it's more like an intersection, a crossroad where things meet.*

This could be the moment Arion foresaw—an event so important that it could be seen from a distance.

Minna is here. I'm here. Mawyndulë is as well, and now there is a scratching without a source. Nothing is accidental. Nothing.

Suri crouched down to study the scratches. They were making a series of pictures. The first was the unmistakable shape of the horn that Suri held. The second appeared to be that of a spear. The butt end started at the horn and the tip was aimed at the last image. It began as a rectangle, taller than wide. As more scratches were added, Suri could see it was a drawing of a door, and not just any entryway.

Suri understood the message but had no idea who was giving it to her or why.

"Who are you?" Suri called out.

More scratches appeared, forming in a new place to the side of the old images. Everyone watched the progress as they appeared.

This time it drew the unmistakable image of an eye. Then another spear was drawn with the point going up away from the eye. The scratches stopped, and after a few minutes Suri said, "Is that all? I don't understand."

That's when Minna yipped.

The wolf trotted to Suri's side and looked up.

"You know what this is all about, don't you? That's why you're here."

The wolf yipped again.

"I hope *someone* knows what's going on," Volhoric said.

"Out with it, Minna. What does this drawing mean?"

In reply, the wolf looked up again.

"That's not an answer," Suri said.

The wolf came over and sniffed the markings, then looked up.

Suri continued to watch, puzzled. Finally, Minna threw her head back and howled. The sound echoed loudly under the dome. The noise startled Imaly, who flinched. Volhoric took a step backward. Mawyndulë raised his hands, but a glance from Suri stopped him.

Minna continued her wail. Howling had always been something the two did for fun—both would throw back their heads and harmonize. This hardly seemed the time or place for forest songs, but little had made sense so far, and the only one in that room Suri trusted was Minna. If Suri's sister felt the need to sing, who was she to argue with the world's wisest wolf?

Suri threw her head back and—

That's when she saw it. High above them was the ceiling of the Airenthenon. The underside of the dome was painted to look like the sky with two people looking down from intertwined wooden chairs. One was a rather homely female Fhrey, but the other . . .

"Who is that up there?" Suri asked.

"My great-grandmother, Gylindora Fane," Imaly answered. "She was the first ruler of our people."

"Not her. The other one."

"Oh. That's Caratacus. He was her closest adviser."

Suri looked up again. "We call him Malcolm."

&

Suri was still looking up when she felt a tug on the horn. No one had moved, and at first, she thought it might have been Minna, but the wolf had gone toward the door. Being held by the strap Suri had looped over her head and under one arm, the horn wasn't being taken from her, but it was most definitely moving. Suri didn't sense any use of the Art. Minna gave another yip from where she waited. Then Suri felt more movement from the horn, a light pull, a gentle tugging in the direction Minna wanted to go.

Yip! Minna scratched at the door.

Suri glanced back at the scratches. "I think I know what to do," she told the others. Then, with a flick of one finger, the door opened. She glanced at the prince, but this time, Mawyndulë made no effort to stop her.

Minna rushed out.

"If you take the horn," Imaly said. "Mawyndulë will be fane."

When it came to choosing who to listen to, Imaly or a recently resurrected Minna, the decision was easy. Suri had no idea how any of it was possible. She didn't know why her dead sister had returned and appeared in Estramnadon of all places, but she also had no idea how fish breathed or birds flew. Mysteries didn't bother her. Seeing Malcolm's face was answer enough, and without another word, she chased after Minna.

No one made an attempt to stop them. The crowd of Fhrey that had gathered at the entrance and down the stairs pushed and shoved to give the pair room to pass. Minna led the way, trotting down to the plaza and then straight for the Garden. As Suri ran to keep up, she noticed a flicker of light, a faint twinkling that appeared to follow closely behind Minna.

Suri heard yelling. The noise didn't come from behind her. It didn't originate from the Airenthenon. Such a disturbance would have been expected. Suri assumed that once she abandoned Imaly and Volhoric, Mawyndulë would exact his revenge. He would do something to make them shriek in pain, but no such commotion rose. Instead, the yelling came from in front of her.

As she approached the Garden, Suri discovered another crowd. This one was only a dozen or so Fhrey, but their shouts were drawing more.

"The Door!" someone cried. "The Door has been opened!"

Those who had gathered stared in wonder, but no one ventured near. Suri noticed wolf tracks in the snow. The ones she followed and an identical set going in the opposite direction. "So this is where you came from, Minna? Is this how you got here?"

The crowd of Fhrey in their flapping winter cloaks backed up as Suri and Minna approached. The wolf trotted past them without a glance, and Suri followed her lead. Once more, she noticed a flicker of light, but now it was more of a shimmer.

Approaching the Garden Door, Suri noticed it stood open about two feet, a little hump of snow pushed up by it. A larger set of tracks led in, but without pause, Minna entered. What was good for Minna was fine with Suri, so she followed. Once inside, the shimmering light took on a more defined form, and Suri realized that what she had been seeing was the ghostly figure of a woman.

ॐ

Behind the door was a sizable room. At its center was a grand but deceased tree. In the darkened interior, the shimmer was more readily seen: a young woman draped in a Rhen-patterned breckon mor, who watched Suri with eager eyes.

"Brin?" Suri said.

"You can see me?" Brin's voice was strange, distorted as if she spoke from the opposite end of a long, hollow log. *"Can you hear me, too?"*

Suri nodded. "But . . . what . . . how . . ." Suri couldn't figure out a way to frame the question. There was too much to ask and too few words.

"I'm dead," Brin replied, and then quickly added, *"at the moment, at least. Hopefully it's only temporary. I must look like a ghost to you—I can't see it myself, but I suspect to you I'm all glowy and see-through. Is that right?"*

Suri nodded again.

"You can see me now because we're near an entrance to Phyre where the barrier between the worlds is thin. They blend a little. Normally you can't—at least you couldn't when Minna and I first found you up on those steps. I can't

believe I was reduced to drawing pictures with the key. Hope I didn't damage it. You really should have learned how to read, you know." Brin frowned and waved her hands in frustration. *"Never mind all that. It doesn't matter. I'll explain later. The real point is that we came to save you. But . . ."* Again, frustration washed her face. *"You didn't need saving, and—and as it turned out—your salvation wasn't the goal after all. Malcolm sent me to get that horn."*

Suri had no idea how someone could be *temporarily* dead. All she knew was that this was indeed Brin. And that left her wondering if she ought to feel sad or not.

"I know this doesn't make sense. I know it all sounds crazy, but it's true. I need to take that horn back with me to the Dragon Camp so Nyphron can blow it. He'll be the one to make the challenge."

"It won't work." Suri frowned. "It has to be blown by tomorrow."

"I know." Brin nodded. *"I heard. But I'm pretty sure I can make it in time. Distances are shorter in Phyre than on Elan, and I can get there through this pool. In the afterlife, I'm* very *fast. You really ought to see me. Since I'm traveling east to west I might have some extra time. I'm not sure how much, but it could help. Roan probably would know better, but she's lost in the Abyss."* Brin threw her head back and clenched her fists in frustration. *"Oh, Grand Mother, I know I'm messing this up, I know none of what I'm saying makes any sense, but there is too much to explain, and I have so little time that I can't—"*

Suri held out the horn. "Here. Take it."

"You sure?"

At the sound of those two words, Suri felt tears rise. Sometimes the Art was magical in the way it wove its patterns. Some were powerful, some complex, but some were just plain beautiful. Suri nodded. "Pretty sure."

As Brin took the horn, Minna yipped.

They weren't alone. Standing by the tree, within the tangle of its bony roots, stood a person.

"You again?" Suri said, recognizing the fellow she'd met in the Garden when visiting Arion's home.

"I've waited a long, long time," he replied, and she noted sadness in his voice, and that Minna had positioned herself between them.

The man wiped his face; he had been crying.

"Are you all right?"

"No," he said, and ran a hand over the trunk of the dead tree. "He killed her. Maybe he didn't create this prison, but make no mistake: Her death is on his hands." The man sounded devastated, bereft. "We all loved her. I didn't think him capable of . . . she gave him immortality. She saved him." He took a step toward the ghost of Brin. "You know where he is, don't you?"

"I don't know who you are talking about. Nor do I know who you are."

"I'm looking for my brother," he said with disgust. "I'm Trilos. Second son of Elan and Eton. First to die. First to be murdered. First victim of Turin. And I'll see him punished for his crimes."

"Your brother has changed," Brin said. *"He's trying to make up for his mistakes. He's working to fix the world."*

"This," he shouted and pointed at the tree, "is how Turin *fixes* things!"

Brin moved a step back.

"But Elan herself told me so."

"She's his mother! After I destroy him, she'll still love *me*, too. She'll say she's disappointed, but she'll still love me. She'll have hope that I, too, can change. But Turin *won't*. He can't. He is evil and must be destroyed. That's what the Golrok is for. The Last Battle of the First War will see the death of Turin, and I plan to bring it about."

"But he's immortal. He cannot die."

"Then there's no reason not to tell me where he is." Trilos took another step forward.

"I don't actually know. It's been many years since I've seen him."

Trilos stared at the ghost of Brin for a moment. "Fine. It wouldn't matter if you told me. He can see the future and will know to disappear. But I'll take the key he gave you." Trilos held out his hand.

The moment he did, Brin retreated back a step.

"It doesn't belong to you, and it shouldn't belong to him. Give it to me."

Suri had no idea what they were talking about, but she didn't like the sound of Trilos's voice. More important, neither did Minna. The wolf hunched her shoulders, fur raised, a deep growl issuing through bared teeth as she slowly crept forward.

This got Trilos's attention. He turned, stunned. "You, Gilarabrywn? You would stop me? Are you aware your name has become synonymous with beasts of destruction? Ironic, don't you think? More than anyone— how can *you* defend Turin?"

Minna's growl only grew louder.

Trilos gritted his teeth and raised a stick he held in his hand as the two faced off.

Unsure what Trilos and Brin were talking about, Suri was certain of one thing: If Trilos fought Minna, he was going to face her, too. Suri guessed he wouldn't be as easy to subdue as Mawyndulë. He wasn't normal. Nothing about him made sense—but there was power within. Hidden and restrained like that of a seed, but there was no mistaking his ability. Suri reached out, searching for a source of her own, but in that place she found none. The tree was dead, the grass gone. A small trickle of strength seeped in through the still-open door. The wind was calm, but people were still gathering outside. Their source was weak and to fight him, she would need more power.

There's another source, she realized then. *There always has been.*

She felt it rise within her, and she blew across old coals, watching them start to glow, the heat rising within her.

So what emerges after a butterfly is sealed in a chrysalis? Suri smiled. *It only took being buried alive to discover the obvious.*

"Brin, go," Suri ordered. "Leave now!"

The ghostly figure of her friend, who was clutching the horn to her chest, didn't hesitate. She retreated toward the muddy pool.

Suri straightened her back, hands up, palms out. She wasn't certain what she would do. This, she felt, wasn't going to be a battle of Artists. Trilos wasn't a Miralyith. He was both something more and something less.

Her first inclination was to weave a shield, a dome perhaps, but she didn't know what she would have to block. She had to be ready for anything.

The truly odd aspect of this confrontation was that she was inside this arboreal tomb—a dark place that smelled of withering wood and rotting soil—and she was facing a menace beyond her comprehension. Suri's understanding of the situation was limited to a spattering of comments and the inadequate hints gifted to her by the Art. All of which amounted to a few charred chicken bones in the dirt as seen by moonlight. Suri, however, was good at reading signs, finding patterns, and foretelling the future from nothing more than cracks and smudges. At that moment, the omens were not good.

If she was honest with herself, they were absolutely horrific. And yet she wasn't frightened or even worried. If anything, she was happy. For years, part of her had been dead, but now she was back, and she was free of her responsibilities to Arion, Persephone, Imaly, Malcolm, and the rest of the world. Suri felt like a girl again who was on a grand adventure with her best friend at her side. Even though the challenge before her held unimaginable danger, Suri didn't care.

This is what life is supposed to be.

She readied herself for the battle.

A voice came from everywhere and nowhere. "Not here, Trilos."

Suri had spent a lifetime listening for the voice of Elan, to hear the faint hidden messages that she gave, but never before had the Mother of All been so clear—so loud. The parental voice boomed with motherly exasperation.

"Have you no respect? You shall not desecrate this place. Try and you will fight me, too."

Trilos gritted his teeth. He shifted his gaze back and forth between Minna and the retreating Brin. Then he turned and looked at the tree. "Hasn't he done enough damage, Mother? When will you see him for what he is?"

Drawing himself up to his full height, he shouted after Brin, "I want that key!"

Brin didn't stop. Entering the murky pool, her shimmer faded.

Minna advanced, growling.

"I won't fight you here," Trilos told Minna. "You have the advantage in this place. But then you knew that, didn't you, O Wise One? Yet your wisdom fails you in this: Turin is evil, and you're aligning with the wrong side. The next time we meet, you shouldn't try to stop me."

Minna appeared unimpressed as she stopped growling. Her hair settled, and with a swish of her tail, she turned her back on Trilos and trotted for the door.

Suri followed.

"I mean it, Gilarabrywn!" Trilos shouted. "Stay out of it."

Suri and her wolf returned to the world of snow and ice. The Garden was filled with Fhrey, who, upon seeing her again, let out a collective gasp. They retreated like a flock of birds. Suri didn't recognize anyone, which wasn't strange given how few Fhrey she knew. But neither Mawyndulë nor Imaly was there.

She would have liked to have spotted Treya, to thank her for her kindness. She had been the only one in Estramnadon to treat Suri with compassion. If Brin hadn't shown up, Suri might have volunteered to be Treya's challenger, except she suspected the unassuming Fhrey had no interest in being fane.

As she walked past those in the crowd, a few of the bravest ones asked, "What's in there? What did you see?"

She didn't bother to answer. She wasn't comfortable with the press of the crowd, and she began moving clear. It was then that she heard a familiar voice.

"Suri?" Nyree called.

Arion's mother was on her way to the door, wrapped in a white winter cloak. Her face was knotted in confusion, fear, and amazement, as if Suri had grown long ears and a snout. No—she probably would have been fine with that. Seeing her emerge from the Door was something else altogether.

"I saw . . . you just came out of . . . but . . ." Nyree sputtered, her eyes shifting between Suri and the Door. The priestess caught sight of Minna, which only served to bewilder her further. Then she narrowed her eyes at Suri. "Who *are* you?"

Suri thought for a moment, and a smile came to her lips as she replied, "I am who your daughter always wanted me to be. I am the hope for peace between our peoples; I am the butterfly; I am the new Cenzlyor." Then she turned to the wolf. "Let's go home, Minna."

⁌

Entering the pool was painless the second time—*third time,* Brin corrected herself. This was her third drowning, though technically only the first one was real. Drowning implied a death. Since she was already dead, this was nothing more than a transition between worlds, which was likely why it was easier—that, and the fact she was more terrified to stay than to go. She hoped Suri and Minna would be all right, and guessed they would be because she had the key that Trilos wanted. Once she was gone, she hoped he'd have no interest in them. For a moment, she thought he might follow her, but given the effort she knew he went through to escape Phyre, she assumed he wouldn't. Despite this, after returning to Alysin, after crawling out of the pool into that wondrous paradise, she looked back. She spent precious seconds watching that surface, but it remained still.

Brin wondered if she could run as fast as she hoped. She hadn't really tested her newfound buoyancy since climbing out of the Abyss, and she wasn't certain if leaving and then returning might have hampered her abilities. Crossing Alysin would be her first test of speed. She took a tight grip on the horn and key, crouched, focused on the door to Nifrel, and ran. She hardly saw the little stone house or the fruit trees. The few people she passed did not appear to move, as if frozen in time. A moment later she was at the mirrored doorway.

Faster than I thought! Brin recalled her previous fears of the queen, of Drome, of the broken bridge, and she smiled. *If I can run this fast, imagine what I can jump!*

"Brin!" Raithe called to her. "Wait."

He and Aria were near the door. Both trotted toward her, grinning as if they knew what had happened, or perhaps they were just happy to see her.

"I did it!" Brin shouted. "I have the horn. I just need to get it back to Nyphron."

They both beamed at her.

"We never had a doubt," Aria said, her hands clasped before her. She hesitated, then took a breath. "Can you tell me something? Was Gifford— was my son happy? Did he live a good life?"

Brin didn't know how to answer. She couldn't lie, not in that place, not to Aria. She endeavored to frame the answer as best she could. "Near the end he did. For the last few years—yes—I think he was happy."

"I still say you shouldn't underestimate him," Raithe told them both. "That man has more reserves than anyone I know. He may have fallen into the Abyss, but—"

"But he's good at falling," Brin finished for him as a new thought dawned. "And Roan can figure anything out." Brin fished the key out from under her armor, which had returned when she entered back into the underworld, and held it up to them. "I need this to get out, but I don't need to take it with me."

"Brin—" Raithe started.

"No, listen. I believe the way back to Elan can be opened and held clear the same way Tressa held open the door to Nifrel. If that's true, I can leave the key in Rel for the others to use if they get out." Brin frowned. "But they'd need to be able to—wait! They can pass from Nifrel to Rel without the key, right? I saw Gifford's hand pass through the portal. He was almost dragged back. So it's possible for them to return to Rel, right?"

"Yes." Aria nodded. "As we told you, limitations here are what people place on themselves, and those who enter Nifrel expect they can also enter Rel."

"You can't leave that key in here," Raithe said. "It's too risky."

"It's also dangerous for me to take it out. Trilos knows I have it. If he finds me before I get to Malcolm—that will be worse. In here, it will be safer for now."

"But Malcolm will want it back. You can't—"

"It won't stay here. If the others don't claim it soon, I'll leave instructions for the key to be delivered to Muriel. She's safe. She's immortal. She can't use the key, and she's Malcolm's daughter. If the others do escape, Gifford will certainly come here. He'll look for you, and you can tell him. But urge Gifford to hurry, because you're right: It won't be safe in Phyre for long."

"Where will you leave it?" Aria asked.

"I don't know yet, but I'll find somewhere safe, someplace they can all find it."

She gave them both hugs, then turned toward the mirror where the face of a golden-armored hero looked back. "I have to go now."

"Good luck, and may Elan's and Eton's blessings go with you," Aria said.

"Give Persephone a kiss for me," Raithe said. "Tell her I understand why she made the choice she did, and I'm not angry. Let her know we can still be together, and I have the perfect place picked out. Tell her, if she still wants me, I'll be waiting for her."

Brin nodded, then steeled herself and pushed into Nifrel. As she did, she remembered Tesh's words once again. *"Promise me one thing—one lousy thing. That if things go bad, you'll run—that you'll run as fast as you can and save yourself . . . Will you promise that much? Please, Brin, promise me that."*

Brin was going to keep her vow and so much more.

CHAPTER EIGHTEEN

Dropping Rocks

When going forward doesn't get you where you need to be, going back will at least keep you moving.

— THE BOOK OF BRIN

Using his wadded cloak as a pillow, Gifford lay on his side in the crook between the wall and the tooth-shaped rock. Doing so messed with his mind because he knew he didn't have a cloak, but he didn't have a head, either. Between him and Tesh, Tressa was curled, head down, knees up, arms pulled tight like a newborn. Her eyes were closed, and she shivered and jerked, as if enduring a nightmare. Of all of them, Tressa suffered the most in death. She'd never had it all that good in life, but in the Abyss, *she* was the cripple. He reached out to her, wishing he could ease her suffering. That's when he realized that helplessness came in at least two forms: those who couldn't do for themselves, and the people who could offer little more than a hand on a shoulder.

Maybe that's how Tressa felt about me when we sat on the porch of Hopeless House.

Being trapped in the Abyss was a lot like his former home. He, Roan, Tressa, and Tesh were a set of lost misfits, ensnared by their own shortcomings.

But I escaped Hopeless House. How did I manage that?

He tried to think back, but everything was difficult at the bottom of Nifrel, and getting harder.

Gifford had been lauded as a hero after his miraculous midnight ride through the Fhrey camp, but that hadn't been what saved him. Odds were good that he would eventually slip back into the familiar role of the cripple. People might still offer him a smile as they passed, but in their eyes would be that old uncomfortable sadness. Eventually they would forget his deed, and so would he. But when that happened he'd still have Roan, and that was all he needed.

On the mornings when he couldn't stand up on his own, when he wet the bed, or when he couldn't find a word without an *rrr* sound to express what he needed, she had been by his side. And during the nights when he doubted himself, when the memory of his heroic deed grew hazy, all he needed was to touch her. That she no longer recoiled was proof of his salvation and the reward for his heroic ride. Roan had saved him; of that he had no doubt.

Why can't I do the same for her?

All of them were piled up like warmth-seeking puppies. Gifford reached for Roan, who had been cuddled against his back. He expected to feel her shoulder but found nothing. Gifford sat up and looked around, expecting to see her elsewhere in the cave, but it was dim, desolate, and Roan was nowhere to be seen.

He stared confused at the place where she'd been.

How can she be gone?

Gifford pushed to his feet and felt the weight—that strange heaviness that climbed onto his back, pulling him down. He knew that load, that drag of pointlessness and despair. He shouldered it now the same way he'd always endured life as a cripple. Hopelessness and the difficulty of standing and walking were as familiar as old shoes.

"I'll be back. Just going to look for Roan," he told Tesh and Tressa, figuring they wouldn't be pleased about losing his light, even as dim as it had become. Still, being in total darkness would be worse, although neither bothered to respond. He wished he could offer words of hope before leaving, but he had none to give.

Baffled as to why Roan would have left and where she would go, Gifford made a quick exploration of the cave, looping around the edges and stepping over the scattered tablets lying on the floor against the back wall.

Where are you?

Logically, he shouldn't worry. They were in the Abyss, a vast wasteland of nothingness. Nothing down there could—

Iver. The name flashed through his mind.

Concern shifted to fear and then jumped to rage. Gifford's light grew brighter as he left their cave. He crossed the black expanse, his feet crunching the frost as he searched among the craggy cliffs for the entrance to Iver's lair. He had difficulty remembering which niche was the home of the carver.

How long has she been gone? Did Iver walk right in and steal her? How could I not notice? Do I sleep that soundly? Does Roan? And why do we sleep at all?

Frustrated by an inability to remember the exact entrance to Iver's cave, Gifford's anger grew. He flexed his fists and noticed that the sword— the one Roan had made for him in Alon Rhist—hung at his side. His armor had disintegrated as he fell, but the sword was still there.

Has it always been?

He didn't think so, but he was glad to have it now.

Voices.

Gifford pivoted sharply and homed in on a dark spot in the cliff.

"She screamed the first time," Iver said, his voice emanating from the dark. "Grand Mother, how Reanna could howl. I stuffed rags in her mouth after that. Didn't want the neighbors to hear."

Gifford ran forward and nearly clipped his head on the top of the tunnel as he came upon them. Roan sat at the feet of Iver, who squatted on a flat rock near the middle of his little chamber. Iver lacked any light, but Roan still glowed a bit, and her light illuminated Iver's sagging face and empty eyes—the visage of a melting monster.

Roan's cheeks glistened with tears.

Gifford advanced.

Roan turned and raised her hands. "Gifford, no!"

Iver scuttled backward, watching him with eyes that weren't circles anymore but rather tall stretched ovals, a pair of black empty sockets.

"I'll make certain he never takes you again." Gifford moved in.

Roan grabbed him, her little fingers clutching his leg. "He didn't. I *came* here. I came to him."

Gifford stopped. "What? Why?"

Roan sniffled as she looked up at him. Her eyes were puffed and red, the ends of her hair wet and chewed. She quivered with emotion, and her fingers squeezed his leg as if he were a floating piece of debris and she were drowning.

"For Brin." Roan shook even harder.

Gifford was dumbfounded. He looked at the cowering, sagging flesh of Iver and then back at Roan.

Is she—she's—oh, Elan, she's going mad. Roan is losing her mind to the Abyss.

Gifford's light dimmed. "Brin? I don't understand."

"We promised. I promised. I told Brin I wouldn't stop trying to find a way out. I've thought and I've thought, and all I can come up with is that the answer lies with Iver. He's been the problem my whole life. I thought it was guilt—the guilt I suffered from killing him."

"What? You came to get forgiveness from *him*?" Gifford glared at the wallowing pile of flesh that had once been the worst kind of man.

"That wasn't it, but he *is* the one who is keeping me here."

Gifford let out a false laugh. "Oh, I can fix that. I can rid you of him *real* quick." He drew his sword.

Iver cringed, lifting saggy arms in defense.

"No! Don't!" Roan shrieked so loudly that it scared both of them. "You still don't understand."

Gifford understood just fine. Roan was losing her mind, and Iver was speeding up the process. He had been the one who broke Roan in the first place, and now he was doing it all over again.

He had always hated himself for not saving Roan when they lived in Dahl Rhen. It didn't matter that he was a cripple or that interfering with a master's treatment of his slave wasn't allowed. No one had actually known what was going on in Iver's roundhouse, but Gifford felt that he should have figured it out and done something. Now the Abyss was presenting the opportunity to make up for past failures.

"He'll never be able to hurt you again."

"It's not him," Roan sputtered as more tears fell from her eyes. "It's not anything he is doing. It's me—what *I'm* doing."

He's got her again!

Gifford had never understood the hold Iver had on Roan and her mother. If it had been Moya in that roundhouse, she would have worn Iver's head for a hat. But Roan and Reanna were timid. Their wills, their sense of themselves, had been eroded by years of degradation. Now he was doing it all over again. He was using guilt and fear to—

"Don't you see, Gifford? I'm the one at fault here."

"No, Roan, you aren't! That's just what he wants you to think. That's how he controls and manipulates. He steals your sense of self-worth. Iver belittles and demeans until you think his beatings and abuses are your fault, but they're not. He's the evil one, not you. You're the victim."

Roan's eyes went wide, and she nodded. "Yes! Yes! Exactly!"

Thank the Grand Mother. I'm still able to reach her.

"That's it. That's the problem. Thank you, Gifford. You're right. I am the *victim*. I always have been."

Gifford was surprised this was coming as such a revelation.

Even geniuses have blind spots, I guess.

"I have to stop being the victim," Roan said with grave seriousness. "There's only one way to do that. Give me your sword."

Gifford understood and handed her the blade. "He deserves it, Roan. Remember that."

Roan stood up and raised the sword in both hands, facing Iver, who continued to cower like a squirrel in a rainstorm. "What you did," she told Iver in a shaking voice, "to me and my mother during all those years of torture is something that no one should endure." She looked at Gifford. "Even though I'm married to the most wonderful, loving, caring man in the world—I still have nightmares because I can't get out from under your shadow or escape my pain. I've hated you for so long, and I've never realized that in doing so, I was dragging you with me. All my hate was tied with fear, regret, and shame. It all made an unbreakable knot that I would never be able to untie. That's the weight that I carry. The one I've always shouldered."

She reached Iver, who stared at her with his dark, elongated eyes that didn't look so monstrous now. They looked terrified.

"Roan, I know I—I know I did bad by you. I—"

"Oh, this hurts," she whispered.

Gifford wondered if she knew she was speaking aloud.

"Grand Mother of All, give me strength," Roan prayed.

She dropped the sword and took a step forward. As she did, Gifford saw fresh tears spilling down her cheeks. "Killing you didn't set me free, so doing it again won't, either."

Her light wavered.

"Roan? What are you doing?"

"The hardest thing I've ever done," she said, her words barely audible.

"Roan, I . . . I . . . ." Iver stammered.

"Shhh," Roan said as she came closer and knelt. "Iver." She said the word gently, as if she were speaking to a child rather than to someone who'd done countless unspeakable horrors. "You were a terrible man. A truly despicable person, but you're not anymore. You're dead. And it's not like I haven't done my own terrible things. I murdered you even though I could have run away, or at least tried to, but I didn't."

She took a steadying breath. "And while you didn't mean to kill my mother, I killed you on purpose. I wanted you dead, so I took your life." She shook her head. "None of us are perfect, least of all me. Everyone makes mistakes. The point is to learn from them. Padera used to say, 'There's always a better way' and she was right." Roan reached out and put her hand to Iver's cheek. "You see, I finally figured it out. I want to hate you for all the things you did, but that's just me hanging on to pain. If I wish to be truly free, I have to let it go." She nodded. "Iver, I—" She took a breath. "I forgive you, Iver." She leaned in and kissed him. "I truly and honestly do."

Gifford stared in wonder as Roan put her arms around the carver and held him close as they both cried.

As they rocked, Roan's light stopped flickering, quit wavering, and began to grow.

↵

By the time they left Iver's cave, Roan was so brilliant that Gifford had trouble looking at her. He was brighter, too, and together they lit up the open expanse from cliff to cliff.

Together they walked hand in hand back across the frost. As they did, Gifford realized he felt lighter than he had even before Brin left. He was thinking of this and staring across at the base of the pillar when Roan abruptly stopped. Her head was up, her eyes wide.

She pointed. "Look! Look!"

Tilting his head, Gifford searched the blackness overhead and was stunned to see a light.

Together they watched as something bright flashed overhead. It looked like a falling star except that it streaked left to right—from the top of the pillar toward the Plain of Kilcorth.

"Brin," they said in unison.

"She did it!" Gifford clapped.

"She's going back," Roan said. "She's going home."

و

Tesh was groggy and squinting in pain at the bright light.

For a moment, he thought Brin had returned, but the light came from Roan, whom he could barely see amid her brilliance. Gifford, too, looked brighter, but Roan was a star.

"Brin did it," Gifford told them, "and Roan has figured out how we can, too."

"There isn't anything pressing us down. The weight is what we carry," Roan explained. "We have no bodies, but our spirits are crushed by our regrets, our hate, our guilt. We're like people who have reached the bottom of a lake by holding heavy rocks. To get out, all we need to do is drop the rocks."

Tesh looked at Tressa, who reflected his skepticism.

"It's true!" Gifford said. "Roan forgave Iver, and when she did, her light—well, you can see for yourself. Then . . . then she made me do it." Gifford frowned. "Trust me when I say it's not easy. You can't just say it. You have to mean it. You have to accept and believe. It's not—well, it's culling hard is what it is, but not really, you know?"

Tesh and Tressa shook their heads.

"What I mean is that . . ." He looked helplessly at Roan, the way he used to when he couldn't find a word without an *rrr* sound.

"He means that doing it isn't physically hard, but it requires admitting you are wrong about something you have always known you were absolutely justified in. That's the battle. You have to fight yourself, sometimes against your own sense of identity. You must sacrifice your pride and dignity as well. It all feels so horribly wrong, like spring giving way to winter, or water falling up. That's what makes it difficult. It goes against everything you believe, but worse, it goes against everything you *want* to believe. And yet once you do it, when you let yourself fall, when you give up fighting and just accept that you aren't going to hate anymore—as terrible as that feels to do—the pressure disappears, and you realize it was an illusion.

That the hate only existed in you, and keeping it is the same as cherishing an addictive poison that's making you sick. Looking back, it doesn't even make sense. But getting there, crossing that chasm—it just seems too wide to jump until you look back and see it was only a crack."

Tesh sat up straighter.

"So, what?" Tressa asked, her voice groggy, her words slurred. "We all have to give Iver a hug or something?"

"No," Roan said. "You have to discover what's weighing you down and let go of it. It will be different for everyone."

Tesh sat back, considering this. It didn't take much study for him to find his burden. He hated the Fhrey, the Galantians, and Nyphron. Roan was asking him to just forget what he'd lived most of his life for.

No, not forget—forgive.

Roan wanted him to kiss Nyphron and say, "Hey, look. I know you murdered my family, my whole clan, burned our homes to the ground and laughed while you did it, then started a war letting my people die to serve your selfish ends. But so what. That's all in the past—friends?"

"You're insane," Tesh told them both. "I can't do that."

"Neither can I," Tressa said.

"You can." Roan knelt down, nearly blinding them. "You just *won't.* But if you don't, you'll stay here. Think about the logic of that. You're willing to let them punish you further? To give them the power to ruin you for eternity rather than forgive? Where's the sense?"

"Not everything makes sense," Tesh threw back.

"Yes, it does. If it doesn't, you're probably not looking at it right."

Tesh was shaking his head. What she was asking was impossible. Even if he wanted to, he couldn't. "It's not like I can just turn it off. I've lived my whole life hating them. You're asking me to do magic here, to just wave my hand to erase my memory."

Roan shook her head, making the light shift back and forth. "No, actually that would be too easy. You *have* to remember. You have to really think hard and pull up all those horrific memories by the roots and then scatter them to the wind."

"You're asking me to unmake myself."

"You're more than hate, Tesh," Gifford told him.

Tesh wasn't at all certain about that. Everything he was had grown from that wellspring. His skill as a fighter was born out of his desire for revenge. His leadership of the Techylors, his fame, his respect came from his need to kill those who had butchered his people. He had always planned to win the war, to slaughter every living Fhrey. And when they were all gone, he would find Nyphron and explain how he had returned the favor of annihilating his tribe and burning down his house. Then, and only then, would he kill the focus of his pain. He could never give that up, never forgive Nyphron and the rest of the Fhrey. Never.

"Tesh." Roan inched closer so that he had to close his eyes. She took his hand in hers.

This was shocking. Roan never touched anyone except Gifford. With his eyes closed, her small hands felt like . . . they reminded him of . . .

"You promised Brin," she said.

Tesh opened his eyes, and was once more blinded by her light. He jerked his hands away and pushed back, shoving himself down the wall.

"Tesh?" Roan called at him out of that horrible light.

"That's not fair!" he said, his voice louder than he planned.

"But you did promise."

"Shut up!" he shouted.

"If you get out, there's a chance you'll see her again," Gifford told him.

"I'll never see her again! We've been here forever. She either succeeded and is back on Elan, probably married with kids, or dead and back in Rel with her parents—her parents and mine. And I'll never see *any* of them—*ever.*"

"It's not too late," Roan told him. "I just saw her—I just saw Brin."

"You're lying!"

"Roan never lies," Gifford reminded him.

Tesh knew that, yet he couldn't help himself. He was trying to hurt her—hurt Roan.

What am I doing?

Roan moved close again. "I saw Brin race across the top of the Abyss, heading for Rel. You can't mistake her light. I think she succeeded, so she's going home."

"We'll never catch her."

"If she stops at Mideon's castle—which she might, if only to see if we got out or to look for Moya—there might be a chance, if we hurry."

"No."

"You promised," Roan said.

"Quit saying that!"

"Do you think Brin knew you were lying to her?" Tressa asked.

Tesh cocked his head sharply and glared, feeling strangely betrayed. "So all the stories are true. You really are a bitch, aren't you?"

"Absolutely," Tressa replied, with no smile, no hint of humor.

"What about *you?* What great hate is keeping you here?" Tesh fought back, feeling terrible the moment he said it, and worse when he saw Tressa's eyes brimming with tears. He ought to know better. He was facing the same pain. This wasn't a game. The anguish they were experiencing was deep and cruel. Tressa wasn't one for tears, so seeing her eyes glisten showed just how deeply he'd wounded her. But misery was a sickness that insisted on spreading, and, like a drowning man, he was willing to shove her under to lift himself up.

Tressa looked down at her hands and mashed her lips together, swishing them around in an attempt to fight the tears. Then she squared her jaw as best she could. "I was expelled from Clan Rhen, punished for years, made invisible and untouchable for the unforgivable crime of turning a blind eye while my husband murdered Reglan and then tried to do the same to Persephone. All those people, the self-righteous geniuses—they figured it all out. Put all the pieces together and found me guilty." She looked up at each of them. "They were all wrong."

"So you hate them?" Gifford asked.

"Of course I do," Tressa said. "I despised everyone on that dahl for as far back as I can remember. Not for anything that they did, but because they couldn't see the *greatness* in me. The kicker is . . . they still don't see me for what I am."

Gifford glanced, confused, at Roan and Tesh.

"You don't see it, do you?" Tressa shook her head, frowned, and looked at Roan. "Even the genius hasn't figured it out.

"Konniger wasn't responsible for Reglan's death, nor did he plan to kill Persephone." Tressa sighed. "My husband was an idiot who needed help pulling his shirt on in the morning. You have no idea how many times the man nearly choked to death because he couldn't manage something as simple as swallowing. He had no ambition and no mind for planning. But I was tired of living in the pit that Konniger's sister called a house. I wanted the lodge and all those fine things beneath its roof. I longed for people to see me as grand, to be respected. That's why I married Konniger in the first place. I didn't love him. But I knew he could get me what I wanted, and I wanted to be Second Chair. Honestly, I wanted to be First Chair, but I just didn't think that was possible. Little did I know . . ."

"What are you saying?" Gifford asked.

Tressa smirked in disbelief. "You still don't get it? It wasn't Konniger at all. It was me. I killed Reglan, Holliman, Hegner, and Krier. I even tried my best to kill Persephone. I tried *real* hard. Konniger did the grunt work, of course, but it was all my idea. I had to force him, threaten and guilt him into it. Oh, the hours I spent belittling his manhood, his courage, not that he was all that strong to begin with. The man was a fool, but good with an ax. That's why I picked him. He was the perfect tool to get all I wanted."

They all stared in silence.

"I had so desired to put that smug Persephone in her place. I planned it for years. I figured out how I could maneuver Konniger into the position of Shield. Then, after killing her husband, all I had to do was threaten Maeve and she declared Konniger would be Reglan's successor. We had to tidy up a bit, of course. Holliman Hunt had to die because he knew too much. But

I got my chair. Then the Fhrey came and everything started to fall apart. I convinced my husband to kill Persephone. I gave Konniger his cloak and sent him on his way. But as it turns out, he was as inept at murder as he was at swallowing.

"Persephone knew. I saw it in her face when she came back. And what did she do?" Tressa's voice was cut off by a closing throat and a shuddering battle against tears. "She made up a story about how Konniger died a hero, fighting the bear. Said it right out loud in the courtyard. She did it to be nice to me. No one believed her because it was such a blatant lie. When people saw through it and sensibly blamed me anyway, Persephone told them not to."

Tressa was losing her fight with her tears as one slipped over the brim and slid down her cheek. "Even after all I did, that bitch, protected me." She wiped her face and nose, a sour expression squeezing her cheeks. "So if you want to know who it is I hate, if you haven't managed to work out this little puzzle, it's really quite easy. It's me. I despise everything about myself. I hate that I was so greedy that I took lives and ruined others. I hate that I returned true kindness with suspicion and anger because I couldn't believe it—because I would never do such a thing as be helpful for no reason. I hate that I only ever thought of myself, and never even got anything for my single-minded efforts. So you see, I'm not leaving—because unlike the rest of you, I belong here. I deserve this. I want this."

Tressa then whirled on Tesh. "So you—you little culling fool—*you* have no excuse." She added a nasty, taunting whine to her voice and said, "So the Fhrey killed your family—so what? They killed a lot of families. What if a pack of wolves had killed them? Would you devote your life to hunting wolves? And what if it was starvation or sickness? Or what if your mother had fallen in a well, or your father through thin ice, what then? What then, Tesh? People die—people die all the damn time.

"You know what else does that? The sun comes up. It rains. Leaves fall. Not here, of course, but back on Elan. Some of it is good, and some of it is terrible, but that doesn't mean you throw your life away. Ask yourself this, hero: The revenge you're after, who is it for? Not your family, not your clan. They've all put it behind them and are happy in Rel. So who is it really for? Who would ask you to throw your life away, to toss eternal happiness aside for their petty desires of revenge? Ask yourself if a person like that deserves such a sacrifice?" Tressa took a labored breath. "I can tell you with firsthand knowledge they don't. Because I am that sort of person. I know I'm a bitch. That's why I can't even stand up."

They heard a cough, and in that dark quiet, it rang as loud as a gong. Looking over, they saw a large drooping man who dragged himself toward them, using the wall for support.

"Iver?" Roan said, surprised.

Tesh watched her. He didn't know the circumstances between them, but from the earlier comments, he gathered they weren't friends.

"Just thought you ought to know," the man said with effort. "It's snowing, so I think they've seen your light, or maybe Brin's. I don't know."

"Who?"

"The Typhons," Iver said with the same miserable tone one might expect from a man delivering home the dead body of a loved one.

Something was strange about this plump man whose bottom was bigger than his top. His eyes were black and long and, as far as Tesh could tell, empty. He didn't approach but kept his distance.

"Always snows before they come. We hide in the little caves so they don't eat us." Iver's voice had an odd quaver. "Light attracts them."

Gifford looked at Roan, his eyes edging toward panic.

"This cave here," Iver said, looking around. "It's too big. They can get in. That's why no one took it. You can come to my cave if you like. Can't even get a finger in there. *Maybe* it will help."

That *maybe* didn't sound hopeful.

"We're going to climb out," Roan told him. "Aren't we?" she asked the rest.

"Absolutely," Gifford said. "Tesh? You don't want to be eaten, do you?"

Tesh shook his head. "Wasn't on my list this morning."

"So you'll try?"

"Why not? Later on, I'll bake a cake in the shape of a castle, and we can eat it while riding on giant swans."

"Sounds like a plan."

"You can come, too," Roan told Iver.

The melted man only shook his head, then held up a wooden figurine. "I wanted to give you this."

Roan took the carving. She stared down at it, and her free hand rose to her lips. "It's my mother. It's beautiful."

"I never meant to kill her, and I—I always wanted to give her back to you. This is the best I can do. Not even certain how I did it. Never been able to do anything like it before, but after you left, after you kissed me—I could."

Iver turned around and with dragging feet headed back into the dark.

CHAPTER NINETEEN

Horizontal Star

The secret to Phyre is realizing that the things we think are real in life are fictions in death, and that which we label as intangible fabrications while we are beneath the sun, are everything when we are in the dark.

— THE BOOK OF BRIN

As if she sat upon a massive throne, Moya lounged in the crenel between two stone merlons, dangling her legs off the front of Mideon's great curtain wall. Crenel, merlon, curtain wall—in her time spent in the Belgriclungreian fortress, Moya had added these architectural terms to her vocabulary, along with a dizzying array of dwarven rebukes and profanity. Jobbie and bawbag were easy enough to grasp after the first few times she heard them—and she heard them a lot. "You're a wee scunner" was a bit harder, but she figured it meant to call a person a nuisance. For a long time, Moya had no idea what "awa' an bile yer heid" meant. She liked the sound and hoped it was something truly terrible that she might add to her regular repertoire. After finally asking, she was disappointed to learn it only meant "get lost." Moya found frequent use for it nonetheless, and it came with the added benefit of at least sounding terrible.

"Why are we here?" she asked Beatrice.

The Little Princess had insisted Moya accompany her to the battlements. But when they got there, they had done nothing but stare out at the Plain of Kilcorth.

"In a hurry to get back to my father's hall, are you?" Beatrice stood before an adjacent crenel, peering out. At her height, she could rest her chin on the stone without bending.

Moya didn't bother answering the jeer that masqueraded as a question. Instead, she rotated, bending her knees and placing them against one merlon while putting her back against the other. She sat at a dizzying elevation, but she held nothing but contempt for heights. Still guilt-ridden, Moya contemplated jumping into the Abyss. Compared with that drop, dangling her toes off Mideon's wall was as frightening as swimming in a knee-deep pond. She'd have done it, if not for Tekchin, who continued to tether her. Although his injuries were extensive, Moya felt the Galantian had been slow in recovering from his wounds, and she suspected Beatrice. *The Little Princess*—Moya's mocking title for her— appeared interested in Moya staying put. Why, she had no idea. After the battle, Moya refused to forgive Beatrice for her betrayal. No matter how much The Little Princess tried to explain, that's how Moya saw it. She had known the tragedy that would occur and had done nothing to intervene. She hadn't even warned them.

"You don't like it here, do you, Moya?" Beatrice asked. The dwarf's voice was soft and gentle, soothing in a way that Moya didn't care for. It felt like a lie.

"Plenty of hard stone and hatred—what's not to like?"

"Imagine it without the guilt. Would it be so bad here if you succeeded in your quest? If you returned to life, lived decades, and then died?"

"No chance of that."

Beatrice hummed to herself. She did that frequently, and Moya realized she despised it just as much as everyone else. It was The Little Princess's way of saying, *Ha, ha! I know something you don't, and I'm not going to tell you.*

"But if it were true," Beatrice pressed. "Would it be so bad? You and Tekchin here together?"

"No," Moya replied. "If it was just me and Tekchin, if everyone else got out, and Persephone was able to win the war—wouldn't be bad at all."

"You need to remember that."

"Why?"

Beatrice placed her little hands on the merlon, as if she were doing vertical push-ups. She lowered her head and sighed. "You have some rough times ahead. You're going to feel . . ." She gave up leaning against the stone. Instead, she folded her arms and rested them on the crenel as if it were a windowsill, and she were laying her head down to sleep.

"What am I going to feel?"

"I don't want to say you're prone to self-loathing, but well, you are. It doesn't take much for Moya to hate Moya. When that happens, you get ugly. You have a tendency to unintentionally hurt those around you. Then you hate yourself more, and matters spiral downward from there. Tekchin won't care. He's strong and understands more than you'll ever give him credit for, but there will be others. People for whom your words and actions will have a lasting impact. She won't be able to understand until it's too late, and what a terrible tragedy that will be for both of you."

"Who are we talking about?"

Beatrice smiled. "You haven't met her yet, and won't for several years—but she'll be a lot like you, much to the dismay of you both." She lifted her head and, resting her chin on folded arms, looked out at Nifrel. "You see, the world is about to change. It will be a very different place from what it was when you were born, which wasn't all that different than when I was born. For so many generations, everything has stayed the same. But upheavals are coming. You and the others have started a landslide that won't be stopped, and the landscape will change as a result. So much is on its way. Writing, industry and engineering, trade, exploration, inventions beyond your imagination, kingdoms and empyres."

"What's an empyre?"

"A huge realm made up of numerous kingdoms." Beatrice frowned. "The upheaval that is necessary to give birth to it is difficult to explain. I've seen what's to come and still have problems grasping it all. The world will become so very different. Yet at its core, everything will be the same. There is a continuous thread that has existed from the beginning—the invisible hand that moves the world forward and another one that opposes that order. We are part of that epic struggle. In the future, many people will refer to the conflict as Good versus Evil, and yet from my viewpoint, seeing it all laid out, I find it hard to decide which is which. That's another problem with seeing the future, by the way. Everyone thinks it's easy. You see something bad is going to happen, so the obvious solution is to stop it. But there are repercussions. Stopping one minor evil might create a greater one later on. You can see how that right there makes things tricky, but that's not all. It's not even the hardest part."

"What is?"

"When you see the whole picture, the colors blend: good and bad, light and dark, up and down. They can flip depending on time and place. For example, right now you don't like me very much. You hate being here, and you hold clear ideas of right and wrong, what you want and don't want. But the next time I see you, you'll be a different person with a better understanding of the world. The present Moya and the future Moya would heartily disagree over many things. And if that can happen to one person, imagine what it's like to see that same shift through the eyes of millions and over thousands of years. Who's right and who is wrong? It doesn't merely depend on who you are, but when and where as well. Everything changes all the time—including yourself. Nothing can be trusted. It's as much a guessing game as a skill, and the goal itself hides or changes faces, or flips altogether."

Beatrice laughed bitterly. "And I'm only an observer in all this. Well, mostly—the ball was kicked to me so I kicked it back. But I'm not actually playing. I couldn't handle it." She shook her head in amazement. "That's what it's all about, though. That's what each day is for—one more step that will bring the story closer to the end. We are merely observers. Still, each of us must play our part. We are only grains of sand, but without us, there is no beach, no place for the final stand. So in a very real sense, we are the footholds that future generations will rise up on to face one another and decide what is right and what is wrong, who wins and who loses, and what those prizes are."

"You seem to be telling me a lot," Moya said. "You're not normally this chatty."

Beatrice tilted her head to one side and smiled. "I envy you, Moya. What you're a part of, what you're about to see. You have a center seat at the great banquet."

"Okay, now you've got me worried. Is something terrible about to happen to me?"

"No—something wonderful." Beatrice pointed out through the crenel.

Moya caught movement beyond the wall. Out on the plain, she saw a light. It streaked like a falling star, only it wasn't falling. The light sped from left to right. Only visible for a few seconds, the sight was phenomenal, moving Moya to tears. "Brin."

❧

Moya wiped her eyes long after the light had disappeared. "Thank you," Moya told Beatrice. All of it finally made sense. The Little Princess had brought Moya up there to lessen her load. The trip wasn't an utter failure. Brin would make it out. Maybe she'd learned something that could save Persephone and the army. The guilt wasn't gone, but the load was lighter. "It helps knowing she'll get out. Did she save Suri?"

Beatrice grinned at her.

"What? You told me everything else. You can't tell me that?"

The dwarf remained silent.

"You're a wee scunner, aren't you? Why don't you awa' an bile yer heid, ya wee jobbie."

Moya was certain she'd unloaded a vile blast of homegrown insults at The Little Princess, but Beatrice remained undeterred. She continued to grin, only she did more than that—she beamed. That smile was powerful and tight, the way a person acted when they were bursting to tell a secret.

Finally, she gave in. "You're not done."

Moya narrowed her eyes. "What do you mean?"

"You don't get to stay here. You're going back, Moya."

"Going back? How's that going to work?"

"Brin has the key," Beatrice said.

Moya looked out at the dim landscape, which appeared all the darker after Brin's passing. "I figured as much, but she's also gone."

"Have a little trust, Moya. I'll give Rain his sword. You get Tekchin up. Tell him I said it's time."

"The two of you have been conspiring against me! I *thought* his recovery seemed too slow."

"We couldn't afford to take the chance that you'd do something stupid like jumping into the Abyss. They're going to need you—so is the world." Beatrice smiled. "No, Moya, you are not done yet. You have a long road of troubles ahead before you can return to me—before you can take your final rest. And you don't have a lot of time. You're in a race now. The queen saw Brin, just like we did. It will take her a little while to figure out exactly what that means. She'll waste time making the same assumption you just did— that once again the key slipped through her grasp. She will fret, scream, and terrify everyone around. Then eventually two things will dawn on her."

"What two things?"

"That a streak of light as bright as that one could never abandon loved ones so long as hope remains."

"And the second?"

"That in this place, light is hope."

CHAPTER TWENTY

Unlocking the Key

In the years to come, my trip through Phyre may become so hazy that it feels like a dream. But I am sure it will never leave me completely. When I lie on my deathbed, I might feel doubt, but not dread, because such worries are born from the unknown, and I have seen what lies beyond.

— THE BOOK OF BRIN

Darkness, absolute and insoluble.

Floating, drifting, rising, Brin held on to the feather and felt like a bubble rising toward the surface where, like all bubbles, she would pop. Yet for a long indefinable moment, she lingered in that peaceful ascension, not at all certain she wanted to reach the surface. Weight, light, and sound waited impatiently. Pain wanted in.

I have to go back. But for the first time, she wasn't sure she wanted to. In that moment of indecision, her bubble bounced against the surface.

It's just so nice to be without pain, fear, and the weight of the world on my shoulders.

"Brin?"

Did she really want to go back to that world of work and hunger? Return to the cold and the heat, the sadness and so much suffering?

"Brin!"

It was so nice seeing her parents again, playing with Darby.

"BRIN!"

The bubble burst.

A bright light hit her, then the sound of splashing water—and pain. She felt it in her chest, a burning married to a terrible weight that pressed down on every inch of her, a heaviness as if she were being crushed. Then convulsions racked her body, and she vomited from both her mouth and nose. All her muscles contracted as over and over she wretched and water gushed—a foul, dirty flood ejecting from her lips as her stomach drove its contents up her throat.

Air! I need air!

"That's it—that's it, cough it all up," a woman said.

Another burst of water was driven from her, and then she could breathe. She managed to pull in an exquisite bouquet of air before it was cut off, this time by a series of violent coughs.

"It's okay. You're fine now."

She didn't feel *fine*. Opening her eyes hurt, but she didn't have the strength to wipe them. Daylight and hazy figures were all she could see. A hand was on her back, a light reassuring pressure. Brin was on her knees, doubled over on something cold and bright—snow? Yes, snow. She could feel it crush under her. Grand Mother of All, was she cold!

Cold as death.

She'd had no idea how literal that phrase was.

Brin blinked enough times to vaguely see out of her left eye. Her right was still blurred. She was on the bank next to the pool.

Ice. The pool is frozen over.

She saw a hole in the middle, jagged pieces floating in black water.

"I need to get you back home, and get these wet clothes off. Are any others coming?"

"I . . ." That was all she could manage before her voice gave out. Her throat felt ragged and torn.

"Don't try to talk yet."

She shook her head.

Brin felt herself lifted by someone's arms.

She let her head fall, let it rock. That felt good, her first nice feeling since returning to life. She fell asleep or passed out. Either way, as she slept, her body must have done the work of living again—heart beating; blood flowing; lungs drawing in air—for when she woke, she heard the crackle of a fire and felt its warmth. She was naked before a hearth, a blanket wrapped around her. She felt hands rubbing, scrubbing hard, shaking her whole body.

She whimpered because being moved hurt. Her head throbbed, and her limbs ached.

"You're doing great," the woman said as she dried Brin's hair.

With eyes cleared of muck, Brin saw Muriel's face. She was in the woman's hut, which looked the same as before except the windows were wreathed in snow. Brilliant sunlight flooded the interior, shooting in at a sharp angle. Brin's nostrils remained lined with slime, and just like after a cold, she guessed it would be days before she was entirely free of the rank smell. Still, through that stench, she smelled something savory, and hunger woke with a fierce, desperate pang, a craven yearning that started her mouth salivating.

How long has it been since I ate?

"Ready for some stew?" Muriel gently lowered Brin's head and moved toward the little chopping table, carefully threading her way through the dangling strings of stones that hung from the ceiling. Muriel found a wooden bowl and returned to the hearth where Brin noticed a blackened pot simmering over neatly stacked coals licked by little flames.

Such a perfect blaze. My mother would be so impressed. Even Padera would have to admit that is one fine cooking fire.

Brin caught herself staring. Not *at* anything, just looking. She didn't want to move, and that included her eyes. She wanted to let her mind roam untethered. She didn't have the strength for anything else. Weak and heavy, her arms hung limp, her hands pooled in her lap, her bowed head making curtains of her hair.

My mother always brushed that aside. Drove her crazy. Did the same to Persephone and . . .

"How long was I gone?" Brin asked, her voice rough but working again.

"A few days," Muriel replied.

"Only days? Are you certain?" Turning her head and lifting her chin, Brin looked once more at the brilliant snow-bounced light and the decorative frost wreathing the windows. "It felt like years."

Muriel knelt down before the hearth, grabbed up a stick, and used it to hook the arm that held the pot. It swung out and away from the fire. "It's the snow." Muriel gestured at the windows with the stick. "Makes the whole world look different. It got cold right after you left. I kept the ice open for you, just in case."

"Thank you."

Muriel pulled a thick rag from a hook and used it to lift the pot lid. She stirred the contents a few times, then spooned two full ladles into the bowl. "Here," she said, holding it out. "Careful. It's hot."

"Thank you, again." Brin struggled to lift her arms, and she was surprised they still worked. She was able to take the bowl, which was warm to the touch. She brought it to her lips. Thick, with a clear broth and plenty of root vegetables, some sort of stew, she guessed, but she didn't put much thought into it. Brin was starved and would have poured the whole bowl down her throat if it hadn't been so hot.

She sat, feeling the heat warm her chest then settle into her stomach. Almost immediately the throbbing in her head eased. The cold that had shaken her body receded. The aches and pains that had stabbed her muscles faded a bit. Brin felt like a lantern whose wick had been lit once more. Tilting the bowl up, she took another swallow, and another, and then—

"The horn!"

Brin looked down at herself, but aside from the blanket she was naked. She looked at Muriel. She didn't have the horn, either. Brin scanned the hut in a growing panic.

I lost it! It didn't come out with me!

When she started to stand up, Muriel placed a hand on her shoulder, pressing down. "I have it. Relax."

That wasn't going to satisfy Brin, and Muriel appeared to know this. The woman got up and plucked the horn from atop Brin's pile of wet clothes. "Is this what you were after? I thought you said you were going to save a friend."

"We thought so, too." Brin took the horn. Its surface was still slick, and a little water dribbled out, leaving a wet stain on her blanket. "Do you know what it is?"

"You mean other than a ram's horn?"

"Yes."

Muriel shook her head and returned to stirring the pot. "But I know it's special."

"Why do you say that?"

"Because you brought it out of Phyre."

Muriel replaced the lid and pushed the pot back over the fire. The metal arm squeaked a bit with the effort.

Brin stared at the horn in her lap. In all the time she'd carried it, she hadn't bothered to look. It seemed like nothing more than an old ram's horn except . . . there were markings. She thumbed over the surface, feeling the indentations. *Writing.* The symbols were hers.

> Gift am I, of Ferrol's hand
> These laws to halt the chaos be.
> No king shall die, no tyrant cleaved
> Save by the perilous sound of me.

> Cursed the silent hand that strikes,
> Forever to his brethren lost.

DOOMED TO DARKNESS AND BEREFT OF LIGHT,
SO BE THE TALLY AND THE COST.

BREATHE UPON MY LIPS; AND ANNOUNCE
THE GAUNTLET LOUD SO ALL MAY HEAR.
THY CHALLENGE FOR THE KINGLY SEAT,
SO ALL MAY GATHER, AND NONE NEED FEAR.

BUT ONCE UPON A THOUSAND THREE
UNLESS BY DEATH YOU HEAR ME CRY.
NO CHALLENGE, NO DISPUTE PROCEEDS
A GENERATION LEFT TO DIE.

UPON THE SOUND OF CHALLENGE CAST
A BATTLE OF CONTENDERS WILL ENSUE,
COMBAT WILL BEGIN AND LAST
UNTIL THERE BE BUT ONE OF TWO.

A BOND FORMED BETWIXT OPPONENTS
PROTECTED BY FERROL'S HAND.
FROM ALL SAVE THE BLADE, THE BONE,
AND SKILL OF THE OTHER'S HAND.

SHOULD CHAMPION BE CALLED TO FIGHT,
EVOKED IS THE HAND OF FERROL.
WHICH PROTECTS THE CHAMPIONED FROM ALL
AND CHAMPION FROM ALL—SAVE ONE—FROM PERIL.

BATTLE IS THE END FOR ONE;
FOR THE OTHER ALL SHALL SING.
FOR WHEN THE STRUGGLE AT LAST IS DONE,
THE VICTOR SHALL BE KING.

"It says the winner will be king," Brin said. She looked at Muriel. "It doesn't say *fane*. That's what the leader of the Fhrey is called."

Muriel shrugged. "*Fane* is actually a name—the first ruler of the Fhrey was Gylindora Fane, and all other leaders adopted her name. *King* is what the world's first ruler called himself."

"Yes," Brin said, nodding. "He did. And the Fhrey couldn't read this anyway, so I suppose it was never meant for them. This is a message for others, for people in the future." She looked toward the windows again, at the slant of light, so sharp the sun had to be low. "Is it morning or evening?"

"Morning. Sun just came up."

"I need to get going." Brin pushed to her feet, surprised she could. That one bowl of stew had done wonders. "I need to run."

"Seriously? That's ambitious. What about the others? Won't they be coming?"

Brin hesitated, wavering on her bare legs. She bit her lip as it began to quiver. "Maybe. I'm not sure, but I can't wait for them. I left the key inside in case they make it."

Muriel's brows rose.

"It's in safe hands, but it'll only be there a short while. If no one gets back to the Rel Gate soon, it'll be given to you."

This made Muriel's mouth drop. "Me?"

"Sorry to impose. You will keep it for Turin, won't you?"

Muriel didn't answer.

"The whole thing—it was harder than we thought." Brin let out a sad little laugh at the absurdity of the statement. She looked again at the windows, at the light creeping across the floor. "I have to get back to the Dragon Camp before the sun sets tonight, or everything we went through will be for nothing. I have to get the horn to Nyphron."

It hit her then, slapped her hard as she remembered the distance. The trip to the swamp was less than a day's travel, but the trip *through* Ith had taken all night. She didn't have that much time, and in her present state, she felt a rising panic. "I really do have to go."

Brin grabbed her wet clothes, which were so soaked they dripped. They were as cold as ice. The soup—that miraculous meal—had helped, but she still felt tired and a bit dizzy. The idea of putting on those wet things, of wearing them out into the winter snow . . . Brin had forgotten the agony of living, but it came back with a crash. Clinging to the blanket, she couldn't help it. She started crying. "In Phyre, I was so fast and strong, but here—it's so cold and there's snow. I have so far to go and—and then there is the swamp. I'll have to wait for that tidal bridge or swim across and hope that *thing* doesn't eat me. Oh, Grand Mother of All, give me strength."

The tunic fell from her hands, and she heard it hit the floor with a sodden slap that sprayed her ankles.

Muriel came to her with a sympathetic frown and pulled her into a hug. "I'm sorry. The world is an ugly place. Trust me, I know. A perfect piece of glorious fruit that has since turned black with rot."

"But I'm supposed to make it better. We went to change things. That's what Malcolm—that's why Turin sent us. He's trying to fix things, and sending us through Phyre was a step in that direction."

"Turin isn't interested in fixing the world. Your mistake was putting faith in him. But then, a lot of people made that error. He is evil."

Brin shook her head. "No—you're wrong about him."

"No, I'm not."

"You are. I know you are." She sounded like an impetuous child even to herself. How foolish she must sound to Muriel. Still, Brin knew she was right, but she couldn't adequately explain. Some things were just beyond the realm of words and gestures. Some truths, the most basic ones, refused to be denied.

"You've known him for what? A few years?" Muriel said. "Turin is my father, I've known him—well, almost since time began. He's cruel, self-centered, unrelenting—"

"He's changed." Brin cut off what she thought might be a long list, all of which was irrelevant. "He's trying to make amends. I know he is. He wants to be good, and he can be."

"Yeah, right. When trees walk and stones talk."

Brin pulled back and stared at Muriel. "What did you say?"

Muriel didn't register her surprise. The woman was dug in, still focused on Turin and working at proving her point. "I just meant it's not possible. Turin is—"

"No. That's not what you said." Brin held Muriel at arm's length, watching her face and searching it for answers. She was looking for verification. "You said, 'When trees walk and stones talk.'" Brin reached up and carefully drew Muriel's hair back from her left ear, revealing a large freckle.

The woman brushed her hand away, annoyed. "What are you doing?"

"The freckle is there. I knew it would be. And you have a space between your teeth. I'm betting you can whistle through it. Can you?" Brin was starting to bounce on the balls of her feet as the energy of excitement grew.

Muriel stared at her. "How do you know that?"

"Because you're Muriel," Brin said.

"I know who I am. And so do you."

"Yes, but I'm in such a hurry—if I didn't hear you say that thing about stones and trees—I would have forgotten to tell you."

"Tell me what?"

"He called you Reely. Mu*riel*," Brin said, listening to how the word sounded. "Mur-*Reel*—*Reely*. It's a nickname. *Your* nickname."

Muriel stepped away from Brin. She staggered backward, threatening to overturn the stool behind her. She didn't respond at first; she didn't have to. Everything was on her face.

"How do you know all this?" she finally asked.

"I've read about you."

"You did what?"

"It's a long story. There are tablets in the Agave, carved thousands of years ago, and I know what they say. Many of them are all about you. Trilos made them."

Muriel's arms fell limply to her sides. She took another step back, and the stool finally toppled with a *clack*. "Did—did you say—*Trilos*?" Muriel remained staring at her. In her eyes, Brin could read the entire story as easily as she had read the tablets.

"Yes, and that's not all. I *met* him."

Muriel bent down, righted the stool, and sat. She was breathing hard. No longer looking at Brin, she studied the floorboards with great interest. "You—you actually saw him? You spoke to Trilos in Phyre?"

"No, not there. I saw him in Estramnadon."

Muriel looked up. "No." She shook her head. "That's not possible. He died and went to Phyre. Everyone—"

"He escaped," Brin told her. "Trilos *was* in Phyre. He was in the Abyss of Nifrel, but he managed to escape. It happened long, long ago."

Muriel was still shaking her head. "No." She stood up defiantly. "He couldn't have. No one can leave Phyre. Not without the key. And if he did, he would have . . . the first thing he would have done is . . . no—no!" She kicked a basket of stones, scattering them across the floor. "Trilos is still in Phyre. He's trapped there. He can't get out. He has to be. He *has* to be!"

Muriel's brow was furrowed. Her gaze shifted around the room as if searching for something. Then she turned sharply, and with an angry, accusing tone, she asked, "If he escaped, why hasn't he come to me? I'm not hard to find—even you found me!"

Brin felt devastated. The answer was unspeakable. If their situations were reversed, Brin thought how debilitating it would be to learn such a thing about Tesh. How many times worse must it be for Muriel? The person known as the Tetlin Witch hadn't found her way to this spot in the swamp by accident. She was like Aunt Needa's dog, Apple, curled up and waiting for the one person she cared for the most—waiting through eternity.

"You know," Muriel said, her eyes narrowing. "Tell me."

Brin hated doing it, and this time the idea of lying did cross her mind, but she couldn't bring herself to do it. She had no experience, no skill at deception, but more than that, the idea repulsed her. Brin was a Keeper, trained to speak the truth and taught to believe in the sacred value of honesty. She could no more deceive than she could fly.

Brin took a breath. "He's forgotten you."

Muriel blinked. "Forgotten me?"

"Yes." Brin began slowly, trying to be as kind as she could, but there was no way to soften this blow. "Trilos sacrificed the one thing he had left, his love for you. He gave up his memories, killing his only joy. The pain, the anguish of that sacrifice gave him the power to punch a hole between the worlds, but it erased you."

Muriel continued to stare at her, and Brin had no idea if Muriel believed her or not. Then the tears slipped down the woman's cheeks.

Feeling like she'd stabbed a friend, Brin reached out for her, but Muriel retreated, raising her hands to ward off the Keeper. Her shoulders rose as her entire body cringed.

"But he saved you, too," Brin offered as a sort of consolation. "He preserved his memories."

Muriel's face remained a mask of despair and bewilderment.

"He wrote everything down, carved it in stone." Brin showed her a smile, but it wasn't much of one. Brin didn't have much to give, but she gave what she had to show Muriel that all might not be lost. "He left himself a record of everything he knew or felt about you, just like I wanted to do with my parents. I did it so future generations would know them as I had. But Trilos—I think Trilos left the memories for himself. He stacked them neatly in Phyre where they would never be touched. That's where I found them. That's how I learned about the two of you. He wrote down how he met you, how you two fell in love. I know everything he felt. Trilos worked at capturing all the little details, pouring all he knew, all he remembered of you into those words. I think he put them there so one day he might somehow reclaim what he lost. But . . ."

"What?" Muriel took a step back toward her.

"I'm not sure he even knows the tablets exist or realizes their importance."

"You said you *read* them?" Muriel grabbed her arms. "What does that mean?"

Brin nodded. "It's a form of communication. Something I invented. Well, Trilos helped, too. It's difficult to explain, but it lets me know everything he thought and felt."

"And you're a Keeper—you can remember it all, can't you?"

Brin thought a moment and recalled the golden field on a spring morning. "Yes. Yes, I can."

"And you met him, so you know what he looks like and where he is. You can find him again and give back his memories." Muriel crossed the small distance between them and grabbed hold of the blanket, tugging Brin close. "Oh please, Brin. Please. I beg you. Please do this for me."

Outside, a wind whipped up. It whistled, then howled. Snow flew past the windows, making them dark, then light, then dark again. Muriel took no notice of the sudden storm. Her eyes were fixed on Brin's. Then she seemed to stretch, to grow taller. As she did, the little door began to rattle.

The Tetlin Witch.

"There's something else," Brin said.

"What is it?"

"When trees walk and stones talk, is a message your father sent me as a reminder. He wanted me to let you know that Trilos is no longer trapped in Phyre. To give you hope that the two of you can be reunited. I'm right about him trying to fix things. He knew I would be in a hurry and would have rushed right out of here without telling you. But that didn't happen because he went to so much trouble to plant that phrase of yours in my head. Your father lived with us for many years, but when he found out that someone escaped from the Agave, he left. He must have been looking for proof that it was Trilos, and when he found out, he sent that message to me in Phyre."

"No." Muriel shook her head. Her face was harsh, cold, and as close to the proverbial Tetlin Witch as any woman could hope to achieve.

Flash! White light burst through the windows as lightning streaked across a winter sky. Thunder cracked, and Brin screamed. Seeing Muriel that way was terrifying.

"You don't know my father," Muriel said through clenched teeth. "I do. He's beyond manipulative and extremely clever. He shouldn't use people like you. You're a nice girl, Brin. And he . . . but, of course, that's why he picked you."

"Malcolm didn't pick me, I—"

"Don't be naïve. Of course he chose you! Nothing happens by coincidence around my father. He controls *everything*. I thought he was done trying to control me."

The wind blew so hard outside that some thatch peeled off the roof, letting puffs of snow spill in. The front door rattled louder. Outside, Brin could hear trees creaking; some cracked. Again, lightning flashed and once more thunder followed.

Brin continued to pour out all she could to stifle the wildfire she had ignited. "I spoke to Elan. She wants Turin to fix the world, to repair the damage he's done, and she thinks he can—she believes he will. And she's known him even longer than you."

"You spoke to her, too?" Once more Muriel studied Brin, this time less out of skepticism and more from awe.

"She told me everything. She believes Turin has changed, or is trying to. He knows how much pain he caused, and that everyone hates him. Especially you." Brin's eyes widened then as the thought struck her. Both sensible and poetic, the beauty shook her. "Muriel, Turin gave us a key of great worth, but it wasn't the one that unlocked Phyre. It's you. *You're* the key. You'll decide everything. None of this was ever about Suri, or a horn, or even Trilos. It's about you. *That's* why he sent me. He wanted us to have this conversation. It's why he sent me the message in Phyre. He sent me to unlock the key."

Muriel stared at Brin. The woman's breathing slowed, and she began to nod. As she did, the wind stopped rattling the door. "He chose very well when he picked you."

Sunlight reappeared, flickering in through the windows. "I'm not saying I believe everything you said, and as much as I hate doing exactly what my father wants me to, I can't deny that our paths travel in the same direction, which means getting that horn to Nyphron in time. And I can help with that. Pick up your clothes."

Brin bent down and grabbed the pile. Her tunic and cloak were dry— dry *and* warm.

"I can't do anything about the distance you must run between Ith and where you came from, that's a struggle you'll face on your own, but you needn't fear the swamp; it will be your friend and aid you in your travel."

"Thank you."

Muriel nodded. "And when you are done with your trip, you'll go to Trilos?"

"Yes," Brin promised. "Although I don't think that will be necessary. There's a good chance he'll be trying to find me."

"And you'll tell him about me?"

"Yes, and I'll do even better than that. I'll do what Trilos did, but I won't leave it in the bottom of the Abyss. I'll write it all down in *The Book of Brin*."

CHAPTER TWENTY-ONE

The Sun Goes Down

Up! Down. Up! Down. This is how we cover ground! I know it is
stupid, but it is true. I wish I had a lot more stew.
— THE BOOK OF BRIN

Persephone looked up at the sound of shouts, hammers, and running feet, and for a moment—for a terrible, horrible instant—she was certain the end had come. She had been watching the sunlight move across the fabric of the tent. Morning had arrived and departed, and the diminished light of a deepening winter shortened the day. She remembered Malcolm's dire tone the night before. Taken together with what she had seen—or thought she'd seen—in his eyes, she felt justified about her unsteady nerves. When a man capable of seeing the future warned of impending disaster by nightfall, it was hard not to be scared of the dark.

Down for his afternoon nap, Nolyn was still asleep in a wad of blankets he had twisted around his body. His little legs, having kicked free of the coverings, were splayed out, taking up much of the bed. Despite what sounded like a battle being waged just outside, the boy didn't stir. Justine, who had also napped, was awake and hastily pulling on her dress. From the look on her face, she didn't want to die wearing only her shift.

"What's happening?" she asked.

"Keep an eye on him," Persephone ordered, jerking on her boots. She grabbed a cloak from the pile and rushed out. Sharp, angled streaks of sunlight were blinding. Men burst through the white, rushing past carrying bundles of rope. Not a weapon was out. This was her first clue to the mystery of the clamor, a positive sign. Then to her left, Persephone saw a tent list dramatically and deflate.

"What's going on?" she asked a man running past.

"Breaking camp, my keenig!"

"Breaking—why?"

But the man had already run by.

Persephone struggled to pull the cloak around her and realized she'd grabbed Justine's by mistake. The nurse was much smaller, and the fabric didn't reach all the way around Persephone, leaving an inch-wide gap showing the dull white of her gown. With a scowl, she rushed to where the tent was collapsing. A dozen men stood around as others worked with shovels and mallets to free the stakes. The tent had been a place for storing raw wool, which had been rolled, tied in bundles, and stacked. By the time she arrived, three more poles had been pulled from three other tents.

"Stop!" she shouted at the workers. "What are you doing?"

They all looked up, startled and nervous. No one responded.

"Why are you taking this down?" She focused on a man with a mallet. He looked familiar to her, but he wasn't from Rhen. Still, she'd seen him often around the camp, usually hauling water or wood.

"We were told to," the man replied.

"By whom?"

"Nyphron, ma'am."

"Where is he?"

Several pointed down the line of collapsing tents, giant flattened canvas footprints that marked the evidence of her husband's passing.

"Well, stop what you're doing and get that wool off the snow and back inside."

As she walked away, one called out, "Does that mean we aren't leaving?"

Persephone didn't answer. She kept on trudging, feeling the hard-packed snow crush under her steps. With every stride, she felt more furious with him.

How dare he order an evacuation without asking me—without even telling me!

She spotted Nyphron down the line of flattened tents, waving his hands and shouting.

"Are you still drunk?" she asked upon reaching him. "What's going on?"

"Scouts just reported spotting the fane's army at the forest's edge. And I personally saw leathery wings circle over the trees just moments ago. We cannot stay any longer."

"We have to stay here."

"Why?"

"Because Malcolm said so."

Nyphron stared at her, confused. "Did you say because *Malcolm* said so?"

"Yes, and he was quite adamant."

"I don't care if he was naked in the snow and swearing like a lunatic. He doesn't command this army—we do."

"But—" she began.

"Persephone, last night the horn was blown. Do you know what that means?"

"Yes, you all explained the whole succession of rulers quite well. And I—"

"I meant, what it means to us?"

She didn't, and had no idea what he was getting at. So she waited to be enlightened.

"After creating his first dragon, Lothian began building an army to attack with. He's extended the Avempartha bridges and marched troops across the Nidwalden. He has the Spider Corps training, and he's made more dragons. A lot more."

"I've heard the reports, just like you."

"What you didn't hear, what neither of us knew until this morning, was that those troops began marching up the same road I built, and dragons are coming with them. They are just inside the trees now. Persephone, the attack has been ordered. They were told to launch their offensive at dawn today."

"You keep saying that as if this is going to be a problem. Will there be a time when Nyphron wants to leave?"

Persephone looked northeast at the trees and saw nothing. She looked at the sky. It was already evening. "And yet they don't appear to be attacking. Why is that?"

"Because every once in a very great while the gods are kind."

"This has something to do with the horn, doesn't it?"

"Yes! Lothian ordered the attack, but last night every member of his army heard that horn blow." Nyphron jabbed a finger in the direction of the forest. "They all know the fane is dead, and they have no more idea what that means than we do. So they wait for new orders. By sunset tonight, either there will be a new fane, or someone else will blow the horn and a battle will be scheduled. Either way, we have a brief window to act in, but we also gain one thing—we now know they have an army complete with dragons."

"I wouldn't make such a point of it, if staying will be an obvious choice."

"The new fane might not choose to attack," she said.

Nyphron looked at her, incredulous. "You can't actually believe that. Our scouts have identified dozens of dragons—*dozens*, Persephone. Suri told me that dragons are made by killing loved ones. No matter who the fane is, how can they stop the war now? No—this change of fane alters nothing, but it has saved us from annihilation. It has granted us just enough time to pull up stakes and fall back beyond the range of their dragons."

Persephone stared over the fallen tents at the misty haze of the forest eaves.

"If you leave, you will lose the war."

"We can't leave," she said.

"Persephone, it's suicide on a grand scale to remain here, open and exposed the way we are. It also serves no point. With Elysan dead and your southern army eaten, we have no reason to remain."

"Timing is everything. We can't leave," she insisted.

"Of course we can. If we retreat just twenty miles, we'll put the Bern between us and them. It's not even a question at this point."

"You're right, it isn't. We aren't leaving."

She shouted to the working men, "Stop what you're doing! Put these tents back up. We aren't going anywhere."

Nyphron's eyes widened. He grabbed her by the elbow and pulled her aside, forcing her feet into deeper snow. "What are you doing?" He spoke low enough not to be heard, but loud enough to infuse his words with anger.

"You aren't in command here," Persephone replied. "You should have asked me before starting any of this."

"I thought we ruled together," he said.

"These men follow me. I don't wish to be cruel, don't want to embarrass you, but—"

"I won't allow your foolishness to jeopardize the lives of hundreds of soldiers," Nyphron said. "I'm not playing here. I'm serious."

"So am I."

"We are in this situation because you gave Suri to the fane, and she gave him dragons. You lost this conflict for us. You don't understand war. I do. We will all die if we don't leave, and leave now. Forgive me, but I can't allow your inexperience to destroy us." He grabbed her by the wrist and began pulling her back toward the tent.

"Stop it!" she told him.

He ignored her, hauling onward. She jerked back but his fingers gripped like a raow, and his arm was iron. She had no footing on the snow. She slipped and nearly fell.

"Let go!" she growled.

The men working on the tents stopped to look. Those digging snow, carrying wood, coiling rope watched the spectacle of Nyphron towing his wife down the path. Not one interfered. No one would dare insert themselves in a fight between husband and wife.

Maybe if he started hitting me—if he drew his sword.

She was certain that if Nyphron threatened to kill her, they would restrain him. But short of that—marriage bestowed certain rights, one of which was the privilege to quarrel with your spouse.

She continued to resist. He jerked hard. She fell in the snow. Rather than let her get up, Nyphron dragged her. The tie of Justine's cloak came loose as she skidded across the snow.

"Damn you!" she screamed at him. "You sonofabitch!"

He did not look at her. His grim face locked on the destination of the tent.

"Stop it!" she shouted, and jerked.

He pulled harder, spinning her. The nape of her dress dipped and snow slipped down the back of her neck, chilling her. "LET ME GO!" she screamed.

Nyphron ignored her, but on the nearby hilltop Persephone saw something move.

The outline of a summit that hadn't changed in ages was different.

No one interferes between a husband and a wife except—

"Nyphron! Nyphron, let go! Let go!" she cried, with new urgency. "Nyphron, let go or you're going to die!"

"Please don't make this worse than it already is," he told her.

"That's exactly what I'm telling you!"

She remembered a moment from years before, back in Dahl Rhen when she was about to face Konniger, and Raithe had told her: *"Persephone, if you have any problem, yell. Yell real loud and then get out of the way. I'll do the rest."*

Nyphron didn't know where the dragon had come from, how *exactly* it was made. In her head, she heard its words again. *"Even now."*

She had to do something, but she came up with nothing. Nyphron wasn't letting go, and he had given up listening to her. Persephone was jerked again, her face nearly hitting the snow. Then she was on her back, her legs kicking like a flipped beetle. She would have been upset at the indignity, except a real horror was drowning her thoughts. For at that moment, she looked back at the hill.

The dragon was gone.

She felt a growing wind that only she understood. Tents, the ones still standing, began to shudder, shake, and flap. It hadn't been snowing, but snow filled the air. It didn't fall; it swirled.

Thrump. Thrump. Thrump.

"The dragon, you fool!" she screamed, pointing up with her free hand.

Persephone was pleased to discover that the terror in her voice finally got through to her husband. Nyphron's concern was finally triggered by her panic. He stopped and looked up. Some had already started running, toppling over buckets and tripping over bundles of wool still blocking the pathway. As the shadow enveloped the entire camp, people screamed. Nyphron finally let go, but it was too late.

The gusts and thrusts stopped as the dragon folded its wings and dropped like a falcon onto the Fhrey commander. One giant claw with sword-length talons landed, pinning Nyphron to the ground. Then that great mouth of vicious teeth opened.

"Stop!" Persephone shouted at the creature. She had rolled to her knees and had both arms raised. "Don't hurt him!"

At the sound of her voice, the dragon hesitated. Its lips pulled back into a sneer, showing still more teeth. One big eye fixed on her, the tall elongated pupil snapping her into focus. The great beast released a deep, ground-shaking growl and let go a snort of hot air that blew back the edges of Persephone's cloak and tossed her hair.

"Please," she told it. Her heart pounded and she wondered how she was able to talk. "Don't."

Nyphron lay on his back in the snow, pinned by the claw as if the roots of a tree had grown over him. His head was trapped between two great talons, the webbing of the claw up around his neck. Barely breathing, he didn't say a word. Although Nyphron was arrogant, self-centered, and frequently unsympathetic, he wasn't stupid. For once, he was perfectly willing—eager—to let *her* command the situation.

"I—I need him alive." Persephone spoke to the dragon but looked at Nyphron. "He's my husband." She turned to those still watching, the ones spellbound by what they saw, or too scared to move. Sikar ran toward them with sword drawn, but stopped short when he saw Nyphron under the claw.

"He hurt you." The dragon spoke with cavernous timbre. The voice could have been that of a mountain or a god.

Gasps escaped the crowd.

"He didn't." Persephone held up her hands, revealing—she wasn't sure what—that they were still there? "I'm all right. I am. He"—again she looked into Nyphron's eyes, speaking to him, willing him to go along— "would never *really* hurt me. We just had a disagreement. Husbands and wives have those. He was angry, and so was I. But he wasn't going to hurt me. *Were* you?"

"No." Nyphron shook his head so slightly it appeared as if he was shivering, and maybe he was. Even the leader of the Galantians might show fear when pinned by an invulnerable dragon. "I only sought to—"

The great claw tightened. Talons dragged, digging deep furrows into the snow, plowing up dirt and last year's grass.

The crowd gasped again, and several retreated. Others raised defending hands to shield their frightened eyes.

Persephone rushed forward and placed a hand on the dragon's claw. "Stop!"

Again, the beast listened. Again, it hesitated.

"This war isn't over. I need him, and . . . he is my husband." She paused. Persephone looked around at the men with mallets and shovels, women with buckets and baskets, so many she didn't recognize, so many strangers. She straightened up and spoke directly to the crowd. "And I am keenig. I know the fane's army is advancing. I know they have dragons. I know our situation appears impossible. But I also know what most of you are too young to remember: That I have done the impossible before—and more than once. And I—"

"I 'member." Habet stepped forward.

Habet, who had been missing all day, reappeared. He was dressed in soaked traveling clothes, looking haggard and sweaty. Without pause or concern, he walked right up to Persephone and the dragon. He reached out and patted the dragon's side three times, smiling as he did. Then he turned to Persephone. "I 'member it all. I was there. I was always there. You gave us food when we was starving, killed the bad bear no one else could, moved us to the sea when our dahl was destroyed, brought back da shiny sword from far away, and had Moya kill that ugly Gula." He made a fierce face, then laughed.

"You remember all that?"

Habet nodded like a pigeon. "I 'member you said, 'trust me.' You said it, and we did it."

She smiled at him, then she turned back to the crowd. "Now I'm asking everyone to trust me again. My command is that we stay here. We do not run. It might seem a foolish thing, but if we leave now, we will most assuredly lose this war. The Fhrey can always make more dragons, so there is nowhere that is safe. They will hunt us down and kill us all. If we stay . . ." She didn't know how to finish. She was working blind, believing in a man who wanted her to trust him.

"You only need to trust me one more time. If I'm right, this war will be over and my reign as keenig will end. But for now—for now we stay."

No one spoke. There wasn't so much as a cough, and the winter stillness was as complete as if the world had stopped. Everything paused, waiting on her to start it again. Persephone dusted snow off her hands, brushed hair from her face, and once more tried and failed to pull Justine's cloak around her. There was just no way to look dignified in an ill-fitting wrap. "Let him go," she told the beast. "I need him. We need him. The world needs him."

The claw opened.

"Return to your hill," she told it. "We may yet need you as well."

Gusts of downdrafts exploded against the ground, throwing up snow and sending bales of wool tumbling. In that blinding swirl of dragon-made blizzard, Persephone walked to Habet and gave him a hug. "Welcome back," she said. "Where did you go?"

"I went for a ride."

❧

Brin raced the sun, and it was winning.

She chased it west, watching as it flew farther and farther away. It shifted from white, to yellow, to a now frightening shade of orange.

The trip through the swamp had been as ideal as Muriel had promised. The word *enchanted* came to mind. The muddy water had frozen, its surface dusted with a thin coating of snow that was just enough to provide good traction. Finding her way was simple: A path had been made for her. The trees themselves had lined up to create a corridor that blocked the wind. Maybe it had always been there, and in the dark, they hadn't seen it. But that morning it felt as if the swamp held her hand.

She felt that hand let go when she reached the field and ran out of the swamp. The last time she was there it had been a beautiful fall day of bright colors and an easy downhill stroll. Now Brin struggled uphill through a frozen, windswept landscape of snow and bare trees. She'd hoped to find Naraspur still tethered, but the horse was gone, and she was left to hike. The sun was well overhead as she began that arduous half circle swing around the mountain. She was feeling strong, and confident, which didn't make much sense. She'd been dead for several days, her body inert and packed in ice-cold mud. No food, no water, no air, and since hopping back inside and taking up the reins of those arms and legs, she'd had only one night to rest. When Arion had woken after her near-death, it had taken weeks for her to recuperate, alternating between sipping water and vomiting it back up. Yet here was Brin, switching back and forth between a fast walk and a trot after already covering what had to be miles.

She hadn't been hungry or thirsty. That was the clue that led Brin to suspect the stew. When it came to the Tetlin Witch, everyone knew that her food and drink were enchanted. In the stories, eating or drinking anything she offered invited disaster. Muriel was a different story, and that tiny breakfast continued to fill her stomach with warmth and strength for longer than it should have.

But by the time Brin cleared the swamp, her stamina was fading. Then thirst rolled in with a vengeance. She took to stuffing handfuls of snow into her mouth as she trudged on. The snow took some of the pain away, but it couldn't satisfy her need for water. She began to grow hungry, too.

She gave up trotting altogether, sticking only to a fast walk. By staying close to a line of bushes that made a snow shadow, she was rewarded with a path of bare ground. Brin was still making good time, but she was rapidly running out of strength. And as the sun, unwilling to wait for her, ran ahead, Brin noticed the cold. She'd been hot and sweating most of the day, but as the shadows lengthened and she stopped running, her wet clothes chilled her.

Then the wonderful line of bushes ended, and with it, the clear path.

Brin stopped at the end of that hedgerow, panting.

This is where we had our last meal together before entering the swamp. I ate an apple. The core might still be around, somewhere under the snow.

Her breath created clouds.

Has that been happening all along, but I've been moving too fast to notice? Or is it getting colder?

She shivered.

It's getting colder.

She felt the clammy grip of her tunic, which was soaked through with sweat. Her legs were tight and tired, her feet sore—where she could feel them. Her toes were going numb. Brin looked ahead, trying to pick a good route. There wasn't one. The world before her was a sea of white. Everywhere, snow was ankle-deep or higher.

Going to slow me down.

She noticed how much taller her shadow was; the sun was setting. Brin clutched the horn to her chest.

"Elan, give me strength. I can't do this alone, and you said you'd be with me."

She waited a moment, hoping for something, a word, a sign. Nothing materialized. Not a single bird chirped.

Brin clamped her jaw tight and pushed forward into the snow. Her speed was instantly reduced. She went from a fast walk to a labored trudge. Soon she was marking the passage of each footfall, concentrating on forcing her legs to move, her feet to land.

Up. Down. Up. Down, she said in her head, mentally ordering her feet to move, matching her footfalls to the beats of the words.

Up. Down. Up. Down. This is how we cover ground.

The second part fell into place with a singsong rhythm. Brin didn't know how she thought of it, didn't know she was thinking at all, but once it was there, she chanted it with gusto.

Up! Down. Up! Down. This is how we cover ground!

She bent her head, watching her own progress. Like a spectator, she observed how snow collected in the tops of her shoes. She could see it packing against the skin of her ankles, and how red her flesh became.

That's not good. That's going to be a real problem. Might lose that foot altogether if this keeps up.

The thought was a disconnected observation, as if this was happening to someone else—someone she felt sorry for, someone she knew was doomed.

Up! Down. Up! Down. This is how we cover ground!

She entered a ravine where a cluster of large, snow-covered rocks created mounds. A few juniper and thyme bushes grew up one slope.

Up! Down. Up! Down.

Brin grabbed more snow and sucked it into her parched mouth.

This is how we cover ground!

The sun was turning red. The day was ending.

She had failed. That poor young woman with the snow-filled shoes was going to die in the snow just miles from her goal. Brin couldn't help feeling sorry for her.

Then she heard the snort of a horse, followed by a whinny.

I've gone mad, she realized as she looked up and saw none other than Naraspur, fully tacked and tethered before her. Looped over the saddle was a skin of water and a bag of bread and cheese.

"This isn't where you were," she told the horse.

Behind Naraspur was a clear trench of packed snow, as if someone had walked while dragging their feet.

Brin lifted her face to the sky. "Thank you, Elan."

❧

Nyphron slipped into the tent. He never spent much time there. This was Persephone's place—hers, the kid's, and the nurse's. It smelled like them. He stood for a moment just inside the tent flap, listening. All three were gone. He didn't know where. The sun was setting, the light soaking through the canvas with a gold color. He moved quickly, lifting the sword off the tent post. The naked blade caught the sun's light and shimmered. *Black bronze.* There was a brilliant gleam, and in the metal, he saw symbols, finely etched markings lining both sides of the blade. For nearly a decade, Nyphron had allowed others to fight for him. Fhrey can't kill Fhrey, but this was an enemy he was allowed to slay.

Since having been thrown on his back, Nyphron had spent time considering his future. All of it distilled down to one of two bad choices.

He could walk out and abandon Persephone and her people. Sikar and the other Fhrey would follow him. They could retreat to Merredydd, hole up there, and watch as the human army was wiped out. But what then? The Miralyith huntsmen would track him down. The rest of his life would be spent fleeing that spineless brat until at last he died in some muddy hole or, worse, was dragged back to be displayed and humiliated like his father had been.

His other option was to force the army to retreat, which would require the new fane to order more dragons. Though the chance of success was slim, this option offered at least the possibility that the new fane might face enough anger back home to give up. As much as he hated the idea, Nyphron might be forced to acquiesce to peace.

Better than dying in a muddy hole.

Nyphron searched for Malcolm but failed to find the infuriating man. This left him but one option. As long as the dragon remained, Persephone would not retreat, and with it as her guardian, he couldn't force her. So Nyphron climbed the hill with the sword in his hand.

The dragon lay where it had been, but in a different stance. In two years, the creature hadn't moved until Persephone screamed, so Nyphron fully expected the beast to remain statue-like now. He didn't attempt to hide his approach or his intent. He held the sword confidently, swinging it with his strides as he climbed the last few feet. He was nearing the top when the dragon's head came up.

Nyphron froze. The beast was bigger than a house, but it jerked up with the speed of a cat. The thing's eyes flashed open and narrowed on him. Its lips rippled up, revealing stalactite fangs.

"You've come to kill me." The Rhunic words rumbled out of the giant mouth.

Nyphron hadn't expected it to talk, not to him. "Your services are no longer needed."

"How rude," the dragon said, surprising him. "Even for a Fhrey, that's ill mannered. So you're a great warrior, then? I'm a little disappointed. I expected you'd be taller—the tales certainly are. Do you think you could kill me?"

The words were familiar. They came from the past. Nyphron had said them himself. A conversation outside Dahl Rhen's wooden gate.

"Do you know who I am?" The beast rose up. Its wings flashed out, and its neck arched up and back.

Nyphron narrowed his eyes. *Not possible—is it?*

"It requires a sacrifice," Suri had said. *"I have to destroy the life of someone dear to me."*

"God Killer?"

The great dragon's lips tightened, showing more pointed teeth. "How's your back? Hitting the snow like that looked really painful."

Nyphron advanced.

"She loves me, not you," the beast declared.

That stopped Nyphron, who paused to laugh. "Persephone?" he said. "I don't care about her. Did you think I wooed her away from you because I loved her?"

"You care about losing."

"I didn't lose. You're dead. And will be more so in a moment."

"I'm in Alysin, and in a few years, she will be, too. But you won't. This battle doesn't end here. This is only the beginning. So tell me, Fhrey, do you think you can kill me?"

⨏

Even Nolyn couldn't sleep through what had happened. Justine, with the boy in tow, eventually found Persephone not far from an enormous claw print where the keenig was busy reordering the camp. The look on the nursemaid's face—which sported a very strained and extremely brave smile—made Persephone wonder if Justine was rethinking her decision to care for the keenig's son. She held out Persephone's cloak, and they traded.

"I grabbed yours by mistake," Persephone said. "Sorry—got a little wet."

Justine nodded blankly as Nolyn hung from her grip like a wet sack. His drooping eyes and long face told the tale of a boy who'd just gotten up, wasn't awake yet, and wasn't happy about it.

"What happened?" Justine asked.

"Nothing, nothing important." The big thing, Persephone knew, was still coming. What that thing was she didn't know, but as the sun was close to setting, she was tired of waiting. "Have you seen Malcolm?"

"Over there," Justine said, pointing north. "Passed him on the way here."

"Show me."

The young woman hoisted a disagreeable Nolyn up on one hip so that the boy's feet bobbed as she walked, his head toppled over on her shoulder. She led the way down between rows of tents until Persephone could see Malcolm for herself. He was standing with his back to her near the edge of the camp, where the mass of regimented tents stopped and the field began.

Persephone stopped Justine. "I see him, and I can take it from here." Conversations with Malcolm weren't meant to be shared, and that was never more true than now. She looked at Nolyn, his head resting against Justine's neck, thumb in mouth, eyes open but only a crack. She had an incredible urge to grab her son and hug him tight against whatever storm was coming. She wanted to shield him, save him, the way she hadn't saved the others. Persephone had had three children with Reglan, but only Mahn had lived to maturity, an adulthood cut horribly short. Now she had Nolyn, beautiful, perfect, and her last chance. Persephone knew she couldn't save him with a hug.

"Take him," she told Justine, trying to sound as calm as possible. "Get him something to eat. It'll be dark soon."

The nursemaid cupped the back of Nolyn's head with her hand as she nodded. Persephone saw a hesitancy there, a lingering apprehensive look. "All right," Justine said with an odd sort of finality, as if accepting a grim and dangerous mission. Then, unexpectedly, she reached out and hugged Persephone. The three of them shared a squeeze that was hard to break from.

Persephone pushed back. "Take him. Keep Nolyn safe."

"I will."

Persephone didn't watch them go. She pushed forward, swallowing the remaining distance between her and Malcolm. He must have known she was there.

He knows everything, but refuses to share.

As she approached, he remained with his back to her, his cloak wrapped tightly against the growing cold.

"Sun's setting," she said.

"Yes," he replied, but he wasn't looking that way. He stared east into the growing darkness at Mount Mador, whose lower half was in shadow, the upper still dazzling with the final rays of the day's light.

"What's going to happen, Malcolm?"

He had his arms folded across his chest, his face red with windburn, his eyes straining to see. What he looked for she couldn't begin to guess. "It's too cold, and there's too much snow."

"Too much for what? Malcolm, you—"

The ground shook, and a terrible roar came from Dragon Hill.

"I tried my best," Malcolm told her sadly. "You must understand that Some knots are too tight to untie. Some must be cut."

Persephone rushed past him into the snowy field, clearing the camp to see north. The dragon had moved again. The beast was in the air, its great wings holding it aloft with regular beats that shuddered the nearby tents, threatening to blow them down. It wasn't alone. Nyphron stood on the hill's crest, holding the black-bronze blade with both hands and aiming at the beast.

The two combatants were caught in the same brilliance of the setting sun. Evening light illuminated the shimmering scales on the gilarabrywn's body, revealing their iridescence. That same radiance transformed Nyphron's armor into a golden mirror. For a moment, Persephone could do nothing except stare. The vision was more than striking—it inspired awe. Compared with the dragon, Nyphron was tiny, but oh so bright, and oh so brave. His little sword gleamed both red and gold, like fire. If she didn't know who the real hero and villain were in that play, Persephone would have been enraptured by the glory, gallantry, and grand heroics of Nyphron.

The population of the camp burst out of the line of tents with shouts and cries. They migrated into the open to better see the spectacle on

Dragon Hill. Hundreds pushed forward for the chance to witness, then became strangely silent.

"Persephone," Malcolm called to her.

She was walking forward, heading toward the hill, picking up speed.

The dragon snapped at Nyphron with its massive jaws. Nyphron swung the sword. Neither landed a blow.

Persephone had hold of her cloak and gown, clutching the skirts in her fists, hiking them as she ran up the slope. A firm hand caught her at the elbow and spun her around.

"Wait!" Malcolm ordered.

"I have to stop it!"

"You can't!"

"It's Raithe! The dragon is Raithe!"

"It's not! He's dead."

She jerked and pulled, but Malcolm refused to release her.

On the hill, the dragon reared and sucked in air. It happened so quickly she didn't have time to think, feel, or choose sides. Fire blasted from the beast's mouth and struck Nyphron, engulfing him in a torrent of flame. Persephone held her breath as she watched with wide eyes, unable to look away. She fully expected to see Nyphron collapse in a pile of ash, but her husband didn't fall, didn't waver.

All around the top of that hill, snow turned to steam, creating a hissing fog. Through it all, Nyphron held the black-bronze weapon high. When the fire stopped, the hilltop was scorched black. Rivers born of melted snow ran. In the following silence, the rushing water was loud. Fog lingered. A heavy mist engulfed the top of the hill. The wind blew, the haze cleared, and the sun continued to glint off shining armor. Nyphron remained on his feet, undaunted and unscathed.

"He's alive," Persephone said.

"Nyphron's armor is etched in Orinfar, and that isn't a real dragon; it's a magical representation of one." Malcolm let go of her arm. "Future generations will know of this moment. Nyphron will always be seen as he is now, a gleaming hero on a hilltop. The story of this battle will be told and retold, and with the passing generations, exaggerated beyond all reason."

"Exaggerated? How could *this* be exaggerated?" Free of Malcolm's arm, Persephone charged up the hill.

The ground was slick with snow, ice, and rivulets of water, and Persephone slid back one step for every two forward. She was halfway to the top when the dragon beat its wings hard. She paused in her climb to look. The dragon appeared to be flying away. Up it went in a spiral, corkscrewing higher and higher. She stood, head back, watching it rise.

Go, she thought, *fly away. You can't beat him. Save yourself.*

The dragon dived.

"Even now," she cried, watching it streak down. They were no longer his words—they were hers.

Plummeting with extended claws aimed at Nyphron and backed with enough force to turn stone to powder, the dragon descended. Persephone wanted to look away but couldn't. She had to see.

Looking brave and valiant, Nyphron aimed his sword at the sky, at the screeching death from above. The moment they collided, the instant the sword blade impaled the dragon, the hilltop exploded. Snapping the bonds that created the beast, the world reclaimed the energy in a sudden violent outburst. The eruption of force threw Nyphron to the ground. The shock wave continued down the hill, radiating out in all directions. Snow burst into the air. Tents flattened all across the camp. And Persephone, like everyone, was knocked off her feet, blown down by a violent gust of air.

ر

When Persephone opened her eyes, Nyphron was standing over her. The sun was still illuminating him so that he appeared a light unto himself, a beacon in the growing darkness, but one that cast a long shadow.

"We are leaving," he told her. No anger, rage, hint of gloating, or insult filled his voice. He merely stated a fact. "Without the dragon, there is—" Nyphron stopped and looked past her.

From behind, Persephone heard the crush of snow as someone approached. Pushing off the burnt, wet grass, she climbed to her feet. Turning, she found Malcolm standing there. In his hands, he held a ram's horn.

"Is that . . . ?" Nyphron asked, his gaze shifting between the thing in Malcolm's hand and the man's face.

Malcolm nodded.

"But . . . how?"

Malcolm stepped aside, revealing a figure sitting in the snow just down the hillside: a woman in a tattered cloak that hung off one shoulder. The hair from her bowed head covered her face. Hunched over and almost prostrate, she appeared exhausted as she sat beside Gifford's horse, Naraspur. Still, Persephone knew her.

"Brin?" She whispered the name, casting it forth as a sacred wish, a prayer, wanting so badly for it to be true. "Brin," she called, louder.

The woman's head tilted. A quivering hand came up and parted the hair, revealing weary eyes, wind-beaten cheeks, and cracked lips.

"BRIN!" Persephone shouted, then ran to the Keeper's side. The keenig tightly wrapped the young woman in her arms. "Oh, Brin, Brin, Brin," she cried.

Malcolm held out the horn to Nyphron. "I promised you the world, and I'm handing it to you now. Blow this. If you do, the war will end, and you'll rule both sides of the Nidwalden."

"I don't want to rule them. I want to kill them."

"I understand. But that's not one of your choices. Once that sun sets, Mawyndulë, with his fleet of dragons and army of Miralyith, will be fane. You can either blow this and fight him for the Forest Throne, or refuse and accept both defeat and your own death. The choice is yours."

Brin's clothes were soaked, and she shivered within Persephone's embrace.

She must be freezing to death.

The Keeper looked so tired, beyond exhausted. She was used up, empty, and withered.

The woman lifted her head clear of Persephone and glared at Nyphron. "Blow it," she begged in a desperate voice. "We all died bringing it to you. I'm the only one to make it back. Blow it. For the love of Elan, do it."

"We all died . . ."

Persephone felt the words as much as heard them. And in that moment, she remembered a girl-mystic with strange tattoos and a white wolf standing in her darkened lodge.

"I came to tell you that we're all going to die. All of us." Suri had said.

But it wasn't *us,* Persephone realized, it was *them.* Everyone she had ever loved had died, even Brin. Yes, she was back, but could anyone fully return from such a thing?

Silence caused her to look over.

With a noncommittal expression on his face, Nyphron took the horn and weighed it in his hand. He sneered at the thing. "Mawyndulë, eh? Lothian's son."

"There's a certain sense of symmetry in that, don't you think?" Malcolm asked.

Nyphron considered this, and a smile tugged at the corners of his lips. He raised the horn and blew.

CHAPTER TWENTY-TWO

The Horn Blower

Turns out, Mawyndulë did not expect his musical debut to be a duet.

— THE BOOK OF BRIN

Mawyndulë sat on the Forest Throne. He'd never done so before. His father wasn't the type to indulge his child with even a momentary sit in the *Big Chair*. Mawyndulë wasn't all that certain what a father did, or was supposed to do, but he figured that since Lothian had been a failure at everything else, it only followed he was a bad father. The throne was about as comfortable as one would expect from a chair made out of intertwined living trees. Thankfully, the bark had worn away, but Mawyndulë still insisted on using a pillow. The seat was also weirdly sized, seemingly built for a giant. The armrests were too high, the seat itself too wide and deep. He had to either sit a mile from the backrest or have his feet stick up in the air like a child. Mawyndulë had hoped sitting there would help him feel more confident, more self-assured. Instead, the throne only made him feel small.

The seat wasn't his yet, but that didn't matter. He was the only Miralyith in the city—assuming the Rhune and her wolf had left. Reports of her taking the road west were plentiful. No one had tried to stop her, least of all Mawyndulë. Those in the city had heard what she'd done, and where she'd been. No one was concerned that she had assaulted their prince, but everyone was fascinated that she had entered the Garden Door. Already the Rhune and her white wolf were slipping into the realm of legend. Mawyndulë had murdered his father on the floor of the Airenthenon, but all people talked about was how impressive the Rhune had appeared in that formal asica, carrying the Horn of Gylindora, and how blue the wolf's eyes had been. Mawyndulë was glad she was gone.

Until he heard the horn blow.

It happened as the sun set. Everyone heard it. The sound pierced the ear like teeth scraping metal.

Now he needed answers.

Mawyndulë was shifting in his seat, trying to center the pillow, when the Aquila were ushered into the throne room by palace guards. The fane's soldiers had heard about Mawyndulë killing his father. They also knew the entire Aquila had been complicit in the act. Mawyndulë had explained the whole thing to them while reminding each he was blessed with the Protection of Ferrol. He also reminded them that he was the only remaining Miralyith within three days of the city. Then he asked for their loyalty. Unsurprisingly, none had refused.

Mawyndulë had considered executing the Aquila right away. He'd almost done it that night, imagining a grand public barbecue right in the plaza. But he'd held off. He wasn't fane yet. He didn't know all the rules, and while he was invulnerable for now, he guessed this wouldn't last. Slaughtering the whole of the Aquila—the leaders of each tribe—might anger too many. It could spark a full-scale revolt. *Best to wait until after I am enthroned,* he thought. *And I want Imaly to personally crown me.* He felt that would be the sweetest victory of all. So he had them imprisoned—all of them, including Vasek and a handful of others he suspected of being sympathizers. Executions would begin the day after his coronation.

Imaly and Volhoric came in first, followed closely by Osla. The two ringleaders held hands like lovers. Mawyndulë suspected the high priest and the Curator hated each other now, but fear made friends of everyone. Nanagal and Hemon came next. They didn't hold hands, but they bumped shoulders as if neither one wanted to be first or last into the room, as if there might be a penalty for either. The five crept forward, huddling in a tight group. Mawyndulë had heard sheep did the same thing because the odd one out got eaten.

While Imaly did nothing, Volhoric bowed.

"Your Highness," Imaly said.

Not "my fane," Mawyndulë noted.

"Who blew the horn?" he demanded.

The fact he had heard its blast at all was a positive sign. It meant he was still Fhrey enough to participate in the ritual. But the fear of not knowing who he would face in battle was making him sick. He felt nauseous.

"How would we know?" Imaly replied. "Being locked in a cellar makes it difficult to be informed."

"Truth be told, my fane, we are in uncharted territory here," Volhoric said.

"So how do I know who to fight?" Anxiety leaked into Mawyndulë's words, which alarmed all of them. Each took a step back.

Mawyndulë's frustration rose. "Don't you have some way of locating it? Did it reach the river? Did it get to Avempartha?"

That was his real concern, his greatest fear. If the horn had somehow managed to travel all the way to the tower, then he could face another Miralyith. Mawyndulë was confident in his ability to defeat any non-Artist, but he doubted he could stand up against even the weakest of his own kind.

I failed in combat against a Rhune. What chance do I have against someone like Jerydd, even as old as he is? If he is the one who blew it . . . the thought terrified Mawyndulë.

"I don't see how," Nanagal said. "Avempartha is three days away."

"Maybe it would be possible with a good horse," Osla said. "It could travel a hundred miles in a day. But it would probably drop dead right after. Still, it *might* be possible, and Avempartha isn't nearly that far . . . is it?" She looked at the others.

"The Rhune didn't have a horse. I'm not even certain their kind can ride one," Mawyndulë replied.

"If I may," Imaly started, "surely there have been reports of the Rhune's movements since leaving the Airenthenon. If you could provide us with what's been reported to you, perhaps we could aid you better."

Oh, yes. You're always the helpful one, aren't you, traitor.

Mawyndulë calmed himself. "Eyewitnesses say they saw the Rhune take it inside the Door, and she didn't have it when she came back out."

Shock washed over the faces of each of the Aquila members, their eyes widening.

Not even Imaly is that good at deception. She did not *expect that.*

Mawyndulë's stomach had been in knots since he'd heard the report. Was he being challenged by someone who was dead? Or had it been that odd, filthy guy in the Garden who had blown it? There wasn't anyone more obsessed with the door than Trilos.

If that's the case, I'm done for. He's as talented as Jerydd. They both can create strawberries. I've never heard of any Artist who can manifest something from nothingness.

When no one said anything, Mawyndulë took a different tack. "What happens if the challenger never comes forth? What happens then?"

The sheep shared more wide-eyed looks.

"Ah . . ." Volhoric opened his yammering mouth again. "That has never happened. The challenger has always been eager to engage, either to fight or quickly concede. In the case of two combatants, they have always been together because the horn was always here. We've given each the chance to blow, and the ritual went on from there. It's not supposed to happen like this. It's just not."

"Is there a time limit? Like between the first and second sounding of the horn? A point after which I win by default if the challenger doesn't show up?"

"Like I said, we are on new ground here, my fane. I suppose it's possible that everything will just washout and start over," Volhoric offered.

"Washout? Start over? What does that mean?"

The high priest didn't look at all certain of himself. "Maybe if the challenge isn't met, the whole process begins again."

"You mean I'd have to blow the horn again?"

Volhoric nodded. "Possibly."

This was almost more frightening than not knowing who had blown it in the first place, and Mawyndulë's anger grew again. "We don't have the horn anymore! We. Can't. Have. A. Do-over."

He pointed at them, sweeping his finger like a weapon. All of them shrank in terror as it passed over them. "Take them away," he yelled at the guards. "Lock them up again. And no meals, not even bread. Until I get real answers, I won't be able to eat, so they don't get to, either!"

The guards herded the group out, leaving Mawyndulë alone on his ill-fitting chair.

All manner of nightmares rushed at him.

Who can it be? A monster? Trilos? My father? A god? Ferrol himself might be coming to dole out punishment for my crime.

As far as Mawyndulë knew, no one had ever murdered a fane then blown the challenge horn. Perhaps this act had broken some universal law and summoned a deity to deliver retribution. In some strange way, he preferred the idea of having to fight Ferrol over having to face his own father. He imagined Lothian returning from the dead still blackened and charred, his eyes angry.

Mawyndulë put his head between his knees and cried.

CHAPTER TWENTY-THREE

Losing Weight

The worst thing people can do to one another is also the best—
provide challenges. How we respond becomes our lives. How we live
our lives becomes the best and the worst parts of our afterlives.

— THE BOOK OF BRIN

Tesh saw that Iver was right about the snow. Small icy flakes pelted them and made a hissing sound where they struck the frost en masse. Gifford led them around the curve of the cliffs out into what Roan's light revealed to be a wide canyon.

She's brighter than Brin was, Tesh thought as he realized he could see from wall to wall. In between was a flat plain of white littered with the broken pieces of the bridge.

Roan had pulled his arm around the back of her neck and was acting as a crutch the same way she used to help Gifford.

I've become a burden.

Tesh looked at Gifford, who carried Tressa in his arms. His light was growing brighter.

He feeds off Roan. He lives for her. Who do I live for?

By the time they reached the base of the big pillar, they heard sounds unlike anything since they'd fallen in. The noise was odd, like thunder made from breaking glass. Down the length of the canyon that zigzagged with the randomness of a mammoth crack, they could see a reddish glow, and it was moving, growing bigger and brighter.

Gifford set Tressa down gently, then tilted his head back and peered up at the long ascent. "They are attracted to your light, Roan. Is there any way you can turn it down? Can you think terrible thoughts?"

Roan shook her head. "I doubt you'd want me to, even if I could. We both need to be as light as possible in order to climb."

Only then did Tesh notice the connection between buoyancy and brilliance. To be without weight was to be *light*.

Roan placed Tesh's hands on the rock as if he were drunk, and they'd reached the door of his home. "I can't carry you. You have to climb. You have to pull yourself up."

Tesh felt that miserable rock: dry, rough, sharp, and cruel. "I can't. I'm just too heavy."

"Yes, you can. You know you can. You just have to decide to do it. You, too, Tressa."

"I'll never climb this thing," she said, looking up and uttering what was close to a laugh. "I don't even know why you brought me."

The sound of the shattering thunder grew louder, and what looked to be sunrise stretched out across the horizon, becoming brighter but retaining that terrifying red color.

"You have to try," Gifford told them. The desperate way he rushed his words decided the matter for Tesh.

"I will on one condition."

"A condition?" Gifford said. "We're doing that again?"

"Don't wait for us."

"You're just giving up again."

"No, I'm not." Tesh nodded toward the red glow. "This could take time, and I already have enough weight to deal with. I can't add fear and guilt on top of it. You and Roan go up. We'll either make it or we won't, but being responsible for your failure won't help."

Gifford looked at Roan, who shook her head. "He's lying, just as he did to Brin."

Gifford frowned, then grabbed Tesh by the shoulders. "I want your word you'll do it."

"You have it."

"No," he said. "I want your word *on Brin's eternal soul.*" Tesh pushed back, but Gifford wouldn't let him go. "I want your word that you'll fight harder than you ever have, that you'll do whatever is necessary to climb this damn pillar. Swear it."

Tesh didn't make a sound.

"Swear it, or so help me we'll stay here and be eaten. Is that what you want? Is it?"

"No."

"And you know us; we'll do it. We are just that crazy. Both of us." He looked at Roan, who promptly and emphatically nodded.

"No one has *ever* called me sane," she said without a hint of humor, but there was something in her voice that surprised Tesh. Her tone was different, more alive, more free. The expression on her face was new, too. She was smiling, and not just with her lips. Her eyes sparkled. Roan was happy. She had always been a closed, cowering, sad person, slow to speak, quiet and meek, the sort to content herself with the corners and dim places of the world where she could hide. But this shining woman was different. She was now able to tolerate Tesh's arm around her shoulder as they walked. Roan was . . . *healed.* The word came to Tesh, and he thought it had never before been so aptly applied.

Gifford was right. They were both crazy.

"You want us to go? Swear it!" He gripped Tesh with powerful arms and slammed him against the rock. "You swallowed your stupid pride to learn how to fight from the very people who murdered your family. You did that for a memory. Are you telling me you won't even try for Brin's sake? She's up there waiting for you. Do you care for her so little?"

The lousy culling cripple.

"I—*loved*—her."

"You still do, you idiot! Just prove it. Swear to me, now. Swear it!"

In the distance, Tesh saw movement. Something was drawing toward them. Far too big to be a giant, this was the size of an open-plains storm, where the clouds billowed up into huge formations, then darkened and rolled in. Typhons were not beings so much as events. They were both the herald and the doom, the portent and the catastrophe. Seeing the horizon approach, Tesh understood how small they all were, and how foolish.

"All right! I swear. Now both of you get out of here."

Gifford stared a moment longer, then nodded. "See you at the top."

The going was easy for a while. Gifford just followed Roan, who hadn't the slightest trouble scaling the stone. Not that it was a hard climb. There were plenty of handholds and small ledges to rest on if they needed to. She didn't. Roan was inexhaustible—him, not so much.

"Need to stop," he called up when they reached another ledge. Gifford had no idea how high they were. All he knew was that he couldn't see the bottom anymore. Tesh and Tressa had faded into the darkness.

"Why?" She looked back down, all that brightness making it hard to see her face clearly.

"I'm tired." He threw himself on the foot-wide jut of stone. "This isn't easy."

"How could you be tired? You don't have muscles, no lungs, no—"

"I don't know how, but I am. Are you saying you aren't even a little weary?"

"No more than walking." She paused, analyzing his question as she did everything. "Actually less."

Roan let go of her holds and dropped down to him, scaring Gifford so badly he yelled. "Don't do that! You could fall!"

She bent low and looked into his eyes. She peered deep, tilting her head left then right as if trying to get a better angle. She was searching for something, peering into his house through the tiny windows of his eyes. "You have weight."

"Of course I have weight. Everyone—every *thing* has weight."

"No, you don't, because you don't have a body. You have no more weight than a beam of light. Any heaviness you feel is something you're carrying. Gifford, you can't climb out with a burden. Don't you understand? That's the whole point of the Abyss. To get out, you must clean house. Can't have so much as a dust bunny hiding under your bed. You need to lose it all: hate, fear, guilt, regret."

Dust bunny? She'd been like this since forgiving Iver. *This is Roan as if there had never been an Iver. This is the woman she was supposed to be before fate threw her off a cliff.*

He shook his head. "I don't have any of those."

"You have something, and you won't make it out unless you let go."

Gifford looked down. The only thing he could clearly see were the three red points of light moving toward the base of the pillar. "Typhons," he muttered. "Do you think Tressa and Tesh managed to climb high enough?"

"I don't know," Roan replied. She sat down on the little ledge beside him and dangled her legs off the edge as if she were sitting in one of her hanging chairs in a roundhouse.

"Have we?" He looked at her, at that brilliance. "Are we high enough, do you think?"

Roan looked down, leaning so far forward that Gifford held his breath. "I think so."

Gifford was seized by a jolt of fear. "Can Typhons climb?"

Roan shook her head. "Doubt it, or they would have already."

Gifford peered back down at the lights that moved in a whirling mist that might have been snow or fog. "Yeah, I guess you're right."

He tried to spot Tesh or Tressa, hoped to see them scaling the pillar somewhere below them but couldn't see anything. "I don't think either of them are going to make it. We shouldn't have left them."

"Gifford?"

"What?"

"Stop," she said. Her eyes locked on him in that piercing manner.

"Stop what?"

Roan took his hand. She placed it between both of hers. "This isn't about them. It's about you."

"Roan, there's nothing."

Gifford was telling the truth. He honestly couldn't think of any guilt or regret that might be holding him back. In his whole life, he'd never hurt anyone—except the Fhrey that had been on the verge of killing Roan, and he didn't have *any* guilt over that. His life was clean of mistakes—at least the sort that a person could feel regretful for. That was one of the benefits of being pitiful: He lacked the opportunity to be an ass.

"Is it me?" Roan asked. She said it gently, inviting him to be honest; letting him know with a squeeze of her hand and the acceptance in her eyes that he could admit anything to her. "Something about me? Is it that I killed Iver?"

"No!" Gifford shouted and took her hand in both of his. For a moment, he forgot they were on a tiny ledge so far above the ground that he couldn't see the bottom. "I love you, Roan. I always have. As far as I'm concerned— you're perfect. Now more than ever."

"Then what is it?"

Gifford sighed. "I can't imagine. I've been happy with you, I really have. Since the Battle of Grandford, my life has been far beyond my greatest hopes. I mean, I really thought—I couldn't imagine that you— that anyone would . . ."

"Would what?" She put a lock of hair in her mouth and began to chew as she leaned closer, those eyes of hers boring in, trying to pry him open, trying to solve the puzzle.

"I don't know."

"Yes, you do. Tell me. What couldn't you imagine?"

He shrugged. "I don't know. I guess—well, okay, I couldn't imagine that anyone would want to be with me, you know?"

"Why?" She stared at him, appearing dumbfounded. With anyone else, he would have known it was an act, and he would have accused her of pretending to be stupid. There were two problems with that, of course: Roan didn't understand *pretend,* and she was anything but stupid.

She really doesn't know.

He pointed up. "Because up there I'm a cripple."

Roan's brow furrowed, and she shifted her eyes side-to-side as she struggled to understand.

"Roan, how can you not see this?" he said in frustration. "Up there I'm grotesque, a hunchback who can't talk or walk. I'm someone to be shunned, someone to throw rotten food at."

Roan stopped puzzling. Instead, her eyes began to blink rapidly. Her lips trembled. "Who threw food at you?"

"Everyone."

"I didn't!" she shouted, her chest rising and falling, her eyes filling with tears.

"Okay—okay, not everyone, but a lot of people did . . . and worse."

"They beat you?"

A bitter little laugh escaped Gifford. "Why do you think I wore long sleeves in summer? Couldn't hide my face, though. Didn't matter. People didn't look at me—still don't. When I walk—" He laughed again. "When I *hobble* by, people pretend I'm not there. They don't like looking, don't like seeing. Don't know why. Maybe they're afraid they can catch my condition. Even the nice people. Even Moya and Persephone . . . I can tell they're pretending I'm normal—but I'm not. They look so embarrassed when they can't understand what I say, as if it's their fault I can't talk. I pretend I don't notice that they feel awkward, and we stand there both pretending—them that they don't really want to be someplace else, and me, that I don't know they want to get away."

"*I never* felt that way." Tears slipped down Roan's face.

How I hate making you cry.

"I know, Roan. You never saw me as different. That's why I fell in love with you. You were the only one who never knew I was crippled."

"But everyone else did," she said.

Gifford nodded.

"Even the nice ones," she added. "Even your friends."

Again, he nodded.

"That's your rock," she told him. "That's the weight."

Gifford stared at her. He stopped breathing. There was a pain rising in him, the sort of hot burning that comes after numbness when toes or fingers come back to life.

I pretended.

Roan was nodding, encouraging him to see, to accept. She squeezed his hand, knowing the anguish was rushing in, all of it coming back in a terrible, horrific assault.

"I pretended for so long, convinced myself that it didn't hurt. But it did . . . it does. The pain is terrible."

"You can let all that go," Roan told him.

He looked at her through blurry eyes. "How?"

"Because now you know."

"Know what?" he begged.

She took his face in her hands, and he felt as if the sun itself were smiling at him. "That you're not a cripple. That you never were."

Like any truth, upon hearing it, Gifford felt stupid. But feeling stupid next to Roan wasn't like being a cripple, and he felt the weight fall as he reached out and hugged his wife, and light filled their world.

"I carried a boulder." Roan kissed him. "You had the same weight, only in countless pebbles."

❧

The silent stillness of that place had been so deafening that to Tesh, wind whipping snow was loud. The flakes had grown big, and they flew in a turmoil, making it hard for him even to see Tressa, who lay only a few feet away. Wasn't just the snow, Roan and Gifford were long gone, having ascended beyond what the snowstorm let them see. The only light at the base of the pillar was the distant but steadily growing glow of red that inched into view like a bloody sunrise.

"Go on, Tesh," Tressa said. She was lying at the base of the pillar, her legs tucked under like a wounded fawn well on her way to being buried. Frosted in snow, her hair and eyelashes were dusted white. She appeared to be a very old woman, withered and wan.

"You say that as if I have a choice." He shouted to be heard over the howling wind.

It's screaming.

Tesh heard the cries carried past them as if lost, disembodied souls were being driven before the red glowing plows.

That's where we all go. We melt, erode away, but still can't escape the Abyss. Maybe not melt—maybe we freeze.

He looked at the icy snow. Maybe it wasn't snow at all.

"You do," Tressa told him, her voice already matching the raspy tone of the blasting snow.

"If I do, you do, too."

"What's *my* choice?" Tressa asked. "To climb up there and do what? Reunite with my beloved husband? Serve the queen?" She tried to laugh, ended up coughing, pretended to spit, then settled for a good long defiant stare through the whirling flakes that clustered on her face. "I'd rather stay anchored here by my pride than face that eternity. But you—you have Brin." She lost her insolence just speaking the name, and Tesh could see a bitter shadow of envy pass through her eyes. "She's a good woman, Tesh. A *really* good woman. If Konniger had ever shown me just a hint, even a suggestion that he could be so much as—as a blister on her foot . . ." She shook off a frown by biting her lower lip, then lifted her gaze and peered up at the pillar. "I'd be up there already. I'd climb that stone if I had to strip naked and kiss everyone's ass who'd ever spat on me. You're an idiot if you don't see that. You're down here, and she's up there waiting. That's just stupid."

"She's not up there anymore." Tesh wiped the flakes from her eyes. Unlike real snow, these didn't melt, maybe because unlike real skin neither of them was warm. "She's gone."

"You don't know how long it's been."

"It's been forever. You know that. Doesn't even matter. I'll still eventually end up here in Nifrel, and she won't."

A sudden burst of shrieks ripped past in the rosy distance. Tesh heard the first jarring footfalls, which made a terrible *whump!* sound.

"Oh." Tressa nodded, acting as if she didn't notice. "So that's it. That's your problem, eh? Even if you make it, you don't, right? But you still have time. You're still young. If you returned to Elan and lived a better—"

"I murdered five people who thought I was their friend. That's not something to erase with an apology."

The rising red light was bright enough to make the cliff walls look like they were covered in blood, and Tressa's face appeared rosy.

"I believed it was justice," Tesh said.

"Whose?"

"Mine, I guess."

"Most of us call that revenge."

"Yeah, I can see that *now*. Thanks for being there for me, Tressa."

Whump.

The ground shook, and some snow fell off the upper ledges of the pillar, raining down with a hiss.

Tressa blinked away a ridge of snowflakes that had gathered once more on her lashes, and for a moment, she lost her hard edge. She was surrendering, giving up, and in that moment, Tressa revealed a woman who in another place and time might have been pleasing. "I'm not getting out of here, Tesh. Not ever. I'll melt away, but if I had any light left, I'd give it to you. I would give you everything I had."

Tesh couldn't help himself. He reached out and hugged Tressa tight to his chest.

The Typhons who had so quaked the Abyss, stopped. For a very long time nothing happened. Then the Typhons slowly began to walk away. What they had come for was gone. The stars that had fallen had flown out again, and the hope that had briefly filled their world was gone. All that remained was the darkness of Tressa and Tesh and the bitterness that rendered them invisible.

CHAPTER TWENTY-FOUR

News from the Tower

I still remember him the way he looked when he came to Dahl Rhen, young, arrogant, selfish, cruel, entitled. When I saw him again, I was surprised to learn that while half a decade of war and the loss of parents had utterly transformed me, it hadn't changed him at all.
— THE BOOK OF BRIN

Mawyndulë stood staring at his room. This chamber-and-a-half filled with a bed, a small desk, some shelves, and a window that looked out on the Shinara River had been his home for the last thirty years. On the mattress was the formal asica he'd worn the first time he visited the Rose Bridge. Beside it lay the gray cloak, the terrible one made by Inga and Flynn—his badge of rebellion. He'd kept it all these years in the bottom of the chest in his closet. Why, he didn't know. Looking at it now, he saw a pathetic thing; the sad efforts of children playing at being adults. On top was the gold chain Gryndal had given Mawyndulë on his twentieth birthday. He'd thought it was a necklace at first, but Gryndal had explained it was to be worn between a pierced ear and a pierced nose. Mawyndulë, who winced when having his toenails clipped, never got around to wearing the gift.

"Aren't you excited to be moving?" Treya asked, her tone far too happy to suit him.

Mawyndulë knew he should be, but he wasn't. He tried to sort out his feelings even as Treya sorted his belongings. This small space had always been his home, the place he'd lived for his entire life. As Treya excavated, he was shocked at how few artifacts she unearthed: an old pair of shoes he loved so much that he'd refused to discard them despite their holes, the winter cloak he'd worn on the night he and Makareta had come together in the Airenthenon, and a rock he had found on the banks of the Shinara that looked like a lumbering bear. They were all added to a small pile of clothing. The little glass fishbowl remained on the table beside his bed. His goldfish had died weeks ago, but he hadn't replaced it. Mawyndulë discovered he both loved and hated the room, and he was bewildered how such contradictions could coexist.

"I'll have the tailor up to take proper measurements for your new clothes," Treya said. "You'll want something special for your coronation."

He frowned at the word. All it did was remind him that someone had blown the horn and no one knew who, or what, he would have to fight.

"I don't care what I wear." He flung himself down on the bed, making the gold chain chime.

"Of course you do," Treya said. "A new fane needs to project dignity to his people."

"I don't think I'm going to be fane."

Treya stopped. She'd been down on her hands and knees, going through the back boxes of his closet, but crawled out and stood to face him. "Why do you say that?"

"Because it's true. I've been challenged. Whoever blew the horn did it knowing they could beat me. Why else would they? It has to be a Miralyith—Vidar or Jerydd probably. I've threatened both with execution if I became fane. I'd blow the horn if I were them." Mawyndulë saw this as the best case. He still harbored fears and suffered nightmares that he might face an undead, charbroiled father. He almost voiced this concern to Treya but held back. He didn't want her to think him a coward.

Treya, he'd come to realize over the last few days, was his only living friend. Not that he had many to start with. Gryndal was on that list.

Makareta transcended it. Then there was Imaly, but she had only pretended to be his friend. She'd done a fine job. Even after everything, he still craved her approval. Mawyndulë wanted Imaly to change her mind about him. He felt he still might prove his worth, show her how wrong she'd been and regain her respect. Mawyndulë also knew this was a fantasy. He'd never had her respect. He ought to have killed her that night in the Airenthenon, but he couldn't bring himself to do it. He hated the ugly Curator. She had stolen his soul, killed Makareta and his father, and yet . . . she was still the closest thing he'd ever had to a mother.

"You'll be fine," Treya said. "You have strength, you have skill, and you have youth on your side. Those others are dusty old Fhrey. Their bodies and minds cannot compete with yours."

"Dusty?" he said, amused. "I thought I was the only one who said that."

Treya smiled at him, an odd, embarrassed look.

"What?" he asked.

Treya looked around the room at the disarray that was Mawyndulë's life. She took a breath and bit her lip.

"What is it?"

"I suppose it doesn't matter anymore. Your father is dead."

"What doesn't matter?"

"I just . . ." She hesitated. "It's been so long. It feels strange to think that I could . . ." She stopped again, looking like she was suffering indigestion.

"Could what?"

"It's a secret, and I've kept it for so long that breaking my silence is scary." She had both hands on her stomach as she looked toward the window as if she wanted to go there, but she didn't move.

Maybe it is an upset stomach. Perhaps she needs to vomit.

"But like I said, it doesn't matter now. Lothian is gone, and my vow was to him. That was the agreement we had. I would be allowed to be near you, to nurse and raise you, but I could never do more than that. I could never tell you the truth."

Treya's expression became pained, and the hands that had lain against her stomach came up and pressed to her cheeks. She shook her head and looked away. "I'm sorry, but—"

"Mawyndulë!"

He gasped. The voice did not come from the room, not from Treya certainly. This was the harsh, demanding voice of a dusty old Miralyith. "Jerydd?"

"I didn't catch you on the privy, did I?" the old kel asked. *"Or on top of some terrified junior councilor's wife?"*

"Of course not!"

Treya stared, confused.

Mawyndulë shook his head and waved a hand at her, then pointed back at the closet. She nodded and went back to work.

Mawyndulë stood and walked to the window. This was it, Jerydd was letting him know he planned to—

"What's going on back there?"

"It's a long story."

"Tragedy or comedy?"

"That's yet to be determined."

"Why haven't you contacted me?"

There were many reasons. The biggest being that Mawyndulë was fairly certain Jerydd knew full well what had happened. The kel was playing some form of mind game, a means of flustering his opponent before the battle. He could hear it in his voice: the confidence, the lack of any true outrage. His cordial manner was evidence he knew more than Mawyndulë did.

Mawyndulë obliged him, but without any real effort. "The Aquila launched an overthrow. They tricked me into killing my father, which obliterated my birthright. But I was able to blow the horn, and none of them were brave enough to fight me. I sort of figured it would end there, but that Rhune we captured ran off with the horn, and someone blew it. I don't suppose you know who that might be?"

Mawyndulë held his breath.

"Actually I do."

Of course you do, you miserable old snake.

"He's here with me now."

Mawyndulë pushed out onto the little balcony. The cold winter air gusted into the room, making Treya squawk as the wind ruffled the bedcovers.

So it wasn't Jerydd? Who then? Was it Vidar? One of the younger Miralyith?

He decided it didn't matter. He'd still lose. All of them were better at the Art.

"Who is it?"

"Nyphron of the Instarya. He's sitting right here in the tower. We're having tea."

ꝇ

"You promised this was going to work!" Volhoric shouted at Imaly.

"I made no promises," she replied.

The five of them were locked in the same cell. Fanes had never had much use for prisons, but they did need to store food. Since people were prone to steal provisions, especially during hard winters, a lock had been placed on the doors to the cellars, which were dug deep into the ground. The location proved to be an excellent place to store the rebellious members of the Aquila as well, although no one appeared to care if they were preserved or not.

Imaly was tired of the bickering and finger-pointing, almost all of which was aimed at her. Only Vasek refrained from the popular new pastime. She guessed he didn't indulge because he alone had gone into the endeavor with realistic expectations.

"You did!" Volhoric insisted. "You said as much."

"Well, then, you should never have believed me, as no one could *promise* to deliver such a thing. That was just foolishness on your part. Honestly, Vol, you should know better."

He stood among the crates of onions, glaring at her with an expression that she could best describe as a befuddled owl—two big eyes blinking in the dark. Outside, it was daytime, and a few slices of light pierced the slats of the door, just enough for her to recognize the hate on her companions' faces.

"I'm only twelve hundred and thirty-two," Osla said in a melodramatic woe-is-me manner, shaking, maybe with the cold, but probably not. "I thought most of my life was still ahead of me."

"Makareta was only a hundred and twenty-eight," Imaly reminded her.

"But I didn't do anything. That lunatic Gray Cloak tried to kill the fane."

"So did you." Imaly drew her collar tighter around her neck. In summer, the cellar's coolness kept the food fresh. In winter, its temperature was near freezing. "How did you think it was going to work out if we failed? Mawyndulë will kill us, just as his father executed the Gray Cloaks."

Osla's eyes went wide, as if this notion had never crossed her mind. Imaly glared as well.

How stupid are these people? Leaders of their tribes, voices in the council to advise the fane, and they didn't see this?

"But someone challenged him," Nanagal said. "We all heard it."

"He's Miralyith," Vasek said. "Only a Miralyith will fight him, so the dynamic will be the same. Nothing will change. Knowing that we tried to prevent the Miralyith tribe from holding power, whoever becomes fane will also kill us and likely abolish the Aquila, assuming they have even a hint of intelligence."

The lock jiggled, and they all fell silent.

The door to the cell drew back, revealing the unmistakable silhouette of Mawyndulë. Two guards with lanterns entered ahead of him, brushing the rest of them back among the roots. Osla began to cry.

"How are you enjoying your stay?" Mawyndulë asked.

His voice was far too light, his expression too pleased. Despite her years of bolstering his ego, Imaly couldn't imagine Mawyndulë being happy at the thought of engaging in mortal combat with any other Miralyith. Something had happened.

"Turns out I was smart not to kill you right away. I was *so* on the brink of it, but it seems you might be useful. If you are, I may be persuaded to let you keep breathing. Interested?"

They all nodded, but no one spoke.

"Good. I need some questions answered. I have obviously been challenged, but not at the Carfreign. Does the fight *have* to take place there?"

Everyone turned to Volhoric, who looked down at his feet and shook his head slowly. "No . . . nothing that I can think of. The Carfreign was actually built by Fenelyus as a stadium for Art competitions. It just seemed the best place to hold the fight. Until Lothian dueled Zephyron, horn challenges had never resulted in an actual battle."

"Never?" Mawyndulë asked.

Volhoric looked up. "No. Gylindora named Navi Lon her successor, before she died." He looked over at Imaly, who nodded. "No one challenged. Ghika was Navi Lon's daughter. Everyone accepted her as fane. My grandfather blew the horn in challenge against her and immediately conceded. He only did that to accommodate the necessary ritual that requires the horn to be blown at least once every three thousand years. If it's not, the Law of Ferrol wouldn't come into effect. When Ghika was killed by the Dherg at the start of the Great War, no one wanted to be fane. Alon Rhist, much to his credit, was brave enough to blow the horn. And when he was killed in battle, once again, no one wanted to be fane. When your grandmother Fenelyus blew the horn, my father—just like his father—blew it, too, and conceded. So no, the only actual succession by combat was between Lothian and Zephyron."

Mawyndulë considered this. "So there are no restrictions on where the fight can be held?"

"Not that I'm aware of. An arena has to be built, so dry land would help."

"An *arena?*" He spoke the word in shock. "What are we talking about here? A building? A stadium?"

"It doesn't need to be much. A circle of a specific size, with the proper torches and incense and such."

"So nothing super elaborate?"

"Not really."

"May we ask why you want to know?" Imaly inquired.

Mawyndulë refused to look at her. "I have been challenged by Nyphron." He had a hard time keeping a straight face as he said the name. "Apparently, the Instarya want a rematch. I suspect some might have missed the show the first time around, and having heard so much, they want to see it all play out again. I am eager to please them."

"How is that possible?" Volhoric asked. "The horn . . . how did it get to Nyphron in time? Isn't he on the other side of the Nidwalden?"

"I have no idea," Mawyndulë said. "But Jerydd says Nyphron blew it. According to him, the Galantian was invulnerable during his visit to the tower, proving he was endowed with the Protection of Ferrol. Nyphron actually petted the dragons. But he won't come here. He insists on meeting halfway. We settled on the bank of the Nidwalden near Avempartha. Jerydd feels this is great for lots of reasons. We will pull back our troops and dragons to our side of the river and allow the Rhune to occupy the other. That way when I win, we can simply destroy them and be done with the war."

"What if you lose?" Vasek asked, his voice coming from the shadows as always.

Mawyndulë leaned to peer around Volhoric, searching for the face behind the question. "Jerydd says if that happens, being at Avempartha will be perfect. Nyphron hates Miralyith. He'll want to kill us all. Jerydd is telling everyone that if Nyphron kills me, they should take it as proof he intends to wipe out the Miralyith. He's convincing the Artists at the river to be prepared to fight if that happens—dragons and all."

"He will break Ferrol's Law?"

"No." Mawyndulë grinned. "He has a better idea. They will kill the Rhunes, then take Nyphron prisoner, lock him away, and rule in his name. Might even torture him a bit. No rules against hurting a fane."

Mawyndulë stepped forward and plucked a turnip out of a bag and studied it with a dull expression. "None of that will be necessary, of course. I should have no trouble killing Nyphron. But I do want this to be done right. I want no excuses, no failure to perform the proper ritual that later prevents me from taking the throne. So each of you will be coming to The Challenge to guarantee that everything is done properly. If everything goes right—you do your part, and I get the throne—then I'll let you go. There won't be an Aquila anymore, but you won't be dead, either. And you, Imaly . . ." He finally faced her. "You will be the one to crown me when I win."

Imaly felt her heart sink, and her great-grandmother shift in her grave.

◈

All of it was a lie. The moment Mawyndulë was properly seated on the throne, he would execute every member of the Aquila—including Vidar, if Mawyndulë could find him. This was a promise he made to himself as he walked through the snow back to the palace.

I wonder how Imaly will like being lied to.

On his way, Mawyndulë slipped through the Garden and paused at the Door. It was closed again, sealed shut, and once more no one could open it. Mawyndulë turned to look at the nearest bench, the one eternally occupied by the enigma who called himself Trilos. The bench was vacant, the Garden empty.

Mawyndulë pondered this for some time. *Did Trilos go in? Is he still inside?*

Normally Mawyndulë hated his encounters with the benchwarmer. But just then, Mawyndulë realized he was interested in what was behind the Door, in how the horn might have gotten to Nyphron, and in several other things. But like his bedroom, Mawyndulë's world was changing, emptying of all the old things he used to know, both the good and the bad.

When he returned to his room, Treya was still there.

His chambers were packed up and cleaned, but she remained seated on the stripped-down bed. "You're back," she said brightly and stood up.

She was smiling. Mawyndulë couldn't remember her ever doing that before—at least not like this.

"You're finished in here. That's good. We need to pack up. We are heading to Avempartha in the morning."

Treya nodded. "I'll get you packed. But there was that one thing I wanted to discuss with you."

"What's that?" In the wake of all the excitement and the relief that all he needed to do was kill an Instarya, he found himself exhausted and wanted to lie down. He'd been having trouble sleeping, but he didn't think that would be a problem anymore.

I could take a nice nap.

"The secret," Treya said. "The one your father ordered me to never speak to you about."

"Oh, right, what was that?" he asked, then yawned.

"I was nursemaid to your brother, Pyridian. You see, his mother Olyona died giving birth, so I was brought in. At the time, I was very young, only a few hundred years old. Your father and I raised Pyridian, and he turned out to be a fine son—a great Artist. He taught both Gryndal and Arion."

"Yes, I've heard." Mawyndulë didn't enjoy hearing how great his older brother had been. He never had. Now that Mawyndulë was about to become fane, listening to the achievements of Pyridian felt disrespectful at best.

"When he died—"

"How did he die?" Mawyndulë asked. "I never heard."

"An accident," Treya said. "Something Pyridian was trying at the academy one night. That's what Gryndal said. The two were the only ones there at the time. Something to do with the Art, I suspect, but I'm not an Artist, am I? Anyway, when Pyridian died, it devastated your father. Didn't do me any good, either."

"Is this the secret my father forbade you from telling me?"

Treya shook her head. "No."

"Getting to that anytime soon?"

Treya looked embarrassed and nodded. "Because Pyridian was dead, your father felt he needed another heir, but he didn't want all the headaches that came with marriage. I was there, relatively young, and, being a Gwydry, I was no threat. He could discard me without repercussions. He knew I would never protest, never cause a fuss." Her voice grew softer and quieter. "When you were born, he planned to send me away, usher me off to some small, distant village, make me disappear. I pleaded with him. I begged to be part of your life. I knew it would kill me to never see you, never hold you. I wanted to guide your first steps, hear your first words." Treya bowed her head. "I think our history raising Pyridian together softened his heart, and he granted me this favor. He said I could be your nursemaid just as I had been with Pyridian, but under the condition that I never tell anyone—especially not you."

She stared at him then. Treya seemed to be waiting for something, but Mawyndulë had no idea what. "So are you going to tell me this big secret or not?"

Treya blinked in surprise. "Mawyndulë, I'm your mother."

While this wasn't the best of jokes, Mawyndulë laughed anyway. The buildup was what did it. Treya really sold the backstory.

"I'm not joking. I am your mother."

The deadpan look on her face was too much. "Thank you, Treya, I needed that. Things have been so serious around—"

"Mawyn, I'm serious. You are my son!"

Mawyndulë stared, confused. Selling a joke was one thing, but this was . . . *she's serious?*

"Treya, you're Gwydry. I'm Miralyith. Of course you're not my mother. Don't be absurd."

She reached out and put a hand on his arm. "But I am. Look into my eyes. You'll see. I'm telling the truth."

Mawyndulë couldn't believe her insolence, this insane insistence that they were related and then her touching him as if she had a right. He pushed her away.

"You know, I wouldn't have thought it possible—not you, too . . ." He shook his head in disgust.

Everyone lies to me! Imaly, Volhoric. They all pretend to be someone they're not!

"You learn I'm going to be fane, discover that all I have to do is kill an Instarya, and here you are claiming to be my long-lost mother. Isn't that convenient? Yesterday, you were a Gwydry palace servant, but today you're the mother of the fane! You disgust me." Mawyndulë stood up. "Don't bother packing. You won't be coming to Avempartha. I never want to see you again."

With those words, Mawyndulë left his chambers, along with the whole world as he'd once known it, and he did so for the last time.

CHAPTER TWENTY-FIVE

Mission from God

For motivation, nothing beats having a god take a personal interest in your work.

— THE BOOK OF BRIN

Brin lay on her side, staring at the bed across from her. There was a sag, a hollow depression in the straw mattress exactly the size of Padera. It wasn't large; the cavity could have been made by a sizable dog. Somehow Brin remembered Padera as bigger; she'd certainly played a larger role in Brin's life—in everyone's life. Hanging in a net bag on the wall was an assortment of spices Padera had received from Grygor. She'd stopped using them after the giant died, but kept them in that bag with all her other cherished items. On the floor was the bolt of fabric for Tressa's dress. As a surprise, the garment was going to have pleats. Brin had planned to make that dress ridiculously beautiful, not just with pleats, but with buttons, too, and a pocket. People would marvel at Tressa instead of sneering in her direction.

Brin started crying.

She had pulled her blanket up to her cheeks because the tent was cold that morning. Now she used the corners to wipe her eyes. More tears came. She wiped again. Didn't help. Brin just gave up then and, burying her face in the cloth, sobbed.

"Brin?" A shadow appeared outside. "Brin, are you awake?"

"Yes." Her voice was wispy, ragged from the weeping.

The flap drew back. More sunlight entered, and Persephone rushed in with it.

"I was so scared," Persephone said and hugged the girl tightly. Then, as if realizing she might be hurting Brin, Persephone loosened her hold. "Malcolm told me you died but might come back. It was so hard to believe."

Brin wanted to hug back, but her arms were too weak to perform a good squeeze. Neither said anything for some time. Then Persephone drew away, wiped her eyes, and sat opposite Brin on Padera's bed so she could look Brin over. Reaching across the narrow gap, she took Brin's hands, warming them in hers. "How are you feeling?"

"Like I've been dead for a week." The answer felt stupid coming out of her mouth, but it was the truth.

After delivering the horn, Brin had passed out. She had no recollection of how she got to her tent. She woke up exhausted, noticed it was morning, and realized the effects of Muriel's meal had long since worn off. She felt horrible. Everything ached—except her head, which throbbed, and her stomach, which both ached and throbbed. It also twisted with simmering nausea. Food and drink were at the side of her bed. She forced herself to nibble and then fell back to sleep. When she woke up again, it was dark. More food had been delivered, and again she ate and drank what she could, then fell asleep once more.

"How long have I been here? How many days have I been sleeping?"

"Just a few. I've visited you often, but nothing excessive." Persephone forced a smile. "Only about once every hour. You were always asleep, and I didn't want to wake you. I usually just sat over here and listened to you breathe. It made me feel better; I don't know about you."

Persephone's face was coated in concern as she rubbed the back of Brin's hand in a slow, circular pattern. She didn't say anything, waiting for Brin, expecting her to explain all that had happened . . . and where the others were. Brin was a Keeper after all—that was her job. But Brin didn't want to tell *that* story. Not now, not yet. It hurt too much, and she was already in such pain.

As if understanding this, Persephone didn't ask. "You still look tired." She reached up and brushed Brin's cheek.

"I am."

Persephone nodded. "You should rest then. We can talk another time. I just . . . Nyphron will be fighting Mawyndulë in a few days near Avempartha. We'll have to be leaving soon, but before I go, I wanted you to know that your mother and father would be so very proud of you, Brin. Of all that you've done for us. Of all that you sacrificed."

"They are," Brin said. "And my mother thinks you are doing a wonderful job as keenig."

Persephone bit her lip and sucked in an uneven breath. Her eyes grew teary as she nodded. "You saw her? You saw Sarah and Delwin?"

"Yes." Brin smiled. "I saw everyone. Even Padera and Darby, too. I always wondered about dogs, where they went. I guess maybe if someone loves you enough . . ." Brin felt the tears rising again.

"What about . . ."

"Yes, Raithe was there. He wants you to know that he understands why you picked Nyphron, and he's not upset. He still loves you, and he waits for you. He—"

Persephone silenced her with a squeeze of her hand. She nodded, wiped away a tear, and didn't say anything for a long time. Then she said, "I'm so sorry, Brin."

That was all it took. She began crying again.

Persephone shifted beds. She hugged Brin, pulling her tight. "It's okay. It's okay," she repeated as if willing it to be so.

Brin dropped her head onto Persephone's shoulder, her brow pressed against the older woman's neck.

"You did it, Brin." Persephone rocked forward and back, taking Brin with her, holding her like a child who'd just woken from a nightmare. "You saved us. You saved them. You saved everyone."

Brin lifted her head. "Not everyone."

Persephone cupped Brin's face, lifted it, and looked into her eyes. "Don't do that. I know what it's like to lose people. I know how it feels when you believe it's your fault. It can eat you up from the inside. Don't let it. You're so young. You still have so much life to live. Don't give in to the grief. You have to go on."

Brin didn't realize she was shaking her head until Persephone took a firmer grip and stopped her.

"You have to, Brin. You must."

"I don't want to."

"It's not about *want*—do you think I wanted to keep eating after Mahn died? Or continue to breathe after Reglan? And when Raithe . . ." Her voice broke. She let go of Brin's face and turned away. "It's not about want. Some things you just have to do; some things you need to do because you can and others can't. Do you understand?"

"Yes. Yes I do."

"Good." She kissed Brin, hugged her one more time, then stood up.

"Wait," Brin said, then paused in thought, recalling her conversation with Moya. *"What good will come from telling her now? She's married to Nyphron. They have a child."*

While all that was true, the more important point was that Nyphron had blown the horn, and the fate of all Rhunes rested in his ability to win against Mawyndulë. Not to mention that it was what Malcolm wanted. He wouldn't have put them through all they endured if it weren't so important.

What benefit will come from revealing his treachery? If I tell her the truth, Persephone will do what she always does. She'll sacrifice herself for her people. She'll do nothing, say nothing. But late at night, she'll torment herself with the ugly truth that she married a ruthless murderer who thought nothing of starting a war to serve himself. Is that what I want to give her?

If Brin kept quiet and Nyphron were to win The Challenge, that day could be bright. Persephone could receive the reward she deserved. The sacrifices would be balanced against the promise of the future: that the world would be a better place.

If Brin told the truth, she'd have to live in silence, knowing that her husband had deceived her, that the father of her child was to blame for thousands of deaths. That she had—

"What is it, Brin?" Persephone asked.

"Nothing."

❦

Brin lay on her bed, listening to the sounds of those preparing to travel as they went about the tasks of breaking down and packing up. The camp had been in place for years, and travel in winter was miserable. More than one person complained, but mostly to themselves. Brin could hear them through the canvas, grumbling and cursing their misfortune. They had no idea what real hardship was, or how lucky they were. None of them knew the price that had been paid for the luxury of their inconvenience.

They will. Brin looked over at the stack of pages. *I can do that much for them.*

The flap of her tent lifted.

"May I come in?" Malcolm asked as he did so anyway. He bent low to get his tall, lanky frame under the roof of the tent.

He smiled at her as he moved in a crouch to sit on Padera's bed, just as Persephone had. Malcolm let his hands run over the surface of Padera's bed, dipping down into the depression the old woman had left. "She seemed bigger than this."

"She gave me your message."

"Yes, I know. I can't see into Phyre, but looking into the Swamp of Ith is an easy task."

"She still hates you."

"A lot of people do, but you know that now, right? You know everything. That's why I sent you. I needed you to know the truth, warts and all."

Brin nodded, and watched as Malcolm crossed his long legs and folded his hands in his lap. He looked clumsy and not at all godlike.

Funny, the Fhrey always looked like gods, and Gryndal acted like one, but they weren't. Malcolm looks like the kind of awkward man whom people ignore—the dull sort that is never noticed, never appreciated. Tressa was right, though. Malcolm is a god, and with the world as his mother, the sky his father, and immortality granted from Alurya's gift, he might be the only true god. Unfortunately, he's the god of evil.

"Is it true?" she asked.

Malcolm raised his brows. "You'll have to be more specific."

"That you're evil."

Malcolm smiled. "*Evil* is an odd word. Somewhat useless, really. It means different things to different people, doesn't it? If you're asking, did I do many terrible things, then yes—I did. I would say I hold the record for that achievement. But am I evil? I suppose that's for others to decide. People like you."

"You sent all of us to our deaths without so much as a warning. You had Tressa lie to us so we didn't even know what we were getting into."

"Yes, I did. I've deceived a great many people."

"Why did you do it?"

"Because it was what was necessary. If there had been a better option, I would have chosen it. There wasn't."

"I don't . . ." Brin shook her head. "I don't know what to make of you. Are you trying to fix the world? Elan says you are, but Muriel says you aren't. Who is right?"

Again, he smiled; once more looking like the same old friendly Malcolm, the one she remembered sitting on the floor of Roan's home, chatting about how Fhrey, Dherg, and Rhunes were all related. "I can't answer that question. Well, I could, but we've already established that I'm not to be trusted, so my answer would be pointless. All I can say is this: You've spoken to my enemies, and the very few people who might still believe in me. I have no idea what they told you, but words can be lies. So I'll ask you to judge me on my actions. Granted, up to this point, it's difficult to know all the things I've done. But you can see where we are now, and if you think about it, you'll see that I've been steering us to this point. The world is about to change, and if it's going to be for the better, you should aid me. That's why I sent you. To grant you the unvarnished knowledge necessary to decide."

Brin nodded.

"Well, then, on to other matters. Can I assume you no longer have my key?"

Brin sucked in a breath. She closed her eyes, with all the expectations of a criminal ready to be executed. Then she confessed, "I left it in a safe place in Phyre."

Malcolm frowned. "That's probably not a very—"

"It's only temporary. I'm hoping the others will be able to get out. Even if they can't, it will be given to Muriel."

Malcolm tilted his head to the right and then the left, considering the implications.

When he didn't say more, Brin spoke up. "I told her that you're trying to fix things."

"Let me guess. It had no effect. She still hates me."

Brin frowned and with a sudden unexpected fit of bravery and self-righteousness said, "You need to fix that."

"Yes." Malcolm displayed a sort of smile, a curious, amused expression. "You have learned a lot. What's more, you've become quick to advise."

Brin flushed. Malcolm didn't look like Ferrol or Drome. He didn't speak with a booming voice, more of a quiet tone, but his words carried a similar weight.

"Sorry," she said.

"You should know by now, that's one sentiment no one need ever express to me." He nodded then. "And you're right. And I *am* working on it."

"Trust is a good first step, don't you think?"

He didn't appear to share her enthusiasm, but neither did he strike her dead. Brin took this as a good sign.

She was still trying to wrap her head around the idea that this unassuming man before her had sort of fought the sky . . . and kind of won. He didn't look anything like how Elan had depicted him: wearing a crown and a shimmering robe that changed colors. The notion that he had once ruled the world and made it tremble seemed so odd. And before that . . .

"What was it like?"

"What do you mean?"

"In the beginning? Before—you know—before everything went bad?"

Malcolm looked at the floor. He appeared sad for a moment, then the smile returned. "It was wonderful. Not at all like now. The world was . . . well, like bread fresh out of an oven. You know what I mean: The smell fills the air and makes everything wonderful somehow, and it tastes so good when it's warm and soft. Fact is, all you've ever known is hard, week-old moldy crust. Back then, colors were different, the light brighter. Everything was just, well, *more*—I guess. It's hard to explain. Everyone who had ever been was here. Not one had died. The world was massive, unexplored, and more people arrived every day: new friends, new loves, and an endless universe was our playground. Instead of fear, regret, and hate, we had only joy, love, and happiness."

"No wonder they hate you," Brin said.

Malcolm's brows rose, and Brin's hands flashed to her mouth as if to retrieve the words and push them back in.

"No—no, you're right. It's true. I ruined all that. And that's why I'm here—why I've come to visit. I have one last task for you. A very, very important job."

"It doesn't involve running, does it? Because I can't even walk. If I could, I'd be—"

Malcolm raised a hand to stop her. "No. But you do need to get up. I've arranged a wagon for you. A nice one with wooden sides and a fringed canopy. There's a bed filled with thick blankets. It will take you days to get to Avempartha, but while you are traveling, I need you to finish this."

He placed a hand on the stack. "You need to write down everything you learned in Phyre."

"I plan to. I will. But as soon as I'm better I need to go—"

"No," he said firmly. "This has to be done *now*."

"You mean *now*, now?"

"Yes, and don't worry about your supplies, you'll have all the ink and parchment you require."

"I don't understand."

"This is why you went, Brin. To be honest, writing what you learned is even more important than retrieving the horn. Stopping the war was crucial, of course. Nyphron will become the first emperor of those born of Mari and the children of Ferrol. Then he'll make an alliance with Drome's children. But that's only a start. Your book will do the rest."

It was a lovely sentiment, but Brin couldn't follow the logic. "How?"

"With it, you will teach the world a new language. From your book, all races will learn to read and write. This will give them a common tongue again, allowing them to communicate with one another as they once did. And in reading your story, they will learn that they are all one people, born of the same five seeds, of the same mother and father. This will open the door for reunification. Brin, I sent you through Phyre so you could see the truth for yourself. I sent you because no one can ever doubt your words. My words, on the other hand . . ." He shook his head and snorted. "No one will ever believe me, no one will listen—and with good cause. I wouldn't believe me, either. But you! Your words are untainted. I sent you into Phyre because you're flawless—perfect."

"I'm not!" she said, feeling the pain return. "How can you even say that? For example, look at how disgusting and messy this tent is?" She glared at him as her lower lip began to quiver. "I've been mean to people, too. I was judgmental. For years, I despised Tressa . . . and . . . and . . . I didn't even help my uncle Gelston after he was struck by lightning." Tears came up and spilled. "And . . . Tesh, Roan, Gifford, Moya, Rain, and Tressa." She wiped her cheeks. "I left them behind! I am not perfect, Malcolm. Not at all."

"You left the key for them. You did so while knowing I would want it back. You willingly angered the god of evil, the creator of murder, deceit, and war, and you didn't even hide the fact. You didn't try to lie to save yourself. That doesn't sound like much of a character flaw."

"I still abandoned them, and Tesh wouldn't have even died if it weren't for me." She stared at the blanket on her bed. Her hands spread out, palms down, sliding back and forth, smoothing it.

"Okay." Malcolm shrugged. "Have it your way. You aren't perfect, but you're close. That actually helps. People are suspicious of those who have no flaws. Knowing you've made mistakes will make it easier for people to believe your writings. Through your words, they will learn to join and work together. But you really do need to hurry."

Brin paused in her efforts to wipe out the wrinkles. "Why?"

"Because my brother is back on Elan. I can't see him any more than I can see into Phyre, but I can witness the effects of his actions. I don't want all that I've sewn up to unravel. He'll follow behind me, tearing my seams apart. He knows about you, doesn't he?"

She nodded. "We've met."

"And I fear you will again. It's only a matter of time." He chuckled. "*Time.* It's endless, yet its rate of passing is never constant. And it's something, believe it or not, I fear I need more of."

Malcolm looked mournful as he got up and went toward the entrance.

Before he could leave, Brin said, "Elan told me, if anyone could fix the world—it was you."

Malcolm pulled back the tent flap, letting the sunlight in. He turned back and said, "Perhaps she has too much faith in me."

"She's not the only one. I believe in you, too."

Malcolm looked skeptical. "Even after all you've learned? How can you, Brin? I created evil and invented the lie. Until recently, everything you knew about me was a fabrication. I used you and everyone else. It wasn't Nyphron who murdered all those people for his own selfish means. He didn't start this war. I put the spark to that flame. I sacrificed Raithe,

Arion, the entire Dureyan clan, all the people of Nadak, and so much more than you could ever know."

"Everyone falls. We all have things that we regret. No one is perfect. You know that now, but you didn't when you were Rex Uberlin. Your mother is right, you've changed, and I think that your trying has to count for something, doesn't it?"

"Perhaps, but the real question is, will it be enough? And only time will tell." Then his gaze moved to the stack. "You might want to take measures to protect that. I fear my brother will not abide anything I had a hand in creating. Be careful, Brin. Be *very* careful."

CHAPTER TWENTY-SIX

The Man in the Mirror

Gifford is like a pearl inside an oyster. From the exterior, no one would ever assume such a treasure lay inside.

— THE BOOK OF BRIN

"Didn't seem as wide before," Gifford said as he stood at the broken edge of the stone bridge and stared across at Nifrel. They had no trouble seeing the far side. Even if the queen's manufactured gray sky weren't lighting the world, the combined shine of Roan and Gifford would have done just fine. After reaching the top of the pillar, the two were once more clad in Alberich Berling's armor. Roan, who had never felt comfortable in it, stripped off the priceless suit. Gifford did the same, and they were surprised that removing the Belgriclungreian armor hadn't put a dent in the light they emitted.

The gap wasn't wide. Gifford could throw a rock across the missing section of bridge. Beyond the gap lay the slate-gray plain—the worn-out battlefield polished and stained dark with the nonexistent blood of uncounted conflicts. After all the time they had spent in the Abyss, seeing the Plain of Kilcorth seemed like waving to an old friend.

Has it been years? It certainly feels like it.

Even the queen's White Tower, which rose a short way to the left, didn't hold the same horror it once had. After facing oblivion in the unending dark, everything else was a good deal more pleasant. And they didn't have the key anymore. Nothing to protect, no rush, nothing to worry about—except how to cross the gap. Unless they found a way, the two would spend eternity on that tiny tongue of stone.

"Don't suppose you have any ideas, do you?" he asked while glancing over his shoulder at Roan.

She gave him a withering look as she continued her pacing between the mirrored door and the severed end of the bridge. She was still fuming for not having realized they should have climbed the other cliff. "Just stupid—just so stupid," she muttered. She'd been saying that for a while.

"Did you even know the bridge was broken?" he asked. "I was nearly hit by the pieces, but you weren't there."

She didn't answer, just scowled as if Gifford was taking the wrong side in an argument with a hated enemy.

"Sorry." He held up his hands, then sighed. "We're going to have to go back down, aren't we?"

Roan groaned.

"It might be fun, you know?"

She didn't appear to know anything of the sort as she continued to frown.

"I mean this time we're armed with the knowledge that we won't splat, and that we can climb back out." He smiled at her. "So it could be like diving. People enjoy diving."

Gifford got to his hands and knees and peered over the edge, looking again for signs of Tesh and Tressa, and wondering if he could see the Typhons. That would be the only real issue—falling on them. He had no clear idea what a Typhon was and didn't feel the slightest need to find out. He and Roan would need to wait a good long time to ensure the things had moved away.

But how long is long enough? And how can I keep track?

Gifford couldn't see the Typhons, and there was still no sign of Tressa or Tesh.

"Well, if it helps, I never would have gotten this far without you." He smiled.

Roan's eyes narrowed, and she began shaking her head. "How could that possibly help? How?" Her brow wrinkled, lower lip riding up. Roan started making a noise in the back of her throat, the prelude to a scream. Instead, she punched both of her thighs with her fists and resumed her pacing. "There's got to be a way. Stupid. Stupid. Stupid."

Roan shoved a lock of hair into her mouth and chewed it as she passed by in her eternal walk; then she halted. She didn't move for a second—just stopped and stared, but only into the distance, not at anything in particular. Gifford knew that when Roan was thinking, she could walk right into a wall and never notice. Whatever she was seeing, it wasn't the bridge or the Abyss. He often speculated on what she did see: crimbals, perhaps, or the gods pantomiming answers to her questions.

"*You* can do it," she said.

"Do what, Roan? We've discussed this before, remember? How I can't actually hear your thoughts?"

She pivoted and showed him her frustrated face.

"You have to give me a hint, at least. Okay?"

"The mirror, the mirror." She pointed frantically. "The door to Alysin."

"What about it?"

"*You* can go through."

Gifford shook his head. "We don't have the key."

"*You* don't need the key," she said, her hair falling out of her mouth as she spoke.

"Roan, I saw you push on it. You knocked, put your nose to the glass. We can't get through without the key."

"That's not what I said." Roan huffed. "I said *you* don't need the key. You're the Hero of Grandford."

Gifford smirked and folded his arms. "I'm not a hero."

She fixed him with one of her impatient glares. She had an assortment; this was the one accompanied with squeezing fists of frustration. "You thought you were going to your death. We all thought you were going to die. Even Padera did. You did, too, didn't you?"

He shrugged. "Yeah, sure, but that doesn't mean—"

"It does!" Roan came to him, knelt down, and took one of his hands. She threaded her fingers into his, as she loved to do. She had once told him that the way their fingers fit, the way they *wove*, was practical evidence of a universal truth. It demonstrated that they were meant to be together. The first time she told him this, he foolishly pointed out the obvious: that everyone's fingers fit together. He remembered how she had smiled and nodded with profound understanding. *Exactly*, she'd said.

"No one—no one in all of Alon Rhist would have dared do what you did that night. Not Nyphron, and not any of the Galantians—and everyone says *they're* heroes, but they aren't, not really. But you are. You risked everything. You, who'd never used a sword or spear before, or sat on a horse—you put on armor and alone rode into the face of the Fhrey army. And for what? Glory?"

"No!" Gifford said, surprised she could even say that.

She laughed softly. The sound was music, ice water on a sweltering day, a warm blanket on a cold night. He loved that laugh. "I know," she said, her eyes full of pride. "You never once thought of yourself. And when Tressa declared she would travel through Phyre, you were the first to volunteer to die with her. Even if it meant leaving me, you couldn't let her die alone. And when I couldn't make it out of the Abyss, you stayed to keep me company. Never even tried to leave. You bravely gave of yourself. More important, you don't even see the miracle in that. I honestly suspect you think everyone is that way, but they aren't. Almost no one is. Gifford, you *are* a hero, a real hero, and I think that means that door is open to you."

Gifford looked across the remaining bridge at the mirror. Even at that distance he could see himself in it, a shimmering light. "Not without you."

Roan's brows went up. "Did you think I was asking you to leave me behind?"

"Well . . . ah, then I guess I don't understand."

"It's just like the Battle of Grandford."

"Still not seeing the path you're walking, Roan."

She rolled her eyes, huffing through her nose again. "You need to go get help."

"Get help? How can I—we don't know what's over there. And anyway, if I go through, I won't be able to come back. I mean, if I belong over there, Roan, I won't be able to come back here without the key."

"Doesn't apply to you," she said with that misty-eyed look of hers. This was the same reverent stare she used to beam at him whenever he gave her cups or that amphora. It proclaimed he was something he wasn't. Gifford would have thought that she would have lost that expression of awe years ago, around the same time she saw him roll out of bed, something that—with his bad leg and twisted back—he literally did, and oftentimes hit the ground in the process. But there she was, as entranced as ever.

"What do you mean?"

"You put your hand through the door back into Rel. Almost got pulled through. You didn't have the key. Tressa did, and she was nowhere near you. The doorway was locked, had to be. Otherwise Drome's minions would have come through. But your arm went right in. It passed *back*. So I have a theory. Maybe everyone can go backward through Phyre and the key is only needed to go forward, or maybe only you can do it. Doesn't matter. You have the ability to move through doors without the key."

"A *theory*?"

She fixed him with a smirk. He knew this look, too, but Roan didn't own that expression. He'd seen Moya display the same twisted smile when anyone suggested she couldn't hit a mark with an arrow, or when someone asked Brin if she could recall—well, anything. "Okay, so your theories usually work—but not *always*."

"This one will."

She wasn't lying. Roan didn't lie, but her eyes didn't match her words.

"Really? Because you don't look confident. To be honest, you look terrified."

"I'm certain you will be able to come back," she told him. "I'm just not positive you'll want to."

"What are you talking about?"

Her light flickered. This was hard for her. She was being brave. "Through that door is paradise. If you go there, you'll want to stay. It'll make you forget all about me."

"No, it won't," he said.

She nodded, but her light dimmed again.

"I *will* come back, Roan. This"—he touched her cheek—"this right here is paradise."

She offered him an embarrassed smile, then nodded. "I'll wait for you."

He stood up, and together they walked hand in hand to the mirror. Their reflection was strange. While Roan was just as magnificent as ever, the man beside her, the one holding her hand, made him jealous. Tall, handsome, confident—everything he wasn't. Phyre had a strange way of twisting the view of things.

"I look so . . . so different," he said.

Roan's face twisted up, befuddled. She peered into the mirror, then over at Gifford. "I don't understand. You look the way you always do."

He laughed. "The guy in there is gorgeous and dashing."

Roan nodded.

"Really?" He laughed, and straightened himself up striking a dramatic, heroic pose. "So this is how I appear to you? This is how you see me in Phyre?"

Puzzlement once more filled Roan's face. "No . . . that's how you've always looked."

Tears welled up in his eyes as Gifford pulled her to him and kissed her. She had no body, but he felt her warmth, and those lips, soft, moist, quivering. Their faces slid past each other, tear-slicked cheeks pressing as he hugged her as tightly as he could. "I love you so much, Roan. And so help me, so help everyone, I will be back."

Then Gifford passed through his own reflection into a world of light, music, and color.

֎

Roan watched Gifford go, saw him pass through. Once he was gone, she was left with only her own reflection in the mirror. Some stranger she'd never known glared back at her through the glass. The stranger looked sick and terrified.

Turning away, she surveyed her tiny realm. Nothing but a broken bridge and the little cave with the door.

I wonder how long I'll be here? This is the first time I've been completely alone since I killed Iver.

After Iver's death, Padera had arranged for Moya to move in with Roan, and the old woman was a frequent visitor. The two took turns watching Roan, who had expected to be executed or severely punished at the very least. Any idiot had to realize she'd killed her owner. Instead, Padera taught her how to cook, and Moya taught her how to live. Yet it was Brin who gave her the greatest gift—admiration.

Roan couldn't understand it at first. The girl visited frequently, asking all sorts of questions. Roan was convinced Brin was after evidence to prove Roan had killed Iver, only she acted so oddly. She would arrive all excited, sometimes bringing little gifts—things she'd found. Brin would ask what the name of a colored stone was, as if Roan knew everything. And then she realized, that was exactly what Brin thought. The girl wasn't looking for evidence; Brin was in awe. No one had ever looked *up* to Roan. But Brin did. Realizing this, Roan discovered that she hated herself a little less afterward. Brin had managed to open the door that Moya and Padera had struggled to bust down, the door to a prison that Roan herself had built.

Now here she was again, alone in the dark. She had shed all her old ghosts and left them below, but she quickly discovered new ones. She was scared that Gifford wouldn't come back, and also frightened that he would. On the other side of that mirror was paradise—some sort of wonderworld that she couldn't begin to imagine. Through that glass was the reward that Gifford deserved; inside was his happiness. But she wasn't allowed in. Roan wanted Gifford to have everything, but she also wanted Gifford—needed him. Padera had given her wisdom, Moya courage, and Brin confidence, but Gifford—Gifford had given her love. She could deal with being stupid, scared, and insecure, but she couldn't go without love.

Gifford was the one who had truly saved her. He was the one true thing, the unbending, unmoving, unbreakable hero of her life. And Roan resolved in her heart that she would wait by that door forever, wait for Gifford—and hope, for his sake, he never returned.

"Roan!"

She spun.

There was no one there, no one near her. The voice came from far away.

Tesh? Tressa? It didn't sound like them, and it hadn't come from below.

"Roan! Over here!"

꙱

"Are you sure that's Roan?" Moya asked. All she could reliably see was the light and a figure within it. "That light is so bright."

"I'm telling you, it's Roan," Tekchin said as they stood on the end of the broken bridge, peering out across the dark gulf.

"You also told me you were too weak to stand, remember?"

"Aye. I think it's Roan, too," Rain said as he continued to fidget with the sword. They had all rushed out of Mideon's castle, and the dwarf was still having trouble with his blade. The pommel of Lorillion kept hitting the handle of his pickax whenever he took a step. He had *clinked* all the way there.

"That was hours ago," Tekchin said with a mischievous smile. "I'm feeling much better now."

Moya frowned at him. "So you're saying you made this perfect recovery in a few hours after being near death for who knows how long?" She put a hand on her hip. "And how exactly are you telling time, my sweet? Besides,

Beatrice already spilled the beans. I know what the two of you have been up to, and don't try denying it."

Tekchin let the battle die and returned to the topic at hand. He pointed at the distant light and said, "It's her, I'm telling you."

"Then why is she so bright? And why doesn't she answer?" Moya held her bow, Audrey, above her head and waved it. "Roan!"

The figure stood up.

"Moya?" Roan called back.

Tekchin grinned. "Mystery solved."

"One of them," Moya said. "Why I love you is still up for debate, along with . . ." She clapped her sides in frustration as she glared at the jagged tongue of stone that had once been a bridge. "How are we going to get over to her? How is she going to get over to us?" Moya looked down into the endless dark. *How did she get up there to begin with?*

"Didn't Beatrice tell you?" Rain asked.

"No," Moya said, a bit of anger slipping into her tone. "Did she tell you?"

The dwarf shook his head. "All she ever tells me is how great I am. Makes me homesick for Frost and Flood, who say they can never understand how me mother didn't drown me the first time she saw me face."

"Nice friends you got there."

"I'm guessing Beatrice assumed you knew there was no bridge." Tekchin inched his way out onto the tongue like a cat on a wind-whipped branch. "You two were here when it exploded, right?"

"We all were."

"Yeah, but I was in pieces at the time. This is the first I've seen it."

"Roan?" Moya shouted. "Do you know how to get across?"

"Working on it . . . sort of." Roan's voice was a chickadee-sized tweet, nearly lost to the overwhelming silence that blew up from the deep.

"What is she doing, do you think?" Tekchin asked.

"Who knows? It's Roan. The bigger question is, where are the others?" Moya scanned the far side and down the length of the pillar as far as she could see. The only one visible was Roan.

Beatrice had gathered up Tekchin, Moya, and Rain and shoved them out the door into the cold gray of the endless Nifrel night. She gave her usual cryptically confusing directions. Rather than telling them to run after Brin, The Little Princess sent them the opposite way.

"You need to go to the bridge first. And hurry! You're running out of time. The queen is asking questions. It won't be long before she decides to come out and investigate for herself."

"But if we have to hurry after Brin, why do we need to—"

"It will all make sense—just go!"

"It's not making sense," Moya muttered to herself. "Stupid Little Princess." She whirled on Rain. "Can you do something? Can you build a bridge?"

Rain looked up at her, startled. "I dig," he said, then pointed out at the nothing that lay between them and Roan.

Moya squinted across at Roan. She wasn't even moving. As far as Moya could tell, her friend was just standing there.

That's when Moya heard the drum, a pounding in the distance off to her right. Soon this was followed by a horn. The sounds came from the White Tower of Ferrol.

ى

"Gifford?" a woman's voice said.

Long hair, bright smile, the woman stood before him in a beautiful gown, her arms held out in invitation.

Gifford wasn't sure what to do, and his hesitation extinguished the woman's smile. Then her eyes clouded as tears invaded that once happy face. "He doesn't know me."

Coming up behind her, a man placed his hands on the woman's shoulders, giving her a slight squeeze of sympathy. He was familiar, a face out of the past, but different—so young.

"Father?" Gifford asked.

The man nodded, then looked at the woman he held before him, the first person Gifford had seen upon entering Alysin.

That should have been my first clue.

His mouth opened, but not to say anything. It just hung agape as he stared at her in amazement.

Gifford had always wondered what she had looked like. As a child, he had fashioned her face out of the best bits and pieces he found in others, the most beautiful, the most kind. That was the memory he carried, a timeless illusion of a goddess that he'd invented. The woman before him looked nothing like he had imagined. This person was young—younger than Roan, younger than himself, not much more than a child. And so small, so tiny and delicate, like a songbird. There were freckles on her cheeks. Gifford had never once imagined freckles. He thought of them as imperfections, and this mother could have none. Her hair was wavy. Her face thin, even a bit gaunt. Her front two teeth were a smidge too large, her small mouth drawing too much attention to them. She could have been Brin's younger sister, or Persephone's daughter, but she wasn't.

Her eyes brimmed with tears as she watched him. In that gaze, he saw pain, fear, regret, longing, and love. A tear slipped down, first one cheek and then the other.

"Mother?" he said.

Her shaking hands went to her mouth as more tears spilled. All she could do was nod in reply—nod and cry.

Gifford had never felt more awkward, never more crippled. He staggered forward and reached out. She extended a hand toward him, and for the first time, Gifford touched his mother. Their fingers clasped, and she drew him to her. She was so small, but her arms engulfed him, her tiny body pressed tight.

"Gifford. Gifford. Gifford," she repeated in a whispered chant broken by sobs. "I've waited so long to hold you. I'm sorry I wasn't there. I wish you didn't have to go through so much all alone. I'm . . ." Her voice failed.

"No, it's okay. It had to be that way. It made me what I am and helped me win my race."

Gifford's father put a hand on his shoulder, making a folded-lip face as he, too, cried, while nodding over and over, agreeing to a million unsaid truths. "I knew you'd do it, my boy. Never had a doubt. Not ever."

"And I got married," he told them. "She's . . . she's wonderful—and she's waiting for me. Right now, Roan is probably torturing herself, thinking I'll never return, so I have to go."

"We know."

"Good, but the bridge is gone. That's why I'm here. We need help. Is there anything you can do?"

His parents smiled at each other in pride as if he'd just taken his first step. "You don't need our help, my love. I heard about your ride and how you started the fire at Perdif with just the clap of your hands. And you managed that on Elan. On Elan! Anyone who can call forth the elements out there won't be stopped by a missing bridge in here. There's always been so much more to you than you've allowed yourself to believe." She looked him over. "And I can see now that you recognize it, too. The Abyss apparently does that for people. Rinses them clean of any prior foolishness. You are not a cripple. You aren't weak, helpless, feeble, or pathetic. You are my son, and a power to be reckoned with."

She kissed him. "But you must hurry. Brin left the key in Rel for you, but only for a short time."

"She did? Where?"

"She didn't say exactly, just that it would be somewhere safe and in a place you could find it."

Gifford swallowed hard. "I'm sorry we don't have more time. I wish—"

"We'll have eons to be together, but for now your place is still on Elan."

Gifford frowned. "No, I won't be coming back. When I die again, I'll be staying with Roan. I suppose I can visit, but I can't leave her."

"Just bring her with you."

"She can't get in."

"Of course she can." Aria smiled. Reaching out, she took the hand of Gifford's father. "Just hold her hand as you enter, and she will be as welcome as you are. Now go, son. We'll be waiting. Go and continue to make us proud."

❧

Gifford had barely stepped back through the door when Roan embraced him.

"You came back!" she shouted. "You didn't have to come back for me."

"It's fine, Roan," he said. "My mother got my father into Alysin, and I can do the same for you. We'll be together, but we can't go there, not yet."

"Gifford?" A voice floated toward them from across the Abyss.

"Is that Moya?" Gifford asked.

"Yes, she's over there with Tekchin and Rain."

Gifford looked past Roan's shoulder at the three figures on the far side.

"Is there any way for you to get across?" Moya shouted. "We have to get out of here! We need to get to Rel. And the queen . . . she's coming!"

Gifford looked at the broken bridge.

"You are not a cripple."

Gifford saw the door to the White Tower opening. Drums beat and trumpets blared.

"Get behind me, Roan."

❧

Moya didn't know what to do. She wasn't sure she could do anything. Something was going on near the door to Alysin. Gifford had appeared, and as far as she could tell, he'd come out of the door itself.

"Did you see that?" Tekchin asked. "Where did he come from? Does that mean he has the key? I thought you said Brin had it."

"That's what Beatrice told me. Stupid Little Princess!"

Moya saw the door to the White Tower open.

"This isn't good," Tekchin said while retreating to the mainland and facing Ferrol's forces. He put a hand to his sword as he rocked his head and stretched his back.

"You can't fight all of them," Moya told him.

"Of course I can. I'm a Galantian. I'm not guaranteeing I'll win, but I'll try."

"All by yourself?"

"What are you talking about? You'll help. And I have the Great Rain with me, and he's got that sweet new sword."

Rain looked like he might be sick.

"We should tell Gifford and Roan to go back." Moya said. "If they can get into Alysin, they'll be safer. We don't need to—"

"Look!" Rain shouted as he pointed across the Abyss.

At first, Moya had no idea what she was seeing. Roan was behind Gifford, who had his hands out as if expecting to catch something. He and Roan were amazingly bright, illuminating their whole side. Looking at them was like trying to stare at twin stars, but it wasn't their light that had caught Rain's attention.

The stone is moving.

The whole of the bridge, and much of the pillar, looked to be melting, boiling, swirling, and rising up like a dark and terrible beast.

"What's going on?" Moya asked. "Is it the queen?"

"No." Rain said. "Run!"

Not waiting for her to listen, the dwarf grabbed hold of Moya's wrist and hauled her away from the edge.

"What are you doing?"

"Remember Perdif?" Rain said as he continued to drag her away.

Moya jerked back, but as was always the case with dwarfs, they were a lot stronger than they looked. "What about it?"

"It's not there anymore."

"What are you—"

All three were thrown off their feet as an earthquake shook Nifrel, and stone exploded into the air.

CHAPTER TWENTY-SEVEN

What Do Butterflies Do?

I thought I had been sent to save Suri, but I left her in danger on the wrong side of the river. As it turned out, I was not supposed to save her at all. I also had not left her in danger. As for the river . . .
— THE BOOK OF BRIN

What do butterflies do?

The question had *fluttered* through Suri's thoughts ever since she left Estramnadon. Nothing in particular had summoned the idea; there certainly weren't any butterflies around, and no caterpillars, either. Winter had settled in, and the ancient forest was asleep beneath a blanket of snow and ice. Suri was retracing the route she'd traveled in the cage, but she was only faintly aware she'd been there before. Occasionally she would recognize a tree or a bend in the road, or she'd walk by a village and remember the curious pale frame of an oddly shaped window that looked like a winking eye. All of it was dreamlike and a little bit eerie, because it hadn't been a pleasant dream. The time she had spent in the cage had been a nightmare, yet even in that screaming white-light-noise of pure panic trapped alone in a rolling box, she had learned something. Suri wasn't a placid pond but a deep well. And in the bottom were those char-white embers, the same ones she had called upon when facing Trilos, the same coals she'd ignited for the first time in the Agave when she—

Minna bounded, darting into the woods, thrashing through the snow, pausing to sniff at the base of a tree, then under a tuft of dead leaves. She crisscrossed the road, leaving a dotted line of tracks in an almost perfect looping pattern. She hadn't changed. She was still the same carefree wolf she'd always been. Some soft-spoken part of Suri's mind suggested it wasn't altogether normal for Minna to be alive. This tiny but sensible thought was shouted down.

Is it altogether normal for me to have sacrificed her? Is it altogether normal for Arion to have been killed by Mawyndulë? Is it altogether normal for milk to turn into butter if you shake it?

Normal, she concluded, was an altogether silly notion. *Normal* was only what *usually* happened. People didn't usually die, but sometimes they did. People didn't usually come back from death, but obviously, that *rule* turned out to be more flexible than she'd first guessed. Suri had seen a raow eaten by a manifestation of the Art, which was created by the binding of natural energy held fast by the power of her own grief. In comparison, Minna bounding through the snow wasn't strange at all.

Minna isn't her real name.

It was the name Suri had given her when they both were young. Gilarabrywn was her true name. That was also the name Trilos knew her by, but how could Trilos know her at all?

How many lives does it take to become the world's wisest wolf?

Maybe wolves were like cats, or perhaps death didn't work the way Suri thought—the way Tura had suggested. Suri had never paid death much mind before, but seeing Brin—or rather, seeing Brin's ghost—made her wonder if being dead wasn't as bad as it sounded.

What exactly was it?

Either way, it was clear Minna had a whole other life that she had never shared with Suri.

Probably more than one.

Suri didn't begrudge the wolf's mysterious past. The notion only made Minna more interesting, more amazing, but there was a lingering concern. "Minna?" Suri said, and the wolf stopped to look back. "Would you like it better if I called you Gilarabrywn?"

The wolf whimpered.

"You like Minna better?"

Yip. The wolf's head jerked up with enough force that her front paws came off the ground.

Suri shrugged and smiled. "Minna it is."

The wolf started off again, then stopped when she noticed Suri wasn't following. Suri stood in the road, her arms held tight around her, each breath making little white puffs. The wolf walked back.

"Minna," Suri said, her voice quiet, nearly a whisper that carried clear in the sleeping bedroom of the forest. "Do you forgive me?"

The wolf leapt up. Her paws landed on Suri's shoulders. A big tongue washed her face. It was warm and slick.

"Okay, okay," she said, laughing. "I love you, too." Suri ruffled the fur on Minna's head and scratched behind her ears. "But next time, *I* get to be the sacrifice, okay?"

Minna trotted forward again, and Suri didn't think she had actually agreed.

The trip to the river had been a long, quiet walk. Suri hadn't met anyone on the road. She was alone with Minna, much the way they used to travel together in the Crescent. In many ways, it felt similar, but not the same. Not the same forest—not the same Suri or Minna. Things were more difficult back then. Harder to find food, harder to stay warm. Now Suri had the Art, and nothing was difficult. That bothered her.

What do butterflies do?

Caterpillars constantly ate and labored to crawl, struggled to avoid being eaten. But butterflies never appeared to do anything, never seemed to have any problems at all. They simply fluttered.

Arion had wanted Suri to go to Estramnadon and stop the war, which would save both the humans and the Fhrey, and she had done that, at least she thought so.

But what now?

Suri was certain of one thing: She was going home. She had wanted to return for so long, and now she was determined to get there. She also knew it wouldn't be the end of her journey. After all, butterflies couldn't return to being caterpillars. They had to be something else. But . . .

What do butterflies do?

On that early morning on the third day, Suri reached the end of the forest and spotted the spires of Avempartha. She could also hear the falls making its low growl. As she came out of the trees onto the riverbank, the Nidwalden looked to be made of black, rippled glass cutting between white banks. Large chunks of ice floated by, having broken off from someplace farther upstream. They drifted lazily, then picked up speed as they bobbed toward the drop, which that morning appeared as a wall of white mist set on fire by the early rays of a new sun.

No bridge led from her side to the tower, and of course, no bridge extended from the tower to the western side. The road merely ended at the riverbank. A tall, youngish-looking Fhrey walked toward her. He stopped the moment he got a clear view and stared at her in shock.

"Hello," she said and waved. Minna trotted up and sat beside Suri, and together the two smiled innocently.

The Fhrey continued to stare, his face filled with concern and laced with confusion. He didn't appear to know what to do with his hands, and he opted to wring them.

Suri hadn't planned what to do when she got to this point. She knew the river was lined with Miralyith, and now they had dragons, too. No longer wearing the collar, she was less concerned about the Miralyith than the dragons—one of which was just up the bank. The beast crouched on its haunches, its wings folded up, its head down, its eyes closed, its whole body covered in new snow. She looked back at the Fhrey, who was still staring. She guessed the dragon was his.

"I'm sorry," she said. "Who was it?"

The Fhrey's eyes widened, then softened. "A friend."

Suri nodded.

"Is it true?" he asked. "Is the war over? I heard the horn blasts. Jerydd said Fane Lothian is dead, and that Mawyndulë will fight Nyphron for the throne *and* the war."

Brin made it.

Again, Suri nodded. "I think so."

"And when Mawyndulë defeats Nyphron, will your side really stop fighting?"

"*If* he wins."

The Fhrey began shaking his head, and tears spilled down his cheeks. His eyes went to the dragon. "I killed her for nothing, then?"

"*Where do you think you're going?*" A familiar voice whispered in Suri's head.

Jerydd.

Suri looked up at the tower. Clouds muted most of the sun's light now, and she couldn't see him. There were too many dark windows, too many hidden balconies, and he wasn't showing himself.

"I'm going home," she said.

"*No, I don't think so. You need to get back in your box where you belong.*"

"Why?" Suri asked.

"*Because you are an abomination that can never be allowed.*"

"Why, what?" the Fhrey Miralyith asked.

Suri smiled, pointed at the tower, then at her own head. "Jerydd is scolding me. What's an abob-nation?"

"*A horror and outrage. That's what you are. The Art is for Fhrey alone. And if you were to get away, you'd teach the Art to more Rhunes. We can't have that—no, absolutely not!*"

Teach? Suri thought and started to nod. "Yes—teach. Tura taught me. Arion did, too. That's what butterflies do; they show caterpillars how to fly."

Looking at Minna, she added, "And how much more beautiful the world would be with more butterflies."

Minna wagged her tail.

Suri smiled back, knowing only Minna could fully appreciate the plan. Suri waited, but apparently Jerydd was done speaking to her. She glanced at Minna, who waited patiently, sitting in the snow. "Isn't that cold, Minna?"

Looking toward the tower, the Fhrey with the dragon spoke, "But you said we have a truce, and I heard the horns. There is no fane at the moment, so by what authority are you—" The Fhrey paused, listening. "That's not right. She's not doing anything. She said she's going home. Honestly, Jerydd, if it wasn't for Ferrol's Law, I'd order her to rip your throat out, not the Rhune's. There is no reason for me to do that."

"C'mon, Minna." Suri walked past the Fhrey and up to the river's edge. She bent down near the water and brushed the snow away until she found a perfect stone. "This is a good one."

Round, slim, and almost flat, the rock had just enough of an edge for Suri to get a good grip on. She picked it up, hummed a little tune, and threw it with an excellent sidearm pitch. As it flew, a span of stone formed. Where the rock skipped, support piers grew, and with each hop, a bridge formed. Fifteen elegant arches crossed the river just upstream from the tower.

The wolf yipped.

"Bet you wish you had hands now, don't you, Minna?"

"Be careful. Jerydd is going to—" the Fhrey started to say when the fine stone bridge blew apart, pelting the river with pebbles.

"That wasn't very nice," Suri said. She saw Jerydd then, a tiny figure on a balcony, his arms spread out.

"You've misplaced your collar, I see."

"Putting me in that cage was more than impolite. Maybe you didn't know I had a problem being locked in small places, but even if you didn't, you were aware how cold the trip would be. Plus, you tricked me, and I'm trying to hold my temper, but you're not making it easy."

"A cage is no longer adequate for you."

Suri felt the draw. There was no noise; it was a sensation that crawled across her understanding, but Suri perceived it as a sound the same way tones and pitches were related to weaves. Usually when pulling power, the pitch was deep and throaty; this one was high and whistling.

He's using the tower, focusing it, funneling it.

When the attack came, it was heavy-handed, like trying to hit a fly with a hammer. Pure power in the form of light and heat, similar to what had killed Arion, was now directed at Suri. She had played this game before. The last time she had bounced the beam back, but knowing there were other people in the tower, Suri deflected it into the river where it hissed and formed a massive cloud of steam.

She looked at the youngish Fhrey who, after that first blast, had taken the precaution of moving away from her and creating a shield. "He has no right to attack you. We have a truce."

"It's okay." She looked down at the wolf standing at her side and smiled. "I wonder how Jerydd would like it if I put *him* in a box."

She felt the draw of power again. Suri looked at the water. Ice chunks flowing toward the falls revealed the power of the current. "It's the river, isn't it, Minna?"

The wolf yipped again.

"You're not powerful at all, are you, Jerydd?" Suri said toward the tower, not certain if he was listening or not, but she guessed he was. Even at that distance, she felt his fear. "All your strength comes from the river and the tower. One boosts and the other funnels the Art. That's why you never leave Avempartha. And it's why you sent Mawyndulë to take me to Estramnadon." She looked up at the sleeping trees, at the snow and ice, at the overcast sky. There wasn't even much wind to draw from. "Without the river, you're helpless."

She sensed it again, that high-pitched whistle as Jerydd pulled the might of the falling current. Suri stepped back, braced herself, and sang a single powerful note of her own. With a thrust of her arms, she slammed shut the source. Like a banging door, she heard it close with a power that echoed. Snow fell from the branches of trees. A few sparrows took flight, and then quietly descended. There was a trickle, which slowed to a drip, and then even it dried up. In its wake was a different world. A quiet world.

The river was gone.

Between the two banks lay a dry bed. A few puddles remained, but mostly it was sand, mud, rocks, and stones—lots of rocks and stones. The whistling that came from the tower had stopped—as had the roar of the falls. In their place was an eerie silence, a dead quiet.

"What have you done!"

"He's unhappy," Suri told the Fhrey on the bank, who stood stunned, his mouth open, his gaze on the empty riverbed. "But now he knows what it feels like to wear a collar. You see, I've discovered something about the Art," Suri explained, speaking to all of them, but then she focused on the Fhrey near her. "*You* know about it." She pointed at the beast. "Anyone who's made one of those does. That power doesn't come from outside." She put a hand to her chest. "It comes from pain, but more than that—it comes from passion and emotion. An explosion of internal feeling fuels it. But it doesn't have to be heartbreak. It can be joy. Do you understand?" She watched the Fhrey. He looked young, but there was no way to tell how old he might be. For all she knew, the Miralyith might have lived a thousand years already. "Maybe you can't. You see, time, it wears away at passion. When you're young, you're so full of life, but age dries up that river. And you Fhrey—well, your lives are so long that you can't keep it flowing. It's the same reason you don't mate for life, isn't it? Arion said that feelings fade and passions pale. Bright fires burn out fast, but while they blaze, they are hot."

Suri looked back at the tower, at Jerydd, who had retreated into the shadows, but she was certain he could hear her. "You're right to be afraid of human Artists, Jerydd. We don't live long, but we live well. We don't have so much knowledge and wisdom, but we have passion, and that makes us strong. We'll always be stronger. We human Miralyith are—" She stopped herself. That wasn't right. Miralyith was a Fhrey tribe. Human Artists weren't Miralyith. Human Artists were . . . "Butterflies—wonderful, beautiful butterflies."

Suri smiled at the Fhrey, who still watched them. "Nice meeting you." She waved again, then looked at the wolf. "Race you to the other side, Minna."

The wolf darted out across the riverbed, chased by a woman who ran like a girl.

CHAPTER TWENTY-EIGHT

The Chariot Race

Some roads feel like they go on forever.

— THE BOOK OF BRIN

"Brin *did* get out, didn't she?" Moya asked as they ran back up the slope, climbing the ridge. One of the benefits of being dead was that she could run and still talk. Breathing, she discovered, was optional. She still did it, but more as a means of calming herself, the way people bit their nails or pulled their hair. Breathing felt normal, a comforting sensation, and she needed it because she wasn't at all certain she knew what was going on.

Roan and Gifford had clearly returned from the Abyss, but she didn't know how. Brin had also returned and already crossed Nifrel in a blink of time, and according to Beatrice, she carried a horn that would allow Nyphron to challenge for leadership of the Fhrey. But no one said anything about Tesh or Tressa. Why this was, Moya didn't know. None of that was important because the Queen of Nifrel was chasing them again. Also, it seemed, they still had a chance to escape the afterlife. However, once more, the details remained hazy.

"Yes," Roan said. "Brin was the first one out of the Abyss. Gifford and I followed later."

"The whole tower is lit up now," Tekchin announced, looking backward as they ran. "She's turning the place out looking for us."

"I meant, has Brin left Phyre?" Moya said. "What I'm asking is: Who has the key?"

"Brin had it," Gifford said. He looked tired as he struggled to keep up.

That was one more thing Moya didn't grasp. She had no idea what had happened at the bridge. One moment she, Tekchin, and Rain were looking across the Abyss at Gifford and Roan, and then everything exploded. When the cloud cleared, a new bridge existed—a thicker, bigger bridge that appeared to have been smashed into existence with as much finesse as ramming a splitting wedge into a log.

Moya was fairly certain Gifford had been responsible. He had been doing something with his hands just prior, and Rain's remark about Perdif supported the idea. That Gifford was doing magic now was, oddly, the most normal issue she had to confront.

"If Brin had the key, why are we running?" Moya asked. "If we can't—"

"Brin left it," Gifford said.

"She did what?"

They cleared the last of the ledges, reaching the top of the ridge. Standing once more where they had first met Fenelyus, they looked down at the sight of Nifrel spread out below. The White Tower blazed, and its light spilled out in all directions, but mostly its tendril roots reached across the plain and up the slope following the path they took. Moya watched with fear as the white lines of light bled out toward them.

"She's coming," Rain said.

"The door to Rel is this way." Tekchin pointed into the forest of bone trees.

"Is that where the key is?" Moya asked. "Did she stash it under a rock or something?"

The very idea sounded absurd.

How can we know which rock? And if Ferrol created all the rocks, won't she know exactly where it is?

"Don't need a key to get back to Rel," Roan said. "People can go backward, just not forward, unless you belong there."

"So does that mean Ferrol can enter Rel?" Moya asked.

This was met with terrible silence.

"Run!" Moya shouted.

᪥

Stepping through the door to Rel, they were greeted by that familiar dull white light of an overcast winter's day. Moya feared they would be leaping into disaster, but it appeared Drome wasn't expecting visitors. The castle across the street was back up. Drome was clearly a stickler for consistency, and Moya wondered if he had a picture to go by, as it all looked precisely the way it had before their ill-fated visit.

They quickly traversed the mountain region with its narrow passages and switchbacks. In no time, they came to that beautiful downhill broad way of white bricks that promised to make the remainder of their flight easy.

"How you holding up, Rain?" Moya asked.

The dwarf was pumping his little arms and legs with serious intent, the pick on his back still clapping hard against Mideon's sword.

"Right as rain," he said and gave her an uncharacteristic grin.

When they reached the homesteads, people came out to gawk.

"Out of the way! Move!" Moya shouted, using both hands to wave them aside.

Husbands pulled wives back; mothers grabbed up children; everyone stared.

"Sorry," Gifford offered the bystanders.

Moya didn't know what he was sorry for: Because he nearly ran down gawkers or didn't stop for polite conversation? Knowing Gifford, it was both.

The white brick road finally leveled out. They entered the sparsely populated fields of grass and wildflowers that surrounded the main valley.

Now that they were back, Moya found Rel lush and peaceful—a pleasant change from the dark. She had to wonder how nice it might seem to Roan and Gifford after the Abyss. She wanted to ask what was down there, how they got out, and why they were suddenly so bright. But that conversation could wait until a day when they were not running for their lives.

Running for their lives. The thought made her smile.

Then she thought of Tesh and Tressa, and the smile died.

What happened to them?

Moya imagined the attack of some monster. Tressa, too slow to run, would have been devoured. Then Tesh would suffer the same fate while buying time for the others to escape. Or perhaps the bottom of the Abyss was some massive sea in a constant storm, and Tesh and Tressa were swept away while the others clung to rocks. She really had no idea. All she could tell was that now that Gifford had time to catch his breath, he and Roan showed no signs of fatigue, and Brin had looked like a star.

What was down there?

"Same tree," Roan said.

Moya assumed Roan was pointing out a tree she remembered seeing on the way up, but this was Roan, and Moya had learned long ago that with her it wasn't smart to ever assume too much.

"What do you mean, Roan?"

"Third time we passed that tree."

Third time?

"That's not possible, we've only been this way twice."

"Third time heading in this direction," Roan corrected.

Moya looked out across the fields. "Which one?"

"That one." Roan pointed, not behind, but ahead of them. "If we pass it again, it will be the fourth time."

If we pass it? If?

Moya, who like all the rest, had been focusing hard on running as fast as they could, now began watching their surroundings in more detail. Miles of tall grass spread out on either side. Not much distinction, nothing to gauge their movement, but there was a single tree. It grew at a distance along the start of what might be a small stream. Looking ahead, Moya saw a little bridge, except . . .

"Does it seem to anyone else like we aren't getting any closer to that bridge?"

"I was thinking the same thing," Gifford said.

"Everyone stop!" Moya shouted, and they all held up, bunching together and looking at Moya.

"What's going on?" Tekchin asked.

"I don't know." Moya held up a hand. She peered around, looking, listening.

She took note of the tree, which appeared to be a fruit tree of some sort, not very tall, lots of branches. Then, as she watched, the tree jumped. One minute it was across from them, the next it was a quarter mile ahead. The shift happened in a blink. Everything had moved—the grass, the bridge, the tree—everything except *the road*.

Only it's not the road that's standing still . . .

Moya moved to the side, off the white bricks and into the tall grass.

Tekchin looked curiously at her. "What are you—" Then he was a quarter mile behind her.

"Get off the road!" she shouted, and waved at them in case they couldn't hear.

That's when she heard the familiar thunder—not in the sky but up the road behind them. A great chariot pulled by four white horses charged down the white brick.

The queen has entered Rel, and she is . . .

Moya couldn't believe it herself even as she shouted, "The queen is *pulling* the road back!"

Everyone leapt off. Rain was the slowest and was hauled another quarter mile back.

"Run!" Moya waited among the meadow fescue, buttercups, and ragwort, watching them race at her. "Son of the Tetlin Witch! Run!"

Everyone was already running as fast as they could, but she felt she had to yell something.

"Go! Now!" Tekchin shouted back. "Don't wait for us!"

"Kinda have to! Can't get out alone." Still, she began trotting forward. "C'mon, Rain!" Moya shouted as Tekchin, Roan, and Gifford finally reached her.

"She's not screwing around," Tekchin declared as he ran beside her.

"Really?" Moya replied. "You think Ferrol normally does things half-assed, do you? That wasn't my impression."

Once Rain was close, they ran again, but it was clear by then that the queen was gaining quickly.

Tekchin looked back. "I don't think we're going to make it."

"Yes, we are," Moya said.

They cleared the fields and entered the villages. People were everywhere. They heard the thunder of hooves on the road, saw the chariot clattering on brick. This wasn't Nifrel. This sort of thing probably never happened here. Screams and cries erupted as the chariot closed the distance and gave no hint of slowing.

The five of them were strung out in a long line, Moya in the lead and Rain to the rear. In the villages, Moya didn't know where to go, and the homes were too close to do anything other than follow the white brick. She hoped she'd be lucky and find it no longer cursed. Luck wasn't with her.

Not long after everyone resumed running, the road jerked back again. An instant later, Rain fell under the hooves and wheels of the queen's chariot. It bounced over his body. A soft, rumpled slap on the bricks and the momentary irregularity that interrupted the thrumming rhythm of the horse's hooves were the only clues to what had happened. The rest of them had just enough time to leap to the side to avoid the same fate.

The horses cried as the queen reined them in. They puffed, snorted, turned halfway, and the chariot was still moving when Ferrol stepped off and approached them.

Moya launched a barrage of arrows, all of which were incinerated in mid-flight. Each one turned to ash sooner than the one before such that the last one ignited and snapped the string it was nocked against. Gifford drew a sword that hadn't been at his side before, but the blade became a shimmering snake. He gasped in shock and dropped it.

"You're bright, my boy, but no match for me," the queen told him.

Tekchin didn't waste his time with the queen, but used his blade on the snake that had turned and hissed at Gifford. He cut the sword in half, then looked at the queen. She waited, watching him. Tekchin frowned and sheathed his weapon.

"Well, that was fun, wasn't it?" Ferrol said. "I haven't had a good chase like that in, oh—" She frowned, then shrugged. "Who in Eton's name really knows?"

Ferrol wasn't as brilliant as she had been in Nifrel. Moya couldn't tell if the general luminescence of Rel diffused her, or if her power was in fact diminished. She certainly had power here, no doubt about that. And she was just as frightening: the same sharp cheeks and razor-thin black lips. Not what Moya would call a looker, yet there was an attractiveness about her, a sort of severe, merciless beauty.

Ice is the same way.

"You have something I want," the queen said to all of them at once, pivoting so that her cape whirled.

The ground began to rumble. All of them staggered, dancing just to keep their feet as the world shook. The queen staggered along with the rest, her confident glare replaced with concern.

"FERROL!" a booming voice issued up from the ground.

"Egat," the queen softly cursed.

A head emerged from the ground. It began as a face of white bricks rising up. "How dare you come into my house like this!" The bricks slipped down as the body of Drome rose up. His beard-wreathed face lacked the happy grin Moya remembered. In its place was an angry frown. Luckily, he wasn't looking at any of them. "I just got my castle back in order, and here you are ripping up my road!"

The queen, undaunted by the massive figure rising up, replied, "Yes, why don't you go fix it, and leave us alone."

Not surprisingly, this did not make Drome smile. "Get out of Rel before I—"

"Before you what?" she snapped.

"Don't test me, sister." Drome rose up to his full height, towering over all of them. His great hands became fists that appeared as giant sledgehammers.

People poured out from the many homes. None came close. They gathered in fearful groups, gazing in amazement at the scene before them. A few held their hands to their faces as if ready at any minute to cover their eyes rather than see what happened. Almost all were at that perfect age, past adolescence and before wrinkles. That was how they wanted to see themselves, or how they *did* see themselves, Moya guessed, remembering how few of her childhood friends had reached maturity.

"Don't be an idiot!" Ferrol shouted. "They have the key, you fool!"

This stifled some of Drome's fury. He turned his gaze to Moya. "Eton's Key? Is that true? Do you have it?"

"No," Moya said. She spoke quickly, feeling that same odd desire to be honest rising up. Luckily, it was the truth. She did not have the key.

Drome bent over, his great shadow covering them in darkness as he studied each. When he spotted Rain, he sighed. "Get up, son!" he shouted, and Rain's head popped up as if the dwarf had merely fallen asleep. He looked about, disoriented. Moya knew the feeling and sympathized. Then Drome focused once more on Moya and Tekchin. "You two don't belong here. Your ambition and skill make you her kind." He nodded at Ferrol. "So if my sister is wrong, why are you here?"

"We"—Moya looked around at the crowd, and she was disappointed not to see a single person she knew—"came back to visit family. The last time we passed through here, we went so quickly that we didn't have much time to reunite. Is there a rule against that?"

Drome looked skeptical.

"She's lying," Ferrol declared. "She's one of mine, and like all of my people, she's selfish, self-centered, and deceitful."

"Hey!" Moya protested.

"They have the key and are trying to escape with it. Moya of Dahl Rhen *has* no family—at least none that cares about her. She has no reason to come back except to—"

"Yes, she does." A small voice spoke up from within the depths of the crowd. "I'm her family—I'm her mother."

A hush took the crowd as everyone paused a moment, turning to look.

From the back, a small woman pushed forward. She was beautiful, young, vibrant, and alive, at least in appearance, and it took Moya a second to recognize her. The last time she had seen her mother, Audrey had looked like the residue of a dried-up mud puddle. Too many years, too much work, and too much misery had ruined her. Audrey the First had been the sort of person who could always be counted on to find the one weed in a field of flowers. Her poisoned outlook found a way to express itself visually, and turned her into what Moya had always thought the Tetlin Witch should look like. All the curses Moya had leveled at the witch over the years were just her way of berating her mother. But this person looked nothing like what she remembered. This person was beautiful.

"And it's true," Audrey told Ferrol. "I didn't get a chance to see my daughter when they came through before." She looked at Moya. "I heard about it. Everyone talked about how she had visited, and they said she might be back. I didn't believe them. Didn't think she would really come—not for me."

Moya felt her throat tighten.

"You're right, my daughter is thoughtless. Didn't even take the time to send me here with a stone. And to be honest, if I wasn't looking at her right now, I never would have believed it. But maybe I should have." Audrey looked unflinchingly at the queen. "I always thought she'd be a failure like me. Turns out, she did all right. Became Shield to a chieftain and then Shield to the keenig. Led troops in battle against your Fhrey *and won*. Turns out I've been wrong about her."

The queen hissed in a breath. "So she has a mother. Who doesn't?" Ferrol strode across the white bricks, advancing on Moya, her white cape sweeping behind her, those thin lips pulled tight like the sneer of a growling dog. "If you're so innocent, why did you run?"

"You were chasing us," Gifford replied. "On a chariot." He pointed at Rain as evidence of the need.

Moya confirmed this with a nod. She was facing the queen but aware of her mother just off to the side, watching her. She was afraid to look over, afraid of what she might see. Moya needed to stay focused.

"Search them," the queen said. When no one moved, she pivoted and looked at Drome. "Do it! We can't let them escape with the key."

Drome frowned but nodded. He pointed to a few onlookers. "Go on. Check them."

Moya held her breath as a man approached Roan.

Gifford saw it too. "No!" he shouted, and stepped between them.

The queen rushed forward. She caught Gifford by the throat with slender fingers and sharp nails. "Yes, you're the bright one—the honest one. You can tell me." The queen placed her other hand on his head, raking his hair with those nails. "Tell me the truth. Do you have the key?"

Ferrol dragged her nails over Gifford's scalp. His fingers wiggled, and his body shuddered.

"Tell me the truth. Do you have the key?"

"No," Gifford replied. The single word escaped through clenched teeth.

"Does anyone else here have it?"

"No."

The queen looked puzzled, more than a little irritated, and for the first time, doubt flashed in her eyes. Then a smile came to her lips, and her eyes narrowed into a sinister, cruel expression. "Do you know where it is?"

She raked his scalp once more, making Gifford shake in a horrible, uncontrolled manner, as if he were a puppet in her hands.

"No."

The queen's smile vanished. "Does anyone here know where the key is?"

"No."

Confusion took over that icy face. She held him for a moment more, appearing puzzled, then Ferrol let go. She looked at each of them, studying every face. "But . . ."

"Are you satisfied now, Ferrol?" Drome asked.

The queen shook her head. "Makes no sense."

"Yes, it does," Audrey announced. "My daughter wanted to see her mother so badly that she defied the Queen of Nifrel."

Moya felt hands on her shoulders. Turning, she saw her mother, only it wasn't the mother she used to know. This one's face looked at her with the hint of a smile that might have been pride in a daughter.

Ferrol glared at Audrey, and to Moya's shock, her mother waved at the queen with the back of her hand as if shooing away a cat. "Go on back, and leave us alone."

"Yes," Drome thundered. "By all means—get out!"

The queen looked disgusted. She huffed at them, then at Drome, and finally without another word, she climbed back aboard her chariot. The horses snorted and charged back up the white brick road. They watched her until she disappeared from sight. By then, Drome was also gone. However, Moya hadn't seen him leave.

Audrey still had her arms around Moya, and with great reluctance she faced her mother. "Thank you."

Audrey smiled back.

"Mom," Moya said, frowning, "I—I didn't really come back here for you. That sounds so terrible after what you just said and did, but it's the truth. And I realize I was wrong. I should have given you a stone, but I—"

Audrey put a finger to her daughter's lips. "I know."

"You do?"

"I'm your mother, Moya, not an idiot."

"Oh? . . . Oh! So you were just . . ." The thought that her mother was actually proud of her slipped away, and left Moya with the old, familiar pain. Once more her mother was finding fault with her worthless daughter. It felt like waking from a dream to find cold reality still there, along with a mother who never had a kind word to say. Moya took a breath. Her shoulders drooped as she nodded. "Of course, you lied. That was clever. Thank you."

Audrey gave her that age-old disapproving scowl, and shook her head, declaring how disappointed she was. "Still think you know everything, don't you!"

"I was just trying to thank—"

"Don't be stupid. I didn't lie to save you."

"Oh. Okay." Moya nodded. "So who did you lie for?"

Audrey rolled her eyes. "I told the truth, you little brat."

"The truth?"

"Didn't believe me at first." The familiar squat figure of Padera waddled out of the receding crowd. "I had to tell her three times and get Arion, and Sarah, and a dozen of the boys who fought in the Battle of Grandford to back me up before she believed it."

"Believed what?"

"That her little girl had done well. That she had more than made something of herself. That she was Shield of the Keenig, champion of the people, and an undisputed hero."

Audrey turned and started walking away.

"Mother?"

"Don't." Audrey waved a hand over her shoulder at Moya. "I know what you think of me. That's fine. I just wanted to say what I said. And I'm glad I could help." Her mother was crying. She sniffled and wiped her eyes. "I'll leave you alone now. I'm sure you have more important things to do."

She retreated, pushing her way through the crowd.

Moya chased after, catching her and trying to draw her into a hug, but Audrey jerked back, frightened. Mother and daughter had so little practice at expressing affection that they both stood dumbfounded, staring at each other. Moya finally gave up. "Mother, I'm sorry."

"For what?"

"For not being a better daughter."

"I just said I was proud of you. You never listen to me, do you?"

"Okay, fine, then how about for not going to your funeral, for not giving you a stone."

Audrey wiped her nose and nodded. "I didn't deserve that. I wasn't *that* awful a mother."

"No, you weren't—you're right, and I'm sorry."

"Well, I eventually made it here."

Moya let go, but they continued facing each other uncomfortably.

"I have a place here," Audrey said. "Not much, but you could stay with me if you wanted."

Moya glanced back at Tekchin, and Audrey followed the look.

"He can come, too."

"It's not that," Moya said. "We're not staying. At least I don't think so, but we need the key." She turned to the potter. "Gifford, what's going on? Did you lie to Ferrol?"

Gifford shook his head. "Can't lie to her. It's like—"

"Yeah, I know, but then . . . I don't understand. You said . . . you didn't know where the key was."

"I don't. I was only told that it was here, and it was safe."

"What?" Moya looked at him, stunned. "How are we going to find it?"

"You could ask," Padera said, squinting at her with that mushed-melon face of hers.

"You!" Moya whirled on the old woman.

"Who else did you think she'd leave it with? Darby?"

⨘

Padera opened the gate for them, then slipped the key back between her breasts. She could hide a hairbrush, a hat, and an afternoon snack in there, which explained why she'd never had much use for Roan's pockets.

"Aren't we supposed to take that back with us?" Moya asked.

The old woman shook her head. "Brin asked me to play gatekeeper for *all* of you. Tesh and Tressa are still down here, right?"

Gifford nodded. "But I don't think they're gonna make it."

"I'll give them a while longer. As I understand it, the bodies you left on Elan won't last forever. I'm supposed to wait, then go out and give the key to a lady named Muriel."

"Then what will you do?" Gifford asked.

Padera laughed. "You mean up there?" She pointed out the gate. "Afraid I'll haunt you? I've lived plenty. I deserve my rest down here with my Melvin and my children. Muriel's supposed to give me another stone, and I'll use it to come back down." She winked. "I honestly can't leave Melvin alone, or he might get eyes for another."

"Fine," Moya said. "But watch out for the queen and Drome."

"I won't need to keep it long, I don't think." She pressed a hand to her bosom. "Which reminds me, you all need to get moving, don't you?"

"Yes," Gifford said and gave Padera a kiss and hug. "Thank you. For everything."

Outside the gate, they found the river. This time it was bathed in light that poured out from Rel, and its waters looked dark and ugly. The crowd was gone, but the stony bank wasn't empty. A person sat on the rocks weeping. She was a Fhrey. The brilliant light of Rel was on her face, glistening off wet cheeks. Her eyes were dark and bagged, her mouth long, open, and quivering.

Gifford, being the helpful sort, surmised the problem and approached the Fhrey. "You've died. You're supposed to go in through the gate," he told her. "That's Rel in there. Everyone you know is waiting inside."

"I tried." The Fhrey shook her head. "I can't pass through."

The five of them exchanged puzzled glances.

"Of course you can," Moya said. "The gate is wide open."

"It's okay. It's nice inside," Roan told her. "Family and friends are waiting."

Again, she shook her head. "Not for me." She focused on Tekchin. "I broke Ferrol's Law. There's a barrier. I can never go in."

Tekchin stiffened as if the Fhrey had somehow threatened him. "Who did you kill?"

The Fhrey didn't answer.

"We have to go," Moya told him.

Tekchin nodded, but continued to linger, looking at the weeping Fhrey and biting his lip.

"I was only one hundred and twenty-eight," she told him. "Just a child. Now what will I do?"

They walked past her, climbing down to the water's edge.

"Where are you going?" she asked.

"Back up to Elan."

"You can do that?"

"Just need a feather," Gifford said.

Roan looked alarmed.

"Relax, Roan," Gifford told her. "It's not a real feather, remember? Just the idea of rising up."

Roan calmed down and nodded.

Soon, everyone was holding up little white tufts and grinning like they'd all just won something. The Fhrey girl got to her feet and walked over to watch.

Moya shook her head while looking upstream. "Dying was horrible, so I can't imagine coming back will be a treat. Still . . . it'll be nice to see the sun again. To feel it, you know?"

"How exactly do we do this?" Tekchin asked.

Moya shrugged and threw up her hands. "Tet if I know."

"You really need to find a new curse," Gifford told her.

Moya looked up. "Probably right."

They all stood a moment longer. Then Moya took Tekchin's hand, and Gifford took Roan's. Rain stood alone. Roan reached out, and the dwarf smiled appreciatively as he took the offer of her hand.

"That's a first," Gifford said.

"I think there will be a lot of firsts in my future—our future," Roan said sheepishly. "I left a lot of baggage in the Abyss."

"You're just going to go back up?" the Fhrey asked.

"Yep," Tekchin said.

She looked back at the gate to Rel, then, pivoting on her left heel to look up the River of Death, she said, "Didn't know you could do that."

CHAPTER TWENTY-NINE

Reunions and Farewells

This was the first time I felt sorry for Nyphron. Given what I knew about him, I doubted it would ever happen again.

— THE BOOK OF BRIN

Persephone stared up at the tower of Avempartha, and, seeing its soaring beauty, she forgot for a moment how scared she was.

Most people were never present at moments of great significance. Those who were, probably never even realized until years later. They always said things like, "I didn't know it at the time" or "If I had only known . . ." Persephone herself had had no idea the Battle of Grandford would be as pivotal as it was. She'd certainly had no idea how monumental that morning had been when she met a certain young mystic, or the one where she was saved by a tall and handsome Dureyan. She hadn't even realized how important a decision she had made when sending the messenger bird to Estramnadon, but as she approached the tower of Avempartha, Persephone knew this was *the* moment when the world would change forever.

After several days of travel and with all the pomp and circumstance their twenty-person delegation could muster, the representatives of the Forces of the West arrived at the banks of the infamous Nidwalden. This grand assembly consisted of Persephone, her son Nolyn, Justine, the Instarya who had been at the Dragon Camp, a handful of volunteers, and Brin, who for nearly the entire trip had sequestered herself inside a wagon. Nyphron was already there, having driven his chariot to the tower immediately after blowing the horn to declare his challenge for the Forest Throne.

Persephone called a halt to their little procession while they were still on the west bank. Not a single Fhrey or dragon had been spotted. They were at a rocky high point overlooking the river and the tower. For several years Nyphron had struggled to find a way to cross, but Persephone couldn't understand why. As far as she could tell, anyone could walk from bank to bank without a problem. The riverbed was dry—the falls absent.

A familiar figure, who until that moment had been seated on a rock in the trees, stepped out. She was dressed in an amazing blue asica that shimmered like water. She wasn't alone, and Persephone stared in wonder at the white wolf by her side.

"Suri!" she shouted and rushed forward. "I thought . . . we all thought . . ."

They met just off the road, where the two embraced.

"I'm so proud of you," Persephone declared. "And Minna!" She felt the wolf brush her leg. "How is it possible?"

"How is anything?" Suri replied, a huge grin on her face.

There was a certainty in her voice, a confidence Persephone had not heard before.

The keenig held her back to look. No scars or bruises, she had all her teeth and fingers, and the asica the mystic wore was amazing. "You're all right? Did they hurt you?"

"They tried."

Persephone's face darkened. "Was it terrible?"

Suri thought about it a moment. "Parts certainly were."

"They put you in a cage, didn't they? That must have been horrible."

Suri nodded. "But . . . not all bad things are bad for you, and not all good things are good. Do you know what I mean?"

"I think I do." Persephone smiled. She was so happy to see Suri, to see her whole and safe again. "You talk like a wise mystic now. Does that mean you ran your Gifford's Race? Did you fulfill Arion's prophecy?"

"Yes, I believe I have." She looked toward the tower. "At least you'll find out soon, won't you?"

"Shall we set up camp here, Madam Keenig?" Hiddle, son of Berston of Clan Warric, asked from where the others waited on the road beside the rocky bluff.

"Yes, I suppose." She looked at Suri. "Is it safe here?"

"The Fhrey withdrew all their forces to the other side of the river. Nyphron is inside the tower. You can just walk over. There's a truce, so no one will hurt you. They take this kind of thing seriously. Unless Nyphron is defeated, I think you'll be safe."

She tapped her lips thoughtfully and added, "However, I wouldn't trust Jerydd, and Mawyndulë is a snake. Imaly and the rest of the Aquila are a little better, but they have no real power." Suri paused and faced her. "But you shouldn't think they are all bad. Some are good. There was Treya who helped me when I needed it most, and a Miralyith who refused to set his dragon on me even though Jerydd ordered him to. And there was also Makareta, who, despite being young and spoiled, was a good person, or might have been." Suri made a crooked face that seemed half smile, half frown. "Makareta had lived for more than a century, yet in many ways, I was older than her." Suri took and squeezed Persephone's hand to emphasize her next words. "I discovered that age isn't measured in years, but rather by the roads we travel. Steep paths build muscles, know-how, and empathy, an easy one, only indifference. You as much as anyone helped teach me that. Thank you."

The river might have been dry, but the dam within Persephone broke with those words, and she began to cry.

"What's wrong?" Suri asked.

"My daughter is all grown up."

The sound of gear being hauled, of tents being laid out came from behind her, and then . . .

"Sir-ee, Sir-ee!" Nolyn shouted. Persephone's son broke free of Justine's hand to run to them, but he skidded to a stop short of the mystic as he spotted the wolf. His eyes grew big, and he drew back in fear.

"This is Minna," Suri told the boy as she bent down. Then she extended an open palm to the wolf. "Minna, this is Nolyn."

"Does he bite?" the boy asked with a concerned voice.

"Only if you call *her* a *he*."

The little boy stiffened. Suri laughed, ruffled his hair, then stood up.

"Treat Minna with respect, and she'll do the same to you. Minna is the world's wisest wolf."

"Can I—can I pet her?"

"That's up to Minna."

"Is it safe?"

Suri thought about this, then shook her head. "Nothing is safe. Nothing you ever do, Nolyn, will ever be safe. Minna will either let you or eat you." She said this with enough seriousness to draw another wide-eyed look from the boy.

"What happened to the river, Suri?" Persephone asked. "I thought—"

"It was in my way," Suri said with casual indifference, as if Persephone had inquired about a branch in the path.

Persephone looked at the dry bed, stunned. "*You* did that? We struggled for years. Does Nyphron know? Oh, he'll be furious."

Suri was back to watching Nolyn, who had inched closer to Minna but was holding his hands together up near his face. "I couldn't have done it before," she explained. "Like I said, not all bad things are bad for you. The river will come back. I like rivers. Locking it up for too long would be wrong. I know that from personal experience. It's already coming back. By tomorrow, the falls will be roaring again."

Nolyn was still staring at Minna.

"Are you going to pet her?" Justine asked.

"She might eat me," the boy replied. "Sir-ee said so." The boy looked up at his mother with asking eyes.

Persephone shrugged. "Life is full of risk, Nolyn, but you should never let that hold you back. You can't let fear stop you from living. Just make certain the chances you take are worth the risk."

The boy reached out and placed a tentative hand on Minna's head. He rubbed, and a great smile grew.

"Is Brin with you?" Suri asked.

"She's in the wagon," Persephone said. "She . . . she died—but she's all right now, I think. I know that must sound—"

"I know what happened," Suri said. "And I wanted to say goodbye before I left."

"You aren't staying?"

Suri shook her head. "Minna and I need to get back where we belong. The storm is over, ma'am," she said with an impish grin recalling their first meeting. "The clouds are clearing out. Minna and I would like to be back in the Hawthorn Glen for spring. We have a lot to do there. And, of course, you and Nolyn are always welcome to visit. I'll introduce the two of you to Fribble-bibble, and teach Nolyn how to pick strawberries and to keep the goulgans out of the garden. On summer nights, the fireflies will dance to the songs we sing."

Suri kissed Persephone and Nolyn, then the mystic and the white wolf walked toward Brin's wagon.

The others watched her go, and then Justine said, "She's not altogether normal, is she?"

"No, she's not," Persephone replied. "She's a butterfly."

❧

Brin worried she would run out of ink. She only had so much and didn't know how to make more. Roan had always provided her with it, never acted the slightest bit irritated when she asked for more. Roan always seemed so happy to help.

Now Roan was dead.

Don't, she told herself. *Stay focused. Keep writing.*

"*I need you to finish this . . . From your book, all races will learn to read and write. This will give them a common tongue again, allowing them to communicate with one another as they once did. And in reading your story, they will learn that they are all one people, born of the same five seeds, of the same mother and father. This will open the door for reunification.*"

The strange thing was that Brin knew she should have run out of ink, and parchment, too. She didn't have that much put aside, and yet every time she reached for a new sheet, one was there. Each time she dipped her quill, it came up full. More than that, in the past she had never written more than three pages without needing a new quill. The end always wore out, split and frayed. This time she had written everything with a single quill.

Brin had worked almost continuously for days. The trip was a bumpy one, and despite Malcolm's promises of a luxurious ride, her bed was crowded in between sacks of flour and barrels of wine. Still, she managed not only to not spill the ink pot, but to write cleanly. Truth be told, even though she rushed her script, racing to get everything that had happened down, her handwriting was better than ever, consistent and splatter-free.

She stayed in the wagon, not realizing they had arrived. She was right in the middle of her final conversation with Muriel when someone rapped on the side of the wagon.

"Go away. I'm busy," she said.

Hearing a whimper, she looked up.

Suri stood outside the wagon with Minna beside her. "I thought you were dead," the mystic said.

Brin very nearly did spill the pot of ink then as she dropped her quill and scrambled off the wagon to hug the mystic.

"I did this before, but you couldn't feel it," Brin told her, then dropped to her knees and hugged Minna as well. "Thank you so much, Minna. I couldn't have done it without you."

Brin scratched Minna's neck, which the wolf appeared to appreciate, given the way she lifted her head.

"Isn't getting back up that river a pain?"

Brin looked over and saw they had arrived at the Nidwalden.

"Not that one," Suri said. "The one outside Rel."

Brin looked at her, stunned. "How do you know—"

"Pulling Arion out was tough. The current was horrible."

"That's right," Brin said. "I forgot."

Suri lowered her head and rubbed her hands together. "Did you see her?"

"Arion? Yes." Brin nodded. "She's fine. She's in Rel. Likes the quiet there, I think."

Suri nodded even as she looked at the ground. "Thank you."

Brin reached up and caught her by the shoulders. "No—thank *you*."

"I wasn't the one who died and came back."

Brin showed an awkward smile. She was going to have to expect that from everyone now. She was the girl who defied death, who traversed the afterlife. She wasn't looking forward to it. "When is this thing happening? The Challenge?"

"Early tomorrow, I expect. You'll have to come visit and tell me how it turns out."

"You aren't going to watch?"

Suri shook her head. "Minna and I are going home."

"I'll see you again, won't I?" Brin asked.

"I think you already proved that." Suri smiled. "One day, after I've ridden that river to those gates, I hope you'll show me around. Show me where to find Arion."

"Oh, I think that will not be a problem. I suspect there will be many waiting at the gate to welcome you."

Suri appeared pleased with this and smiled.

"In the meantime, you should learn how to read. I can't believe I was forced to resort to drawing pictures!"

"C'mon, Minna, time to go home. I just know those goulgans are in the garden. Won't they have a surprise when we get back?"

‰

More than Mawyndulë and the Aquila had come. Hundreds of Fhrey arrived to witness the event. Persephone could see them lining the far bank of the river as they made their approach, little shifting figures of brightly colored clothes standing out from the snow. The crowd started at the bank and disappeared under the shadowy forest eaves, where she could see tents. Now that the river was starting to flow again, the Miralyith did them the courtesy of extending bridges across the water from both banks, meeting at the tower. They were impossibly long, thin structures made of the same sort of stretched stone as the tower itself. None of it looked the slightest bit safe.

"Amazing," Persephone said to Nyphron as they walked across the new span.

She tilted her head back and peered up. "The tower is incredible. Is Estramnadon like this?"

"No," Nyphron said. "Nothing is like this. Avempartha is a Miralyith structure."

They were walking to a pre-challenge meeting inside the tower, dressed in their best clothes. She wore her finest breckon mor, which was, in fact, her *only* breckon mor—the same wrap she'd worn for years. Nyphron continued to wear his less-than-polished bronze armor.

As they approached, horns sounded, and the doors opened. A contingent of Fhrey dignitaries met them, each dressed in fine silk robes of purple and white. The one in the lead was a large elderly female. She and the others bowed.

"My lord," she said, "allow me to introduce my—"

Nyphron cut her short. "I know everyone, Imaly. As Curator of the Aquila, you gave the Right of Challenge to my father."

"Yes." She nodded with a grim look. "That was an unpleasant affair, but not without value. The indignities Zephyron endured were what finally opened the eyes of many to the injustices suffered by your tribe."

"And yet you did nothing." His inflection was just shy of insulting.

The Curator showed no evidence of offense and continued to stand straight, her hands intertwined in a penitent manner. "We did what we could. The fane was a Miralyith."

"Imaly," Nyphron said in a suspicious tone. "I can't help thinking you're trying to tell me something."

"She'd rather you win The Challenge than I." A young Fhrey in white-and-gold robes approached, his heels clicking on the polished floor. Persephone recognized him as the arrogant prince who had tried to kill Raithe in Dahl Rhen. He hadn't changed, except for his clothes: shimmering robes that were colorful but ugly.

"Ah, yes, Lothian's pup." Nyphron laughed. "The fool who would be fane."

Mawyndulë's eyes widened in anger. "How dare you speak to me in such a way!"

"I plan to do much more than speak to you, child. I fully intend to cut you into little pieces and feed them to my dogs."

Nyphron had no dogs, but Persephone guessed intimidation was a valuable asset in combat, an aspect she didn't—and couldn't—understand.

"I'll enjoy destroying you!" Mawyndulë shouted, but his voice was high and reedy.

"Children should remain quiet while the adults speak, but then I can see you weren't raised right." Nyphron turned to Imaly, dismissing the prince. "When and where?"

"You wretched—" Mawyndulë began.

Imaly raised a hand and interrupted. "Your Highness, if I may? The Challenge will take place tomorrow when the sun first hits the falls. We have a ring built on our side of the—"

"Why your side?" Nyphron said. "Why not ours?"

"The Challenge is a Fhrey tradition, not a Rhune ritual. It should take place on native land."

"It's the Rhunes' fate, as well."

"It should be held at the Carfreign," an old balding Fhrey said. His tone carried more than a little bitterness. "That's why it was built."

Another old Fhrey shook his head. "That's not true, Jerydd. The contest can be anywhere, or do you now profess to be an expert in the ways of Ferrol as well as being the kel of Avempartha?"

"Volhoric is right," Imaly declared. "But we did agree to meet you halfway by coming here. You can at least cross the river, can't you?"

Nyphron considered this for a moment, and Persephone was pleased to hear him give weight to the right of the humans to witness but less so that he still referred to them as Rhunes. Finally, Nyphron replied, "If it gives the rest of you a better view of me killing this little brat—absolutely."

"That *brat* is the next fane," Jerydd declared.

"I'm not a brat! I am the—"

"You'd honestly rather have *him* for your fane?" Nyphron asked.

"Everyone knows of Nyphron's hatred of the Miralyith," Jerydd said. "If you are crowned fane, you'll eliminate all of us."

"I don't believe that is true," Imaly broke in. "Nyphron is a fine example of a Fhrey. He knows that a fane can't launch an indiscriminate, comprehensive slaughter of a seventh of the population and still retain the blessing of Ferrol. Don't believe in foolish rumors, Jerydd. You are only here because you are the host for this event. We—"

"I am here because I am Mawyndulë's only true adviser. The rest of you are traitors."

"No one knows what Ferrol will decide tomorrow," Imaly said.

Rumors, it seemed to Persephone, had gripped both sides of the river.

Immediately after Nyphron had blown the horn, Persephone sent word of the event to all ten clans. Less than a week had passed, and already there was wild talk. One insisted Nyphron and Persephone planned to live in Estramnadon after expelling the Fhrey from the city, and that they might force members of the Ten Clans to resettle there. This was a widely hated idea, so much so that there was already gossip of rebellion. A few—a very few—even suggested that having achieved his dream of conquest, Nyphron would turn on the Ten Clans. One story went so far as to suggest that Nyphron had started the war only to see himself on the Forest Throne and merely used humans as fodder for his ambition. His marriage to Persephone, their son, and her continued support went a long way toward quelling this notion. But the truth was, Persephone didn't know anything for certain. She didn't know if Nyphron could win.

Mawyndulë and this Jerydd person appeared particularly confident. And if Nyphron did win, she had no idea what he'd do. He was her husband, and she the keenig, but he might soon also be a fane with a fleet of dragons and an army of Miralyith. Sadly, Persephone's grand scheme to end the war did not extend beyond that. She had never intended to rule. Keenigs were only expected to lead until the crisis was over. *But what then?*

Will the Gula and the Rhulyn Rhunes live happily together? Left to themselves, the clans will war. Territories will form and fights for domination will flare up, battles over minor slights. Chaos will spread and mire mankind in perpetual desolation. Misery, disease, war—these will be the offspring of the sacrifices everyone made.

"I think we are done here." Mawyndulë bared his teeth. "Sleep well, Nyphron, and don't forget what happened to your father. I hope you are a morning person. I am."

ℒ

Night came, and Nyphron held no illusions. Tomorrow would bring the greatest battle of his life against his greatest fear—magic. No sword could kill it, no shield block it. He had a plan, but plans almost always failed. His father, who had been equally confident, had been destroyed in a similar combat, which left Nyphron with a terrible sense that this might be his last night beneath the stars.

"You can do it, can't you?" Persephone asked as the two sat before the campfire. She stared at him with those human eyes, the ones he'd never learned to read. Other Fhrey were easy; he could relate. Men—Rhunes—were harder; they saw the world differently, responding at times in unexpected ways, but generally predictable. Women—ordinary human females—were beyond reckoning. And Persephone was no ordinary woman. Whatever he saw, or thought he saw, in those eyes would be what she wanted him to see.

"I don't know," he replied.

She lowered her head sharply. That wasn't the answer she wanted.

The two were on the west bank only a few hundred feet outside the tower. Night had fallen in the forest, but the mist rising from the now thunderous falls managed to catch the last rays of sunlight, creating a sparkling white cloud. The tower also caught the sun, but only at the top. Nyphron had watched the shadow creep up its side, swallowing Avempartha in darkness. Jerydd had granted him a room in the tower where he had stayed for the past week, but with the arrival of Mawyndulë, the atmosphere had changed. Nyphron preferred to spend that night in the woods; there would be fewer snakes to guard against. Tents had been pitched on the west bank. Nyphron hated them. After escaping the Dragon Camp, he was once more forced back under canvas.

If I survive, I'll never sleep in a tent again.

This was one of many vows he'd made to himself. He'd spent a large part of that day making lists.

I need to do this one thing. If I succeed at this last challenge, that's all I have to worry about.

"When we first met, you never had doubts." Persephone pulled her checkered wrap tighter. A breckon mor they called it, the woman's version of the thick folded blankets the Rhulyn men wore, although Nyphron had never understood the difference.

"I always have doubts. Only a fool doesn't."

It would be just him and Mawyndulë in that arena. No one else could interfere. And if his plan didn't work. If he screwed up just a little . . .

"You'll win," she told him.

He was surprised at the confidence in her tone.

"You really believe that?"

"I've had four children," she told him. "They might mean little to you, but they are everything to me. I lost the first three. Their deaths nearly killed me. Nolyn is my last chance." She sat up and pointed to her tent. "He's right over there." She turned back and faced him. "Tell me, Nyphron, tell me the truth. What will Mawyndulë do if you lose?"

"He'll order his Miralyith and their dragons to cross the river and slaughter everyone, then he'll press on and continue his rampage."

"That's what I think, too, and yet our son is right over there in that tent." She nodded. "Yes, Nyphron, I really believe you will win."

He stared at her for a long moment. "Thank you," he said. "And I'm sorry for dragging you." .

"You should be," she snapped. "But tomorrow morning, if you manage to kill Mawyndulë, saving me, your son, and all mankind from annihilation, I might be willing to forgive you."

"Well . . ." he smirked. "In that case . . ."

"You should try to sleep."

"Not sure that will be possible. I'm going to go for a walk. Try and clear my head."

She nodded, and in her eyes he saw sorrow. Even as he walked away into the trees, he knew it hurt her that she wasn't enough. That night especially, she would wish for him to stay with her. Perhaps she suspected he was off to spend the night with another. He wasn't. He merely needed to be alone. For the first time in five hundred years Nyphron was frightened. Maybe he was getting old. He'd never felt this way before. The Galantians had roamed the known world without fear, but that was before he'd watched his father—the man who'd taught him to fight—die in the arena. Nyphron wasn't afraid of death; a glorious passing was optimal. Humiliation was what terrified him. He could still see the embarrassment Lothian had made of Zephyron. He didn't want to die a joke.

"You'll do fine."

Nyphron spun.

Moonlight spilled through the forest canopy and illuminated Malcolm, who sat sideways on a log.

Oh, great, Nyphron thought.

Malcolm had propped one leg on the fallen trunk; the other hung down, swinging back and forth. Perched as he was, Malcolm appeared like some kind of mischievous crimbal king. Nyphron hadn't felt comfortable with him since the death of Shegon. The not-quite-a-man revealed himself by shedding layers like an onion until Nyphron didn't know what to think. But in the depths of the forest and bathed in moonlight, Malcolm was eerie.

"Mawyndule is young and arrogant," Malcolm said. "You are equally egotistic but much older."

"I thought you had run away again."

Malcolm smiled, and in that pale light, Nyphron felt cold.

"I do need to leave, but before I do, there is a matter of the debt between us. I trust you haven't forgotten your promise."

"So you're finally going to reveal what you want?" The vow had hung over Nyphron's head for too long. He wanted it to be over with. "Do you want land? A title? Riches? My firstborn, perhaps?"

"No, I want you to not kill Mawyndulë."

"What do you mean? Are you saying you want me to lose? To die? Because I—"

Malcolm rolled his eyes. "Of course not. You'll still win, but you need to spare his life."

"The Challenge is to the death—you understand that, right? After someone dies, that's how you know who won."

"You're the victim of a mistaken assumption. The victor only needs to obtain a verbal surrender from the defeated to satisfy the rule that there is but one of two challengers. If you obtain that, then the torches will flare, go out, and the ceremony will end."

"How do you know?"

"Because I was the one who established the rules and created the horn."

Nyphron laughed. "Are you now claiming to be Ferrol?"

"No. Ferrol had nothing to do with any of this. She has been imprisoned in Phyre since I killed her, leaving you, her poor children, on your own and forced to fend for yourselves. Being the guilt-ridden uncle that I am, I took steps to help out. So yes, I know the ritual because I designed it. It never was intended to be to the death, but that's how it ends up in the future—how it has to be. The whole point of the horn and Ferrol's Law is to keep you monsters from slaughtering one another, and it has worked remarkably well." He seemed to consider his statement, and added, "That is, until recently."

Nyphron was left staring and weighing one of four possibilities. Malcolm was either drunk, insane, lying, or—the really unlikely option—telling the truth. Nyphron had no way of knowing, and decided it didn't matter. But he still owed the debt, and none of the rest would erase that.

"Why?" Nyphron asked. "Why ask such a thing? Mawyndulë is a greasy stain on the face of Elan. Why do you care if he lives or dies?"

"Because you are to be fane. Jerydd has started a wildfire of *rumors*, convincing his followers that as fane you will order their executions. If you were to kill Mawyndulë the way Lothian killed Zephyron, the Miralyith will revolt, just as the Instarya did. But the Miralyith are ten times more powerful. They have dragons, and as a tribe have already broken Ferrol's Law twice and killed one fane."

The bewilderment left Nyphron's face as he considered this.

"Defeat him," Malcolm said. "But don't kill him. Make your first act as fane to be one of mercy. Take the unprecedented step of pardoning Mawyndulë—a Miralyith. Let him live as a sign to them that Jerydd is wrong about you—that all of them are mistaken."

"I can't allow Mawyndulë to fester like a disease inside of Erivan. I am only the son of Zephyron, and look at the trouble I made."

"Mawyndulë will not be in Erivan. He is an outcast."

"What?" Nyphron looked at him, puzzled.

"He broke Ferrol's Law."

"He broke—but how—who did he—?" Nyphron straightened up. "He killed Lothian? He killed his own father to be fane?"

Malcolm nodded. "He hopes that if he wins this challenge, he will force Ferrol to readmit him to Fhrey society. If you make him surrender, he will be nothing. Demonstrate mercy in full view of all. Show everyone that the days of the cruel Miralyith rule are over and that a fair and just fane sits on the Forest Throne again. Do that and you will be more than respected—you will be loved. Wars don't end by deaths but because someone stops killing."

"Spare me your sappy philosophy—unless you claim to have invented war, too."

Malcolm opened his mouth to speak, but said nothing and then closed it.

"I won't be fane, though, will I? I'll be emperor. Isn't that what you said?"

"I did. The fane is the ruler of the Fhrey, but that title, that woody chair will be too small for you."

"And you swore I'd rule the world."

"And you will, so long as you keep your promise."

CHAPTER THIRTY

The Challenge

So I realize now that The Book of Brin *can never actually be "done." There will always be more to chronicle. A new chapter is required this morning—a very important one—and I want a good seat to write it from.*

— THE BOOK OF BRIN

In the dark, Moya fell farther behind.

Tekchin was out in front like an irrepressible hunting dog, looking back and waving encouragement. Maybe there was something inherent in being Fhrey that made it easier to recover. Moya still felt dead. She had suffered the worst. Maybe her body hadn't been as well preserved as the others, or maybe she had swallowed more muck on the way down. It could also have merely been Moya's bad luck. She reentered a dead body like the others, but hers refused to wake.

According to everyone else, they had managed to crawl out, spitting and spewing muck from their noses and mouths. They vomited, gasped for air, then lay on the snow, staring up at stars. But Moya hadn't come out of the pond. Tekchin said he had to drag her limp body from the icy pool. He beat on her, slapped her face, turned her over and tried pushing the mud out of her lungs. He squeezed, let go, squeezed, let go. The rest believed her body had been abandoned for too long. Maybe Tekchin did, too, but he wouldn't give up. No one knew where he found the strength. Then Moya coughed. More of a gurgle, Rain had said. She retched black water, then air went in. Moya's first memory after jumping into the river and imagining herself floating up like a feather in a dream was of being colder than she'd ever been, of feeling like her insides had been ripped out, and of being held tight as a vise by Tekchin, who cried when she opened her eyes.

Muriel took them in, dried, fed, and encouraged them by confirming that Brin had already passed that way and been successful in returning with the horn. She provided them with travel food and drink, and Muriel also revealed that the Dragon Camp was no more. The Challenge was about to be held at the tower of Avempartha, which was where Brin, Persephone, Nyphron, and a few others had gone to decide the fate of both races. The rest had retreated to Merredydd—in case Nyphron lost.

"If you head north from here, you might catch those going to Avempartha," Muriel had told them.

Moya, whose head was still mostly filled with mud, had never thought to ask how Muriel knew this. Not until days later had Moya considered that, for a hermit who lived deep in a swamp, Muriel was surprisingly well informed. But then she was also the Tetlin Witch, and the daughter of Malcolm, whom Moya finally conceded was some sort of god. Moya also discovered she was beyond such concerns. Dying and coming back to life made all other crazy things far less suspect. Then came the long hike with weak bodies. The swamp was more considerate. They had little trouble going north, where they found a broad, level greenway. Soon they entered the Harwood, and progress slowed.

After clawing out of the black pool and vomiting for several minutes, their throats were sore, and no one's voice worked well. Conversations were minimal and restricted mostly to nods and headshakes. So when Gifford said, "We need to who-wee," she had wanted to cry.

How difficult must it be for him to go back into that prison after being free, she had thought.

Yet Gifford showed no outward sign of regret. Moya imagined she'd have spewed an abundance of profanity the moment she tried to take her first step, but Gifford resumed his struggles without complaint. Watching him, she thought she could still see the dashing hero within. At the very least, she understood where that bright light had come from.

Tekchin, doing his best hunting dog imitation, guided them through the night away from the Goblin Coast and up to Harwood Heights, where they reached the Bridge Road. Most of them collapsed at that point. Muriel's meal had worn off, and the effect hit them like the worst hangover ever. Progress after that was slow, although the road was broad, flat, and packed by recent travel.

"A score of people came this way no more than a day ago," Tekchin explained as he studied the wagon ruts and footprints that cut the snow.

"I'm not sure which I'm more impressed by," Moya said, lying carelessly in a snowdrift. "That you have the skill to read trail marks in the dark, or that you have the strength to bother. To be honest, I'm too exhausted to decide." She breathed deeply, feeling the pleasant cold of the snow beneath her overheated body.

"It's not dark," Tekchin said. "Sun's coming up."

"Says you." Moya took another wonderful breath. "It's not the end of the world if we're late to this thing, right?" In the past, Moya had used exaggerated phrases to indicate something wasn't serious, but at that moment, she realized the wheels had come off *normal* and overstatement had lost a lot of territory. "I mean, we're done. We did our part, right?"

"I can see my breath, but I'm sweating. Is that normal?" Roan asked.

"You've likely got Black Pool sickness," Moya said.

"I do?" Roan stared at her, stunned.

"Moya!" Gifford scolded.

"Sorry, I'm delirious."

"That means you probably have it, too," Tekchin said.

"Is there really such a thing?" Roan asked.

"Of coss not," Gifford said. "Get up, Moya."

"Why?" She looked at him with her best Padera imitation. "I like it here. Very comfortable."

"We have to get moving."

"Again, why?"

"Because we do."

"That's not a . . ." Moya looked over and found Gifford wasn't looking back. He was staring up at the forest canopy. She sat up and lost her humor. "What's wrong?"

"Don't know—but something." Gifford scanned the snowy branches.

"Like with the trees?" Roan asked.

Gifford nodded. "Elan is talking, I think."

Most of the trees were pines, and they swayed softly in a gentle wind . . . creaking and whispering to one another.

They all began looking around.

"Goblins?" Tekchin asked, putting a hand to his sword.

Rain started to reach for his pickax, then remembered he had a sword now, too.

Gifford shook his head. "Not this place, not now."

"Something to do with The Challenge?" Tekchin asked.

"We need to go, can't be late," Gifford said.

"Why not?" Moya asked.

"Two challenges coming." Gifford continued looking up into the canopy. "Two battles. We can't be late."

"Still haven't said why, Giff."

"It will be bad."

Just then, they heard the distant blare of trumpets.

⁂

Trumpets announced the gray light of predawn.

The Fhrey officials were still busy putting finishing touches to the wall of intertwined brambles, but torches already burned blue flames. Drums followed a loud fanfare and beat to an ominous rhythm—the heartbeat of an ancient people. Persephone walked at Nyphron's side as they led a tiny procession out of the tower and across the bridge to the eastern bank.

Persephone had offered to spend the previous night with him, if only to provide the warmth of body heat and see that he slept well, but Nyphron had refused, saying he'd sleep best alone. Persephone felt she ought to be more upset than she was that her husband preferred to spend what might be his last night away from her. Instead, what concerned her most was that if she couldn't be of use to him on the eve of his possible death, she'd be of little use in the days to follow.

If he loses, we'll all die. If he wins . . .

Only that morning had she allowed herself to imagine a world without the war, a time without the Fhrey's oppression or clan divisions. Should Nyphron win, an era of building would follow, but it would not be a time of reconstruction, since the old foundations will be erased. Everything that followed would be new and limited only by what she and Nyphron decided. Their combined imagination and wisdom would set the cornerstones for the world to come. Nyphron, she was certain, would focus narrowly on military defense, and perhaps further conquests. She would leave those to him, for that was where his talent lay.

She would take on the traditional role of homemaker, only her home would be the known world. And in that short walk toward the tower, Persephone decided there would no longer be Rhunes living in huts, cowering in fear of starvation, the gods, or one another. Human cities would rise, rich in the bounty of Avrlyn fields, open trade, and a greater understanding of their neighbors. She recalled a day on the beach in Tirre when she and Raithe had spoken about the future.

Raithe had wanted Persephone to abandon her people and run away with him. He called her hopes of winning the war nothing more than fantasies.

"I would call them dreams," she had told him. *"And maybe that is all they are, but I believe in them because they are worth believing in."*

Looking back, Persephone realized Raithe had had a dream, too—impossible for her to accept at the time, but a beautiful one nonetheless.

"I have the perfect place picked out," she remembered him saying, then he described a bluff overlooking the Urum River. *"I'm not saying it has to be just the two of us. I'm not asking you to leave the ones you love behind. Bring whoever you want."* It had been a long time, but she thought he'd said something like that, and then he talked about a magical place with abundant game and rivers filled with fish. *"Then we might be able to do some good,"* he'd said. *"Maybe we can build something that will stand."*

Persephone finally saw the wisdom in his words. *There will be human cities, and the first—the greatest—will be on a bluff overlooking the Urum River, in a place that is perfect.*

Watching Nyphron step into the light of that morning dressed in his bronze armor under the gaze of the great tower of Avempartha, she felt pride. No matter how the fight ended, she and her band of unexpected heroes had changed the course of the future, not only for the Rhune clans, but for the Fhrey tribes, as well. Two peoples had been given hope and a fair chance for peace. Suri had told her once that a storm was coming and that everyone would die. The signs were all there. Elan herself shouted a warning at them. No one thought anything could be done, but Persephone couldn't understand why a warning would be given if no chance existed. Her whole life had led to this moment, to this tiny opportunity to escape what everyone had believed to be inevitable.

What more could anyone ask?

The drums grew louder, the rhythm faster as they reached the circle that had been cleared of snow for combat. The sky began to lighten, and birds, newly returned to the north, began to sing.

Mawyndulë appeared out of the forest. He was alone, dressed in a green asica, with a broad smile on his face. Everyone looked, but no one spoke to him as he approached the ring of brambles and torches. Not long after, five Fhrey dressed in purple and white emerged. One was Volhoric, the high priest of Ferrol, who entered the ring with a thurible burning agarwood incense, and he began walking around the arena while singing softly. The last act in the play was about to begin.

⁓

Brin could see everything from the balcony, but because the falls were once more roaring at full fury, she wouldn't be able to hear what was said. This hardly mattered, as the ceremony would be in Fhrey, which she couldn't understand all that well. She'd learned some of the Fhrey language in the process of sending messages, but there was a significant difference between being able to code and decode rudimentary messages and understanding rapidly spoken dialogue with all its accents and nuance. This was another shortcoming of being alive. In Phyre, she had understood everything anyone said, regardless of the speaker.

As expected, a large crowd had formed around the arena, composed almost entirely of Fhrey. The importance of a Rhune Keeper of Ways would not be acknowledged in that maelstrom of anxiety. Persephone had inquired and gained permission for Brin to watch the proceedings from the relatively quiet calm of the tower and had given detailed directions for an east-facing balcony ideally suited. The instructions included a series of hallways, stairs, and doors, which were not as easy to navigate as Brin expected, so she wasn't at all certain she'd found the intended spot. In fact, she was pretty sure she hadn't, as this terrace looked generally south, providing a stunning panorama of the falls directly below. Still, it wrapped far enough around a spire that she could see most of the arena on the east bank as well as the bridge on the west. Looking down, Brin could see other east-facing terraces. One—likely the intended one—was crowded with spectators. So her mistake had an unexpected benefit: Brin was the only one on her balcony.

She had brought her book to work on. The Challenge was perhaps the most historic event ever, and she hoped to record it as it happened. Down below, both Nyphron and Mawyndulë had appeared. They stood stiffly as an official-looking Fhrey performed some kind of ritual that Brin imagined would take a while. Ceremonies usually did. She set out her blank pages and used her ink pot to anchor them against potential wind, then sat with her back to the tower's wall and looked up at the sky. No clouds. No breeze. Warmer than usual. It felt like the whole world was holding its breath. Brin guessed that both Eton and Elan were watching. Being winter, it was far from warm, and Brin pulled her breckon mor around her shoulders. The thick wool wrap was one that her mother had made. Maybe it was all in her head, but it seemed to keep her warmer than any other.

Out of the corner of her eye, she noticed movement. Someone had joined her on the balcony. Brin couldn't expect she would be able to keep the perch all to herself, but she had hoped she might, and this was a disappointment.

"So that's the book."

Brin looked over. Her new balcony-mate was a familiar Fhrey in a dingy cloak.

"I watched you writing long before you were born. Studied you fumbling with the markings. In the future, this fascination you have with scribbling becomes quite popular. There will be well-established institutions created to teach it. Children will learn how to make proper sentences with verbs, nouns, and a well-defined structure of agreed-upon rules." He paused, thought, then added, "Well, mostly agreed-upon."

Brin said nothing. She sat frozen, watching.

Trilos crossed the terrace to the rail and looked down, peering at the falls far below. "Did *he* ask you to write the book?"

"Malcolm isn't here," Brin blurted out.

She hadn't forgotten Trilos, or her promise to Muriel, but she hadn't thought she would encounter him again so soon. Everything from her time in Phyre felt like a dream, and seeing him again got her heart thumping.

"I believe you." Trilos turned, and his gaze focused on the blank pages, the ink, and her packed satchel.

"That's the whole history of the world, isn't it—including firsthand descriptions of my brothers and sisters and their new realms in Phyre, I presume?" He grinned at her, then the grin twisted into a smirk.

"Yes, but that's not all. There's a woman, who lives in a—"

"It's all propaganda, you know."

"What does that mean?"

"Propaganda? It's a lie made to foster a specific point of view. To make people believe what you want."

Brin shook her head with passion. "I am a Keeper. I do not lie."

"I know your reputation. That's the best part. He picked a remarkable author—a woman so pure she was able to climb out of the Abyss. No one can doubt your word."

"Everything I wrote is true."

"To you it is, but one person's truth is often another's lie."

"No." Brin shook her head. "The truth is the truth."

He smiled at her, a look that lacked warmth and was absolutely devoid of kindness. "You wrote about this war, didn't you?"

"Yes."

"Did you write how the barbarous Rhunes imperiled thousands of years of Fhrey civilization? How they threatened to destroy the world with their selfish, single-minded lust to breed and consume?"

"Of course not." Brin no longer felt comfortable sitting on the floor of the balcony. She didn't like the way Trilos towered over her. She pushed to her feet, but moved slowly as if fearful of startling a dangerous animal. "That's not true."

Trilos pointed to the east. "It is to them—and it *is* true. By their standards, your people are crude and dangerous. That's what propaganda is: taking away some truths and emphasizing others in order to warp reality to tell the story *you* want others to believe. Your book is what Turin wants the world to accept."

"He wants to heal the world, make it better. He's trying to—"

"No. He's attempting to escape justice . . . again."

"Justice?" Brin had heard Tesh use that word in much the same way. "Turin is working to correct his mistakes, fix the world. That's what this is all about. He's working to unite the three races again."

"Yes! And that is the most insidious part of all. Right now in Phyre, there are generations of people who long for the day when they can make my brother pay for the disaster he created, but through your book, Turin will be embraced by a new generation of the living. These people know nothing of his past. They will be convinced he is the *savior* of the world. Your retelling of what happened makes him look like the hero, not the villain. And when those people die, they will take that false impression to Phyre. Few will believe . . . at first, but then more will die, and more, and more. Phyre will fill up with Turin supporters, people who have no choice but to believe the heartfelt reports of a flawless woman who climbed out of the Abyss. His poison will spread and infect everyone. Don't you see? Turin can't open the doors to Phyre right now because everyone inside hates him. But given enough time and a constant influx of brainwashed Turin advocates, what do you think will happen? Opinions are changed, and Turin wins. He gets everything he wants without any punishment for the pain he's caused—not even guilt. Turin—the villain—will be reborn as the hero." Trilos took a step toward her. "I don't want him to win."

Brin didn't like Trilos's face. It had grown hard, angry, mean. He was breathing through his nose, his nostrils flaring with each breath.

But that isn't his *nose. That isn't* his *body. Trilos took it from someone and is wearing it like a coat.*

"Without your book, everything falls apart. Turin's grand plan turns to dust." Trilos took another step closer, to stand between Brin and the knapsack.

"Even without my book, people will remember what happens here today." She tried not to look down. She didn't want to draw attention to the pack, to the book.

Maybe he isn't thinking what I think he is.

"No, they won't. They'll remember it wrong. People always do. Memories are as pliable as clay. But the written word . . . your book could make the difference. I don't see the future anywhere near as clearly as Turin, but even I know that much. You're putting a lot of time into your writing, a lot of yourself. It's important to you. Sort of the child you never had, the legacy you'd like to leave behind. I'm not without compassion. Perhaps we can make a trade."

"What do you want?" Brin asked.

"Eton's Key."

ॐ

Persephone felt as wound up as spun wool as she stood behind the barrier, watching two Fhrey exit Avempartha, carrying long, double-bladed poles. They handed one to Nyphron and the other to Mawyndulë. Nyphron took his and lifted it with both hands spread apart. He spun it with remarkable speed so that the blades hummed. Mawyndulë looked at the weapon with disgust. He threw it on the ground and wiped his hands on his clothes.

An announcement was made in Fhrey. No translation was given for the few Rhunes present. This was an ancient and sacred ceremony that was a covenant between the Fhrey and their god, and it had nothing to do with men. The drums rolled, then as the face of the sun cleared the trees over Erivan, and its light bathed the arena, the two combatants entered the ring.

The blue torches flared as each of them passed.

ॐ

Mawyndulë knew the rules; they both did. He and Nyphron had each witnessed their fathers perform the very same ritual. Mawyndulë hoped to make a similar point and guessed his opponent planned the reverse. Nyphron wouldn't set foot in that ring if he didn't have a better scheme than his daddy, and Mawyndulë knew what it was.

The armor.

All that shiny bronze wasn't for show, and it wasn't to protect Nyphron from Mawyndulë's mastery of the ule-da-var that Nyphron spun with skillful ease and Mawyndulë had left lying on the grass. Nyphron was wearing Orinfar armor. Probably had the runes scratched on his sword, too.

Mawyndulë had seen how well it had worked at the Battle of Grandford, and he wasn't a fool. He, too, had planned for this.

He thinks I'm overconfident. That I'm too stupid to realize how clever he's been in dressing for the occasion. He's in for a big surprise.

Mawyndulë had practiced for this challenge ever since learning it was Nyphron who had blown the horn. He speculated about the Instarya's plans and plotted his solutions. He'd come up with two—not nearly as many as he would have liked given the threat to his life. But two were better than none. Maybe there were more that someone like Arion or Gryndal could have thought up, but not him. The idea that he should have paid more attention to instruction, tried harder, and not relied on the expectation that he would be fane by virtue of his birth fluttered across Mawyndulë's thoughts only briefly.

The other Miralyith had more time, more years. They are dusty but learned from one another. I'm on my own here. I have to do this all by myself.

Mawyndulë didn't know exactly what to expect. How could he understand the mind of a barbarian who used a sword as a daily utensil? He'd tried imagining being Nyphron, but that was impossible. He was just as likely to picture life accurately as a slug.

He thought Nyphron might rush him right at the start before he had a chance to set himself. That worried Mawyndulë quite a lot. The sight of those long spinning blades on the ule-da-var was frightening, and he never did well under pressure. He remembered when Arion had thrown the wineglass at him. This time instead of stones dropping, it would be his head hitting the ground. He was also uncertain if an Art-crafted shield would protect him against the runes.

Can an Orinfar-etched sword penetrate a magic barrier?

Mawyndulë's mind returned to the present with a jolt.

Nyphron stood across from him in a crouch, his feet planted wide, whirling that long pole, moving it hand over hand in an elegant, fluid motion that made the blades blur and the wind sound eerily like birds in flight.

He's trying to frighten me, attempting to impress. What a futile strategy. A sharp pole could never intimidate a Miralyith.

Then a new thought crossed Mawyndulë's mind.

What if I'm giving him too much credit? His father must have known what he was getting into as well, and look how stupid he was. And the armor doesn't even cover all of him. His face is still exposed. I could end this right now.

Mawyndulë planted his own feet, grateful that Nyphron had given him the opportunity. He centered himself, drawing in power. They weren't inside Avempartha, which would have been ideal, but the waterfall was close enough. He was a kid entering a snowball fight with a massive stack of ready-made balls at his side. Tapping the water's power was easy and helped convince him that Nyphron was a fool. Choosing to fight there instead of the Carfreign Arena was moronic and demonstrated how ignorant of Artists Nyphron was.

Let's see how dumb you really are.

Mawyndulë had the fire weave down so well he could have managed it drunk. Three flicks of his fingers pulled in power, a squeeze of his left hand condensed it into heat, and a thrust with his open right palm sent the heat out, igniting into a flame that burned not off fuel, but his own will augmented by the power of the falls.

Nyphron raised his arms to shield his face, and the torrent of fire washed over him.

All around, the crowd gasped.

No one cheered.

Despite the power of the falls, Mawyndulë knew *his* power, *his* stamina, wasn't unlimited, and rather than tapping out, he cut the blast short after several minutes. Nyphron had not fallen, and his armor continued to gleam just as brilliantly as before.

Okay, so you're not as dumb as all that. Fine. No problem. I expected this.

As Mawyndulë was catching his breath, Nyphron moved. The two were not far apart, only about thirty or forty feet. The arena size had been set in an age long before the Art was discovered, and the space was intended for people to fight with ule-da-var poles. Once seen as the height in combat weaponry, they were now ridiculous relics that no one knew how to use, though Nyphron appeared more than a little adept at handling his. He leapt forward with stunning speed and whirled the pole so that all Mawyndulë saw was a blur. The blades struck five times before Mawyndulë knew what had happened. The first was aimed at his neck, the second his leg. The third and fourth swings swiped at his midsection, and the last one was so powerful that it broke the ancient blade when it slammed against Mawyndulë's Art-woven shield.

His magic had worked perfectly—none of the strikes had come close to hurting him—but despite this, Mawyndulë screamed in fear. He'd never cried out like that before, didn't know he could—he sounded like a child or, worse, an animal.

Everyone laughed.

All around the circle, Fhrey whooped and guffawed, hooted and slapped thighs. The sound was loud, and it lingered. Even Nyphron laughed at him. He laughed so hard he stopped his attack and allowed Mawyndulë to retreat. Then he, too, tossed away the ule-da-var as useless.

He never intended to kill me with that. He knew it wouldn't work. That was his fire blast. His test to see how stupid I am. Not stupid—no, but scared. He found that out. Everyone did.

Mawyndulë's face was hot, flushed with embarrassment. Humiliation quickly turned to anger.

Time to stop playing games.

Mawyndulë began his weave, and outside the ring, a tree was uprooted. The crowd stopped laughing as the giant trunk listed, tipped, and came down, aimed at Nyphron. The Instarya leader dodged aside, but that wasn't necessary. The tree snapped in two, failing to fall inside the ring. Mawyndulë summoned four severed branches the size of his own arms and fired them like spears at Nyphron. They flew for a few feet, then splintered to a halt at the edge of the torch-lined ring.

Mawyndulë winced as he belatedly remembered that the arena was a sphere that nothing could enter.

Nyphron looked at the broken branches lying outside the circle and smiled at Mawyndulë. Then he drew his sword.

Terrified, Mawyndulë fumbled at his next weave. This was always meant as a secondary choice, an emergency cast. His fingers were shaking.

I didn't bend my forefinger far enough. This isn't going to work!

Nyphron strode forward, raising his blade.

Damn! Damn! Damn! I did it wrong. I know I did!

Then Nyphron stopped. He began to struggle as the ground beneath him grew into a thick mud. To Mawyndulë's great joy and relief, Nyphron began to sink.

Mawyndulë had seen Arion and Gryndal do this in their battle. He wasn't nearly as capable. The ground didn't tar, didn't bubble up, didn't just swallow him as it had when Gryndal had cast it on Arion. Nyphron had time to push out and jump away to firmer ground. Not knowing what else to do, Mawyndulë extended the mud, expanding the affected ground, chasing him around the ring. Nyphron was too quick, and Mawyndulë didn't know how to suck him down fast enough.

Grass!

Mawyndulë focused on the blades and ordered them to grab at Nyphron's legs, but he had already buried most of the grass with the mud. Those blades that did get a grip, Nyphron hacked away with his sword.

Mawyndulë was rapidly running out of ideas. He had one left and wasn't confident it would work. Pushed to desperation, he began the most complex weave he'd ever tried. Concentrating on the ground, he searched with the Art for allies.

There have to be some inside the ring. It's winter, so they'll be sleeping deep, but hopefully not too far down, not beyond the depth of the sphere.

Ants, small biting ants, not as many as Mawyndulë hoped, but enough to do the job, he thought. Assuming they could do anything at all. The number one rule of The Challenge was that only the two combatants could harm each other. But as he so recently discovered, no one and nothing could enter the ring, either. Maybe since they were already inside, the ants were no different from a sword or an ule-da-var.

They were cold, hibernating against the winter chill. Mawyndulë changed that. He summoned heat and transformed the interior of the arena into a springtime glade.

Wake up! Wake up!

Nyphron was still hacking away some of the grass and paused to look at the changes in the ring, puzzled. His little mind was trying to work out what was coming, but there was no way for him to anticipate this.

Finding the thread that linked the waking ants, Mawyndulë wove a message into their communication. Not a language, but a matter of signals existing in the natural world. Elan was able to tell trees when to shed leaves, birds to fly south, bees to gather nectar, and ants to work together as an army. Mawyndulë merely altered the marching orders.

Climb! Crawl under! Find skin! Attack!

He repeated the order and summoned every insect he could locate in the area within the circle of torches. Those beyond heard, too, but like the tree and branches, they couldn't enter the sphere. Those inside, however, responded admirably. And when Nyphron finally realized what was happening, the look on his face was a gift Mawyndulë planned to treasure for a lifetime. He didn't scream, but grunted, growled, and cursed in anger and anguish. This time no one laughed.

Nyphron began hitting himself, punching the armor he wore in an attempt to kill the invaders that were underneath. He succeeded, but only killed a few, and Mawyndulë's army continued to climb up his body. Thousands ravished him, biting and stinging. In a fit of torment, Nyphron threw down his sword and began unbuckling the armor.

The instant his sword hit the ground, Mawyndulë liquefied the soil beneath it, and the blade sank. Then, as Nyphron stripped off his protective plates, Mawyndulë sucked them away and out of sight. Once the armor was beneath the surface, he dried the dirt. Nyphron would have to dig through hard soil to retrieve any of his precious gear, and he didn't have any tools to work with.

Off came the gleaming armguards. Off came the shining chest plate, revealing a simple tunic. Mawyndulë could have blasted him, but waited, letting him remove all the metal first. And with each dropped piece, Mawyndulë swallowed up all of Nyphron's defenses. For the sake of a few ants, the Instarya was committing suicide.

CHAPTER THIRTY-ONE

Fate of the Future

The river is back. The Parthaloren Falls are making far too much noise. I'll never hear anything up here—but it is beautiful. Scary, but beautiful.

— THE BOOK OF BRIN

"I don't have the key," Brin told Trilos.

She didn't like that her voice sounded like a guilty child. She—who had suffered death and returned with wisdom beyond any living man, who had faced the wrath of gods and climbed the Alysin Pillar, who had spoken with Elan herself—felt as frightened as an abandoned infant. But this was Trilos, second of the Aesira, younger brother of Turin, older brother to Ferrol, Drome, and Mari, and the only other being to escape the Abyss. And he had done so without Eton's Key. He was easily the closest thing on the face of Elan, besides Malcolm, to a real god, and this time she didn't have Suri or Minna to help. Brin's one relief was that she was telling the truth. She didn't have the key—not anymore.

Trilos studied her. "Were you anyone else, I'd suspect you of lying, but you're incapable of that, aren't you?" Trilos asked. He hadn't moved. His foot was inches from the knapsack.

It doesn't matter. I can always write it again.

But something told her that wasn't true.

"Did you give it back to Turin?" Trilos stared, but Brin didn't answer.

She also didn't look at him, her focus lingering on that foot so close to her little satchel.

"But you really do need to hurry . . . I don't want all that I've sewn up to unravel."

Was that the reason, or had Malcolm known Trilos would find her? Had he knowingly kept silent? If so, why? What was about to happen that Malcolm didn't want to tell her? What couldn't she know? Was there more to this moment than Brin could see, some ripple effect that would play out across future centuries, a horizon that only Malcolm could perceive? Had he not wanted to spoil the moment because it needed to be unexpected? Or did he really not see this?

"You don't know my father. He's beyond manipulative and extremely clever. He shouldn't use people like you."

"No. You didn't." Trilos answered his own question. "But why not? You saw him. You warned Turin. But you didn't return the key. So if you don't have it, you must have hidden it somewhere."

Brin held her breath as Trilos bent down and picked up her pack. He opened the flap and looked inside.

"Not in here, either." He continued to peer. "Thought you might be trying to trick me with a narrow definition of *have,* but I should have known better, shouldn't I? You're so pure. Not only can't you lie, you can't even mislead. You're quite the hero—good and honest to a fault, or maybe you're just innocent. New snow is that way, but time melts everything." He hefted the pack, appraising its weight. "Quite a bit of work you've done here. It'd be a shame to lose it all."

"You might want to take measures to protect that," Malcolm's words of warning, which had been so soft before, rang in her head.

"Tell me." He lifted the pack and joined her near the railing. "Where is the key?"

"If you destroy my work, I'll just write it again," Brin said. She was trying to sound brave, but her voice was weak. Seeing the bag so close to the edge scared her. Writing it once had been a magical feat, and not just by the way the ink had refilled and the pages never ran out. Brin knew she would never get the chance to do it again.

Trilos knew it, too. He laughed, and in his eyes, she saw the truth—his truth—that *The Book of Brin* wasn't the only thing that would go over the rail.

⁂

Amid all the hoopla, no one noticed the five near-frozen, previously dead adventurers returning from the grave.

They stumbled their way down the road and past a handful of tents and smoldering fire pits. Not a soul was in camp. That morning, everyone was at the river. An army of Fhrey was gathered on the far bank.

"Looks like it has already begun," Tekchin said.

⁂

"You can't destroy my book," Brin said.

"Of course I can."

Brin reached for her bag. Trilos swung his arm, dangling the pack above the roaring falls, making her heart stutter.

"Stop! You don't understand. I put *your* memories in it, all your thoughts of Muriel, the ones you wrote about on tablets in the Abyss. You have to read them. If you do, you'll regain what you lost, what you sacrificed to get out of Phyre. The joy of your life."

For the first time, she saw surprise on Trilos's furrowed brow. He looked at the bag, then back at her.

"It's true!" Brin shouted at him. "You know it is. I don't lie, remember? If you destroy that bag, you'll obliterate what used to be the most important part of you. Something so powerful, it gave you the strength to escape the Abyss. They're your own thoughts, your own words. Words you wrote to yourself."

Trilos pulled the bag back, his expression troubled, his eyes struggling to work out this new problem.

"On those pages lies the love of your life. Her name is Muriel, and she asked me to give your memories back. She begged me. They are in your hand right now."

His eyes shifted left then right. "I don't know anyone named Muriel."

"You called her Reely."

Trilos squinted, struggling to think. That name didn't seem to bounce off anything, either.

"It's all in there. I'm the Keeper of Ways for my people. I remember things very well. I wrote it all down exactly as I found it, precisely the way you wrote it on the stone tablets in the Abyss. Don't you understand? You're right. You did help me develop writing, but you did it so that I could find, read, and return your lost memories. The stone tablets you left in the Agave, in the Abyss—they're your memories, your joy is in that bag. Don't throw it away."

Once more Trilos looked down at the bag.

"I don't lie," Brin said. "I don't even mislead. It's not a trap. It's the truth. And maybe you're right, and there isn't one single, perfect set of facts. I know you don't believe in *my* interpretation because I'm young and naïve, but how do you know that *your* truth is the right one? You could be wrong, too."

"No, I can't." Trilos continued to look down at the bag in his hand. "Because I don't care about the truth."

Brin took a breath, letting her muscles relax.

He believes me.

"Just read the words," she implored him. "Read and remember."

Trilos shook his head. "That's not how it works. Your friend Suri could tell you if she were here." He looked at the bag with a melancholy stare and nodded. "There was a gap. I knew how I escaped. I just couldn't recall what memory I sacrificed. Now I know."

"Yes, and your memories are here!" Brin shouted at him. "You preserved them."

"I'm sure they are. But what does it matter?"

"Because you can get them back."

Trilos shook his head. "No, I can't. You don't understand how it works. The power comes from anguish. If the loss was temporary, there would be no sacrifice. I wouldn't have had the power to punch through the worlds."

Brin was confused. "Then why write all of it down?"

"A suicide note, I suppose. You said that you spoke to this Reely person?"

Brin nodded.

"And you told her what was on the tablets?"

Again, Brin nodded.

"Well, there you have it. I must have foreseen that you would deliver the message. I took the time to write everything down so she would know what happened, and, I assume, how much I cared for her."

Down below and off to the east, she heard people shouting. The Challenge was being fought, and she wasn't even watching.

"I sacrificed someone obviously very dear to me. I must have done so because stopping Turin was more important."

With his free hand, Trilos reached out and grabbed Brin by the throat. She screamed.

"With Eton's Key, I can open the gates to Phyre, and all those now trapped who know of Turin's treachery can rise against him. I need that key. I don't care who I lost in the past, and I won't mourn your passing now. Tell me where it is, and I'll spare your life."

❧

Outside the ring, everyone was screaming at Nyphron, trying to stop him from stripping off his armor. They knew, even if he didn't, the mistake he was making. They, of course, weren't in the battle, and they didn't have thousands of unseen ants eating them. With all his armor except his boots off, Nyphron began clawing at his clothes.

"Here," Mawyndulë told him. "Let me help you with that."

Three fingers flicked. A squeeze of his left hand and a thrust with his open right palm sent a torrent of flames out. This time Nyphron caught on fire and burned. His clothes were set ablaze, his hair igniting.

Mawyndulë let him continue to burn. It taxed him, weakened him, but this was the big finale. Nothing so marvelous as the display his father had entertained the crowd with, but a win was a win.

Mawyndulë eased off and watched with grinning satisfaction as Nyphron fell to the ground, just as Lothian had.

No one was laughing anymore.

Everyone outside the ring was silent. Hands covered faces. A few even whimpered.

ର

As Moya and the others started across the wafer-thin bridge toward the tower, the watching crowd went silent.

Moya looked behind her at Roan and Gifford. Both returned her stare, confused. Something bad had happened. Something terrible.

"Are we too late? Where do we need to go, Gifford? What must we do?" She wasn't an Artist and couldn't speak to trees, yet at that moment, she felt it: The world was screaming with an unmistakable urgency. Moya experienced it as an irrational fear, a dread unlike anything she'd ever known. It washed over her in a rising panic that had no apparent source.

Then, in that moment of surreal stillness, she heard a single scream from overhead.

Gifford jerked his head up. "Bwin?"

High above, Moya saw two figures on a balcony overlooking the falls. A Fhrey holding Brin's pack shoved a woman to the edge.

Gifford was right. It was Brin.

ର

Trilos held her against the rail. "Tell me where the key is. Now!"

Her feet were coming out from under her. All she had to hang on to was Trilos. Looking down, she saw only the roaring white mists billowing up like a meeting of many angry clouds. The morning sun cut across the falls, turning water droplets into sparkling gems.

Her stomach had climbed into her throat, and she swallowed it back down, forcing her body to relax. Her heart and lungs were pumping of their own accord, doing what they were expected to. Only things had changed. The worst part of death was the unknown, and death was no mystery to Brin.

"Go ahead," Brin told him, her voice hard and steady. This was the articulation of the shining woman whom Brin had seen in the mirror to Alysin. "I've been there, remember? It's not so bad." She thought of the fruit that had tasted like anything she wanted and the warmth of the hearth in Mari's home. Then she remembered Tesh. He was still down there, feeling alone and forgotten in the Abyss. She had left him, but now her work was done. The horn had been delivered and the book written. Plus, she didn't have the key. That treasure was locked safely away in the one place Trilos would never go looking.

Trilos glared. His mouth jerked down in a severe frown that appeared painful. He was breathing hard through his nostrils again, making them flare, and for a moment, the world paused. The roar of the falls was still there but fainter somehow, and the shouts of spectators had stopped entirely as she and Trilos teetered on the brink of eternity.

"You've lost your fear of death. Of course you have! Turin thinks of everything, doesn't he?"

"Bwin?" a voice came from below.

Gifford? Brin managed to turn her head far enough to see them. Moya, Roan, Tekchin, Rain, and Gifford were crossing the bridge below.

They made it! Roan found a way out of the Abyss for her and Gifford, at least. And everyone but Tressa and Tesh have come back to life. It worked. They found Padera and—

"Friends?" Trilos asked. "You don't care if I kill *you* . . . but . . ."

"No. Don't!"

"Did you know that Turin isn't the only one who can see the future? Any Aesira can to some degree. But he ate the fruit of Alurya, and it granted him more than just immortality. Most of the time I don't bother because the future changes so quickly, but if I *really* concentrate, and focus on one thing at a time, the way I did with your writing . . ."

Trilos dropped Brin's pack on the balcony's floor, but still kept one hand on her throat. He stared at the horizon. "Ah, yes. There's Gifford and his wife, Roan, enjoying a happy life. And what's this? A perfect child, not twisted like him or broken like her, but a wonderful, beautiful baby." Trilos smiled as if amused by some joke. "They want to name it after you. Imagine that. It's a boy so they'll use the male equivalent: Bran. And he'll be the perfect protégé. You'll teach him to read, and write, and tell him everything you know. After your death, he goes on to form a religion based on *The Book of Brin*. The world's a better place because of the story you wrote, the things you did, the sort of person you are. Unless . . ."

Trilos's tone dropped, filling with a deadly seriousness. "I think I'll kill *her*, not him, and it won't be quick. Roan is a sensitive sort, isn't she? Doesn't like to be touched? I'll make her husband watch. Without Roan, Gifford will be crippled forever, but in a different—much more terrible— way. His pain of living without her will be so much worse than sending them to Phyre together. And you should know that some horrors are so great that we take them with us into the afterlife. Some regrets are so indelible that they can make Phyre less a reward and more an eternal torture."

"Please, I'm begging you." Tears filled her eyes.

"All you have to do is tell me where the key is. Tell me, and I promise I won't hurt you or any of your friends. I'm not cruel. I don't want to hurt anyone. All I want is to open the doors to Phyre and free those who are trapped. I just need the key. What do you say?"

He waited.

Because Tressa and Tesh weren't with the others, there was a good chance that the key was still with Padera.

But what if they brought it with them? The risk is too great.

Trilos's only interest in the others was as leverage to make her obey. He had no idea that they, too, had been in Phyre. He would have no reason to suspect they knew anything about the key. She was his only connection to it.

"Turin entrusted the key to you," Mari had said. *"And he isn't a trusting person."*

"You are the only one that matters." Aria had told her. *"Don't you understand that? This hasn't been about Tressa, or Moya, or any of the others."*

This is about me! Brin finally understood. It had been her story, which was at its end. The rest would be written by others.

All I need to do to help save the world is . . . let go of it.

Brin gritted her teeth, and with one last breath and all her strength, she shoved backward. For all his foresight, Trilos didn't see that coming. She fell away from him over the rail, over the edge. Trilos tried to save her, but only caught her breckon mor. The clasp of the pin that held the garment snapped free.

As she plummeted, mist sprayed Brin's face, and her hair flew back. She wasn't afraid. She'd done this before. She knew what she was leaving behind and what lay ahead. Her work on Elan was done, but she had unfinished business on the other side.

Hang on, Tesh. I'm coming.

⚬

Brin's small figure fell backward over the edge, making one full flip before disappearing into the mist. There was no scream. No cry other than from Moya, Roan, and Gifford. Tekchin and Rain were mute. The five stood frozen on that delicate expanse of bridge, looking up in shock.

"Nooooo . . ." The word escaped Moya as a moan.

Where the strength came from, she didn't know, but Moya ran. What she did couldn't have been called a sprint, but she threw everything she had into the effort. Before they crossed the remaining distance to the tower, Tekchin and Rain passed her, their swords drawn.

The three of them climbed multiple sets of stairs before finding an opening. When Moya reached the balcony, she collapsed from exhaustion, struggling to breathe. She had nothing left.

Tekchin and Rain were at the railing, looking down.

"Where's the Fhrey?" Moya asked. "Did you see which way he went?"

"No," Rain replied. "Are we sure this is the right balcony?"

Tekchin reached down and picked something up.

"What's that?" Moya asked. "Is it her pack?"

"No, it's a shawl—Brin's breckon mor." He looked around. "There's nothing else."

&

It's over, Mawyndulë realized. *I've won. I'm Fhrey again. I'm finally fane! Except . . .*

The cold, it was still there. The empty sense of internal nothingness lingered within him.

Something else was wrong. Nyphron wasn't screaming.

Mawyndulë had blasted him with enough fire to cook a bull, but the Instarya hadn't made a sound, and worse, he was moving. He ought to be shrieking. Lothian had screamed plenty. But Nyphron was quiet, and his movements weren't the thrashing panic Mawyndulë had expected. Instead, the warrior rolled on the ground, putting out the remaining flames from the few tatters that had been his clothes.

Then Nyphron did the impossible. Naked, hairless, and coated in mud, he stood up and smiled.

Mawyndulë wasted no time. He summoned another blast and hit Nyphron with a second round of fire. This time Nyphron didn't fall or pat at himself. The fire did nothing more than dry the mud. And as it did, some of the filth fell from Nyphron's skin.

Mawyndulë stared in horror. The Instarya's body was covered in tattoos. The Orinfar blanketed every bit of his skin—even the scalp of his head where his hair no longer remained.

In an instant, Nyphron closed the distance between them. He had no sword, dagger, or weapon of any kind. He didn't need any. His fists were more than enough. The first blow dropped Mawyndulë on his back. Then the Instarya hit Mawyndulë again. Then again. The jarring pain brought bright lights and jolts of agony. Somewhere around the fifth or sixth blow to his head, Mawyndulë began to lose consciousness.

"Something seems to have gone wrong there, didn't it?" He was in the Talwara again, and Arion had just . . .

"Yeah, you threw a glass at me!"

"Imagine if it had been a knife, a javelin, or a ball of fire. And instead of stones, what if those rocks were people's lives? Perhaps if you had learned how to concentrate on more than one thing at a time, they wouldn't all be dead right now."

"Arion, they aren't people; they're stones."

"Lucky for you, or should I say lucky for them? Now pick up those poor dead bodies and try again."

But there would be no second try, and no paradise for Mawyndulë.

Nyphron was killing the prince, beating the scrawny brat to a bloody mass of soft, sloppy flesh. It's what he had wanted to do for so long. What he had wanted to do to all of them. He'd waited years for this. Even so, his arm slowed. His fists stopped.

If he'd had his sword, Pontifex, the culling little Miralyith would have been dead six times over, regardless of the promise Nyphron had made. Being forced to use his hands had saved the kid's life. Somewhere between shattering the prince's nose and cracking his jaw, Nyphron decided not to kill him. He attributed part of his change of heart to having already worked out much of his anger and that he had the satisfaction of beating the boy to the point of blacking out. He guessed some of his hesitation had to do with distaste for killing a thirty-three-year-old kid. Plus, Mawyndulë was unconscious. Instarya didn't kill helpless fellow Fhrey, and a Galantian certainly shouldn't. This was just one of the many differences between his tribe and the Miralyith.

The final decision came after his fever broke, and Malcolm's words landed in fertile soil.

"Demonstrate mercy in full view of all. Show everyone that the days of the cruel Miralyith rule are over and that a fair and just fane sits on the Forest Throne again. Do that and you will be more than respected—you will be loved."

He lingered over the boy, his hands planted in the mud to either side of his head. His own sweat dripped off his nose onto the prince's blood-splattered face. The kid was breathing a gurgling breath—still alive. That was good, he thought, because no one was cheering. Maybe if they had, that would have made a difference. But the world beyond the ring was silent. He even heard a few gasps. That's what sealed it. Looking up, he saw disgust and horror on the faces around him. He'd seen those faces before. He'd worn that grimace—the day he watched Lothian kill his father.

Miralyith were in the audience. They were watching him.

Nyphron didn't need to be loved, but the idea of a revolt of the Miralyith—the same Miralyith who controlled a fleet of nearby dragons—was sobering.

Nyphron stood up and found Volhoric. "What are the rules? Can I let him live?"

At his words, the crowd whispered in surprise.

The high priest was caught off guard and stammered. "I—I—ah—yes. But—ah, he has to concede."

Nyphron grabbed the kid by the neck and pulled him up. He spat in Mawyndulë's face and used his thumbs to wipe the blood out of his eyes. He slapped one cheek and then the other. "Wake up! Do you want to live or not?"

"You should kill him," Jerydd said. The kel was nearby. With hands lost in his long sleeves, he spoke softly so none of the others could hear. "Letting him live isn't wise."

Looking around, Nyphron studied the expression on the faces of those who had likely seen him as some sort of barbarian a minute ago—the ones who probably wondered if a vicious Instarya from the frontier would be a better ruler than Lothian's son. Maybe it was wishful thinking, but they appeared a little confused and a lot hopeful.

The kid slowly opened his eyes.

"Say you concede. Give up, and I won't kill you."

The little prince blinked. He spat blood and teeth.

"Can you talk?"

He didn't say anything, just blew bubbles.

"Can he nod in response?" Nyphron asked in the direction of where Imaly and Volhoric stood.

"Ah . . ." the high priest looked lost. "I don't know."

Nyphron noticed the burning blue torches. "Listen carefully, kid. Your life may depend on this. I'm going to ask you a question. If you say yes, this might be over, and you'll live. I won't imprison you or anything like that. You just need to leave and not cause any trouble, okay? If you say no, I'll respect that, but then I'll have to kill you. I'll have no choice. I've got no weapon so it could take a while. You ready?"

Mawyndulë managed to nod.

"Okay, here goes. Do you concede this contest to me and relinquish your claim to the Forest Throne?"

There was a pause. For a moment, Nyphron thought Mawyndulë might refuse, and for a brief instant he felt a small amount of respect for him. Then the kid opened his mouth.

"Ye-sss," came out as a hiss.

Instantly the blue torches flared brilliant white, then went out with a loud snap.

Volhoric stood up and turned to the gathered crowd. "It is done," the high priest of Ferrol announced. "Congratulations, Nyphron. You are fane."

"That may be," he said while standing up and accepting the clothes thrown at him, garments pulled off his people's own backs. "But I am also emperor."

CHAPTER THIRTY-TWO

The Book of Brin

I can see the arena below me where The Challenge will take place in just a few minutes. Some Fhrey are walking in a circle conducting a ritual. The day is beautiful. The sky is clear. The sun is

— THE BOOK OF BRIN

Mawyndulë couldn't see very well. His face had swollen up so that one eye was entirely closed and the other remained little more than a narrow slit. With his jaw broken in two places, he couldn't actually talk. He was missing several teeth, the absence of which left frightening gaps that his tongue refused to leave alone. And his right hand was broken. He only found that out when he tried to wipe the blood from his eyes, and his fingers ignored him. He hadn't noticed his hand because that pain was being eclipsed by the throbbing in his head, which was so intense that Nyphron might still be hitting him. Oddly, when Nyphron *was* beating his face flat, Mawyndulë hadn't felt much at all. He couldn't hear very well, either. Everything was dull and muffled, as if his battered head had also been jammed into the mud. After the fight, he had managed to crawl off to the side of the arena. He pushed himself into the snow. The cold felt good, and that was all he wanted. But as he lay listening to the shouts and cheers, his mind began to ponder.

I should have let Nyphron kill me.

Mawyndulë wanted to be dead. No sense in living anymore, he had no future, and the present hurt worse than anything he'd ever known. Death was terrifying for anyone, and so much more for a young Fhrey deprived of centuries of life. For Mawyndulë it was worse. Most had the reassurance that everyone made the same journey when they died, but his trip would be different. Mawyndulë wouldn't go to Phyre.

So where will I go?

The idea that he would be alone in some horrible place scared him. Not that he had a choice. He was going to die right there in the snow thickets on the bank of the Nidwalden. He couldn't see, couldn't speak, even had a hard time breathing. No one would help him.

How long does it take to die from cold? Maybe I should throw myself off the falls.

Mawyndulë couldn't see his way there, but only needed to walk toward the roar. At some point, he'd fall in the river and things would take care of themselves. The reason he hadn't thrown himself in already was that it required getting up. Committing suicide demanded too much effort.

"That didn't work, did it?" someone said.

Mawyndulë had heard a lot of people talking. Most as they walked past.

"He outwitted you. An unforgivable error for a Miralyith to make when facing an Instarya."

He's speaking to me. Whoever it was sounded close. *Someone lingering to gloat?*

Mawyndulë heard a rustle as the person crouched, getting closer still. "Don't let him see you coming next time. Give him no warning. Just kill him."

Next time?

Mawyndulë managed to open his one narrow eye. Everything was fuzzy. Someone was there, but he couldn't tell who. Only that he was in a dingy cloak and carried a knapsack over his shoulder.

"He got some of what he wanted, but not all. The world is back in balance—so to speak—but not exactly the way he had hoped. I gave it a good hard wobble, and I didn't walk away this time. I have his prize, and more than anything else, that will gnaw at him." He indicated the sack, which was filled with parchments, some peeking out the top. "The thing he really wanted is here—his happy little future where he gets to be the hero. I have his key and I suspect he has mine. Not a bad trade. This is far from over."

The snow crunched as the person bent down. "And you, he forgot about you. Looks like everyone did, but I haven't. That makes you another blind spot in his vision. We can use that to our advantage. He wants a religion, fine, we'll give him one, and together we will tear down everything he builds. Then I'll get the key and the real war will begin. He won this round, but he won't win again."

"Who?" Mawyndulë managed to hoot out of his mangled mouth.

"The invisible hand, of course. Rex Uberlin."

ও

After The Challenge, Nyphron had lingered to speak with the Aquila. The discussion was in Fhrey, and they spoke fast and used unusual words. Persephone had problems keeping up. She felt awkward, and after witnessing the contest, she felt drained. The war was over. She wasn't keenig anymore. As strange as it sounded, she was something Nyphron called *empress*. Second Chair, chieftain, keenig, empress—so many titles for one person. Strangely, the Fhrey were celebrating their defeat. Persephone's people celebrated as well, the sort of unbridled revelry that only came from utter ignorance of the future. Tomorrow was a day away, but for now— joy. Persephone walked alone back through the first floor of Avempartha. The two big doors were open at both ends, making it easy to navigate the trip across the river. The main floor was a grand anteroom decorated by shimmering banners forming a nexus for dozens of stairs, corridors, and a great many closed doors. Perhaps later, the celebrants would find their way inside, but at that moment Persephone was the only one crossing through.

"Seph!"

She stopped. *No one calls me that—no one since . . .*

Her eyes searched the shadows until she spotted five figures coming down a stair, five familiar faces she never thought she'd see again.

"By Mari's hand!" she exclaimed.

The day after the fight, they held the coronation inside the tower of Avempartha. Light permeated the walls of the tower, seeping through the stone as if it were smoked glass, making the interior of the citadel an illuminated world of wondrous color and beauty. Ceilings stretched in tall, airy arches, meeting hundreds of feet above the floor. Tamed by the walls of the tower, the roar of the nearby cataracts was a soft, muffled, undeniably soothing hum. Shimmering banners hung from the lofty heights, each displaying the symbols of the seven tribes of the Fhrey. Despite the two armies lined up outside, and the growing sense of celebration, the world inside those curved walls felt peaceful, still, and silent.

The coronation was conducted on a balcony about midway up the tower. Volhoric spoke a good deal in Fhrey. So did some of the others, but the high priest was clearly leading the ceremony. Persephone stood beside her husband as the high priest placed a golden circlet on Nyphron's head, and that ended it. The war, however, still needed to be wrapped up.

Nyphron, who was still fearful of some future Miralyith rebellion, ordered all the gilarabrywns to be destroyed. This was met with widespread grief for those who had given their lives to make them. At Persephone's gentle urging, a memorial was built at the top of Avempartha. Swords that had the names of the Fhrey who had given their lives were placed in racks, and over them was an inscription that told how their sacrifices had saved thousands of Fhrey lives by creating a peaceful end to the war.

Despite this, fights broke out. Hiddle, son of Berston, was killed, and a Fhrey badly beaten. Nyphron resigned himself to dividing the races. He declared the banks of the Nidwalden to be *ryin contita* or off limits to both human and Fhrey. The Fhrey were ordered to remain in Erivan, forbidden from crossing the river. Men were likewise prohibited and would remain in Rhulyn and Avrlyn. This declaration would be self-enforced, meaning that the Fhrey had Nyphron's permission to execute any man found on their side and the Rhunes had the same privilege.

Lost in between, Avempartha would remain vacant, an obvious slap to the Miralyith and punishment for Jerydd's capture of Suri. Still, it was far better than the Artists expected from their new fane.

The question of where Nyphron would live was quickly answered. Two days after his crowning, he decreed that for the next three thousand years the Fhrey would be separated from their fane. He wanted nothing to do with the Forest Throne, Estramnadon, or Erivan. Nyphron would, in effect, banish the Erivan Fhrey just as they had banished the Instarya. The Aquila would be led by Imaly, but no Erivan Fhrey—no *elves*—would be allowed to cross the Nidwalden until Nyphron's Uli Vermar ended. Then, and only then, would they be allowed to cross the river, where Nyphron's heir would present the horn for The Challenge.

All of this was met with stoic calm and silence from the Fhrey leaders. Nyphron's announcement that he would not directly rule them, and that no Rhune would be allowed to cross the Nidwalden, eliminated much of the tension. The fact that Nyphron was keeping the Horn of Gylindora didn't go unnoticed by Imaly. She fiercely argued that the fane should never have possession of the horn, as it circumvented the right to challenge. Nyphron wasn't moved by Imaly's arguments, and the final meeting between Rhunes and Fhrey ended on a less-than-cordial note. Nyphron ordered stakes pulled up, and both groups left the banks of the Nidwalden.

≈

Gifford and Roan rocked together in the back of the wagon as the imperial host rolled west. Neither knew where they were headed, and Gifford honestly didn't care. Even after several days' rest, he remained exhausted. Where they had found the strength to hike from the Swamp of Ith to Avempartha, he couldn't fathom. Rain was with them, but Moya and Tekchin were in a different wagon. The one Gifford, Roan, and Rain rocked in was filled with bushels of grain and barrels of wine.

They bounced and shimmied along the Bridge Road that cut a straight line through the Harwood. Sitting down on the bed of the wagon, with its high wooden sides, all Gifford could see were the snowy tops of huge trees. Rain was being his normal quiet self and spent much of his time looking at the sword he now carried. But in truth, all of them were quiet. The loss of Brin had killed any sense of pride or feeling of victory.

"Who do you think did it?" Gifford asked his wife. "Who killed Bwin? If I could find him, if I could do that much . . ."

Roan shook her head.

"What?" he asked.

"Whoever was up there didn't kill her."

Gifford narrowed his eyes at his wife, confused. Sitting opposite them among bags of grain, Rain's head came up off his chest.

"He didn't push her. She jumped."

Gifford considered this for the first time. "The key is still inside Wel." He sat up, excited. "Maybe she can—"

Again, Roan shook her head. "Her body is gone. Even if she can find it, it'll be too late. She won't return to us, but I think she went back for a reason."

"Tesh and Twessa?"

Roan smiled.

"Do you think she can help them?"

"I think there are few things beyond Brin's ability to conquer."

"Then I think the Typhons should look out."

They bounced along in silence for a time. Rain shifted position. He had made an awkward but comfortable seat out of the grain sacks and sat back down. "Any idea where we're going?"

"Southwest," Roan said.

"Yes, but to where?"

Gifford tried to shrug and failed. It was taking some effort to adjust to his old body. "Oh—that's wight. You have a destiny to fulfill!"

"How are you going to manage that?" Roan asked. "You, Frost, and Flood were banished from Belgreig."

Rain nodded, then shrugged. "Don't know." He picked up a feather that was lying in the bed of the wagon, having fallen to the floor when he moved the bags of grain. He spun it absently between his fingers. "Persephone and Nyphron were talking about building a new city, and I was thinking for now that Frost, Flood, and I could help. Belgriclungreians are good at that."

"What about your future wife?"

"Oh, I'm sure I'll be heading in that direction, eventually. I'm sure I'll know when the time is right."

Gifford was nodding, but Roan was staring at the feather Rain twirled. "That's not a feather."

Gifford and Rain looked at each other then back at her.

"Sure it is. I think it's from a duck," Rain said.

Roan was shaking her head adamantly. "No—it's not."

She reached over and plucked it from the dwarf's hand. "Look." She pointed to the tip where the hollow shaft had been cut to a point. "This is a quill. One of Brin's." Roan got to her hands and knees and crawled over the bags and around the wine barrels. "She was in here. And—"

Roan snatched up a bundle. She drew it back and set it on her lap. Unfolding the wool wrap revealed a bound book.

"Bwin's book," Gifford said.

Roan opened the cover and flipped through page after page of black marks on parchment.

"Can you weed it?" he asked his wife.

Flipping back to the first page, she caught a lock of hair, twirled it into a tight string, and put it into her mouth.

CHAPTER THIRTY-THREE

The First Empyre

I shall henceforth endeavor to piece together all that is known of such said era, which is now recognized by all contemporary scholars as the Age of Myth and Legend. I will record in honest detail and objective discourse how Novron the Great did win the Elven War and establish our grand empire through courage, valor, and for the love of Persephone, a simple farmer's daughter.

—MIGRATION OF PEOPLES by Princess Farilane

On her sixty-second birthday, the day the city was to be officially named and dedicated, Persephone woke up coughing. Her chest hurt from the hacking, and she rolled over and spat into the bucket beside the bed. She steadied herself before coughing and spitting again.

More blood than usual.

Bringing up blood wasn't good, and the fever, chills, chest pains, and sore throat weren't much of a warm hug, either. Even so, she'd had those other ailments for weeks, and the blood was a relatively new occurrence. The way it stained the interior of the bucket left her uneasy, as if she had one foot off the edge of a cliff and the other was slipping.

She lay across the bed on her stomach, staring down until she noticed the sunshine coming in the windows. Spring mornings had a different kind of light, a softer, more hopeful radiance. *Happy light,* she thought. Along with the morning shine came the sound of hammering, distant shouts, and laughter mixed with birdsong. For a moment, Persephone believed she was back in the lodge in Dahl Rhen. Her hand fanned out across the covers searching for Reglan, but that side of the bed was empty—had been for years.

This isn't Dahl Rhen.

People called the outpost New Rhen or Rhenydd in the Fhrey tongue. Old Rhen was on the other side of the Bern and Urum. This place, *this* side of the rivers, was known as Avrlyn—"the Green Land" in Fhrey, but for Rhunes it had always been "the Forbidden Lands." A man had once been killed for being where they were now; that man's son had long dreamed of coming back. He never made it.

Persephone swallowed. That hurt, too. Everything did these days. She rolled over, so she could see out the window. Her bedroom was up five stories. The height still disturbed her, but it provided a perfect view of the city.

By Mari, it's ugly.

What had been a lovely green hill overlooking the Urum River had been torn into a muddy mess. After so many years, all they had managed to accomplish was to scar Elan's face, turning a natural beauty into a hideous blemish. Nyphron wasn't one for the Eilywin tradition of natural harmony. He and his staff of Belgriclungreian designers had their own vision of how the world ought to be. Straight roads, square buildings, and stone—lots and lots of stone. Thousands of men and hundreds of dwarfs labored on scaffolds, using wheels and pulleys to lift brick and block. None of the buildings were finished, and everyone suffered equally under temporary roofs of wooden planks. The Grand Marchway, as Nyphron euphemistically called it, was a line of muck this time of year. In summer, the mud dried, but the city was infested with biting flies and broiled in unrelenting heat. In winter, everyone froze because the buildings were up high, made of stone, and there weren't any natural windbreaks.

Persephone would have preferred a log lodge.

The way Nyphron kept adding to the city, she wondered if it would ever be finished, but her husband was intent on dedicating the place that afternoon. He had a special ceremony planned where he would unfurl the dragon banners and give a speech from the balcony of the palace, the dome of which was still under scaffolding. Persephone rolled back and collapsed, a rasping in her chest. She felt exhausted and hoped she would feel better soon. Nyphron would want her with him for the dedication.

She heard a light tap on the door as if a mouse was rapping, and without a pause Justine's head peeked in. The woman who had once been Nolyn's nurse had become Persephone's. "Are we awake?"

"You seem to be, so it looks like we are," Persephone croaked out, then coughed again.

Justine stepped inside. Sunlight splashed across her face, revealing the growing threads of gray invading the woman's once dark hair.

When did that happen?

"How are you this morning?" The woman had a serious concern in her voice, a tone that was practically suspicious.

"Better."

"Are you just saying that because I sound worried?"

"Scared you, huh?"

Justine nodded with a series of fast shallow bobs and a false smile.

"Do I look like I did last night?" Persephone challenged. She had no idea what the answer to that question might actually be, but given that she no longer felt like hungry rats were nesting inside her chest, she took a gamble.

"No," Justine conceded. She dragged the word out with reluctance while studying Persephone's face, "But you always look fine in the morning."

This was true. Persephone's mornings were usually her best times. Her afternoons were iffy, and her nights, horrific. The last one hadn't only scared Justine—who had actually cried at one point—but Persephone had felt that second foot slip, too. She'd had trouble breathing, a great deal of trouble. She felt as if she were drowning, and once more recalled the face of Morton Whipple—that poor little boy hadn't changed a bit; he was still trapped under the ice.

"Can I get you anything? Water? Food?"

Persephone shook her head. This made Justine scowl. "You *have* to eat."

"I'll just spit it out again if I do."

The worry crawled back onto Justine's face.

"Maybe later," Persephone offered.

Justine slowly nodded. "If you're up to it, there's someone here to see you."

"Nolyn?" she asked.

Justine shook her head with a sympathetic frown. "No, he's with Sephryn and Bran. They're helping with decorations. Do you want me to get him? He's not far away. He asked me to let him know if . . ."

"If what?"

"Do you want me to send for him?"

"No, he was here all last night. He slept in that chair, or tried to, and I feel better, don't I?"

"You tell me."

"I have a better idea. Why don't you tell me who this visitor is?"

"An old friend, although he doesn't look as old as he should. He's waiting. I told him I had to see if you were up to a visit."

"Who is it?"

Justine smiled, and without answering, she returned to the door, opening it wide. "Malcolm? She'll see you now."

The man hadn't changed a bit. No gray hair on him, no potbelly, no wrinkles around his eyes. He could have been one of Nolyn's older friends. Persephone had come to terms with him being far from ordinary. He could see the future and gave brave adventurers keys to the underworld. Malcolm had helped her from the very start, and ultimately, he was responsible for the Rhunes winning the war peacefully. She would forever be in his debt.

"Malcolm!" she shouted and then coughed.

"Watch yourself!" Justine snapped.

Persephone held out her arms. Malcolm crossed the room in three long strides and embraced her.

"It's been so long," Persephone said. "I thought I would never see you again. Have you visited with Nyphron?"

"No," he replied softly, sitting on the bed beside her.

Judging everything to be satisfactory, Justine grabbed the empty water pitcher and left the room.

"Have you seen Nolyn? He'll be thrilled. And you must meet Bran, Roan's son. The boy is growing like a salifan plant. He's taller than I am now."

Again, he shook his head.

"What about Moya, Tekchin, and Sephryn? Oh, you probably don't know their daughter, do you?"

"I haven't seen anyone. I came here only to see you."

This didn't surprise her. Persephone wished it did, but she'd guessed it the moment he entered. The man's timing had always been impeccable, and she realized now that Malcolm never showed up anywhere by accident. The last time he'd appeared out of nowhere was just before Padera died.

"What—ah—what do you think of the city? Nyphron is very proud of his creation. Has a whole army of—oh! Did you hear Rain has been crowned the new dwarven king? Frost and Flood can't believe it. He's pardoned them. They say they will go home after finishing Nyphronronia, but I wonder if that will ever happen. Nyphron keeps making it bigger. They're actually putting in waste tunnels that Roan suggested. That's a huge project. Personally, I think the dwarfs just like digging holes."

"Persephone, it—"

"You can call me Seph. You've known me long enough."

He smiled. It was a sad smile. "Persephone, it doesn't end here."

"You aren't wearing your leigh mor." She pointed at his tailored tunic.

"I'm afraid they're falling out of fashion. All the young people are wearing tunics now, and jackets. You've probably seen them. And the girls, they have these dresses where the top halves are stitched tight—fitted to their bodies. Not exactly decent. They say the new clothes are more freeing, but I've seen the way the men look at them, and it isn't luxury of movement that these girls are after."

"I think it helps if you understand that it doesn't end here," Malcolm went on.

Persephone looked down at the bed. When she looked back up, her lower lip trembled. "Malcolm . . . Malcolm, I think I picked wrong. I think I failed. I think I messed everything up."

"No, you didn't." He took her hand in his and gave a soft squeeze.

"But Nyphron is—" She rolled her eyes. "*Nyphronronia!* He's actually going to name it that."

"No—no, he won't."

"Of course he will. They're having the ceremony this afternoon. His arrogance has gotten the better of him." She took a breath. "He should name it after Nolyn, but he won't let his son have anything. The two are already at odds. Do you know what Nolyn means? Do you know why I picked it?" She sighed. "I fear I chose wrong . . . I only thought . . ."

"Persephone, when the ruins of Alon Rhist have lain buried for so long that no one remembers what the strange bluish stones sticking out of the ground are, or how they got there, the age you lived in will be remembered as an age of myths and legends. People—your people—will live in an era of unparalleled prosperity. This city will stand for centuries and never have need for walls. Raithe's dream of living in the land of green will be magnified beyond his ability to imagine."

At the sound of his name, tears slipped down her cheeks.

She nodded. "Nyphron should name the city after Raithe. It's really his city—his dream finally realized. He always wanted to make something good and lasting." She fixed Malcolm with an intent stare. "Will it? Will this city, will this empire and the peace it was built on stand forever?"

"Forever?" Malcolm looked pained. "That's a very long time."

"Will it last?"

Malcolm shook his head. "I don't think so."

"You don't *think* so? You know everything, Malcolm. You knew to come here today."

He bowed his head and sighed. "It was supposed to last. That had been the plan, but there is a dark spot on the landscape of the future, a shadow into which I cannot see. Wasn't there before, but it is now. *The Book of Brin* went into that hole."

This surprised Persephone. "Roan has Brin's book. She's been teaching Bran to read it."

Malcolm shook his head. "She has but a tiny portion, the first part, the flawed part. The rest disappeared with Brin. That wasn't supposed to happen. Many things shouldn't have. The Belgriclungreians weren't supposed to attack the Fhrey, and the Fhrey weren't supposed to learn the Art and nearly annihilate the world with it." Malcolm shook his head in dismay. "Two steps forward, one step back."

"Why does that happen?"

"I'm not sure, but I'm certain it's not good."

Persephone felt the rats waking up in her chest, and felt a weight pressing down. It was getting harder to breathe again. She looked out the window at the morning sun. It was such a pretty day. "Do you see *anything* hopeful? Or was it all for nothing?"

"Not for nothing. I won't let it be for nothing. I'm not the sort to give up."

"But can you see anything positive in the future? Tell me something encouraging, Malcolm. I need to hear that things will work out, that there is hope for my people—for all people."

Malcolm nodded. "I see a baby, a descendant of yours, crying in the dark. Born on a cold night in a despicable city very near here. His parents have been murdered, and he is forgotten and ignored. The woman who takes him from his dead mother's arms will abandon him in a gutter less than a week after he takes his first breath. He has no chance of survival, and the fate of the world rests with him."

"That's not helping, Malcolm." Persephone wiped the tears from her face. She could feel the fluid welling up in her chest, and the rats building a nest in there didn't like it one bit.

"Then let me tell you something that will. I'm going to make you a promise." He leaned in and whispered, as if he feared someone might be listening, "I swear I'll be there on that cold night when he cries alone in the gutter." He squeezed her hand, and she knew this was meant as a covenant, a solemn vow he wasn't making lightly. "When the world turns its back, I'll pick him up and deliver him to safety, and I'll watch over that child when he faces his most difficult challenges. I'll do this for you so through his strength a woman very much like yourself will one day sit on the throne of the world and rule with wisdom and compassion and change everything."

Persephone rubbed the pain in her chest. "The one who you speak of, this man from the gutter who will save the world, will he be as courageous as Moya and as steadfast as Gifford? Will he be as selfless as Raithe and Suri and as intelligent as Brin and Roan? Surely, he must be all these things to ultimately succeed where they failed."

Malcolm frowned and looked down at his feet.

"What's wrong, Malcolm? Tell me the truth."

He frowned and shook his head. "No. The man I speak of will not be great. He'll be a terrible person, detestable, murderous, cruel, and untrusting."

Persephone stared, bewildered. "How could—I don't understand. How can such a person make the world better."

Malcolm's head snapped up, and he looked as if she had slapped him. He appeared deeply hurt. She could see the pain and shock in his eyes—eyes that were deeper than any man's should be. He looked away, staring out at the horizon. As he did, she saw tears well and slip down his cheeks.

Then he sucked in a weary breath. "Because I hope that no one is beyond redemption, and anyone can correct the misdeeds of their past," he told her in a weak voice. He took another breath. "I believe this to be true. I *have* to."

Malcolm let go of her hand, stood up, and started for the door.

"Malcolm?" she said, stopping him.

He turned.

"What *will* they name the city? You said it wouldn't be *Nyphronronia*, and we both know you can see the future. So, what then? Later today, at the dedication, I doubt I'll be in any condition to attend. So tell me what will Nyphron call it?"

Malcolm paused a moment then replied, "Percepliquis."

"Percep—the city of Persephone?" She looked stunned. "But— but why?"

He offered her one last sad smile. "In memory of you."

ℰ

Muriel knew who was knocking at the door to her little hut before she opened it. She knew before the knock. She had known hours ago, but made him knock anyway. She felt it was good for him to wait. She might have made tea, could have set out wine. The occasion was so rare it certainly warranted it. Muriel didn't bother. They weren't friends, and this wasn't to be a cordial meeting.

Muriel had been in the process of sewing up a bag of goose feathers, the tiny down plucked from the chests of hundreds of waterfowl. She would have a wonderful pillow when she was done, but finishing it would need to wait. She got up from her stool and opened the door.

She hadn't seen him in the flesh in centuries. Hadn't so much as bothered to eavesdrop or even sneak a peek. She could, and had, in the early days. Not that she was at all interested. Muriel just wanted to make sure he was leaving *her* alone. He promised to keep his distance, but he was also a habitual liar. However, until that day she'd never even caught him spying. That was the first wrinkle in her perfectly made bed, the one where her father wasn't just the architect of all that was bad in her life but in the world as a whole. She hadn't expected him to really leave her alone, but he had. He respected her privacy as well, which was as jarring as seeing rain fall up. Sending the key to her was the second wrinkle. Muriel preferred a smooth, simple bed to lie in. Wrinkles were not just unsightly, they were uncomfortable.

He didn't look any different, couldn't. Neither of them ever changed, at least on the outside. His hair could have been cut, or grown out, but it wasn't. The clothes were different. The last time she'd seen him, he'd worn his full regalia: a magnificent robe that changed color, a scarlet, living mantle that enveloped and stroked him with affection, and, of course, the Crown of Light. He had none of those old trappings. The man standing in her doorway wore a stained wool shirt with the sleeves rolled up to the elbows. The front was left loose, tie strings hanging, his collarbone showing, a pool of sweat in the cleft. His pants, though rolled up to the knees, were wet; the hair on his calves slicked.

He walked *across the inlet. He actually walked here. Probably thinks that impresses me.*

He had a crude spear over his shoulder with a bag tied to it.

Not a bag, another shirt.

He had food in it. Berries were staining the bottom a reddish blue.

"I won't forgive you," she greeted him.

"I know," he said, setting the spear down, leaning it against the wall to the right of the doorframe.

They stared at each other for a long time, like the game where one tries not to blink.

Out in the yard, her ducks waddled and quacked and birds sang. All of them were oblivious to the historic meeting.

"Are you going to ask me in?"

"No." She folded her arms.

"Then why invite me?"

"Who said I invited you?"

He looked at her then with a winsome smile. Seeing her reaction, he quickly buried it. "You kept the key so I would come. I consider that an invitation."

"It's been sixteen years. Why come now?"

"I was visiting a friend in the area."

"Those people you sent—they were very convincing. That's why you sent them, isn't it? To soften me?"

"Did they?"

"I invited you, didn't I?"

He smiled again. "But you still haven't asked me in." He tried to look around her, seeking a glimpse inside her hut.

"And I won't." Muriel pulled the key from around her neck and held it out to him.

He looked at it for a long moment. "No," he finally said, shaking his head.

"What do you mean, *no?*" She paused to look at the chain she held out to make certain the key was still there. It was, and she frowned, confused.

"I didn't come here for that. The key is yours."

Despite her foreknowledge of the meeting, this she hadn't expected, and she stood holding the key in her hand, the little chain dangling. "Why?"

"Birthday present. I'm sure I missed one—most of them, I think. You need a really good gift to make up for that many."

Muriel lowered her arm, her hand still clutching Eton's Key. She continued to glare. He was being charming, which meant he was up to something dreadful. "Why?"

"Because I trust you."

"You shouldn't." She said it with intentional venom. She felt it important to remind Turin just how much she hated—how much she *loathed*—him.

"I know." Her father shrugged in that irritatingly sensible way of his, the way that disguised the monster he was. "But one has to start somewhere."

Silence. She watched him, studied his face. She was wrong. He did look different. She didn't know how, but he appeared older somehow, or maybe just tired. "Why give it to me? Why now? Is it because Trilos has escaped, and you think I won't use it?"

He showed no hint of expression on his face, no sneer, no eye-rolling, none of the familiar contempt. "I want you to hold it until you are ready to forgive me. Then—"

She laughed so loudly it sounded like a cackle and disturbed the nearby birds. She shook her hands at him, waving off any such ridiculous notion. "I can *never* forgive you." Her voice was raised; she expected that. It shook; this surprised her. "Not after what you did. Not after *all* you did."

He chose to skip over her comments. "Then, when you are ready to forgive me, I want you to use it."

"Use it?"

"Yes. To let them all out."

She narrowed her eyes at him. "I don't understand."

He looked surprised. He took a step closer, just one. His hand reached toward her. What would she do if he dared to touch her? The question wasn't answered, for he stopped. He studied her face, puzzled. "You can't see it, then?"

"See what?" she asked, wondering if this was another trick, one more manipulation. Her father was an expert at steering cataclysmic events. He could throw a pebble into a pond, and if he did it early enough, that simple action could change the fortunes of millions.

Is this a pebble? Or a lie?

He was speaking of the future. All of the Aesira had some of the vision. Muriel wasn't one. She was second generation, and would have lacked the talent altogether except her father had tricked her into eating Alurya's fruit. That single bite was all it took to do the damage, to make her immortal and to give her the sight. Being Aesira, *and* having eaten an entire fruit, made Turin's vision peerless, while Muriel's was hazy at best. She could see anywhere in the present clearly, but the deeper into the future she peered, the foggier things got.

"You'll understand when the day comes," he told her.

"Which will most certainly be when trees walk and stones talk."

She watched him, wondering if this was part of some master plan. With him, it had to be. "You're not telling me something."

"I rarely tell *anyone* anything." He offered her a smile. "If I did, you might think less of me."

"That's not possible." She didn't know why she said it. The words just came out. Maybe she wanted to hurt him. That was usually the only reason she ever spoke with her father.

When he failed to reply to her declaration, she added, "Trilos is looking for you." Her tone was meant to have a vengeful quality. She was issuing a proclamation of doom, letting him know he wouldn't get away with everything. In reality, it felt more like spitting in the wind.

"I heard. He'll be wanting to kill me, I suspect."

"Can he?"

He shrugged. "You more than anyone know there are worse things than death. But yes, I think it's possible. Trilos is smart. He's probably already figured it out, or soon will."

"That would be . . . bad. You in Phyre? The prison warden sentenced to being locked up? You're very unpopular."

He did reach out then, as if to touch Muriel's face, and the question was answered. She recoiled.

Turin stood on the stoop with his hand still out, forgotten, as he looked at her. Not shock—her reaction wasn't unexpected—but the shift in his expression was sudden. A grimace of pain stole over him. He lowered his arm, bowed his head, and looked at the ground between them. "You really should be rooting for *me* more. I know you don't believe it, but I'm trying to fix things."

"Fix what?"

"Everything."

"And you think you can? Do you see so far as that?"

She expected he would say that he did; such was his way. Everyone knew he could see what would happen, but he used that knowledge against people. He lied about what he saw so no one could trust his visions.

"No," he told her. "Not so far as that. And the maze keeps changing. One day I think I can, and the next, no. And now . . ."

"What?"

"Maybe I'm getting old." He shrugged. "But I do hope that one day I can make it up to you—some of it, at least. But I'm not very good at that."

"At what?"

"Being good. It takes practice, I suspect. And I think I get it wrong a lot. I sacrificed Brin, did you know that? I sent her to her premature death— twice." His shoulders slumped. "I judged it was for a good reason, only things didn't work out the way they were supposed to. And then there's Persephone. She just died. Did you know? Probably not. You never met her. I ruined her life, too. Stole her one chance at true happiness. That's part of what brought me here."

This surprised Muriel. She believed everything always worked out the way her father wanted. Knowing the future made that a foregone conclusion, or so she thought. Either he was lying again or something else was happening. She hated him. That fact had been the foundation of her universe for so long that this new development threatened to upend everything. The unknown was always terrifying, and for the first time she was afraid not *of* her father, but *for* him—for both of them.

"I did the same to Tressa," Turin said. "And Tesh, and . . . well, the list goes on and on, doesn't it? Was I right? Was I wrong? I honestly don't know. I can't tell the difference between what I want and what is right. I don't know how. I believe Alurya could have taught me, but . . . well, with my track record, there's no one I can trust, right?"

There was that face again, tired—no, exhausted.

"Wait here." She went back inside and grabbed an old satchel off the peg near the washbasin. She normally used it to gather mushrooms and berries. Returning to the doorway, she held it out. "Take this."

For once she saw confusion on her father's face. A pleasing sight. "Why?"

"You can't waste time checking back with me."

"Checking with you?"

"Stop lying!" she yelled at him. "This is why you came here. You know it. I know it, so just stop!"

Her father didn't reply.

"See, this is you being you—*being awful*. This is what you have to stop. Take the bag."

He took hold of the shoulder strap and studied the satchel.

He could be faking. Her father was the master of lies and deceit, evil and treachery, so this could all be an act. The one truth that lingered, the one pestering question that stopped her from completely giving up on him was . . . why? What did he stand to gain by coming there, by giving her the key? Maybe he was up to something she couldn't see. He usually was, but it was also true that if anyone could fix the world, the one she would bet on—the only one she thought might be able to do it—was her father.

And if there is even the smallest chance he's telling the truth . . .

Muriel wasn't ready to bet on him, and she certainly wasn't going to root for him. Still . . .

"I'll watch you."

This made his brows rise suspiciously.

"I'll check in from time to time . . . when I'm bored," she clarified. "Each time you do something I approve of, every time I feel my hatred of you lessen, I'll send you a . . ." She thought a moment, looking around. She caught sight of the bags of feathers and smiled. Grabbing a little white tuft, she held it up. ". . . a feather."

"Why?"

"It's a symbol of rising, of renewed spirit, an embodiment of hope."

He nodded, and she saw a smile rising.

"You realize that even with my help you have an *extremely small* chance of success."

He leaned over and peered inside the hut. "You have *a lot* of feathers."

"I was going to make pillows."

He looked down at the bag he held. "So if I fill this up, do you think you can forgive me?"

"You won't manage to. It would take an eternity."

"No, not that long. I'm sure I'll finish before trees walk and stones talk." He winked.

She smirked and held up the feather. "Small feathers—big bag."

"But if I do?"

She shrugged. "Maybe."

He nodded. "That's fair." He looked at her, and for a moment, she thought he might try to touch her again. He didn't. "It will be a long time, I think, before we meet again."

"I don't have your sight, but I'm guessing this is the last we'll *ever* see each other."

"So much faith in me. I'm overwhelmed." He looped the strap of the satchel over his head, letting it hang across his chest. He clapped it against his side and picked up the spear again. He offered a wave, but not a goodbye.

He followed her front path, walking down toward the garden. When he was nearly to it, thunder cracked.

Turin looked up, his mouth open.

Surprised again, she thought. *Two miracles in one day. I'm on a roll.*

He continued to stare skyward as from out of the blue a single downy feather descended. He held out his hand and caught it. Turin stared at his palm for a long curious moment, then turned. "I thought—"

She showed him her empty hand. "Don't cheat next time or no feather."

"Cheat?"

"You want to do this? Do it as a man, not as Rex Uberlin. Sending people through Phyre is an unfair advantage."

"I no longer have the key, so that ought to be easy." Her father looked back at the tiny white fluff in his hand and grinned.

"It's just a feather," she told him.

"No, it's not. It's—" He stopped, and swallowed several times, then sucked in a shallow breath. "It's evidence that you hate me a little less."

"A very little bit. The weight of a feather, in fact." She smirked.

"It's a start." He waved to her. "It is a start."

Malcolm kissed the feather and slipped it into the satchel. Pulling it shut, he continued on his way.

Muriel stood in her doorway, watching until he passed beyond the hill and out of sight.

Michael's Afterword

BACKGROUND INFORMATION

In February 2011, three critical things happened in my writing career. First, I finished the edits on *Percepliquis*, the sixth and final novel of my debut series The Riyria Revelations. Second, Orbit (the fantasy imprint of Hachette Book Group), announced they would be picking up that series and re-releasing it. And Third, I began work on my next novel.

I had decided to rework the first serious manuscript I had ever penned. This wasn't my first novel (in fact, it was my 9th), but it was the first one I thought might have a chance of being published. Originally penned in 1986 and titled *Wizards*, it is the contemporary story of a man who accidentally receives the power to do just about anything. Inheriting such an ability initially led to selfish pursuits. Later, he discovers the power's origin and that there is another person with the same skills opposing him in a classic Good versus Evil scenario. Throughout the book, he must learn not only how to survive but discover how to win in a battle where he is greatly outmatched.

I liked the idea, but back in the mid-eighties, I simply didn't know how to write well enough to produce a decent book. I felt confident that I now had the talent and skill to fix the problems. I retitled it *Antithesis* and got to work. I spent an entire year researching, reconstructing, and rewriting. Then I stopped because I was mistaken. The book didn't merely require a few corrections; it wasn't worthy to begin with. Rather than release a mediocre novel, I shelved a year's worth of work and walked away.

By then, it had been four years since I had written a book. I had spent that time editing and publishing The Riyria Revelations via two separate routes. Initially, it was released as a six-book self-published series (2008 to 2010), then afterward through one of the largest publishers in the world. Orbit fast-tracked the series, and they released all six books in three two-book omnibus editions from November 2011 to January 2012. Given it had been so long since I had written an original manuscript, I began to wonder if I still could.

For my next attempt, I started playing around with an origin story to my world of Elan—the tale of Nyphron. Writing something as extensive as Riyria generates a great deal of world building background, but very little of what I know actually makes it to the page. So I started contemplating what eventually became The Legends of the First Empire series.

While I was doing that, the Riyria books were being reintroduced to the world (in a much bigger way than I could have done on my own), and a need for more Riyria arose. My wife (and more than a few newfound fans) missed the pair, and in Robin's case, depression actually set in. She lamented that I could revisit Royce and Hadrian anytime I wanted to, but with her limited imagination, she was cut off from their adventures. And so I began writing the first two Chronicles to sate her, and to remind myself I could still spin a tale.

Still, I was mindful that I needed to create something new. I was at a crossroads. I never had planned to be a fantasy writer. It just turned out that after nineteen novels, it happened to be the fantasy genre that first gained traction. I suspect most authors are in no short supply of book ideas. I had dozens filling my head. I wanted to try my hand at science fiction, horror, and what-if books. There was no end to the number of tales that excited my imagination. But I was published now, and it wasn't only my desires that were in play. Orbit hoped for another fantasy series, and my readers wanted (and still do desire) more Royce and Hadrian. Doing something completely different might be asking too much of those who were now my supporters. The sophomore curse was upon me, and that might hinder acceptance of anything too different. I felt readers would be most accepting of another fantasy series, especially if it was set in the same world.

But there was something else I needed to face. I had lied in The Riyria Revelations, and I felt terrible about leaving that unaddressed. A great deal of Elan's history, the mythology of the gods, and the Novronian Empire's foundation were garbled tales altered over the centuries. I knew this when I wrote Riyria, and I felt a nagging need to reveal the truth. With that in mind, I returned to creating what I planned to be a little trilogy that would cover Nyphron's story and the origin of the First Empire. My hope was to knock it out quickly, then move onto new worlds. That didn't happen.

LEGENDS ORIGIN STORY

The story began its conception as a biography of Nyphron, written mostly in his point of view. He and his band of valiant adventurers would be a platoon of soldiers in a rebellious territory where they were not wanted. Nyphron would develop an atypical appreciation of humans, and when ordered to slaughter a village, he would refuse. The plot was designed to escalate from there, which was interesting but weak. There wasn't enough there, there.

The story grew as I studied Iron Age Britannic history, looking for inspiration. I added Raithe, the human hero-warrior, and Persephone, the Queen Boudica of her people. I had the foundation for a love triangle building. Here is where the story entered its infancy, and I began writing what was then titled *Rhune* (the other books would be neatly named *Dherg* and *Fhrey*).

I got off to a rocky start when I began the series. I went with a different style, one that resembled other fantasy writers who I had read since entering the genre. Usually, no one—not even Robin—reads my books before they are finished, but I wanted to ensure I was on the right track. I wasn't. Her response was, "I'm not sure who wrote this, but I would much rather read a book by Michael J. Sullivan. Can you please tell him that?" She was right. Instead of trying to be someone else, I went back to being me.

Another major piece of the series fell into place when I decided to drop Nyphron's point of view and focus on Persephone and Raithe. In this version, Nyphron had his group of warriors, Persephone had her misfits, and Raithe was a loner. But a funny thing happened. In building the Galantians, I realized they were unforgivably dull. A bunch of variously skilled warriors was not only boring, but they were also clichéd. No matter how much I tried to breathe life into their characters, they remained flat. On the other hand, Persephone's group exploded onto the page. They had depth, emotion, and humor. I found myself drawn more and more to them. As a result, the Galantians faded into the background. At the same time, Suri, Moya, Roan, Gifford, Padera, and Brin started to take center stage.

I was halfway through what would become *Age of Myth* (altered when Del Rey didn't care for the use of so many invented terms for book titles), that I realized I didn't want to write a story about Nyphron and his Galantians at all. I desired a different kind of story, a better one. Suddenly, the series stopped being something I wanted to quickly breeze through, and it became important to me.

THE MESSAGE

One of the things I was looking to accomplish in this series has to do with Albert Schatz, or to be more precise, people like him. Albert discovered the second antibiotic after penicillin, the one that cured tuberculosis and many other horrific bacteria-based illnesses. Unfortunately, Albert was a subordinate. His supervisor, Selman Waksman, took credit by carefully erasing Albert's name from documents and keeping him away from meetings where he might gain recognition. Waksman won the Noble Prize, and Albert Schatz has been mostly forgotten. Likewise, the astronomer Henrietta Swan Leavitt suffered a similar lack of recognition because she was a woman in a male-dominated field. And then there is Albert Einstein's wife, Mileva Marić. She was a genius in her own right, but other than fellow Serbians, most don't know anything about her.

The list of individuals who improved the world, but due to the prevalent culture or minority status, have been nearly lost to our collective memory is staggering. This made me wonder: How many in the history of Elan have been forever forgotten. This notion became a driving factor in the Legends series as I aimed to reveal the truth regarding historical facts that would later be usurped by those in power.

In Riyria, unlikely heroes meant skilled and strong men who weren't particularly virtuous and, therefore, unlikely to do good deeds. In Legends, I sought to present truly unlikely heroes, the sort that had no hope of being great and no chance of changing the world. I realized this was what had made Tolkien's work so profound to me as a boy.

Hobbits are unlikely heroes because no halfling could ever be expected to take on the might of Sauron, but they were also not children. They did not grow up and become heroes; they always were; they just didn't know it. To me, that was the genius of Tolkien's works. Through his hobbits, the reader follows innocent, seemingly powerless characters sent into unfathomable horror. I was riveted while wondering how they could possibly survive, much less succeed. This is one of the ideas I wanted to convey through my series both as a means to captivate readers but also as a message of hope that ordinary people can achieve extraordinary accomplishments. I wanted to remind us that the disadvantaged can win, and they've done so many times. I know such things are possible because I am just such a hobbit who once dreamed of being an author.

THE BIG MISTAKE

Armed with this new plan, the series' focus shifted in the middle of *Age of Myth* and blossomed in *Age of Swords*. This second book steered away from the tired hero-warrior destined to save the world and moved toward the band of broken misfits who team up to win. And that is one of the reasons why it became my favorite book of the series.

I finished my planned trilogy with *Age of War*, which concluded many of my story arcs. But Robin was quick to point out there was still much to do. "What about that damn door? And what's up with Trilos and Malcolm?" I also had been operating under a mistaken assumption: That people reading Legends would have first read Riyria, and as such, they knew who won the war.

I was left facing a series of repetitious battles, which did not excite me in the slightest. But there was also the ability to explain some of the background information that was known only to myself. For instance, in Riyria, it is the elves rather than humans who have gilarabrywns. So how did that come about?

Frustrated by my own shortsightedness, and without clear direction, I began writing one more book to finish out the war. It was going to be bad; I knew that before I started. I was just going through the motions of completing previously referred to events, hoping to find my way as I went. And then . . .

THE JOKE THAT WASN'T

So my new book began with Suri being captured and taken to Estramnadon, leaving the others to rescue her. They held a meeting to discuss how to do that. All the characters pitched ideas as they struggled to find a way to cross the impassable Nidwalden. Brin suggested there were legends of secret crimbal doorways where you entered in one place but came out somewhere else. Upon hearing this, Tekchin made a joke. "There is a door right in the center of Estramnadon. If we come out there, we can easily get to Suri. The only problem is it leads to the afterlife, so we'd all need to die to use it."

I assumed this was nothing more than a clever bit of humor for about ten seconds. Then I thought . . . what if . . . no that's stupid . . . but it could work on SO many levels . . . no, it'd be too hard, there is too much heavy lifting. In that instant, a cosmos of ideas rushed in. I could make exploring the bowels of Phyre into a whole new world that would be worthy of a novel. I could draw on Dante's *Divine Comedy* and the Trials of Hercules. Both works fit the era of myths that I was aiming at all along. Doing so could fully explain the Door, Trilos, Malcolm, and so much more. I could do what I did at the end of Riyria, where I pulled in all the previously met characters for a big finale. But this time I could include historical people as well. I would be able to reveal the full truth about the gods. From there, I saw the chance to not only tell the origin story of the empire but of the whole world. That did it. I wanted to write this story. I needed to write it.

CHALLENGES

I faced a lot of problems right from the get-go. The biggest was if everyone was already dead, where was the threat? And if there is no threat, where is the tension? Without that, the story would be dull and boring. Also, what were the mechanics? How would they die? How could they come back? Would they be spirits or keep their bodies in the afterlife ala Greek myth? The biggest dilemma was if my party had to die to enter the afterlife, then Suri would have to as well. Clearly, I had issues. I ended up solving most of these problems easily enough. But I was faced with one insurmountable obstacle: This new tale was much larger than a single book. If I was honest with myself, it was on the same scale as everything I had written in this series up to that point, but I wasn't going to let that stop me.

My attempt to condense everything into one novel resulted in a Cliff Notes version of a story. Upon reading the results, my wife let me know I had failed. "Too rushed. Too many missed opportunities for high drama. Not enough emotional impact. It reads more like a textbook than a novel."

Fine. I went back and grudgingly expanded the tale. This was difficult because I didn't have a good place to divide the story. Unlike my other books where everything neatly ties up, these characters were engaged in an ongoing quest that would require being suspended mid-story. It wasn't unlike how Tolkien's *Lord of the Rings* had been released, and I felt the similarity was a bit eerie, but in a good way. I hated not being able to provide a wrapped up ending for readers, but I was pleased with how the story was shaping up.

In this second version, the fourth book divided as they entered Nifrel. I knew it was better, but not great. Robin agreed that I still had too much in too little space. A sixth book would be required. And so I rolled back to the end of *Age of War* and started rewriting the end of the Great War for the third time. Even with the expanded page count, I still was forced to cut large sections and topics I didn't have time to address. Some examples include additional background on Gath, Melen, Bran, Atella, Havar, Sile Longhammer, and many others. Of course, now I had to divide the story twice, and interestingly new breakpoints were starting to reveal themselves.

My newly expanded tale had two exhilarating climaxes. Both of which occurred at places that evenly divided the single long story into three normal-sized novels. Rather than shy away from the problem, I embraced it. Instead of artificially creating quiet moments, I cut the books at these times of high drama—cliff-hangers. I'm sure everyone is familiar with this technique. Television series' season finales often end with cliff-hangers. And the entire concept goes back to western serials, which were designed to keep magazine subscriptions high. I felt if I had to incorporate the technique, I wanted to make the best cliff-hanger I could. I knew I'd get pushback from readers. However, I suspected then—and still believe now—that once all the books are available, the irritation of having to wait will fade to the land of *when I was young, oh the troubles we had to face.*

I'm sure some are wondering why I didn't just create a single massive volume? Well, it isn't because I was trying to maximize income. Nor was it (as some have accused), a ploy by my publisher, which, by the way, is me.

There are several reasons. First, the book would be hugely inconsistent with the other installments, and I like the symmetry we now have with two closely-related trilogies. Second, it would have added years to the release date of the follow-up to *Age of War*. And lastly, the cost of production for the hardcover would be far higher than three separate novels. Why? Because we'd have to switch to Smyth-sewn bindings, which is usually reserved for textbooks and volumes in law libraries.

FUN FACTS

Some readers have accused me of killing the main character, meaning Raithe. When I heard this, I was shocked. Except in very early conceptualizations, he was never expected to be a primary character. In retrospect, I realize that part of the reason people elevated his importance was that the opening scene of the first book appears to start with him. The reality is, it doesn't. The first character mentioned in the series is Brin, and she has been my "main" all along. The fact that you don't discover this until the very end is something that provides me a great deal of amusement. Aside from her, the other primary protagonists were Persephone, Suri, and Malcolm. These four people carry the story. It is their actions that move the plot forward, and the rest provide them with support.

There are a fair number of homages in this series. The White Brick Road of Rel, the Wicked Queen Ferrol, and Roan extinguishing her with water are but a few of the references to *The Wizard of Oz*. The chapter Astray in a Gloomy Wood is in deference to the start of Dante's Inferno, as is the name of the Belgriclungreian seer, Beatrice. Also inspired by Dante, are guides to the various realms of the underworld. Originally, Arion was the guide in Rel, and she did quite a bit of explaining as to how things worked in the land of the dead. Through the various edits, we now have the characters make many of the discoveries. Yet I still have Fenelyus as the guide in Nifrel and Raithe in Alysin.

Oh, and here is a fun fact for Riyria Chronicle readers. In case you haven't figured it out. I'll reveal the identity in a secret-coded non-spoiler message to those who are well-versed in my world: *Yes, it was Makareta*.

THEMES & TRIBUTES

Redemption and forgiveness are central points of focus in both Riyria and Legends (although in both cases, you don't discover this until you're very near their ends). Legends place a greater emphasis on finding the courage to forgive oneself—something that everyone can probably relate to. Selflessness and the ability of people to rise to the occasion when times are dire is also shared between the two series. A noble sentiment that we are seeing played out daily at this particular time in our own history.

There are more connections and references to other works, other subtle themes as well. I will leave these discoveries to those who enjoy such things.

A WORD ABOUT HEROES

Finally, I must say a few words in recognition of the one person who, if you enjoyed this series, you are most indebted to—my wife Robin. She has been your secret advocate for many, many years. As my alpha reader, she provides my first and most trusted feedback and helps shape my novels more than anyone. These last three books were in an abnormally poor condition when she first received the tales. This was mainly due to them being constructed outside of my usual process. Instead of a well-defined structure, I was working in the ad hoc chaos of trial and error. If not for her, the result might have been terrible.

At times, I was throwing ideas at her to see what stuck. We fought many an epic battle over details, both large and small. Luckily, Robin—has a strong personality and was able to stand up to me and make her opinions known, revealing some uncomfortable truths. Not an easy task. Tears have been shed. But the story is far better because of her courage and tireless efforts to make this the best story possible.

I offered to put her name on the cover because she deserves it, but she refused. I offered to dedicate this series to her as I did with the final Riyria volume. Again she opposed the idea. Instead, she provided the Tolkien quote to reflect the difficult time in which this novel was written. Rather than take credit, she chose to offer hope to our readers.

The stories I write might be fantasy, but the depiction of the feelings people share for each other is real. The unlikely heroes, some who we never see or hear about, are as well. They are out among us right now, risking their lives and those of their loved ones. They are sacrificing all they have to help save the world. If you take anything away from this story beyond distracting entertainment, consider remembering this Book of Brin quote: *I had always worshiped heroes in stories. I had no idea I was surrounded by them.*

Robin's Afterword

Hey all, Robin here. I'm back! Thanks again for all the complimentary things you've been saying about my afterwords. It's one of the reasons I keep doing them.

Well, we are done! It's been a very long time coming. How long? I'm not 100% sure, but I do remember seeing a very early version of Chapter One of the first book in April of 2013. So that's six books in seven years, which doesn't sound all that impressive. But during that time, we also released *Hollow World* (Michael's sci-fi thriller) and all four of The Riyria Chronicles. So that makes eleven books in six years—a feat I'm pretty proud to be a part of. Since Michael started publishing books in 2008, he's released one or two books every year. Here's a breakdown.

- 1 book years: 2008, 2012, 2014, 2015, 2016, 2017, 2019
- 2 book years: 2009, 2010, 2011, 2013, 2018, 2020

Putting out three books in ten months was more than grueling. And the books of the "second half" of the series had to go through rushed beta and gamma programs. For the audiobook recordings (the date of which is set well in advance), I was doing copyedits in a "just in time" fashion. This meant I was emailing Tim chapters at 2:00 AM for a 10:00 AM recording. Now, it turns out that it all worked out well, but I was more than exhausted by the process.

Is all this a preamble to something? Yes. For the next series (of which Michael has two books finished, neither of which I've read), they will be coming out once a year, so I can slow down a bit. The good news is there are no cliff-hangers!

I know there are more than a few people who wait until all books in a series are released before they start with the first one, so binge away! I'm looking forward to a full-series reread, myself. It'll be a great deal of fun to just sit back and enjoy the tale, rather than looking for plot holes, consistency errors, or typos. I can't wait!

For those that might be curious about such things, I did a series tally. If you take out the non-story elements (Table of Contents, Author's Notes, Afterwords, Glossaries, and the like) the entire series weighs in with the following statistics:

- 181 Chapters
- 2,763 pages (8 1/2" x 11" with 12 point font)
- 766,699 words

Okay, let's dig into my impressions of this book and the series as a whole. Well, first and foremost, it's clear that this is "Brin's Book" (not to be confused with The Book of Brin). Brin is certainly center stage, and now we get to see just how important her masterwork is. The fact that it disappears makes a great deal of sense because the mythology of the Gods in the Riyria books is quite different, and I suspect that's due to Brin's book being snatched up by Trilos.

Will it show up again? I have no idea. As I said, I've not read any of the books in the next series, but I do recall at least a passing mention of a scholar of ancient texts in Riyria with the name Farilane. And, we know that the second book of the new series is also called that. So, I suspect if nothing else, she'll be searching for the full Book of Brin.

Okay, now for something that might sound odd. I loved that Brin died! From a story standpoint, it prevents her from re-creating what Trilos stole, but, more importantly, I think her returning to Phyre is the only chance that Tesh and Tressa have. In their last scene, it was evident (at least to me) that they had no possibility of getting out by themselves. Still, I'm 100% sure that Brin will be able to rescue them.

With enough persuasion, she may be able to convince them to climb out on her own, but if that doesn't work, I'm sure she can make a sling and carry each one out strapped to her back. After all, we've seen it's possible to use eshim in the Abyss, even if it's not easy to do. After all, both Iver and Gifford managed it. Iver was able to create the figurine of Roan's mother, and Gifford made a sword appear when his anger against Iver was at a peak.

Another aspect about her death that I loved is her crying out, "Hang on, Tesh, I'm coming." It's a direct repeat of Suri's proclamation to a near-dead Arion at the end of *Age of Swords*. So fun! And, yes, I just used "fun" in the context of someone's death.

Now, some beta readers wanted to have another scene with Brin while in Phyre, and there may even be some future readers looking for the same thing. I can understand the desire, but, personally, I think it would have been a colossal mistake. I mean, it's not like we don't know what's going to happen. And to have a scene showing her return would be treading over old ground. There is absolutely no doubt in my mind that Tesh and Brin have a cozy little place on a hill overlooking a river in Alysin that's just a stone's throw away from Raithe's and Persephone's home. For me, I don't have to see the reunion to know it happens.

Which brings me to another issue. I'm okay with Tesh remaining dead. If he were to return to the land of the living, there would be a whole host of problems. First, he would be apart from Brin. Second, he would be tried and punished for the murders of the Galantians. And third, Nyphron's destruction of Duryea and Nadak would come out, and that's really something you don't want to know about your new emperor. Since Alysin is so idyllic, staying dead means Tesh will get to his final reward sooner. I'm good with that!

I mentioned in one of my other afterwords that I couldn't figure out whether Malcolm was good or evil, so imagine my surprise when he turned out to be both! For people planning to read the Riyria Revelations, keep your eyes open for tales about Kile and the White Feather. When you come across them, you'll know the true origin of where those stories come from.

Okay, so one of the highlights of this book has to be the reunion of Suri and Minna. I'm thrilled that the pair are returning to the Hawthorn Glen and a well-deserved simpler life. Suri deserves a rest. She went through a lot. Oh, and I'm so glad that one of my fears didn't come to pass. I was really concerned that Suri's friendship with Makareta would result in yet another gilarabrywn. In general, I'm not able to change Michael's mind on "big plot issues," and I'm glad we didn't have to duke it out over that one.

Michael never treats death capriciously, and at the time of Minna's passing, I totally understood her need to die from a story standpoint. Still, that knowledge didn't make me cry any less. But I still understood it. I NEVER thought we'd see her again. Now, not only is she alive, but we find out she is much more than first imagined. The fact that Trilos didn't want to face off against her was quite telling. Loved it!

Another personal favorite of mine is getting all the lore about the afterlife. Throughout the last two books, we've visited, Rel, Nifrel, Alysin, The Abyss, and the Sacred Grove, and it was great learning about them through the progression of the plot, rather than through an infodump. I'm glad that people in Alysin can get their loved ones in upon invitation. I don't think paradise would be as wonderful if someone you loved were stuck in a different realm.

I really enjoyed meeting Mari, and although I didn't expect to meet Elan, I loved that we got to hear the full story of Turin from the source. Oh, and while I'm here. I know some people have been a bit confused by all the various gods, and they have been asking for a summary, so here it is:

- Eton - God of the sky, Grand Father of All.
- Elan - Goddess of the earth, Grand Mother of All.
- Alurya - firstborn of Eton and Elan goddess of plants and animals. Her fruit bestows immortality. She is now a dead tree in the Sacred Grove.
- Typhons - ancient gods of giants. There are three of them Gar, Erl, and Toth. Currently, they are trapped in the Abyss of Nifrel.
- Aesira - the five gods created by Elan by stealing teeth from Eton which includes Turin, Trilos, Drome, Ferrol, and Mari.
- Turin - (aka Rex Uberlin, Caratacus, and Malcolm) father of Goblins (Ghazel). Also the bringer of war and lies.
- Trilos - (aka The Three, The Old One or the Ancient One) - first

to die by Turin's hand, lover of Muriel. He escaped the Abyss by tricking the dwarfs.

- Drome - Twin of Ferrol and father of Belgriclungreians (dwarfs). In the afterlife, he rules Rel.
- Ferrol - Twin of Drome and mother of Fhrey (elves). In the afterlife, she rules Nifrel.
- Mari - mother of Rhunes (humans. In the afterlife, she rules Alysin.
- Muriel - daughter of Turin, lover of Trilos, also commonly known as the Tetlin Witch, like Malcolm, she is immortal having eaten Alurya's fruit.

The last favorite thing of mine regarding this book was the ending. As far as I'm concerned, I think Michael nailed it. I loved, loved, loved that it ended with Malcolm and Muriel and that she gave him the first of what I hope to be many feathers. The fact that she's open to reconnecting with her father makes me all warm and fuzzy, but I fear she will be a tough judge.

Well, I could go on and on, but I only have so much space. But, if you are interested in more commentary from me, I am writing a "Making of" bonus ebook. If you are a Kickstarter backer, you'll receive it automatically. If you weren't, you could get a free copy by requesting it at https://michaeljsullivan.survey.fm/making-of-legends-ebook.

Before I go, I want to take a moment to talk to those people who haven't yet read the Riyria Revelations. Please, do. There are so many connections between Legends and Riyria that it's really worth checking out. Plus, having read Legends, you'll be "in the know" making you better equipped to see through Michael's lies.

Also, if you think you might like what we are calling "The Bridge Series" (a.k.a. The Rise and the Fall), we'll be doing Kickstarters for it as well, and if you want to sign up for early notification you can do so at https://michaeljsullivan.survey.fm/ks-notify.

Okay, one more thing I'd like to cover, and then I'll be off. I'd like to thank the members of our creative team whose incredible efforts made this book possible. First, to Marc Simonetti, who not only created the fantastic cover for this book but all the books in the series. Next, I'd like to thank Linda Branam and Laura Jordstad, two fabulous copyeditors who worked under incredibly aggressive timelines. Hopefully, we'll have more breathing room with the next series. And, of course, we can't forget to mention Tim Gerard Reynolds, the amazing narrator for the book.

Usually, Michael and I are in the studio during the recording, and Tim has the helping hands of a recording engineer and frequently a director. But because of the Coronavirus, Tim recorded in his home studio, which meant he had to wear multiple hats. We received the "dailies" and reported back areas where adjustments were required. He took care of those before sending them off to Audible. Because Tim had to wear so many hats, the recording took longer than usual. However, we were still able to meet the release day, so good job to Tim and the post-production mastering people at Audible.

I would also like to thank an army of beta, gamma, and early Kickstarter readers who contributed their selfless time and effort to make this book as good as it is. Normally, I would call these people out by name. But, the deadline was so tight that there wasn't time for the coordination involved in getting permission to use all of their names. So, even though they aren't listed here, I still want to publicly offer our thanks.

Last and not least, I'd like to thank the various logistic support individuals. For instance, the people at Grim Oak Press (especially Shawn Speakman) who handles the distribution for the hardcovers and paperbacks. I'd also like to thank the people at LSC Communications, who provided the printing during the height of the Coronavirus. And, of course, my continued thanks to all the people at Audible Studios, especially Esther Bochner and Kristin Lang.

And that's it for me. Both Michael and I would like to thank you for your continued support. We'll do our best to keep the books coming, and hopefully, you'll find them worth your time to continue reading.

Kickstarter Backers

Our eternal thanks go out to the following people (and to those who chose not to be recognized publicly), for being patrons of the arts and making the hardcover edition of this book possible by pre-ordering through our Kickstarter project.

— A —

@ddlt1 • @renaissancemari • Brian A. • Eric A. • Karla Saldate A. • M. C. Abajian • Terri Abbett • Jaxon Oliver Abbott • Winston Percy Abbott • Chuck Abdella • Julian Abernethy • Shilpa Robz Abraham • Thérèse Abrams • Abraxas • AC & AK • Simoneta Gomez Acebo • Iris Achmon • Josh Acocella • Rafael Acosta • Thomas Acquinas • Szilágyi Ádám • Andy Adams • Colin Adams • Frederick Adams • John Adams • Jon Adams • Kevin & Helen Adams • Rob Adams • Sam Adams • Iain Add • Michael & Heather Adelson • Anna Adler • Daniel Adler • Scott Adley • ADM • Lee Adolfson • Adrian & Roberta • Sandu Elena Adriana • Adumbratus • Afterperihelion • Svetoslav Agafonkin • Arjun Agarwal • Natasha Aguiar • Kawika Aguilar • Eddy & Rebecca Aguirre • Matthew Brian Aguirre • Donna Ahlrich • Balal Ahmad • Priscilla Ahn • James & Diana Aiken • Garrett Aikens • Ajvz • Geoff Akens • Khaldoun Al-Qaysi • Rahaf Alahmadi • Dan Alber • Drew Alcaide • Andrew Alderman • Michael Alerich • Scott A. Alexander • Heather Aley • Kristel Alger • Adel-Rehman Ali • Misha Ali • AliiKatt • Seth Alister-Jones • Husain Aljamri • Harrison Alldred • Brin Leah Allen • Caitlin & Liam Allen • Cody L. Allen • Jay Scott Allen • Julie Marie Allen • Sami Almudaris •

Alston • Raul Alvarado III • Jesselyn Alvarez • Barrak Alwazzan • Alwin • Alyksandrei • John Ambrose • Ben Ames • AmethystOrator • Anamue • Peter Andersen • Brian Anderson • Carol Beth Anderson • Chris Anderson • Colin Anderson • George Anderson • Graeme Anderson • Julie Anderson • Katharine Anderson • Kris Anderson • Luke Anderson • Nathan Alan Anderson • Richard "Tripp" Anderson • Sadie Anderson • Sean Anderson • Sean L. Anderson • Tom "Squeat" Anderson • Troy Anderson • Elin Anne Anderssen • Tyler Andor • David Andre • Andrea • Rebecca Andreasen • Andrei • Dennis Andrews • Joseph Andrews • Lesley Andrews • Androsso • Jocelyn Andruko & Mitchell Farmer • Angela & Cid • Jacek Aninowski • Chrissy Anjewierden • Catrina Ankarlo • Emily Ann • Mahir Annama • Joanna Anthony • Summer Applebaum • Paul Aquino • The Arata Clan • Nandinho Araújo • Ricardo Araujo • Dylan Arbuthnot-Olk • David Arcuri • Maryrose Arcuria • Wei Shi Lindon Arelius • Tamara Arens • Sue Armitage • Mary-Helen Armour • Carl & Mya Armstrong • Matt Armstrong • Wesley Armstrong • Cassie Arneson • Aubrie D. Arnold • Jordan Arnold • Melissa "Squirrely Murlley" Arnold • Colin Asbill • Matthew Ash • Quint Ashburn • Ashli • Dyrk Ashton • John Fredrik Asphaug • Chad Atchison • Dagny Athena • The Atkinson Family • Elijah Atkinson • Brent Auble • Jon Auerbach • Marco Auger • Augustine • Erica Augustine • Devan Ausiello • Authoraaronp • Matt Avella • Garrett Avery • Marcus William Avery • Alice Aviles • R. J. Ayres • Arya Azar • Andrew, Rachel, Sophie, Molly & Abby Azzinaro

— B —

B-Hill • Alex B. • Anurag B. • Ariane B. • Dina B. • Dustin, Amy, Owen, Molly & Zoey B. • Glen B. • Jacqualine B. • Justin B. • Marius B. • Richard B. • Sierra B. • Michael Baar • Michael Babb • Nathan & Tracy Bacon • Jacob Bahr • Chris Bailey • Heidi Bailey • Kelvin Bailey • Keri & Patrick Bailey • Michael Bailey • Patrick Bailey • Chris Baima • Isaac & Cameron Baird • Shirley Baird • Charlie & Sarah Baker • Gary & Sarah Baker • Jeff Baker • Anand Bakshi • Linda Balder • Joseph Baldwin • Meghan Ball • Rob Ballew • Tyler Ballew • Nic Baltas • Ben Balzarini • Maciej Banasiak •

Naqheeb Bandukwala • Donovan Banh • Preston Bannard • Tom Bannister • Tony Baraconi • Callum Barber • Joshua Barber • Heather Barcomb • Caldwell Barefoot • Yasmine & Royce Barghouty • Ariana Barkley • Doug Barkus • Aaron & John Barlow • Ed Barmettler • Maria Barna • Bryan M. Barnard • David J. Barnard • David Barnett • Baronen • Christopher Barr • Stephen Barr • Josh Barratt • Benjamin Barreth • Maura Barrett • Nolan Barrett • John W. Barron • Bart • Jan Barthold • C. L. Bartley • Alfred & Michael Jonathan Basaldella • Emily Bass • Wes Batcheller • Barrett Bates • Stephen Bates • Susan Bates • Nicholas T. Battaglia • Paul Batty • Berta Batzig • Marc Baudry • Stefan Baumgä • Shaun Baxter • David Bean • Tyke Beard • Abby Beasley & Caitlin Grady • Dana Beatty • Craig Beaumont • Mark D. Beaumont • David "Friend of Jesus" Beccue • Nate "The Kaiser" Beck • Brian Becker • Nicole A. Becker • Brent Beckman • Anne Beckmann • Maile Beckwith • Mike Dedan • Adam Bedard • Danielle Bednai • Marta Bednarz • Cheryl Beebe-Skynar • Henry Been • Hossain Behbahani • Dana Belden • Christian Bell • Chuck Bell • Douglas Bell • Jessica Bell • Steph, Rita & Lily Belle • Omer Bender • Emily Benger • Shane Benich • Michelle Beninati • Benjamin • Nolan Bennett • Travis Benning • Erin Benson • Shane Benson • Amanda Mae Bentley • Dirk Berger • Larry & Laurie Berger • Justine Bergman • Sara Bergstresser • Mary Catherine Bernadette • Sharla Bernard • Ben Berndt • BernieCH • William & Sydney Berroteran • The Berry Family • Alexis Briel Berry • Corey M. Berry • Nathaniel Besenski • Peter Bess • Kaleb Best • Nathan Best • Oliver Beuchat • Shannon J. Beyer • Nelson Bezanson • Aru & Rati Bhargava • Sanjeev Bhatia • Anna Bianchi • Maria Bianchi • Nate F. Bibens • David Bicheno • Sara Bickersmith • Anthony Bickerstaff • Ralph Biddle • Christian Billen • Jon Billings • Jayne Billington • Adam T. Billups • Chris Bilodeau • Chris Biolo & Tom Schmidt • Sarah Birchard • Rochelle Bird • Christopher Birkheimer • Javier Birriel • Kevin & Jyoti Birtcher • Matt Bisgyer • Joshua Bish • Jodi Bishop • Michael J. Biswas • The Bitterman Family • Jessica Björklund • Ross Björklund • The Black Roths • Jonathon Blacklo • Laly Blasco • Mathias Blikstad • Aaron Block • Karin & Dietmar Bloech • The B. Blount Family • Ben Blount • Ian &

Lisa Blum • Tylor Blythe • Angelique M. Keppler Bochnak • Billie Bock • Lynne Bockelman • Scott & Michelle Boeck • J. Bogze • Nicholas R. Boileau • Mircea Boistean • Ashley Bolduc • Matthew Boley • Elizabeth Bollinger • Lucas Bombardier • John H. Bookwalter Jr. • Jasen Boothe • The Boreham Family • Rikke Borgaard • Halli Borgfjord • Andy Bosher • Becky Bosshart • Brian Boswell • Riaan Botha • Arielle & Cameron Botta • Terry Bouchard • Elizabeth Bougie • Kris Boultbee • Andy Bowden • Chad Bowden • David Bowden • Jason Bowden • Elise "The Cat" BowerCraft • Robert Bowling • Kayleigh Bowman • Matt "Doc" Bowman • Benjamin Ray Boxley • Justin Boyd • McKayla Boyd • Timothy "Doc" Boyd • Michael Boye • Kevin Boyer • Jessica Boyette-Davis • The Boyle Family • Iain Brabant • Angela Bradley • David M. Bradley Jr. • Joe Bradley • Orin R. Brady • Sandy Brady • J. Leigh Bralick • Bram • "Forever a Butterfly" Brandy • Lisa Brandy • Brad Branstetter • Brant • Lindsay Noll Branting • The Brass Family • Lauren Bratt • Mark Braud • Florian Brauer • Neil Breault • Milou Breedveld • James Stewart Breen • Ethan & Ben Breese • Kim Breitwieser • John Breland • Alex Brener • John Brennan • Steve Brenneman • Carmen Brenner • Brent, Kat & Eben • Thomas & Joanne Brewster • Hannah Bridge • Kyle Bridges • Sarah Bridges • The Brim Family • Henry T. Brimhall II • Shane Bringhurst • Ashley Britten • Svemir Brkic • Julien Brochet • Brock • Kelly Diana Brogdon • Michael Brooker • Jaye Brooks • Quinn Broughton • Dana Broussard • Frank Broussard • Rachel Brousseau • Annaïck Brout • Austin Brown • Chris Brown • Christina & Terry Brown • Curtis Brown & Joshua Labonte • Forrest Brown • Joe "Brownsloth" Brown • Matthew Brown • Michael Brown • Miranda J. Brown • Steven M Brown • Theo Brown • V. Brown • Jordan Brownfield • Doug Browning • Jana Broz • Bruce • Claire Brumley • Michael Jay Brunt • Lauren Bruschkewitz • Michael Bryant • Joanna Brzeska • Ryan Buchanan • Michael Buckley • Danielius Buckus • Amit Budhu • Laura Warren Buehler • The Bugge Family • Jerryn Bunnell • Stephen Burchfield • Terence Burdett • Randy Burdick • Elwood Burgess • Everett Burke • Micah & Shaina Burke • Robert E. Burke • Jamie & Zeb Burks • Jennifer Burns • Jeri Burns • Phil Burns • Benjamin Burroughs •

Cassandra L. Burton • Jenny Busby • S. Busby • Janek Busch • Jeremy Busey • Tony Bussert • Nathan J. Bussey • Janet Butler • Megan Butler • Josh Butt • Nicholas Buttram • Alex Butuza • Robert Buurman • Joris Buys • Kenneth L. Bynon

— C —

Amy C. • Bev C. • Carley C. • Cynthia H. C. • Erin C. • Julien Froment C. • Nancy C. • Nikaya C. • Justin C' de Baca • Courtney Cabaniss • Gerald Joan Meizon Cacas • Cadius & Ramora • Josh Cain • Hilary Caldwell • Joshua Callahan • Callie & Cory • Tatiana & Chancie Calliham • Clay Calvert • Ross Cameron • Trevor Camp • Dustin Campbell • Lance C. Campbell • Rob Campbell • Clinton Canady IV • Sarah Cancellieri • Kevin Candiloro • Candy & Justin • Cannon Maverick Inc. • Clay Cannon • Sean Cannon • Tanner Luke Cantin • Terri A. M. Cantrell • Jennifer Caracappa • Marnilo Cardenas • Rosie Cardno • Alfredo R. Carella • Carolyn J. Carideo • Nicolette Carklin • Ty Carl • Steven & Elizabeth Carley • Allison Marie Caron • Alex Carpenter • Jodi Carpenter • Joseph H. Carpenter IV • Ines Carradice • Aidan Carrasquilla • Brandon Carter • Carolyn Carter • Clint Carter • Jennine Carter • Michael Caruso • Peter Casale • Tricia Cascio • Beth Case • Casey • Austin & Brenda Casey • Brian Casey • Casey, Orrin & Catherine • Justin Cassens • Kevin Cassidy • Pedro E. Castillo • Eddie Castro • Joe Castro • Victor Cata • Nick Catalano • Tammie Causey • Kevin Cavanagh • Tim "Starmarc" Caves • Fenric Cayne • Heather Cease • Amar Ćerimagić • Jamie Cerrato • Chad • Jason Chad • Krishna Chaitanya & Gourangi • David Lars Chamberlain • Laura Chamberlain • Preston Champ • Jaime Chan • Kevin Chan • T. S. Chan • Tony Chan • David Chanda • Monica Chandler • Paul & Shirley Chandler • Howie Chang • Rawee Chanphakdee • Maya Hainze Chapman • Rebecca Chappell & Anora Wilson • Amanda Eliza Charles • Charlotte • Jordan Charlton • Anthony Chatfield • Linda Chau & Yulong Sun • Jesse Chavez • Brian Cheek • Brent Chelewski • Yu-Wen Chen • Melissa & Alan Chettle • Richard Chiang • Kristopher Childress • Noel Chin • Lance Ching • Chip • Leigh Chittum • Luke Chmilenko • Jennifer

K. Choi • Chopper • Arunav Choudhury • Choupinou & Choupinette • Chris • Chris & Hause • Chris & Hema • Casey Christensen • Cynthia Christensen • Dylan Christian • Mikaela Christiansson • Mia Christin • Derek Christman • Olivia Christopher • Christy, Jollin, & Abby • Danielle Chritchley • Shannalee Chugg • ChX • Adam N. Cioffi • Robert Claflin • Jasmine Clancy • Brandi Clark • C. Clark • Dave Clark • Jarad Clark • Jenelle Clark • Michael Clark • David Clayton • Tony Clayton • CleanestSprout • Alex Clement • Joshua Cleveland • Francis & Charles Clifford • Greg Clinton • Mike Clougherty • Richard & Vanessa Rivas Clouston • Michael Cluff • CMHMZAN • CMT • Peter Coates • Darcie Cobos • Lisa Cockrell • Ben Cohen • Larry Coker • Ryan Colbeth • Mathew Colburn • Ab Colby • Jason S. Colby • Jenny Colby • Antonino Cole • Ashton Cole • Ryan Cole • Kris Collar • Bruce "Hoss" Collins • Josiah Collins • Justin Collins • Lawrence Collins • Todd Collins • Raymond Colon • Collin Coltman • Todd M. Colu • Willow Elisabeth Colvin • John G. Comas • CompuChip • Conflux • Pet Connection • Brandon Connors • Benjamin Conrad • Christopher Conrad • Gretchen Conrad • Susan Contreras • Al Cook • Elise Cook • Ed Cooke • Richard Cooke • Christine A. Cooney • W. Coop • Michelle Cooper • Jessica Cooperman • Brandon Coppernoll • Anke Corbeil • Sarah Corbeil • Trevor Corlett • Jordan Cornelius • Arletta Kelley Cortright • Kelley Cortright • Lachlan Corvec • Rin Corvetti • The Corvin Family • Cory & Kaylea van Vliet • Sarah Cosco • Cosmo Cosler • Cosmin • Anthony Cossio • Chantelle Costa & Cameron Nevens • Tyson Y. Cote • Bob & David Cottingham & Vickie & Katie Thornton • Larry Couch • Violet Coulton - all my love, Grangrad McCall • Damon J. Courtney • Stephanie & Namira Couturier • Donna Coviello • Andrew Cowell • Jonathan & Alexandra Cowles • Brian Cox • Caitlin Cox & Alex Mellnik • Clayton Cox • Jim Cox & Cooper • Adalyne Coy • Leo Coyle • Matthew Coyle • Tyler Coyle • Jacob Crabb • Brian Crabtree • Daniel F. Craft • Craig • Greg Crain • Anya Crane • Jeffrey Crane • Jeremy Crane • Kyler Danger Cravath • Chris Creech • Ben Crew • Shawn Crimmins • Brian Croce • Nathan B. Crocker • Jens Cromheecke • Kevin Cronic • Peter K. Crookes • Michelle D. Crosby • P.

L. Cross • Rhiannon "Rodeo" Crothers • Brian & Billy Crouch • Trevor & Justina Crow • Andrew Cruise • David Crumbley • Aaron "Crumpy" Crump • Cygnus Crux • Mark Cummings • Michael Cummings • Richard J. Cunn • Lark Cunningham • Lynley Anne Cunningham • Sam Curran • Denise Currie • Cole Currier • Chris Curry • Glenn Curry • Curtis • Nick Curtis & Kelli Cross • Lesley Curvers • Mary Cusick • Nate Cutler

— D —

D-Train • Brett D. • Dominik D. • Elizabeth D. • Garren D. • Leolani D. • Mikee D. • Giuseppe D'Aristotile • Sapphire D'Chalons • Brian Dabbs • Addie Daher • Daimadoshi • Marianne Dainton • The Dake Family • Blaž Dakskobler • Dale of the Line of Haldor • Sean & Katrina Dalton • Dani Daly • Elizabeth Daly • Leon Daly • Joel & Dianna Damir • Dan • Dane • Daniel • Danielle • Mike Danielson • Danilo & Trine • Ilia Danilov • Martin Daniš • Bogdan "BigTheo" Danisch • Patricio Danos • Isaac "Will It Work" Dansicker • Jeff Dansie • Peter Dasso • Chas Daugherty • The Daughertys • Dave • Emma Marie Davenport • David • Anthony Davis Jr. • Boyd Davis • Colton M. Davis • D. Lynette Davis • Donald & Joanna Davis • Ian Davis • Julie Davis • Leslie A. Davis • Randy & Lori Davis • Rocky A. Davis • Saucy Davis • Scott Davis • Luke Davitt • Wendall Dayley • Dazzle • Bob, Merilin & Kirsi De Brabandere • Chris de Eyre • Amber "Æm" de Haan • Marcel de Jong • Martha Charlotta de Jonge • Gerber de Lange • Jeffrey de Lange • Elodie de Peretti • Wendy de Peuter • Dénes Deák • Stuart Deakin • J. C. Dean • Melissa Dean • Shawna JT Dees • Isak DeFay • Emmeline DeGolier • Jean Dejace • Marci DeLeon • Brian Christopher Dell • Mark W. Dell'Orfano • Scott Dell'Osso • Terry Dellino • Anna Demchy • Sheldon & Brittani Dement • Jessica Demers • Melina Demertzi • Diane S. & P. J. Dempsey • Jessie Dena • Justin Denbow • Susan Denbow • Andrea Denekamp • Stephen Denney • Ollie Denning • Paul Dennison • Ken Denny • Ryan Depuy • Wonko der Verständige • Max Dercum • Adam Derda • James Michael Derieg • Deryk, Crystal, Sabryn & Sey • Joe Desiderio • RaeAnn Desmarais • Traci DeStena • Peter Devine & Gina Jiang • Andrew DeVore • Dave Dewey • Dustin DeYoung •

DeZilber • Jake "Karrde" Di Toro • Patricia Diani • Paul Diaz • Jeffrey Dick • Tobias Dickbreder • Anthony Dicostanzo • Zachary Didur • Geoff & Janene Dietrich • Gaetan Dietsch • Ethan Dietz • Bret Dillingham • John DiMaggio • Crystal Dinh • Betsy Dion • DiscountShrimp • Laura Dizon • Dlakeprince • Dmsaelee • Zathras do Urden • The Doan Family: Randy, Marla, Colin & Evan • Andrew Dobry • Aileen M. Dodge • Michael W. Dodge • Christopher Kenneth Doelker • Dogpoop • Andrew Doherty • Matthew Doka • Caroline Dollinger • Miguel Domingo • Donna • Máire Donohue • Nathan Dorsey • Martin Dotzauer • Shannon Douglas • Jacob Doukas • Oscar Dovalo • Nate Dowd • Michael Dowds • RIP Ronnie Downes • Dan Downton • Alycia, Jesse & Alyenna Doyle • Mary Kate Doyle • Thomas J. Doyle Jr. • Karen Drab • Tomas Drab • Maxine Drake • Weston Dransfield • E. L. Drayton • The Driscoll Family • T. J. Driver • Tara Drost • Tina Druce-Hoffman • DT • Mengmeng Du • Amelia Dudley • Maleh Duenas • Colm Duffy • Lisa M. Dugan • Lauren Duggar • Nathan Duke Sr. • Will Duke • Andrew Dulany • Bernhard Dumphart • Michelle Puterbaugh Dunaway • F. Jason Duncan • Christyn Dundorf • Russell Dunk • The Dunlap Family • David Dunn • Elise & Alex Dupuis • Woody DuRant • Eric Durfee • Mama Dust • Vince Dutra • Herman Duyker • DVG • Anna Dy

— E —

EAG • Ken & Kristin Eales • Chuck Earley • Ben Eastham • Joanne Easton • Dain Eaton • Mary & Suzan Eaton • Ryan Eaton • Heather Eberhart • Blake Ebert • Brandy Eckman • Steven Ede • Bryan Edelman • David Edmonds • Bethany Edmonson • Paul T. Edmunds • Wade Edwards • J. D. & Liz Egbert • Samuel & Connie Ege • Nathan Eggleston • Lukas Eichler • Dan Eisen • Evan Eisenberg • Eivind • Robin Eker • Kjetil Vinjerui Ekre • Bilal Elbarrani • Evan Elder • Alyssa Elery • Thomas Elfing • Mohamed Elk • Lindsey Ellertson • Ian Elliott • Jasmine M. Elliott • Malana Ellis • Jared Ellsworth • Matt Ellsworth • Sara Elson • Bryan Elstad • Sean Ely • Elysia • Christian Emden • The Emgushov Family • Emil • Lori Emry • Andrew Enano • Matt Enberg • Travis Enfield • Angie Engelbert • Alex Engelhardt •

Kory Engle • Eon • Catherine & Alley Erhardt • Eric & Susan • Pierce Erickson • Erin • Gabe Erwin • Jill S. Erwin • Daniel Eslinger • Joel Espina • John D. Esser • Etel • David William Etherington • Monroe Etherton • Paul Eugene • Diana Evans • Paula Evans • Ryan Evans • Evelyn & Clara • Peter J. Evenson • Ashby Everhart Jr. • Joshua Ewer • Morgan B. Ewers

— F —

Maja F. • Brian L. Fabbi • Irene Fabig • Iga Fabry-Byczkowska • Magdalena Fabrykowska-Mlotek • James Fahringer • Victoria Fair • Anne Falbowski • Urs Falk • M. Falvey • Sophie Falvey • Anthony Farana • The Fariello Family • Jackson A. Farnsworth • Jessica Farnsworth • Farrell • Mitchell Farrell • Louis Fata • Emma Faubion • Alexander E. Faulkner • Mathue Faulkner • Michael Faulkner • Ser Lambert Fawkes • Michael Fazio • Jeremy Feath • Febin • Carol Feeney • Michael Feeney • Sander Fekene • Emma Fell • Sven Felske • Angela Femrite • Carmelo Fenald • Andrea Fennell • Natalie Shannon Fennell • Sam Fenner • Bruce Fentin • Chris Fenton • Hudson Daniel Ferguson • Shani Ferguson • Paula Fernández • Meredith Ferneyhough • Fernleaf • Jacob Ferrell • Robert Fiallo II • Randall Fickel • Patricia Fie • The Field Family • Cari Fifield • Paul "Akimotos" Fijma • Michelle Findlay-Olynyk • Shawn P. Finn • The Finnegan Family • Kyle Finnegan • Nicole & Patrick Finneran • Simon Fiorucci • Dan Firth • Karen Goeckeritz Fischer • Andrew Fish • G. Fisher • John Fisher • Brooke Fishman • FitzJuno • Derek Fitzpatrick-Jolley • Five Fillies Farm • Cameron & Desma Flagg • Tom Flaherty • Courtney Flamm • Vince Flaxfield • Cassiopeia Fletcher • Tristan Fletcher • Chris Floden • Manuel A. Flores • Andy Flowe • Mikaela Floyd • Ann Flumerfelt • Holly Flumerfelt • Foca • Shawn A. Focht • Sylvia L. Foil • Joshua Foltz • Gordon & Liza Forbes • Patrick Forbis • Donald Jesse Force II • David Forcey • Jermaine Ford • Mark & Michelle Ford • William Ford • Callum J. Forrest • Daniel Forrestel • Forry • Jonas Forshell • Matthew Forsthoefel • Hannah Forsyt • Darryl Fortunato • Ember & Tad Foster • Jerome E. Foster • Quentin Foster • J. Foubert • Greg Fougere • The Fowler Family • Cathy Fox • Jessica Fox • FoxyVixen • The Francisco Family • Franco •

Elizabeth Francois • Mason Frandsen • Franks • Josh Franks • Jon H. P. Frantzen • Jeffrey Frederick • Ian Tyler Fredrickson • Adam Freeman • Spencer Freeman • Kelly French • Manny Frescotta • Jess Freund • Phil & Sarah Freund • Åsa Frid • Rachel Friedli • Phil Fritzsche • Michael Frost • Cody Fry • Miguela Fry • Sabina Fuchs • Fuentez • Fufi • Tanner Fuhr • Daniel Fullem • Nicholas & Rachel Fuller • Donald Fulmer • Meg Funk • Anita Fuqua • Randy Furr • Yurii "Saodhar" Furtat • Arthur Fyles

— G —

Chantel "Epeolater" G. • Choko G. • Mariah G. • Mathias G. • Vitaly G. • Grant Gabbert • Brian Gacki • Denis Gagnon • Gerald Gaiser • Robert Gaissmaier • Kevin Gaither • Larry Gaither • Patrick Galizio • The Galligan Family • Liz Gallo • Rohan Gandhi • Rumen Ganev • Jonathan Ganey • Ari Gani • Kristyl Gano • Elora Garbutt • Guilherme Garcia • Jonathan Garcia • K. Garciga • Amanda Rae Gardner • Christine Gardner • Kelly Gardner • Kelly & Mikel Gardner • Kat Garibaldi • Andrew Garinger • Alan Garretson • Josh Garrett • Keith Garvin • Brandon Gary • Vik Gashi • Cedric Gasser • Brian Gaudet • Cody Gaudet • James & Lexi Gauthier • Sarah Gaxiola • Celeste GB • Kenneth Geary • Bryan Geddes • Jan Clemens Gehrke • Snævar Geirsson • Tamara Gentry & Cody Todd • Matthew Geoffroy • Ashley George • William Gerboth • Mathieu Gervais • Sheri L. Gestring • Courtney Getty • Leila Ghaznavi • Shreyaa Ghosh • Giacomo • Hennie Giani • James & Elizabeth Gibson • Ryan Gibson • Casey Giddens • Alexander S. Gifford • Andrew Gilbert • Mark Gilbo • Ginger Gilbreath • Jeff Gilkison • Cody Gillespie • Stuart Gillespie • Claire Gilligan • Kayden, Levi & Arielle Gilpin • Gimli Good Boy • Stephen Giordano • Maurice Giroux • Julia Given • Tom Gladney • Patrick Glancy • Israel Glasser • Richard Glodowski • Damon Glover • Ira Gluck • Jeramy Goble • Gargi Godbole & Omkar Kolangade • Kriti Godey • Carman Godfrey • Yamir Godil • Lenny Godinho • Wolfgang Goetz • Cary Goggin • Charles H. Goldberg • Noah Goldberg • Emily Gonyer • Gabriel Paz Gonzalez • Gonzo • Melissa Gooda • George A. Goode • J. Goode • Gabriel Goodman • Olya, Joseph & Roman Goodrick •

Melissa Goodwin-Dikkers • Samantha Goodwin • Bhavik Gordhan • Dylan Gordon • Hugh Gordon • Gary Gorman • James L. Gorman Jr. • Justin & Lisamarie Gorman • Michael Gorman • Joshua Eli Gossett • Michael Gouker • Connor Gowin • J. Daniel Grabau • Victoria Graca • Alejandro Grados • Robin Graf • Travis F. Graham-Wyatt • David Graham • Kris Graham • Robert Graham • Ryan Graham • Pat & Kate Gramling • Nicholas & Natalie Granofsky • Gary Gray • Greg Gray • Kerry Gray • Dion F. Graybeal • Todd Grayson • Damon Green II & Leslie Green • Gail Goldner Green • Jason T. Green • James D. Gregory Jr. • Karalee Gregory • Tyler Griesinger • The Griffin Family • Andrew Griffin • Brian Griffin • Christopher Griffin • Kelly "AzureSky" Griffin • Robert W. Griggs • Ruth Grill • Robert Grimes • The Grinstead Family • Brad Grinstead • Kasper Grøftehauge • Pat Grogan • L. Ethan Gros • Estelle Grosjean • Alex Grossman • Adam & Cortney Grove • Crystal Growe • Gilles Guerin • Andrew Guerra • Knut H. Guettler • Troy Gunnell • Katja Günther • The Gurglesplats • Sheri Gurney • Michael Gurry • Mia & Isa Guthier • Cameron Guthrie • Aly Gutierrez • Guymon Brothers Three • Fallon R. Guynn • Francisco X. Guzman • Gabriel Estepan Guzman • Michael Guzzo • Noreen Gwilliam

— H —

Andrew H. • Ellie H. • Emma H. • Gaurav H. • Jeff H. • Phillip H. • Wes H. • Kenny Ha • Jonathan Haas • Tyler Hackett • Jason K. Hackworth • William C. Haddock • Liz & Bryan Haeussler • Jon Hagen • Justin & Stephanie Hagler • Derek Hahn • Ray Hahunga • Gary Hake • Jono Hakes • Runar Håland • Halcyon • Patrick Haley • Dave "Sarge" Halgren • Brody, Joanna, Elayna & Edwin Hall • Glenn Alan Hall • Mike, Morgan & Emmett Hall • Nathan C. Hall, MD, PhD • Chris Halmos • Tim Halsey • Esko Halttunen • Halyna, Joshua & Sebastian • Nicole Ham • Ben, Melissa & Callie Hamilton • Bradley Hamilton • Lama Hamilton • Pamela Hamlet • Audrey Hammer • Spencer Hammond • Lissa Hammonds • Vivian Hammons • Samuel Hamrin • John Han • Daddy Hancock • James Hancock • Kristian Handberg • Harrison Hanes • Gregory Richard Wayne Haney • Jennifer

Hanicq • Jeffrey M. Hann • The Hansen Family • Denise Hansen • Luke, Penny & Emma Hansen • Jim Hanson • Kimberly Hanson • Matthew Steven Hanson • Nichole Haratyk • Matthias Harder • Jordan Harding • Daniel Hardy • David Harfst • Ann JMS Harlan • Jacob Haronga • Mark Harrington Jr. • Brandon W. Harris • Christopher Harris • Damien Harris • Kenneth Harris • C. C. Harrison • Chad Harrison • Margaret Harrison • Andrew RJ Hart • Nicholas Hart • Ryan Michael Hart • Yo & Kevin Hartley • Michelle Hartline • The Harvey Family • Brandt Hasser • Doug Hastings • Rodney Hatcher • Tom Hatfield • Rick Hauert • Chris Haught • Martin Haugland • The Haure Family • Sam Haurie • Thomas B. Hauser • Phil & Courtenay Havers • Atle H. Havsø • Melissa & Nate Hawkins • Natalie & Joseph Hawkins • The Hawtons • Josh & Meaghan Haxton • Melissa L. Hayden • Matthew Hayes • Tim Hayes • Timothy Hayward-Browne • Trevor Hayward • Gus Hearn • Heather • "Daydreaming" Heather • Sean Heffernan • Espen Agøy Hegge • Matt Heiberger • Bryan E. Heil • Mike Hein • Sarah Heineman • Nathan Heinrich • Chris Heintz • Bart Helder • Heleen & Martijn van Hagen • Carol Helfenbein • Kyle V. Helliar • Peter Helmes • Cole Helms • David Hemminga • Kevin Hempe • Sebastiaan Henau • C. S. Henderson • Drew Henderson • Jocelyn Henderson • Joey Hendrickson • Björn Henke • Bobby Henry • Henry, Isabel & Max • John Henson • Quigley Moz Herimpo • Jacob Heron • Chadrick Hess • Jim Hess • Kenneth Hess • Hevs & Shmeey • Lori Hewlett • Andrew Heydorn • Douglas Hickel • Simon Hickey • The Hidinger Family • Patrick High • Ellis & Edwin Hild • Alex Hildebrand • Bryan, Joy, Alamea, Kai & Miliani Hill • Dan Hill • Jo-ann Hill • Kay Hill • Kevin HIll • Mark Hill • Gabe Hilliard • Mark Hindess • Kenneth Hines • Andrew Hinson • Daniel Hirsch • Chantel Hirschel • T. Hise • Eric Hitch • Kevin Hjelden • Hjellis • Carmen Ho • Hanh Hoang • Stephen Hobbs • Greg Hoch • Daniel Hochster • William B. Hockaday • John Hocking • Manuel Hoell • Christina Hoffman • Douglas Hoffman • Garrett Hoffman • Jeff Hoffman • Andrew Hogg • Linda Hojlund • Steven J. Holden • Chris Holdren • Andrew Holl • Amy Holland • Consuela Holland • Patrick Holland • Simon Hollingsworth • Scott, Jacquelyne, Sevilla & Aba Holm •

Cole S. Holman • Corinna Holmes • Lena & William Holmes • Michael E. Holmes • Tamara L. Holsclaw • The Holsworth Family • Bob Holt • Christian Holt • Howard "MajorNerd" Holton • Kara Holtzman • Allen Holub • Kristiina Hommik • Wai Chung Hon & Mark Sanasie • Brendan Hong • Danny Hood • Luke Hooper • Adam Hoover • Jessica Hoover • Jeffrey Hope • Alan Hopkins • Mike Hopkins • Noah, Elliot & Olivia Hopkins • Sabine Horak • Florian Hörath • Elynn Horn • Mari Horn • Alysa Hornick • Ira Horowitz • Brian Horstmann • Paul Horvath • The Houles • Thomas Houseman • TJ & Stephanie Hove • J. R. & Kimberly Howard • MaryAnne Howard • S. D. Howarth • Angela Marie Howe • Harvey Howell • Zach Howell • Katherine Howett • Santiago Hoyos • Hrerikl • Christopher Alan Huddleston • Kimberly Hudna • Curtis & Andrea Hudson • Dan Hudson • The Huffman Clan: James, Mia, Jones & Taeli • The Huffman Family • Megan Huffman • Rachel Huggins • Dundi Thompson Hughes • Jon Hughes • Lizzie Camstra Hughes • Ron Hughes • Austin Hughey • Jonathan Hui & K. K. Miller • Caleb Hulbert • Leland Hulbert • Isaac & Joseph Hull • Jeff & Anna Hullihen • Carol & David Humm • Nathan Hundley • Rebecca Hunt • Joshua & Nina Hunter • Sean Hurley • Johannes Huster • Jaqueline Huth • Yurie & Kathryn Hwang • Jeremy Hylen

— I, J —

I love Annika, Mark & Mikkel so much! • I Love Jenny • John Idlor • Martin Ignacio • Curt Iiams • Paz Ilan • Chase Iles • Marcus Ilgner • Matthew Infantino • Paul Ingalls • Russel Ingle • Mike Ingram • Ioana • Andreas Irle • Michael Irmler • Torian Ironfist • Jeremy & Stacy Ironside • Yannick Isaac • Carl Isganitis • Debbie Isley • Anjeannette Ison • Marion Istrate • Ivana • Paul A. G. Ivany • Amber Ivers • Brad Ivie • Ciro Izarra • Owen J. • Rima Jabbour • Jacinda & Kaitlyn • Jack • Aron Jackson • Bo B. Jackson • In memory of Ellen Kurikka Jackson • Kairah Jackson • Martin Jackson • T. W. Jackson • Bob & Eddie Jacob • Brittany, Jonathan & Dallas Jacobovitz • T. C. Jacobs • Matt Jacoby • Catherine Jacqué • Jan Jakobsson • Chris A. Jalian • Justin James • Kati James • Jamin • Amy

Jamison • Bob Janc • The Janeiro Family • Victoria Jang • Sally Qwill Janin • Eleazar A. Jarman • Erik Jarvi • Jasmine & Yale • Jason - AKA "Traveling Cloak" • Anam Javed • Gary Jay • Jaya • Lasantha Jayasinghe • Jaymian • JD • Jeb • Jeff • Jeff, Brittany & Sherlock • Jeff & The Goodwin Family • JefffreybNeuschatz • Jen • Jason Jennelle • Jason Jennings • John Jerse • Lei Jess • JNM • Jokito Jo • Chelsea Jobe • Tom Jobes • Kyle Jodrey • Joe • Johana of House Barreto • David Johansen • Jessica Johansen • Carl Johansson • Henrik Johansson • Raney John • Alicia & Geoffrey Johnson • Amber L. Johnson • Casey, Marissa & Parker Johnson • Collin & Sophia Johnson • Cynthia Johnson & Deborah Taylor • Dennis Johnson • Eleanor Mallory Johnson • Emily Johnson • Erin & Jerrod Johnson • Fred W. Johnson • Jacob Johnson • Jason C. Johnson • Jeff Johnson • Kelly Troy Johnson • Larry "Keith" Johnson • Tyler Johnson • Will Johnson • David Johnston • Jacob & Jennifer Johnston • The Jolley Family • Jon & Tom • The Jones Family • Andrew Jones • Beau Jones • Jason Jones • Nathan, Jessica & Noah Jones • R. Nickolas Jones • Raven Jones • Rebecca & Shawn Jones • Sarah Jones • Stephen F. Jones Jr. • Tai'anne Mara Jones • Jonna, Anthony & DonnaLucia of Aurora, IL • David Jordan • Tim Jordan • Joseph • Josh, Bina & Ava • Josh & Emmalee • Loretta Joslin • Kathrin Jost • Dan Josua • Sunshyne Joubert • Caleb Journot • The Jovanovich Family • Joyelle • Kala Judd • Samuel Judd • Judy • Julia • Rafal Jung • William Jung • Juraj & Andy • Just a Paramedic • Justin

— K —

K, Scout & Baloo • Freda K. • James K. • Shaz K. • Michał Kabza • Joshua Kail • Kainoa • Naveed Kakal • A. M. Kalmus • Chinmay Kamat • S. Kammerzell • Kanab • Brett Kane • John Kiwi Kane • Youwan Kang • Pulkit Kansal • Andy Kao • Michael Kaplan • Robert Karalash • The Karaliai Family • Eli Karasik • Karen • Karis • Eliza Karlowska • David Karlton • Jaimison Karp • Richard B. Karsh MD • Emerson Kasak • Karmen Kase • Sean Kashino • The Kastelic Family • Christopher "Lobo" Kaster • Kimberlee Katekaru • Lorenzo Katin-Grazzini • Katy • Jacob M. Katz •

Armin Kaweh • Kaya • Kaye • Andrew Keane • Eoin Kearney • William G. Keaton • Mark Kelley • Sean V. Kelley • Erin Kello • Christopher & Erika Kelly • Michael A. Kelly • Emily Kelsey • Brian Kelso • Sam Kemble • Jordan Polly Kemp • Elizabeth & Spencer Kenning • Kent • Kepi • Jose T. Kercado • Julia Kerr • Patrick Kerr • Marissa Kerrigan • Mark Kerrigan • Gijs Kerstens • Kessia • Tracey Jordaan Kester • Erika Keswick • Nina Kettler • Kevin • Nelli Khamraeva • Tuba Khan • KHW • Adam Kice • David "Cinderella Man" Kiddell • Matthew Kidder • Nancy Kidder • Kikos • Nick Kilburg • Jehoshua Kilen • Kilmian • Kim • Hannah Kim • Oliver Kim • Les & Sue Kimbro • Russell Kinch • Benjamin King • G. King • MaryEllen King • Patrick M. King • Ryan King • Shawn T. King • Vaughan King • Lori Kingston • Andrew Kinsey • Russell Kirby • Bill & Susan Kirchner • Bradley Kirk • Doug Kirkland & Stacey Drohan • Christopher Lee Kirth • Alen Kiseljak • Bodhi James Kish • Amie Kissel & Daniel Cowlin • Justin Kita • David Kitching • Adam Kittelson • Daniel Klaassen • Matt Klassen • Matt Klawiter • Joyce Klein • Maxime Klein • Arienne Klijn • Krzysztof Klimonda • Bret & Dena Kline • Daniel Klovning • Jordan J. Klovstad • Bethany & Emma Kluge • Matthew Paul Klure • Matt Kluting • Jessica KluznCannon • Kurt Kneller • Danielle Knight • Michael Knight • Will Knox-Walker • Theodore Kobus • Angella & Matthew Kocian • Pascale Koenig • Jens Ulrich Kögler • Michael S. Kokowicz • Dr. Denny Kolkebeck • Andrew Konicki • Jing Koo • Alex Kopel • Dustin "The Iron Viking" Koppelman • Marten Kops • Brian Korten • Zachary Kosarik • Konstantin Koslowski • Mike Kossian • Brynn Kostelecky • Morgan & Rob Kostelnik • Joseph Kotzker • Joshua, Lily & Sawyer Kovach • Dorothy Ann Kovats • B. R. Kovich • Lochlan Kozlowski • Kevin Kramer • Alex & Sarah Krause • Jaime Krause • Brian Kreider • Markus Kreipe • Steve Krepelka • Bruce Kretschmer • Taylor Krieg • Kristen • Kristina & Markus • Kally Kruchten • Michael J. Krueger • Wulf C. Krueger • Caroline Kruger • Bob Kruithof • Noah Kruss • Tony Kuehn • Nick Kuhn • Aaron Kung • Tiffany Kung • Kimberly Kunker • Margy Kuntz • Larry Kuperman • Kevin L. Kurth • Eyal Kurz • Rabi Kutob • Kyle

— L —

Danny L. • Kerstin L. • Lillian L. • The La Loggia Family • Kyle "Spacecat" Laauser • Mélanie LaBarre • Paul Labbe • Llorente Lacap • Laurie Lachapelle • Mary Lai • Sophie "Moon Warrior" Lai • The Laird Family • Jane Lake • Tom Lake • Peter Lakshmanan • Calen Lambert • Katelyn & Koriel Lambson • Lamefx • Brad Landress • Florian Landsteiner • Adam Lane • Joshua P. Lane • Phoenix Lane • Jeremy Lange • Shirin Lange • Walt Lange • Jan Langhorne • Bradley Lankford • Kan Laohverapanich • Patrice Lapointe • Lara • Damien Larcombe • Rae Larick • LaRocque • Dora Larrabee • Bjarte Larsen • Mark Larsen • Shawn F. Larsen • Rebecca Larson • Bryan J. Lash • Chris Last • Scott Latter • Lau • André Laude • Laura • Laura & John • Joel Lavoie • Kim Lavsa • Greg Lawlor • Jack Lawrence • Laura Lawrence • Jason Lawrie • Shirley Lawson • Brett Laymon • J. Lazz • Justin Leach • Darrell Leadbetter • Michael Leaich • Andreas Leathley • Babette M. LeBlanc • Ben Lederman • Benjamin A. Lee • Bob Lee • Darren Lee • Garrett Lee • Joel Lee • Lani Lee • Nicole Lee • Sandra K. Lee • Taylor Lee • Zachary Lee • Mat Leeds • Jack Leek • Brian Lefebvre • Lefteous • Orange Leg • T. J. Legge • Rainer Lehr • Erynn Lehtonen • Tiffany Lei • Adam Leibig • Megan Leifker • Holger Leimeier • Michael Leinen • Carly R. Leis • Mark T. Lemke • Jerry & Zachary Lencoski • Vladimiro Lenino • Christiaan Lennaerts • Michael Lenzo • Leo • Paul Leonard • Raoul Leonard • Hailey Leone • Kevin O. Lepard • Rolf Lerch • Tarin Leslie • Amy Lesniak & Jeff Briggs • Jared Lessor • Nathen Leung • Guillaume Levesque • Aaron Levi • Daniel & David LeVine • Joshua Lew • Alia Lewis • Deighton M. Lewis • James A. Lewis • Kyle Lewis • Laura Lewis • Olivia Lewis • Todd M. C. Li • Tyler Libey • Judy Liday – Educator & Friend • Bob Lienemann • Eric Lienhard • Ken Lifland • Mike Lightbody • Dominic & Alina Lill • Jeffrey P. Limmer • Chad & Cole Lindaman • Stephen Linden • John Linder • Adrienne Haataja Lindgren • Lindsay • Leila Lineberger • Roxanne Lingenfelter • Brooke R. Lingle • Lisa Link • Ken Lipinski • Chris Lira • Lisa, Nathan & Sebastian • Patricia Liu • Rainy Liu • Tellina Liu • Jaimée Livingston • Liz • Whit Lloyd • Eric & Gwenn Lochstet • Bradley Locken • Dylan Lockwood •

Jonas Lodewyckx • Mitchell Logue • The Lokos Family • Bill Lombardi • Chris Long • Sarah Longlands • Brent Longstaff • Barbara Lookerse • Arya Loomba • Georgia Loomes • Julia Looney • Kevin Looney • Darlene Lopez • David Lopez • Nicholas Lopresti • Kiss Lorant • Frank Loreti • Christian Loroff • Nathan Loutr • Holly Louwagie • Gábor Lovasi • Stewart Love • Louise Lowenspets • Maja Lozanac • Casey Lozier • Boris Lubarsky • Mark Lubischer • M. Jones Luce • Sam Ludford • Luh • Andrea Luhman • Lynda Lum • Garry Lundberg • Suzanne Lundeen • Kyle Lundquist • John Lupo • Luthie & Eggie • Sasha Luthra • Des Lynch • Duncan "Kordwar" Lynch • Jae Lynch • Michael B. Lynch • Paul Lynch • Sean Lynch • DeeDee Lynn • Bob Lyon • Steve Lyon • Andrew Lyons • Kristy Kimberly Lyons

— M —

Abhishek M. • Ashley & Brittney M. • Axel M. • Bryce M. • Caleb M. • Camille M. • Chris M. • Connor M. • Garrett M. • Gary & Pam M. • Javier M. • Karen M. • Kati M. • Lucy Ma • Peter Ma • Tiffany Ma • Caleb Mabe • G. Bradley MacDonald • Dimitrios, Petra, Erika Angelika & Nikolaos Machikas • Brigette MacKenzie • Grace Mackie • Romney, Spencer & Tanner Madsen • Haley Mae • Baby Magaldi-Ruiz • Thomas Magers & Yi Hui Chang • Allie Mages • Jason Magnan • Jacob Magnusson • Nipun Mahajan • Gavin & Sarah Mahaley • Emmanuel Mahe • Maia • Todd Maines • MajikJack • Eaten Mak • Vincent Mak • Eric & Diane Malchodi • Danielle Maley • Tom, Tyler & Zachary Maley • Brendan Mallon • Andra Malmé • James Malone • Thomas W. Malwitz, Jr. • Giorgi Mamadashvili • MamaRooGrande • Naveen Mandadhi • Manessah • Ra'eesah Mangera • Kenneth Mann • Adam Mansell • N. Manzanares • Danielle Mar • Lahman Marcel • R. J. Marchetti • Tonia Marcum • Margaret • The Marinovich Clan • Marise • Mark • Mark & Rachel • Carly Markey • Bailey Markins • Tobias D. Markowitz • Michael Marks • Andrew Marmor • Pedro Marroquin • Steven Mars • Gene & Zi Marsh • Jordan Marsh • Don Marshall • Jonathan Marshall • Nick Marshall • Marco Martagon-Villamil • Craig Martens • Ivan Martens • Barry L. Martin • Brandon "N1" Martin • Brett Martin • Doug

Martin • Kai Martin • Katherine Martin • Lucas Martin • Richard Martin • Sean Martin • Shannon & Lori Martin • Ty Martin • Jenny J. Martinez • Jorge Cordero Martínez • Miranda Martinez • Richard Martinez • Beth Martinson • Laura Martz • The Marvel Family • Mareike Marx • Shaylla Mason-Wright • Beth Mason • Kris Mason • Esben Mastberg • Vince Masten • The Mathat Family • Clarece Mather • Amy Mathew • R. J. Mathews • Amrita Mathis • Chris Matosky • James Matson • Matt • Rebecca Matte • Matthew • Dexter A. Matthews • Jacob Matthews • Ryan Matzke • Zachary A. Matzo • Layla Maurer • Mark Mawdsley • Charlene Maxwell • Stephen May • Nathan Mayberry • Guy Mayer • Lysane Maynard • Josh Mayoral • Lindsey Mayoras • Omar Mazin • Steve Mazurek • Kirsten & Aiyven Mbawa • Lily McAlister • Michael McAulay • Steven McAuliffe • John, Kat & Penny McBee • David McBride • Nate, Sarah, Owen, Kate McBride • Chad McCance • Andrew McCarl • McCaro • Dr. Brendan McCarthy • Kelly McClenahan • David F. McCloskey • Jean McClure • Shane McCollum • John McCormick • Debbie McCoy • Mark McCoy • Kyle McCray • The McCreary Family • Heidi "Raven" McCreary • Ryan McCredie • Kevin McCullen • Andrew Lee McCullough • Andy McCullough • Ed McCutchan • Berkley McDaniel • Bobby McDaniel • Gerald P. McDaniel • Hunter McDole • Steven T. McDole • James McDonagh • A. McDonald • Allison McDonald • Michael McDonald • Jennifer McDougall • Bryan McEntire • Campbell McFarland • Adam McGee • Mack McGehee • Michael McGlothlin • Sean David McGrath • The McGraw Family • Miles McGuire • Ryan S. McGuire • John R. McGuirt III • Michael McHugh • Stephanie McInnes • Rob McKenzie • Patrick McKernan • Justin McKinlay • Jack, Kayleigh & Henry McKinley • Bobby McKnight • The McKnights • Michael, Saoirse & Kieva McLaughlin • Christopher Bishop McLeod • Beth & Terry McMahon • Mitch McMahon • William McMahon • Colleen McManus • Ian McNatt • Laura McNaughton • Denise McWilliams • James Meadison • Nate Mealy • Jed Mecham • Monica Medeiros • Arno & Goran Međimurec • Edgar I. Medina • Morena Medina • Sherwin Meeker • Abbie Meeks • Renée Meeks • Drew Meger • Aaron Meier • Charlotte & Nicolai Meier • Stephanie Meier • Tanya Meikle •

Briony Mejorado • Amber & Brian Melican • Melissa & Leo • Ashley & Megan Mellenthien • Rylan Memmott • The Menda Family • Cris Mendoza & Will Rielly • Stacy Menees • The Meo Family • Deanna Mercer • Mike Mercer • Jason K. Merchant • Nicole Merkulovich • Ben Merot • Christine & Parker Merriman • Chad Merritt • Emmett Meskis • David, Caitlin & Eleanor Messina • Ian Tyler Metz • Wompa D. Mewssiah • Adam Lee Meyer • Robert & Deborah Meyer • Michelle Meyering • MFS • Michael • Michaelangelo & Mona Lisa Ondevilla • Miriam Michalak & Jaap Kosten • Michelle • Mike, Kellie & Binx • Mikheil • Jerome Miklo • Kirk Miles • Monica Mileti • Todd Millee • Millen • Eric Miller • Galen W. Miller • Grant Fitz Miller • J. Lance Miller • Joe & Debbie Miller • Michael Miller • Nathan J. Miller • Sean Miller • Tony Miller • Daniel J. Milligan • Erin Millner & Bran Stoneman • Kendall Mills • Nathan Mills • Elizabeth Milne • Sean & Allison Mince • Mark Miocevich • David Mishler • Michelle Mishmash & Chris Kesler • Trata Misir & Simran Misir • W. Miskovetz • Shruti Misra • Linda Mit • The Mitchell Family of Harrisonburg • Annarose Mitchell • Bradford Mitchell • The Ras & Toie Mitmug Family • ML • Edie Mobley • Matt Moffet • Kumail Hussain Mohammed • David Moldawer • Jakob Moll • Joe Molnar • Nabeel Moloo • Lee Monamy • Joseph Mondragon • Jess Monica • James Monsebroten • Kyndra Monterastelli & Anthony Tran • Swapna Mony • Scott Mooney • Andrea Moore & Martin Eichman • Dan Moore • Dustin Moore • Jordan Moore • Matthew Sonshine Moore • Mike Moore • Paul Raithe Moore • Sabre Addington Moore • Charles & Anna Moorhead • Jason & Daniel Moos • Serge Mora • Lucien Morales • Aaron & Corrie Moran • Cynthia Moreno • Daniel Moretti • Jasmine Morgado • Clifford J. Morgan • Morgan & Dino • Marleigh Morgan • Marvin D. Morgan Jr. • Victor Morgan • Melissa Morrisey • Jim Morrison • Meghan & Adeline Morrison • Francis Morrissette • Rena Morse • Stuart Morse • Brandon Morton • Luka Mosashvili & Tamar Nadirashvili • Mo Moser • Moses • Katie Mosharo • Konner & True Moshier • Eric Moss • Rachelle Gwendolynne Moss • Calvin Moy • Elias Moya • Jeff & Kelly Moyer • Mr.Grome44 • Mrbill2705 • Steve Muchow • Nathan Muilenburg • Kaushik Teshlor Mukunda • Brian Mulvey • Rachel Mungra • Nancy

Munson • Austin Murch • John Murphy • Philip Murphy • Sean Murphy • Sig Murphy • Hana Murray • Julie Murray • Sabrina Musson • Tony & Ben Muzi • Sean Myer • Anna Mykkeltvedt • Eric Mylius • Jamie Mynott

— N, O —

Andrew N. • Rhel ná DecVandé • Axel Nackaerts • Dominique Nadaud • Stephan Nagel • Michael Nagy • Joseph M. Nahas • Subash Nair • Brett Nance • Sid Nanda • Nanni • Jimmy Napier • Kristina Napier • Joe Narcisi • Narrew • Nathapong Narumitrekagarn • Stephen Nash • Natalie • Wendy Natividad • Fabian C. Naumer • Marty Navaroli • Axl Nazario • Jim Nazifi • Elizabeth & Amanda Neal • Dwayne & Denise Need • Kelvin Neely • Patrick Neff • Valerie Neff • Bev Nelson • Jessica Nelson • Kate Nelson • Robert "Holyoutlaw" Nelson • William Netterville • Jason Neustaedter • Dr. Paul E. Neveux, Jr. • Tracy Robison Newman • Newt • Roger & Leslie Neyman • Samantha Nguyen • Lucas Nicholes • Sandy Nickell • The Nickels • Erik Nickerson • Nicole • Joshua Niday • Anita Nielsen • Peter J. Nierenberger • Nikolai • Chrissy Nilsen • Nina • Juliana Nine • The Niu Family • Shante Nixon • Tyler Nixon • Genie Nizigiyimana • Josie Noble • Tiago Nodari • Patrick Noffke • Keith Nolen • Wayne Nordick • Øyvind Nordli • Michael Nordmann • Maureen Nordmark • Cole Norman • Dr. Charles Norton III • Dan Norton • Frank Norton • Paul Norton • Anthony, Devyn & Royce Noto • Margie "Max" Novak • Benjamin Novo • Dino Nowak • Francisco A. Nùñez • Samuel L. Nussman IV • Steffen Nyeland • Andreas Nystedt • Sounde O • Claire O'Brien • David O'Brien • Adam O'Connell • Stefanie O'Connell • Pablo Ortiz Monasterio O'Dogherty • Rick O'Donnel • Jonathan O'Donnell • Neil O'Dwyer • Timothy O'Neil • Joseph O'Neill • Joanne O'Reilly • Bas Oberndorff • Janet L. Oblinger • Sean & Melissa Obrock • Oliver Ockenden • Calley Odum • Michael Offutt • Mosby Oliphant • Phillip Olive • Owen & Kathryn Oliver • Linda Ollila-Scherbring • Craig Ollinger • Curtis & Tina Olyslager • Þórhanna Inga Ómarsdóttir • Michael Oney • Mariëlle Ooms-Voges • Sam Oquendo • Antonio Santo Orcero • Oric • Andrea Orjuela • Orlena • Tim Ormsby • CeCe Orquieza • Renee Orr • Kim Ortega • Jennifer Orton •

Troy Osgood • Joshua Ostrander • Lucia Ott • Kirsten Otting • Conny Otto • Otus • Ron Owens • Katie & Kyle Oxford

— P —

Brad P. • Jackye P. • Jett P. • Pavel P. • Daniel Pach • The Pack Family • Lea W. Padgett • Johannes Paetsch • Richard Page • Christine A. Palmer • Matthew Paluch • Stefan Panevski • Licia L. Pannucci • Tony Pantev • Sotirios Papaefthymiou • Alexandra Papas • Romy Papas • Andrea Pappalardo • Daryl Parat • Scott Pare • Emmanouil Paris • David Parish • Calvin Park • Jeremy Park • Jason & Lynn Parker • K. P. Parker • Michael S. Parker • Rob Parker • Jessica & Justin Parr • Jacob "Laura's Lover" Parry • Zachariah "Law Jedi" Parry • James Parsons • Raymond Partlow • Alexander Pasik • Atit Patel • Chirag A. Patel • Jay Patel • Stuart Paterson • M. Patino • Kevin "Xog" Patraw & Maggie "Yukaige" Jessberger • Jennifer Patterson • Victor & Casper Patterson • Nathaniel Patton • Phillip Paul • Paulo, Tasho & Benson • Robert Pavel • Dom Pavlek • Katie Pawlik • Jacob Pawson • Deric Paxson • Steve Payne • Micah Payson-Lewis • James Payton • Bill Pearce • Ben Pearson • Greg Pearson • Joel Pearson • N. Scott Pearson • Stephanie Peck • Pedro • Joshua Peel • Stephen Peers • Steven Peiper • Autumn PeLata • Joseph R. Pellagatti • Andy & Jacob Pendergrast • Jacob Pendergrast • The Pendleton Family • Lisa M. Pennie • Marge Pepe • Laurier A. Pepin Jr. • Patrick Perrault • Lincoln & Kennedy Perry • S. Perry • Dave Pesano • David Peters • Mark Peters • Nathaniel W. Peters • Timothy Peters • Trevor Peters • Dale W. Peterson • Jay Peterson • J. C. Petock • John Petrila • Momchil Petrov • Bjørn Tore Pettersen • Jesper Pettersen • Oreo Pettigrew • Olivia Pfleider • Patricia Pfleider • Justine Phelps • Skylar Phelps • Matt Philben • Robert Philbrick • Philina • Philip • Philipp • The Phillips Family • Joyce & Gary Phillips • Katie Phillips & Tom Morris • Virginia "Gini" Phillips • Philly • Michael Philpott • Bonnie J. Phlieger • James Phoenix • Dominik Pich • Jim Pier • Jennifer L. Pierce • Michael Pierce • Travis "Xuul" Pierce • Mackenzie D. Pierson • Leslie Pietila • John Pietrzyk • Liam Pietrzyk • Victoria Pietsch • Pigwig • The Pike Family • William Pike • Patrick & Sarah Pilgrim • Katy

Pilkington • Chanthu Pillai • Zahid Pirani • Joseph Pisano • Sean Pitman & George Tice • Clara Pitts • Ian & Mia Spredemann Plasencia • Sharon Su Plasser • Jake Platfoot • David Plaut • Rick Plevak • Carl Plunkett • Suzi Po • Gjergji Poçari • Mario Poier • Therona Baral Pokhara • Anthony Polcino • Sarah Clardy Polk • Shawn Polka & Evangeline Zikos • Annette & Matt Polsky • Jack Pond • Kenny Pooh • Thomas & Amber Poon • TJ Poon • Jen Porn • Beverly Porter (Pollack) • J. Ryan Porter • Jena Porter • Shelley Porter • Zach Porter & Family • Calvin Post • Kris Post • Wieneke Post • Shawn Posthumus • Cody Poteet • Shana Potter-Monroe • Edward Potter • Matt Potts • Max Potts • Brianna Poulos • Alena Povoliaeva • Kevin Powell • Ryan Powell • Franklin E. Powers, Jr. • Kayty Powers • Derek Pozel • Elisa Prada • Craig Prather • Gianna Pratten • Andrew Preece • Benet & Daphne Press • Tim & Serina Pressey • Morgan Pretty & Laura Tan • Dan Price • Joseph P. Price • Logan Price • Will Prier & Melissa Fuller • PRJ • Chris Prohaska • Betty Prorak • pTeranodons • Fiama Puccini • Cameron Pugh • Mike Pugliese • Tony Pulickal • Emilia Marjaana Pulliainen • Chris Pullman • Gregory A. Purdom • Elaine Puri • Matthew Purse • Kimberly Purser

— Q, R —

Heather Quigg • Jay Quigley • Ben Quinn • Andrea & Brian Quinney • Luis Quiñones • David A. Quist • Katie R. • Christomir Rackov • Joe & Cindy Radvany • Terri Ann Rae • Christine Ragan • Tristan Ragan • Becky Raine • Akilan Rajendran • Logan Raj Rajendran • Slobodan Rakovic • Jesse Rambo • Marcos Ramirez • Ramis • Aditya Ramkumar • Michael Ramm • Amanda & Charles Ramsey • Ramy • Dan, Joelle, & Rosalia Kirk Randall • Karthik Rangarajan • Ranger the Labrador • Raphael • Katie Rapp • Mikael Rask • The Rathburn Family • Daniel & Emily Ratica • Kate Rausch & Brian Bosman • Johnny Ray • Ryan Ray • Mike Raymond • Razzinos • Realm Makers • Steve Reaume • Rebecca & Matt • Steve Reckelhoff • Ellie Red • Redrabbit • Chris Rees • Tana Reeve • Jen Regan • Kyle, Carissa, Mel & Gwen Reger • Charlie Regnier • Kevin Rehman • Cody Reichenau • Bob Reichert • I. Reid • Maggie Reid • Brian

Reilly • Jim & Lórien Reilly • Jonathan Reilly • Bradley Reis • Stephanie Reisenbuchler • Teri J. Reiten • Michelle Reith • Elyse Reitter • Renee Relin • Amber Rendmeister • Becky Renfroe • Rengman • Bailey Renner • Lisa Whiting Renshaw • Drew Repasky • Kayce Resha • Sarah Retza • Henrik Reuther • Chris Rhine • Crystal Rhinehart • Rhyolyn • Mike & Tammie Rice • RichaCollins • Sonja Richardson • Christophor Rick • John Riddell • The Riders • George Ricky Rieckenberg • Ernst Riemer • Grant "WereTiger" Rietze • Dana Riggle • Audrey Riggs • Riley & Alexa • Shawn Riley-Rau • Keri Riley • Seamus Riley • Jett Rink • Keegan Rinker • Jason Rippentrop • Taylor Ritchie • The Rivadeneira Family • Osvaldo Rivera-Gonzalez • Nector Rivera • Smooth Rivera • Billy Rixham • RJ & Benji Lynn • Joel Roath • Robbie • William Robbins • Gary Rober • Edwin Roberson • SaraBeth Roberson • C. Roberts • Chris Roberts • Clifton Roberts • Derek Roberts • Elise Roberts • Adele Robinson • D. Keith Robinson • Michael Robinson • Richard K. Robinson • Matt Roccuzzo • Rochester87 • Roderick • Steven R. Rodgers • Monica Rodrigues • Miguel Rodriguez • Rhio Rodriguez • Thomas R. Roedel • Chris Rogers • Hassan Rogers • Yuri Melinda Roh • Robert Rohe • Jose Rojas • Kuba Rokosz • Autumn Rolon • Brian Romand • Colin Rome • Stacey Romeo • Craig & Meg Romero • Robert Romore • Ronnie, The Bear & Radcliffe • David Roos • Matt Roos • Victoria Rork • Allison Rosa • Dylan Rose • Esther Rose • Jon Rose • Kathlyn Rose • Kyle, Marie & Reese Rose • Suzanne Rose • Kristen Roskob • Evan B. Ross • Todd L. Ross • Anders Rossland • Pål Asmund Røste • Mathias Rotestam • Adam Rouse • Parrain Roux • Cathy May Row • Matt "TipTurkey" Rowbottom • David Rowe • Chris Roy • Devraj Roy • Sagnik Roy • Jeffry Royce • Roz • RPC • RSwanson • Cheryl Ruckel • Adrian Rudloff • John Rudwall • Jay Rumple • Hemal Ruparelia • Dale A. Russell • J. P. Russell • Rae J. Russell • Matt & Clare Rutley • Charles Ryan Jr. • Marc Ryan • Nicholas Ryan • Ryan Ryerson • Andrea Ryffel • Mladen Ryhard • The Ryk Family • Ryan Rymer

— S —

Alex S. • Audrey S. • Eric S. • Jacob S. • Mahima S. • Matt S. • Michelle S. • Tim S. • Matthew, Breanna & McKinnon Saagman • Arthur Ariel

Sabintsev • Dillon Sabo • Joseph Sabo • Gabor Sacharovsky • Daniel V. Sadler • Sam & Tiffany Sadler • Nejc Saje • Mark Sakulich • Douglas Sakurai • Daniel Sal • The Salamanca Family • Tony Salva • George Salway • Kushil Samarasekera • Robert Sample • Catherine Sampson • Shayne Sampson • Matthew B. Samspon • Monika "Mon" Samul • Jason Sandau • Mik & Laura Sander • Catherine J. Sanders • Dawn Sanders • Alex Sandilands • Tacho Sandoval • Dunning Sanger • Jerusha Santiago • Sara & Travis • Amy Sarfinchan • Michael Sargent • Abhilash Sarhadi • Justin Sarver • Satyr • The Saumur Family • Ames D. & Linda L. Saunders • McKenzie Saunders • Brian Saurwein • Michele Savides • Glen Sawa • Sax is my Axe • Samuel & Din Scarborough • Scarlettpdx • Lea, Lawrence & Lukas Schack • Robert Schaefer • Jake Schafer • Jeff Schafer • Enola Schaff • Christy M. Schakel • Jacob Scharre • William Scheer • Anna Scherer • Michael Schiefer • Marc Schifer • Whitney Schiffler • Gus Schlanbusch • Catherine Schmidt • David Schmidt • Bryn Mae Schmiege • Doug Schneider • Thibaut Schneider • Tiana Schowe • René Schult • Roy Schultz • Ryan Schultz • Nolan Schwab • Angela Schwartz • Eric Schwartz • Jeremiah Schwartz • Mark, Sydney & Sloan Schwindt • Jeremy Scofield • Johnett Scogin • Scott • Brandon Scott • Nate Scott • Sabra Scott • Daniel Scrutchfield • Sam Seah • Ryan Seaman • Sebastian & Sabrina • Rhea & Dan Secor • Nancy Sedwick • Austin Segrave • Megha Sehgal • David Seid • Ari, Erinn & Nathan Seifter • Tannik Seldon • Carol Sembach • Suzan Sempels • Jose Javier Soriano Sempere • Daniel Sepulveda • Gopakumar Sethuraman • A. C. Severin • Eric T. Severson • Rick Severson • Jay Sevier • Chris Seymour • William J. Seymour • Daniel & Georgia Sgranfetto • Brett Shand • Shane • Anil Shanker • Mark Shannon • David Shapiro • Zach Shapiro • Scott Shaputis • Brandon Sharp • Patrick Shaver • Cameron Shaw • Or Light Shawat • Diane Shearer • Claire Shedden • Rob Sheffield • Jenny Sheldon • Matt Sheldon • Anthony Shenberger • Paul Sheppard • Ashley Sherman • Kerri Sherriff • Clarissa Shetler • John W. Shioli • Shiro • The Shivorderpstrassepy Family • Shannon & Brandi Shockley • Charles Shopsin • Jon Shuerger • Maria Shugars • The Shumates • Daniel

Shunfenthal • Patrick Shurr • Heath Shurtleff • Stephen & Bryn Shutt •
Shyam • Laura & Matthew Siadak • Matt Sich • Taha Siddique • Toine
Siebelink • Matthew Siedman • Brian Sieglaff • Nicole Siemens • Teddy
Sigman • Sigurine • Barbara Silcox • The Silsby Family • Pedro Silva •
Rhonda M. Silva • SilverMt • Rob Silverstein • Gregory Silvius • Steve
simas • The Simpson Family • Elaine Simpson • Susan Lee Simpson • Andy
Sims • Carlee Sims • David Simser • Joseph, Kristin & Clara Simunac •
Kainoe Sinclair • Sinkleir • Anthony Sinnott • Steven Sintermann • Mary
Sisock • Sithrebel • Sarah Sjoberg • Mike Skaggs • James Skala • Skallen •
SKennedy & MunsterFam • David Skerke • Daniel, Carmen & Darren
Skidmore • Niklas Sköld • Tracy S. Skrabut • Sky • Jay Slade • Claudia
Slaney • Jesper Slattengren & Lisa Schutte • Ella & Dorian Sloat • Bryan
Smith • Calvin Smith • Carly E. Smith • Christine L. Smith • Cierra Smith •
Elizabeth Smith • Eric Smith • Evan & Brittany Smith • Jackson Marco
Smith & Calvin Remi Smith • Jeff Smith • Katie Smith • L. Joe Smith •
Nicole Smith • Paul & Scott Smith • Randy Smith • Ryan Smith • Tiffany
Finlynn Smith • Zachary Smith • Zackery & Michelle Smith • Kim Smits •
Maria Snelgrove • Peter Snelgrove • The Snell Family • Davis Snider •
Jennifer Grouling Snider • Sydney Snider • Jesse & Brittany Snyder •
Kayla Snyder • Robin Snyder • Stephen A. Snyder • Tommy L. Snyder •
Danny Soares • Jarosław Sobi • Mattias Söderholm • Stan Sokorac • Brady
Solheim • Christina Solheim • David J. Soloski • Steve Soltz • Miroslav
Sommer • R. Sommerfeld • Robin Sones • Mark Sonnenberg • Jörg
Sonnenberger • The Sonntag Scholl Family • Soomp • Henrik Sörensen •
Matthew Sorenson • Jose Alfonso Torres Soto • Jacob W. Soucy • Andy
Southmayd • Francisco Spaghi • Jennifer Spangrud • Jeff Sparks • Paolo
Spaziosi • Christina Speir • Jane Spencer • Jennifer Spencer • Michael
Spencer • Matt "Bigfish" Sperry • Silke Spiel • SpiRaLzzzz & The Gufreda
Family • Mike Spitzer • Splabes • Sprijnkle • Kyle Springs • Andrew
Sprow • Eric Spurgeon • John Squire • Sarita M. Sridharan • Seth St.
Amand • The Stachniak Family • M&M Stachowski • Doro Stadler • Dr.
Michael Stafford • Derek Stahl • Leah Stain • Stefan Stammler • Mike

Stamp • Jackie Standaert • Deanna Stanley • Devlon Stapleton • Tristan & Adalynn Statner • Leon Stauffer • Brent Steele • Robert Steele • Robbie Van Steenburg • Kim Køhler Steensgaard • Stephanie Steenstrup • Larson Steffek • Jim & Calvin Steger • Erik Stegman • Chaim Steinberg • Maria Steingoltz • Doug Steinker • Edward Steinsho • Steven Stelma • Matthew A. Stenning • Cory Stepan • Steph • The Stephan Family • Tim Stephens • Mike Stern • Andrii Stetskyi • Tom, Tess & Ben Stevens • Ryan Stevenson • Sarah Stevenson • Stewart & Melodie • Debra Stewart • Dianne Stewart • Erek Stewart • Joshua Stewart • Kevin Stewart • Lori M. Stewart • Matthew Stewart • Michelle Stewart • Nick & Lacie Stiffler • Stiliyana • Joshua Stingl • Andrew Stinson • Ken Stith • Michael Stocks • Sean Stockton • K. Stoker • Elisabeth Libby Stone • Wes Storhoff • John Stork • Melicent Stossel • Sarah Strack • Josie Straka • Alexander Strandberg • Daniel W. Stratton • Thom Stratton • David Straub • Eric Streck • Strella • Cameron Strickland • Carole & Bill Strohm • Jenn Strohschein • Marcello Strologo • Stuart & Judith • S. Stuart • Corinna Stübing • Geri Studer • James Sturtevant • Sreevidya Subramanian • Craig Charles Suiter • Ben Suitt • Imraan Sulaiman • Andrew Sullivan • Darren Sullivan • Elliot Sullivan • Joe Sullivan • Kevin "Quentin" Sullivan • Shawn Sullivan • Shawn & Lorrie Sullivan • Stephen Sullivan • Ben Summers • Ray Surman • Ian Sutherland • Jessica Sutherland • Thanuja Suwarnan • Sven • Emily Swadron & Kendra MacDonald • Nate Swalve • Kyle Swank • Patrick Swanson • Jesica Swanstrom • Lincoln Swartz • Dustan Swartzentruber • Kevin Swartzlander • Larry Swasey • Michael Sweitzer • Laurie Swensen • John Henry Swenson • Jason Swiger • Sam Swihart • K. H. Swyers • Saad Hasan Syed • Marisa Syhlman & Tessa Lindman • Sylvia • Jeff Symes • Kathy Szabo • Johnathon & Rachel Szaefer • Carol Szpara

— T —

Alex T. • Brandon T. • Marcin Tabaka • Alex Tabor • Kristin Taggart • Katarina Takahashi • C. Corbin Talley • Nicholas Talty • Brian Tanabe • Jade Tang • Gowtham Kumar Tangirala • Hannah Tangney • Leslie

Tanner • Veronica Tanner • Tara • Péter Tarján • Tash • Andrea J. Tass • Taube • Brian Taube • Gregory Tausch • Alexander & Thurston Taylor • Luke Taylor • Michael D. Taylor • Warren Taylor • Zenobia Taylor • Ayman Teaman • The Tedder-Kings • Caleb Tedder • Myles Templin • Daniela Teofilova • Teresa • Rick TerKeurst & Stephanie Maxwell • Hope Terrell • Jonathan Terrington • Joshua Tesmer • Stephanie Tettamanti • Neen Tettenborn • Sherry Tew • Mr. Tezak • Sibel Tezkan & Amanda Chang • Quinn Thacker • Rachael C. Thacker • Thedave • B. Theriault • Kraig Theriault • TheShaner • Andrew Thomas • Eugene Thomas • Glenn Thomas • Greg Thomas • Justin Thomas • Tanya Thomas • Terence S. Thomas • John G. Thomason • Abbey Thompson • Andrew Thompson • Bridget M. Thompson • Vicky A. Thompson • Peter Thomson • Phil Thorn • Marcus Thornson • Stephanie Thorpe • Ashton Thorsen • Kaitlin Thorsen • Gardar Thorsteinsson • Britta Threshie • Thriftcriminal • Cameron Thrower • Jeff Tiemann • Ryan Tillotson • Tim! • Reyn Time • Mat Timmerman • Scott Timpe • Tina & Marco • Geoffrey Rae Titus • Tobi • Kelton Tobler • Todd • Ian K. Todd • Will Todd • Vicky Tolonen • Meine Toonen • Stefan J. Torres • Torsten • The Toton Buds • Joseph Towe • Robert Towell • Chase Townsend • Kat Tracey • M. J. Tracy • William C. Tracy • Sofia Trainer • James Traino • Sean Trainor • Lauren Tran • Nathan Travis • The Treesons • Gina Trieb • Travis Triggs • Al "The Beard" Trinidad Jr. • Jedidiah Tritle • Manuel Tropper • Troy • Michael Tsai • Chassity Tsaprailis • Evan Charles Tucker • John Tucker & Heather Hisel • Aaron Tufts • Teresa Tung • Jeff Tungate • Turned_Alchemy • Karen Turner • Nathan Turner • Niki & Toby Turner • Stanford Turner • William F. Turner III • Birgitte Turøy • Joonas Turtiainen • Shannon Tusler • Tycen • Mitchell Tyler • Christopher Tyner • Aris Tzikas

— U, V —

Gabriel Ubieta & Lysell Robles • Ihsan Ul-Haq • Ståle Undheim • Josh Upton • Kollin Upton • Daniela Uslan • Marcus Utley • Pete Vagiakos • Teresa & Elizabeth Valcourt • Art Valdez • Richard B. Valdez • Bridgette

Valente • Tess Valerie • Stan Valnicek • Lynley J. Van Allen Brinkman &
Christopher L. Fleegal • Elise & Elena Van Clief • Pier van der Graaf •
Harro van der Klauw • Paulien van der Meer • Ron van der Stelt • Calvin
Van Dorn • Mathias Van Giel • Frits van Hertum • Patricia Van Onckelen •
Janis van Ryswyk • Elle Vance • Youri Vandevelde • Jan Vanhulle • Joseph
Vanucchi • Kristy VanWyhe • Harsh Varia • Alexey Vasyukov • Lindsey &
Caleb Vaughan • Russell Ventimeglia • Teresa Verho • Joan Vernon • Tunde
Veto • Kari Vic • Noah Vick • Matthew Vidalis • Balaji Vijayan • Vikyle •
Michael & Abby Villacrusis • Isidro "Sid" Villarreal • Bruce Villas, MD •
Chris Vinson • Lucas Virgili • Sarah Vissaux • M. Vitagliano • Layton
Vitanza • Andrew Vivian • Vlar • Cheryl Vo • The Vochis Family • B. A.
Vojslavek • Bryce Vollmer • Miranda Vollmer • Iwan von der Ratzeburg •
Oliver Vonderheid • Elizabeth Vorpahl • Rhea & Dan Votipka • Bart
Vrakking • Tuan Vu • Ron Vutpakdi • Zubin & Priyanka Vyas

— W —

Brian W. • Nick W. • Pamela Wadhwa • Joshua Wagner-Smith • Randal
& Lucy Wagner • Wagner/Slavich • Avery & Olivia Walker • Gordon
Walker • Lee Walker • Allen Wall • Michael D. Wallace • Justine Walley •
Anders Walløe • Jennifer L. Walsh • Pat Walsh • Hazel Wanderer • Inge
Binfield Wang • Jade Wang • John K. Wang • Steve S. Wang • Carole-Ann
Warburton • Susanne Ward • Lareb Warda • Alan Warenski • Greg Wargo •
Stephen Waring • Diane Warner • John Warren • Simon Warshal • Mack
Wartella • Kenta Washington • The Waterloo Andersons • Chris Watkins •
Craig Watkins • Tyler Watkins • The Watring Family • Charles Watt •
Joel Watts • Jeffrey L. Wayman • Wburningham • Matthäus Wdowiak •
Malachi Weaver • Sara Webb • Stephanie Webb • Crystal Weber • Cyrus
Weber • Eric Wegner • Madison Wehrer • Erika Weilage • Chaim Simcha
Weinberg • Eric J. Weis • Barda Weishaar • Jonathan Weiss • Seth
Weissman • David Welch • Carson Welker • Charles G. Weller III • Kevin
Wellman • Wendy & Daniel • Harald Wenzel • Beau West • Doug & Jeanne
West • Keith West, Future Potentate of the Solar System • Paul K. West •

Tara Westbrook • David Western • Sonora A. Weston • Terry Westphal • Kristina Wetterman • Doug Weyek • Weylin • Thomas J. Wheatley • Dan Wheeler • Jennifer C. Wheeler • Joseph Wheeler • Meighan Wheeler • Andrew M. White • Brian White • Sam White • Stephen Robert White • Clay Whitehead • Jeff & Laurie Whiting • Philip J. Whyte • Pam Wickert • Beverly Wideman • Danielle Wiegert • Alex Wieker • Nate Wiens • Christopher "Mr. Bear" Wigelbeyer • Kesed Wilbur • Rex Wilburn • Lindsay Wilcox • Ron Wilcox • Brad & Becky Wild • Kelcie Wildeman • Anissa Wiley • Kelley Wilkens • Zebulon Wilkin • Jason Wilkins • Michael F. Wilkinson • Matt & Becca Will • Pieter Willems • Stephen Willems • Tim Willemstein • Brandon & Daniella Willey • William & P. J. Patters • Austin Williams • Bryan M. Williams • Chris Williams • Joel Williams Jr. • Kambric Williams • Scott M. Williams • Rachel Kolconani Williamson • Jeanne Marie Willis • Scott Willis • L. Wills • C. Wilscam • Bernie Wilsea-Smith • Amaya Wilson • Barbara L. Wilson • Durand Wilson • Marshan Wilson • Michael "V. B." Wilson • David Winter • Ian Winter • Lauren & Eric Winter • Nicholle Winters • Matt Winton • Daniel Wise & Suzie Smith • David Wise • Jacob Wise • Clarissa Witherly • Holly Wittsack • Ben, Zach & Steve Witzel • Scott Witzeling • Sissel Wiull • Andrea Wolfe • Jeff Wolfe • Megan Wolfenbarger • Jessica Wolfram • Mirjam Wolfsbergen • Eddy Wong • Jean Wong • Nicholas & Margaret Wong • Jason C. Wood • R. Scott Wood • Elle Woodruff & Presley Faykus • Evy Woodworth • Frank Wooler & Melissa Dankert • D. P. Woolliscroft • John Woosley • Victoria Worlow • Rebekah Wortman • Wren • Charles & Christine Wright • Jake Wright, PE • Kyle Wright • Sean "Stick" Wright • Caleb & Anna Wunderlich • Wxaith • Rikkert Wyckmans • Stacey Wyman • Mark Wyse • Molly & Ken Wyss

— X, Y, Z —

Xiaosy & The Bigs • Katherine Xu • Valerie Y. • Tapas Yagnik • Yogesh Yagnik • Susan Yamamoto • Elizabeth "Neighborly Michaela" Yang • Lemuel Yap • Keith Yarborough • Brian A. Yates • Gail Yates • Kyle

A. Yawn • Chista Yazdani • Mark, Becky, Addie, Milo, Emery & Abel Yedlowski • Wabash Yeti • Vincent Yeung • The Yilmaz Family • Ray & Zeke Yolo • Benjamin & Natosha York • Lawrence B. York • Valerie York • Caitlin J. Young • Daniel Young • Julie & Mark Young • K. Young • Ryan Young • Yoyoreader • Anders M. Ytterdahl • Richard Yu • Allie Zaenger • Aaron Zander • Robert Zangari • Brandon Zarzyczny • Zan Zastrow • Karen Zeigler • Elliot Zeiler • Elizabeth Zeitz • Ludwig Zemrau • Sean Zephyr • Jehnytssa Zetino • Jing Zhu • Anastasia Zhurikhina • Lisa Zidar • Perrin Zideos • Anthony Zieli • Sandra Zielinger • Kristina Žilec & Ivan Horvat • Chad Zilla • John Zimmerman • Drew Zingleman • Adam Zobler • Andrew R. Zodda • Emile Zola • Peter Zola • Martin Zoln • Kálnoky Mátyás Zsigmond • Zwieciu

About the Author

Michael J. Sullivan is a *New York Times*, *USA Today*, and *Washington Post* bestselling author who has been nominated for eight Goodreads Choice Awards. His first novel, *The Crown Conspiracy*, was released by Aspirations Media Inc. in October 2008. From 2009 through 2010, he self-published the next five of the six books of The Riyria Revelations, which were later sold and re-released by Hachette Book Group's Orbit imprint as three two-book omnibus editions (*Theft of Swords*, *Rise of Empire*, *Heir of Novron*).

Michael's Riyria Chronicles series (a prequel to Riyria Revelations) has been both traditionally and self-published. The first two books were released by Orbit, and the next two by his own imprint, Riyria Enterprises, LLC. A fifth Riyria Chronicle, titled *Drumindor*, will be self-published in the near future.

For Penguin Random House's Del Rey imprint, Michael has published the first three books of The Legends of the First Empire: *Age of Myth*, *Age of Swords*, and *Age of War*. Grim Oak Press distributes the last three books of the series, and they are titled *Age of Legend*, *Age of Death*, and *Age of Empyre*.

Michael is now writing The Rise and the Fall Trilogy. These three books are set in his fictional world of Elan and cover a historical period after the Legends of the First Empire and before the Riyria Chronicles.

You can email Michael at michael@michaelsullivan-author.com.

About the Type

This book was set in Fournier, a typeface named for Pierre Simon Fournier (1712–1768), the youngest son of a French printing family. He started out engraving woodblocks and large capitals, then moved on to fonts of type. In 1736, he began his own foundry and made several important contributions in the field of type design; he is said to have cut 147 alphabets of his own creation. Fournier is probably best remembered as the designer of St. Augustine Ordinaire, a face that served as the model for the Monotype Corporation's Fournier, which was released in 1925.